W9-AEJ-984

PRAISE FOR *WHAT THE WIND KNOWS*

"I don't often find a book I can't put down, but I devoured *What the Wind Knows*. It's magical, atmospheric, and compelling, a book that will haunt you for a long time."

—Rhys Bowen, *New York Times* and #1 Kindle bestselling author of *The Tuscan Child*, *In Farleigh Field*, and the Royal Spyness novels

"Amy Harmon brings a tragic and fascinating period of history to life with a poignant love story that plays out across time and oceans. Skillfully woven around vividly depicted historical events and figures, this is a page-turner, hard to put down until the end."

—Helen Bryan, international bestselling author of *War Brides*, *The Sisterhood*, and *The Valley*

WHAT
the
WIND
KNOWS

ALSO BY AMY HARMON

Young Adult and Paranormal Romance

Slow Dance in Purgatory
Prom Night in Purgatory

Inspirational Romance

A Different Blue
Running Barefoot
Making Faces
Infinity + One
The Law of Moses
The Song of David
The Smallest Part

Historical Fiction

From Sand and Ash

Romantic Fantasy

The Bird and the Sword
The Queen and the Cure

WHAT
the
WIND
KNOWS

AMY HARMON

LAKE UNION
PUBLISHING

Published by Lake Union Publishing, Seattle

www.apub.com

Amazon, the Amazon logo, and Lake Union are trademarks of Amazon.com, Inc., or its affiliates.

ISBN-13: 9781542040075 (hardcover)
ISBN-10: 1542040078 (hardcover)
ISBN-13: 9781503904590 (paperback)
ISBN-10: 1503904598 (paperback)

Cover design by Faceout Studio, Lindy Martin

Printed in the United States of America

First edition

To my great-great-grandmother,
Anne Gallagher Smith

Let us go forth, the tellers of tales,

and seize whatever prey the heart long for,

and have no fear.

Everything exists, everything is true,

and the earth is only a little dust under our feet.

—*W. B. Yeats*

PROLOGUE

November 1976

"Grandfather, tell me about your mother."

He was silent as he smoothed my hair, and for a long moment, I thought he hadn't heard me.

"She was beautiful. Her hair was dark, her eyes green, just like yours are."

"Do you miss her?" Tears leaked out the sides of my eyes and made his shoulder wet beneath my cheek. I missed my mother desperately.

"Not anymore," my grandfather soothed.

"Why?" I was suddenly angry with him. How could he betray her that way? It was his duty to miss her.

"Because she is still with me."

This made me cry harder.

"Hush now, Annie. Be still. Be still. If you are crying, you won't be able to hear."

"Hear what?" I gulped, slightly distracted from my anguish.

"The wind. It's singing."

I perked up, lifting my head slightly, listening for what my grandfather could hear. "I don't hear a song," I contended.

"Listen closer. Maybe it's singing for you." It howled and hurried, pressing against my bedroom window.

"I hear the wind," I confessed, allowing the sound to lull me. "But it isn't singing a very pretty song. It sounds more like it's shouting."

"Maybe the wind is trying to get your attention. Maybe it has something very important to say," he murmured.

"It doesn't want me to be sad?" I proposed.

"Yes. Exactly. When I was little, about your age, I was very sad too, and someone told me everything would be okay because the wind already knew."

"Already knew what?" I asked, confused.

He sang a line from a song I'd never heard in a voice both warm and rolling. "The wind and waves remember him still." He stopped singing abruptly, as if he didn't know what came next.

"Remember who still?" I pressed.

"Everyone who has ever lived. The wind and the water already know," he said softly.

"Know what?"

"Everything. The wind you hear is the same wind that has always blown. The rain that falls is the same rain. Over and over, round and round, like a giant circle. The wind and the waves have been present since time began. The rocks and stars too. But the rocks don't speak, and the stars are too far away to tell us what they know."

"They can't see us."

"No. Probably not. But the wind and water know all the earth's secrets. They've seen and heard all that has ever been said or done. And if you listen, they will tell you all the stories and sing every song. The stories of everyone who has ever lived. Millions and millions of lives. Millions and millions of stories."

"Do they know my story?" I asked, stunned.

"Yes," he whispered on a sigh and smiled down into my upturned face.

"And yours too?"

"Oh yes. Our stories belong together, Annie lass. Your story is a special one. It might take your whole life to tell it. Both of our lives."

1

EPHEMERA

"Ah, do not mourn," he said,
"That we are tired, for other loves await us;
Hate on and love through unrepining hours.
Before us lies eternity; our souls
Are love, and a continual farewell."

—*W. B. Yeats*

June 2001

They say that Ireland is built on her stories. Fairies and folklore inhabited Ireland much longer than the English or even Patrick and the priests. My grandfather, Eoin Gallagher (pronounced galla–HER not galla–GUR), valued the story above all else, and he taught me to do the same, for it is in the legends and tales that we keep our ancestors, our culture, and our history alive. We turn memories into stories, and if we don't, we lose them. If the stories are gone, then the people are gone too.

Even as a child, I found myself entranced by the past, wishing I knew the stories of the people who had come before me. Maybe it was due to an early acquaintance with death and loss, but I knew someday I would be gone too, and no one would remember that I had ever lived. The world *would* forget. It would go on, shaking itself free of those who had been, sloughing off the old for the new. The tragedy of it all was more than I could bear, the tragedy of lives beginning and ending with no one remembering.

Eoin was born in County Leitrim in 1915, nine months before the famed Easter Rising that changed Ireland forever. His parents—my great-grandparents—died in that rebellion, and Eoin was orphaned without knowing either of them. We were alike in that way, my grandfather and I—both orphaned young—his loss cycling into mine, my loss becoming his. I was only six years old when I lost my parents. I was a little girl with a tied tongue and an overly active imagination, and Eoin stepped in, rescued me, and raised me.

When I struggled to get the words out, my grandfather would hand me a pen and paper. "If you can't say them, write them. They last longer that way. Write all your words, Annie. Write them and give them somewhere to go."

And so I have.

But this story is like no other tale I have ever told, no story I have ever written. It is the history of my family, woven into the fabric of my past, etched in my DNA, and seared into my memory. It all began—if there is a beginning—when my grandfather was dying.

"There is a locked drawer in my desk," my grandfather said.

"Yes, I know," I teased, as if the locked drawer had been something I'd been trying to break into. I'd actually had no idea. I hadn't lived in Eoin's Brooklyn brownstone for a long time and hadn't called him "Grandfather" for even longer. He was just "Eoin" now, and his locked drawers were of no concern to me.

"Don't sass, lass," Eoin chided, repeating a line I'd heard a thousand times in my life. "The key is on my fob. The smallest one. Will you get it?"

I did as he asked, following his instructions and pulling the contents from the drawer. A large manila envelope sat atop a box filled with letters, hundreds of them, neatly ordered and bundled. I paused over the letters for a moment, noting that none of them appeared to have ever been opened. A small date was written in the corner of each one, and that was all.

"Bring the manila envelope to me," Eoin instructed, not raising his head from the pillow. He'd grown so weak in the last month, he rarely left his bed. I set the box of letters aside, picked up the envelope, and returned to him.

I opened the clasp on the envelope and carefully upended it. A handful of loose pictures and a small leather-bound book slid out onto the bed. A brass button, the top rounded and dull with time, rolled out of it last, and I picked it up, fingering the innocuous item.

"What's this, Eoin?"

"That button belonged to Seán Mac Diarmada," he rasped, a glint in his eye.

"*The* Seán Mac Diarmada?"

"The one and only."

"How did *you* get it?"

"It was given to me. Turn it over. His initials are scratched into it—see?"

I held the button to the light, turning it this way and that. Sure enough, a tiny *S* followed by a *McD* marred the surface.

"The button was from his coat," Eoin began, but I knew the story. I'd been steeped in research for months, trying to get a feel for Irish history for a novel I was working on.

"He carved his initials into his coat buttons and a few coins and gave them to his girlfriend, Min Ryan, the night before he was executed by a firing squad for his involvement in the Rising," I said, awed by the tiny piece of history I held in my hand.

"That's right," Eoin said, a small smile flitting over his lips. "He was from County Leitrim, where I was born and raised. He traveled the country, setting up branches of the Irish Republican Brotherhood. He was the reason my parents became involved."

"Unbelievable," I breathed. "You should have the button authenticated, and put it somewhere safe, Eoin. This has got to be worth a small fortune."

"It's yours now, Annie lass. You can decide what happens to it. Just promise me that you won't give it to someone who won't understand its significance."

My eyes met his, and my excitement over the button fizzled and fell. He looked so tired. He looked so old. And I wasn't ready for him to rest—not yet.

"But . . . I don't know if I understand it, Eoin," I whispered.

"Understand what?"

"Its significance." I wanted to keep him talking, to keep him awake, and I rushed to fill the void his weariness left in me. "I've been reading about Ireland—biographies and documentaries and collections and diaries. I've been doing research for six months. I have so much information in my head, and I don't know what to do with it. The history after the 1916 Easter Rising is just a garbled mess of opinions and blame. There's no consensus."

Eoin laughed, but the sound was brittle and mirthless. "That, my love, is Ireland."

"It is?" That was so sad. So disheartening.

"So many opinions and so few solutions. And all the opinion in the world doesn't change the past." Eoin sighed.

"I don't know what story I'm going to tell. I'll arrive at one opinion only to be swayed by another. I feel hopeless."

"That is how the people of Ireland felt too. That's one of the reasons I left." Eoin's hand had found the book with the worn leather cover, and he caressed it the way he'd stroked my head when I was a child. For a moment we were silent, lost in our own thoughts.

"Do you miss it? Do you miss Ireland?" I asked. It wasn't something we'd talked about. My life—our life together—was in America, in a city as alive and vibrant as Eoin's blue eyes. I knew very little about my grandfather's life before me, and he'd never been eager to enlighten me.

"I miss her people. I miss her smell and her green fields. I miss the sea and the timelessness. She is . . . timeless. She hasn't changed much. Don't write a book about Ireland's history, Annie. There are plenty of those. Write a love story."

"I still have to have context, Eoin," I argued, smiling.

"Yes. You do. But don't let the history distract you from the people who lived it." Eoin picked up one of the pictures, his fingers trembling as he brought it close to his face to better study it. "There are some paths that inevitably lead to heartache, some acts that steal men's souls, leaving them wandering forever after without them, trying to find what they lost," he murmured, as if quoting something he'd once heard, something that had resonated with him. He gave me the picture in his hand.

"Who is this?" I asked, staring down at the woman who gazed fiercely back at me.

"That is your great-grandmother, Anne Finnegan Gallagher."

"Your mother?" I asked.

"Yes," he breathed.

"I look like her," I said, delighted. The clothes she wore and the style of her hair made her an exotic, foreign creature, but the face looking up at me from decades past could have been my own.

"Yes. You do. Very much," Eoin said.

"She's a little intense," I observed.

"Smiling wasn't the thing to do in those days."

"Ever?"

"No," he chortled, "not *ever*. Just not in pictures. We tried very hard to look more dignified than we were. Everyone wanted to be a revolutionary."

"And is that my great-grandfather?" I pointed at the man standing next to Anne in the next picture.

"Yes. My father, Declan Gallagher."

Declan Gallagher's youth and vitality were preserved in the yellowed print. I liked him immediately and felt a surprising pang in my chest. Declan Gallagher was gone, and I would never know him.

Eoin handed me another picture, a photo of his mother, his father, and a man I didn't recognize.

"Who's he?" The stranger was dressed like Declan, formally, in a three-piece suit, a fitted vest peeking out from behind his lapels. His hands were in his pockets, and his hair was slicked back in careful waves and was short on the sides and longer on top. Brown or black, I couldn't tell. His brow was furrowed slightly, as if he wasn't comfortable having his picture taken.

"That is Dr. Thomas Smith, my father's best friend. I loved him almost as much as I love you. He was like a father to me." Eoin's voice was soft, and his eyes fluttered closed again.

"He was?" My voice rose in surprise. Eoin had never talked about this man. "Why haven't you shown me these pictures, Eoin? I've never seen any of them before."

"There are more," Eoin murmured, ignoring my question, as if it required too much energy to explain.

I moved on to the next picture in the pile.

It was a picture of Eoin as a young boy, his eyes wide, his face freckled, and his hair slicked down. He wore short pants and long socks, a vest, and a little suit coat. He had a cap in his hands. A woman stood behind him, her hands on his shoulders, her mouth grim. She might have been handsome, but she looked too suspicious to smile.

"Who's she?"

"My grandmother, Brigid Gallagher. My father's mother. I called her Nana."

"How old were you here?"

"Six. Nana was very unhappy with me that day. I didn't want to take a picture without the rest of my family. But she insisted on a picture with just the two of us."

"And this one?" I picked up the next photo. "Tell me about this one. That's your mother—her hair is longer here—and the doctor, right?" My heart fluttered in my chest as I stared at it. Thomas Smith was looking down at the woman beside him, as if at the last moment he'd been unable to resist. Her gaze was cast down as well, a secret smile on her lips. They weren't touching, but they were very aware of each other. And there was no one else in the picture with them. The picture was oddly candid for the time period.

"Was Thomas Smith . . . in love with Anne?" I stammered, strangely breathless.

"Yes . . . and no," Eoin said softly, and I looked up at him with a scowl.

"What kind of answer is that?" I asked.

"A truthful one."

"But she was married to your father. And didn't you say he was Declan's best friend?"

"Yes." Eoin sighed.

"Oh wow. There's a story there," I crowed.

"Yes. There is," Eoin whispered. He closed his eyes, his mouth quivering. "A wonderful story. I can't look at you without remembering."

"That's a good thing, isn't it?" I asked. "Remembering is good."

"Remembering is good," he agreed, but the words came out with a grimace, and he clutched at the covers.

"When was the last time you took a pain pill?" I asked, my voice sharp. I dropped the pictures and rushed to the pills stacked on his bathroom counter. I shook one out with anxious hands and filled a glass of water, then lifted Eoin's head to help him drink it down. I'd wanted him to be in a hospital, surrounded by people who could take care of him. He'd wanted to be home with me. He'd spent his life in hospitals, caring for the sick and dying. When he was diagnosed with cancer six months ago, he'd calmly announced he would not be receiving treatment. His only concession to my tearful ranting and cajoling was that he would manage his pain.

"You need to go back, Annie lass," he said a while later, the pill making his voice dreamlike and soft.

"Where?" I asked, heavyhearted.

"To Ireland."

"Go back? Eoin, I've never been. Remember?"

"I need to go back too. Will you take me?" he slurred.

"I've been wanting to go to Ireland with you all my life," I whispered. "You know that. When should we go?"

"When I die, you'll take me back."

The pain in my chest was a physical thing, biting and twisting, and I bore down to combat it, to extinguish it, but it grew like Medusa's hair, the writhing tendrils slipping up and out of my eyes in hot, wet rivulets.

"Don't cry, Annie," Eoin said, his voice so weak that I did my best to quell the tears, if only to save him from distress. "There is no end to us. When I die, take my ashes back to Ireland and set me loose in the middle of Lough Gill."

"Ashes? In the middle of a lake?" I asked, trying to smile. "Don't you want to be buried near a church?"

"The church just wants my money, but I hope God will take my soul. What's left of me belongs in Ireland."

The windows rattled, and I rose to pull the drapes. Rain beat against the panes, a late spring storm that had been threatening the East Coast all week.

"The wind is howling like the hound of Culann," Eoin murmured.

"I love that story," I said, sitting back down beside him. His eyes were closed, but he continued to speak, softly musing like he was remembering.

"You told me the story of Cú Chulainn, Annie. I was afraid, and you let me sleep in your bed. Doc kept watch all night long. I could hear the hound in the wind."

"Eoin, I didn't tell you the story of Cú Chulainn. You told me. So many times. You told me," I corrected him, straightening his blankets. He clutched at my hand.

"Yes. I told you. You told me. And you will tell me again. Only the wind knows which truly comes first."

He drifted off, and I held his hand, listening to the storm, lost in memories of us. I was six years old when Eoin became my anchor and my caretaker. He'd held me while I wept for parents who weren't coming back. I wished desperately that he could hold me again, that we could start over, if only to have him with me for another lifetime.

"How will I live without you, Eoin?" I mourned aloud.

"You don't need me anymore. You're all grown up," he murmured, surprising me. I'd thought he was fast asleep.

"I'll always need you," I cried, and his lips trembled again, acknowledging the devotion that underscored my words.

"We'll be together again, Annie." Eoin had never been religious, and his words surprised me. He'd been raised by a devout Catholic grandmother but left the religion behind when he left Ireland at eighteen. He'd insisted I attend a Catholic school in Brooklyn, but that was the extent of my religious upbringing.

"Do you really believe that?" I whispered.

"I know it," he said, opening his heavy eyelids and regarding me solemnly.

"I don't. I don't know it. I love you so much, and I'm not ready to let you go." I was crying in earnest, already feeling his loss, my loneliness, and the years that stretched before me without him.

15

"You're beautiful. Smart. Rich." He laughed weakly. "And you did it all by yourself. You and your stories. I'm so proud of you, Annie lass. So proud. But you don't have a life beyond your books. You don't have love." His eyes clouded and searched the space beyond my head. "Not yet. Promise me you'll go back, Annie."

"I promise."

After that he slept, but I could not. I stayed by his side, hungry for his presence, for the words he might say, for the comfort I'd always drawn from him. He awoke once more, panting from the pain, and I helped him swallow another pill.

"Please. Please, Annie. You must go back. I need you so badly. We both do."

"What are you talking about, Eoin? I'm right here. Who needs me?"

He was delirious, floating in pain, beyond sentience, and I could only hold his hand and pretend I understood.

"Sleep now, Eoin. The pain will be easier to bear."

"Don't forget to read the book. He loved you. He loved you so much. He's been waiting, Annie."

"Who, Eoin?" I couldn't hold back the tears, and they dripped on our clasped hands.

"I miss him. It's been so long." He sighed deeply, his eyes never opening. What he saw was in his memory, in his pain, and I let him ramble until the mumbled words became shallow breaths and restless dreams.

The night ended, and a day dawned, but Eoin didn't wake again.

2 May 1916

He's dead. Declan is dead. Dublin is in ruins, Seán Mac Diarmada is in Kilmainham Gaol awaiting the firing squad, and I don't know what's become of Anne. Yet here I sit, filling the pages of this book as though it will bring them all back. Every detail is a wound, but they are wounds I feel compelled to reopen, to examine, if only to make sense of it all. And someday, little Eoin will need to know what happened.

I intended to fight. I started Easter Monday with a rifle in my hands that I put down and never picked up again. From the moment we stormed into the General Post Office, I was up to my elbows in blood and chaos in the makeshift first aid post. There was very little organization and a great deal of excitement, and for the first few days, no one knew what to do. But I knew how to bind wounds and staunch blood flow. I knew how to make a splint and dig out a bullet. For five days, under constant shelling, that's what I did.

I moved through the days in a dream, never resting, so tired I could have slept on my feet, my head bobbing in time with the artillery rounds. Through it all, I couldn't believe it was happening. Declan was euphoric, and Anne was moved to tears when the gunboat started firing on Sackville Street, as if the use of big weapons solidified our dreams of a rebellion. She was sure the British were finally listening. I teetered between pride and despair, between my boyhood dreams of nationalism and Irish rebellion, and the sheer destruction being meted out. I knew it was futile, but I was compelled through friendship or loyalty to take part, even if my part was only to see that the rebels—the whole ragtag, idealistic, fatalistic lot—had someone looking after their wounded.

Declan had made Anne promise to stay out of harm's way. She, Brigid, and little Eoin were holed up in my house in Mountjoy Square when Declan and I joined the Volunteers marching through the streets, intent on carrying out our revolution. Anne joined Declan in the GPO on Wednesday, kicking in a window and climbing over the jagged edge to reach him. She hadn't even noticed the blood streaming from a slice on her left leg and palm from the broken glass until I made her sit so I could tend to it. She told Declan that if he was going to die, she was going to die with him. Rage and threaten as he would, she turned a deaf ear and made herself useful playing messenger between the GPO and Jacob's factory, since no one would give her a gun. The women were much more able to move about without being questioned or fired upon. I don't know when her luck gave out. The last time I saw her was early Friday morning, when the flames creeping down both sides of Abbey Street made abandoning the post office unavoidable.

I had started evacuating the wounded to Jervis Street Hospital with a stretcher I'd begged off a St. John Ambulance worker. He gave me three Red Cross armlets as well so that we wouldn't be fired upon—or stopped—as we moved south on Henry Street to Jervis and back again. Connolly's ankle was shattered, but he wouldn't leave. I left him in the care of Jim Ryan, a medical student who'd been there since Tuesday. I made the trip three times before darkness fell and barricades prevented two Volunteers—boys from Cork who'd come to Dublin to join the fight—and me from returning. I told the boys to get out of the city. To start walking. The rebellion was over, and they were needed at home. Then I went back to the Jervis Street Hospital and found an empty corner, folded my coat beneath my head, and collapsed, only to be awakened by a nurse, who was certain that the hospital was going to be evacuated due to the flames that had followed me from the GPO. I went back to sleep, too spent to care. When I awoke, the fire had been contained, and the rebel forces had surrendered.

The staff at Jervis Street Hospital told the British soldiers that I was a surgeon when they came to round up the insurgents, and miraculously I wasn't detained. Instead, I spent the rest of the day attending to the dead and dying on Moore Street, where forty men had tried to secure a line of retreat from the burning GPO. Civilians and rebels alike had been mowed down by Crown forces. Women, children, and old men had been caught in the crossfire, and their dead faces were covered in soot. Flies buzzed round their heads, some of them burned beyond recognition. In my heart of hearts, I could not divorce myself from some of the blame. It is one thing to fight for freedom; it is another to condemn the innocent to die in your war.

That is where I found Declan.

I said his name, ran my hands down his blackened cheeks, and he opened his eyes to my voice. My heart leapt. I thought for a minute I might be able to save him.

"You'll take care of Eoin, won't you, Thomas? You'll take care of Eoin and my mother. And Anne. Look after Anne."

"Where is she, Declan? Where's Anne?"

But then his eyes closed, and his breath rattled in his throat. I lifted him up, over my shoulder, and ran for help. He was gone. I knew it, but I carried him to the Jervis Street Hospital, demanded a place to lay him down, and washed the blood and grit from his skin and hair and straightened his clothes. I bandaged his wounds, which would never heal, and then I carried him through the streets again, up Jervis, across Parnell, through Gardiner Row, and into Mountjoy Square. Nobody stopped me. I carried a dead man on my shoulders through the centre of town, and the people were so shell-shocked, they looked the other way.

I don't think Declan's mother, Brigid, will ever recover. The only person who might love Declan more than Anne is Brigid. I am taking him home to Dromahair. Brigid wants to bury him in Ballinagar, beside his father. And then I'll come back to Dublin for Anne. God forgive me for leaving her behind.

T. S.

2

THE LAKE ISLE OF INNISFREE

I will arise and go now, for always night and day
I hear lake water lapping, with low sounds by the shore;
While I stand on the roadway, or on the pavements grey,
I hear it in the deep heart's core.

—*W. B. Yeats*

I flew into Dublin, smuggling the urn of Eoin's ashes in my suitcase. I had no idea if there were international laws—or Irish laws—about transporting the dead and decided I didn't want to know. My suitcase was waiting for me at the baggage claim, and I double-checked to make sure the urn hadn't been confiscated before renting a car to drive northwest to Sligo, where I would stay for a few days while I explored nearby Dromahair. I hadn't adequately prepared myself to drive on the wrong side of the road and spent much of the three-hour journey to Sligo weaving across the road and screaming in terror, unable to enjoy the landscape for fear I would miss a sign or hit an oncoming car.

I rarely drove in Manhattan; there was no reason to own a car. But Eoin had insisted I learn how and get a driver's license. He said freedom was the ability to go wherever your heart called, and growing up, we'd driven up and down the East Coast on little vacations and adventures. The summer I turned sixteen, we spent July crossing the entire United

States, starting in Brooklyn and ending in Los Angeles. That is when I learned to drive, traversing long stretches of highway between small towns that I would never see again. Over rolling hills, through the red cliffs of the West, across the expanse of nothing and everything with Eoin at my side.

I'd memorized "Baile and Aillinn" by Yeats as we drove, a narrative poem filled with legend and longing, death and trickery, and love that transcended life. Eoin had held the dog-eared copy of Yeats's poetry, listening to me stumble through lines, gently correcting me, and helping me pronounce the Gaelic names of the old legends until I could deliver each line and verse like I had lived it. I had a passion for Yeats for his love of the actress Maud Gonne, who gave her love to a revolutionary instead. Eoin let me ramble on about things I thought I understood—but only romanticized—like philosophy and politics and Irish nationalism. Someday, I told him, I wanted to write a novel set in Ireland during the Rising of 1916.

"Tragedy makes for great stories, but I'd much rather your story— the one you live, not the ones you write—be filled with joy. Don't revel in tragedy, Annie. Rejoice in love. And once you find it, don't let it go. In the end, it is the one thing you won't regret," Eoin had said.

I was not interested in love beyond what I could read on a page. I spent the next year pestering Eoin to take me to Ireland, to Dromahair, the little town where he'd been born. I wanted to attend the Yeats festival in Sligo, which Eoin said wasn't far from Dromahair, and perfect my Gaelic. Eoin had insisted I learn, and it was the language of us, of our life together.

Eoin had refused. It was one of the few times we fought. I spoke in a bad Irish accent for two months to torture him.

"You're tryin' too hard, Annie. If you have to think about the way your tongue is movin' in your mouth, then it doesn't sound natural," he'd coached, wincing.

I redoubled my efforts. I was relentless in my fixation. I wanted to go to Ireland. I went so far as to call a travel agent to help me. Then I presented the arrangements, complete with dates and pricing options, to Eoin.

"We're not going to Ireland, Annie. It's not time. Not yet," he said, a stubborn set to his chin, rejecting my travel brochures and itineraries.

"When will it be time?" I wheedled.

"When you've grown."

"What? But I'm grown now," I insisted, still holding on to the accent.

"See there? That was perfect. Natural. No one would know you're an American," he said, attempting to distract me.

"Eoin. Please. It's calling me," I moaned theatrically, but I was sincere in my fascination. It did call to me. I dreamed about it. I yearned for it.

"I believe that, Annie. I believe it is. But we can't go back yet. What if we go and we never come back?"

The thought had filled me with wonder. "Then we'll stay! Ireland needs doctors. Why not? I could go to college in Dublin!"

"Our life is here now," Eoin argued. "The time will come. But not now, Annie."

"Then we'll just visit. Just a trip, Eoin. And when it's over, no matter how much I love it and want to stay, we'll come home." I thought I was being so reasonable, and his adamancy confused me.

"Ireland is not safe, Annie!" he said, losing his temper. The tips of his ears were red, and his eyes flashed. "We're not going. Jaysus, Mary, and Joseph, girl. Let it go."

His anger was worse than a slap, and I ran to my room and slammed the door, crying and raging and making childish plans to run away.

But he never yielded, and I was not a rebellious child; he'd never given me anything to rebel against. He didn't want to go to Ireland— didn't want *me* to go to Ireland—and out of love and respect for him,

I eventually gave up. If his memories of Ireland hurt him so deeply, then how could I insist he return? I threw away the brochures, retired my Irish accent, and read Yeats only when I was alone. We kept up the Gaelic, but Gaelic didn't make me think of Ireland. It made me think of Eoin, and Eoin had urged me to pursue other dreams.

I began to write my own stories. To craft my own tales. I wrote a novel set during the time of the Salem witch trials—a young-adult book that I'd sold to a publisher at eighteen—and Eoin had spent two weeks with me in Salem, Massachusetts, letting me research to my heart's content. I wrote a novel about the French Revolution through the eyes of Marie Antoinette's young lady-in-waiting. Eoin happily arranged his schedule, reassigned his patients, and took me to France. We'd been to Australia so I could write a story about the English prisoners who'd been sent there. We'd been to Italy, to Rome, so I could write a tale about a young soldier during the fall of the Roman Empire. We'd been to Japan, the Philippines, and Alaska, all in the name of research.

But we had never gone to Ireland.

I've gone on dozens of trips by myself. I've spent the last decade of my life absorbed in my work, crafting one story after another, traveling from one location to the next to research and write. I could have gone to Ireland alone. But I never did. The time never seemed right, and there were always other stories to tell. I'd been waiting for Eoin, and now Eoin was gone. Eoin was gone, and I was finally in Ireland, driving on the wrong side of the road, with Eoin's ghost in my head and his ashes in the trunk.

The anger I'd felt as a sixteen-year-old girl—the injustice and confusion at his refusal—reared in my chest again.

"Damn you, Eoin. You should be here with me!" I cried, pounding on the wheel, my eyes filling with tears, causing me to narrowly miss plowing into a truck that swerved and blared its horn in warning.

When I arrived at the Great Southern Hotel—a stately, pale-yellow establishment built a few years after the Irish Civil War—in Sligo at sundown, I sat in the crowded parking area and said the Rosary for the first time in years, grateful to be alive. I stumbled into the hotel, bags in tow, and after checking in, I climbed a staircase that reminded me of pictures of the *Titanic*, which was strangely symbolic of the sinking feeling I'd been battling since leaving New York.

I collapsed onto the big bed, which was surrounded by heavy furniture and papered walls in various shades of purple, and fell asleep without even removing my shoes. I awoke twelve hours later, disoriented and starving, and stumbled to the bathroom to huddle in the ridiculously narrow tub, shivering while I tried to figure out how to turn the hot water on. Everything was different enough that it took a moment to adjust but similar enough that I grew impatient with myself for the difficulty I was experiencing.

An hour later, washed and dried, dressed and pressed, I took my keys and headed down the ornate staircase to the dining room below.

I walked down the streets of Sligo in tragic wonder, the girl in me gaping at the smallest things, the grieving woman devastated that I was finally there and Eoin wasn't with me. I walked down Wolfe Tone Street and over to Temple, where I stood beneath the bell tower of the enormous Sligo Cathedral, my head tipped back as I waited for it to ring. William Butler Yeats's face—with white hair and spectacles—was painted on a wall next to words that proclaimed this "Yeats country." The painting made him look like Steve Martin, and I resented the tacky display. Yeats deserved more than a shoddy mural. I passed by the Yeats museum in stony protest.

The town sat higher than the sea, and here and there, the long strand, glistening and bared by the tide, peeked out at me. I'd walked too long, not paying attention to how far I'd gone, my eyes gobbling up what was immediately around me. I ducked into a candy shop, needing sugar and directions back to the hotel and to Dromahair if I was going to attempt another afternoon behind the wheel.

The owner was a friendly man in his sixties, selling me on sour licorice and chocolate caramel clusters and asking me about my visit to Sligo. My American accent gave me away. When I mentioned Dromahair and an ancestral search, he nodded.

"It's not far at all. Twenty minutes or so. You'll want to take the loop around the lake—stay on 286 until you see the sign for Dromahair. It's a pretty drive, and Parke's Castle is along the route. It's worth stopping for."

"Is the lake called Lough Gill?" I asked, catching myself just in time and pronouncing it correctly. *Lough* was pronounced like the Scottish *loch*.

"That's the one."

My chest ached, and I pushed thoughts of the lake away, not ready to think about ashes and goodbyes just yet.

He pointed me back in the direction of the hotel, telling me to listen for the bell tower on the cathedral if I got turned around. As he rang up my purchases, he asked me about my family.

"Gallagher, huh? There was a woman named Gallagher who drowned in Lough Gill, oh . . . it had to be almost a century ago. My grandmother told me the story. They never found her body, but on a clear night, folks say you can sometimes see her walking on the water. We've got our own lady of the lake. I think Yeats wrote a poem about her. He even wrote about Dromahair, come to think."

"'He stood among a crowd at Dromahair; his heart hung all upon a silken dress, and he had known at last some tenderness, before earth took him to her stony care,'" I quoted, lilting immediately into the Irish accent I'd perfected in my youth. I didn't know the poem about a ghost lady—it didn't ring any bells at all—but I knew the one about Eoin's beloved Dromahair.

"That's it! Not bad, lass. Not bad at all."

I smiled and thanked him, popping a piece of chocolate in my mouth as I traipsed back across town to the hotel that reeked of time and bygone eras.

The candy man was right. The drive to Dromahair was beautiful. I plodded along, gripping the wheel and taking the turns slowly for my own safety and the safety of the unsuspecting Irish traveler. At times, greenery rose so thick on either side of me, I felt goaded by the canopy that threatened to enclose the road at every turn. Then the foliage broke, and the lake glimmered below, welcoming me home.

I found an overlook and stopped the car, climbing onto the low rock wall that separated the road from the drop so I could drink it in. From the map I knew that Lough Gill was long, stretching from Sligo into County Leitrim, but from my vantage point, looking down on her eastern banks, she seemed intimate and enclosed, surrounded by squares of stone-lined farmland that rose from the banks and onto the hills on every side. An occasional home dotted the hills, but I didn't imagine the view could be much different from what it had been a hundred years before. I could have easily climbed the wall and made my way down the long grassy slope to reach the shore, though it might have been farther than it looked from above. I considered it, knowing I could take the urn with me and have the dreaded task behind me. Part of me wanted nothing more than to dip my toes in the placid blue and tell Eoin I'd found his home. I resisted the call of the water, not knowing if the terrain to the lake's shores was marshy beneath the grass that stretched below me. Being stuck up to my hips in boggy mud with Eoin's urn was not in the plan.

Ten minutes later, I was pulling down the main street of tiny Dromahair, searching for signs and symbols. I was not sure where to begin. I couldn't start knocking on doors, asking questions about people who had lived so long ago. I walked through a church cemetery, eyeing the names and dates, the clusters that indicated family, the flowers that indicated love.

There were no Gallaghers in the small graveyard, and I climbed back into my car and continued down the main street until I saw a small sign that said "Library," underlined by an arrow pointing down a narrow lane no bigger than an alleyway.

It was little more than a stone cottage, with four rough walls, a slate roof, and two dark windows, but libraries were great for research. I rolled to a stop in a gravel space not big enough for more than three patrons and turned off the car.

Inside, it was smaller than my home office in Manhattan. And apartments in Manhattan were notoriously small, even when they cost two million dollars. A woman, maybe a few years older than I, hunched over a novel, and books that needed to be reshelved were piled on her desk. She sat up and smiled vacantly, still lost in her story, and I stretched out my hand in greeting.

"Hello. I know this is strange, but I thought maybe the library was a good place to start. My grandfather was born here in 1915. He said something about his father being a farmer. My grandfather went to America in the early thirties, and he never came back. I wanted to see"—I waved my hand helplessly toward the broad window that gave me a view of a little alleyway and not much else—"where he was from and maybe see where his parents are buried."

"What was the family name?"

"Gallagher," I said, hoping I wouldn't hear the story of the woman who drowned in the lake again.

"It's a common enough name. My own mother was a Gallagher. But she's from Donegal." She stood and made her way around her desk and the piles of books she clearly had no room for.

"We have a whole collection of books written by a woman named Gallagher." She stopped in front of a shelf and straightened a stack. "They were written in the early twenties but professionally reprinted and donated to the library last spring. I've read them all. Delightful, really. All of them. She was ahead of her time."

I smiled and nodded. Books by a woman with a common last name weren't exactly what I was looking for, but I didn't want to be rude.

"What townland?" she asked expectantly.

I stared at her blankly. "Townland?"

"The land is divided up into townlands, and each one has a name. There are roughly fifteen hundred townlands in County Leitrim. You said your great-grandfather was a farmer." She smiled ruefully. "Everyone in rural Ireland was a farmer, lovey."

I thought of the painfully small village I'd driven through, the cluster of homes, and the little main thoroughfare. "I don't know. Isn't there a cemetery? I thought I could just explore a bit. It's a small county, isn't it?"

It was her turn to stare at me blankly. "There are plots in every townland. If you don't know the townland, you'll never find the grave. And most of the older graves don't have headstones. It required money to have a headstone, and nobody had money. They just used markers. The family knows who is who."

"But . . . I'm family, and I have no idea," I blurted, oddly emotional. Jet lag, near-death experiences, and needles in haystacks were catching up to me.

"I'll call Maeve. She was the Killanummery parish secretary for almost fifty years," she offered, her eyes widening at my distress. "Maybe there are some church records you could look through. If anyone knows something, it will be Maeve." She picked up the phone and dialed from memory, her eyes flitting uncomfortably between me and the stack of books on her desk.

"Maeve, this is Deirdre at the library. The book you've been waitin' for is available. No, not that one. The one about the bad-boy billionaire." Deirdre was silent, nodding, even though the woman she was speaking to couldn't know she was being agreed with. "That's right. I peeked at it. You'll like it." Her eyes swung to me and away again. "Maeve, I've got a woman here. All the way from America. She says she has family from the area. I was wondering if there are parish records she could look at. She's wantin' to find where they're buried." She nodded again, sadly this time, and I guessed Maeve was telling her what she already knew.

"You could go to Ballinamore," Deirdre said, moving her mouth from the receiver, as if Maeve had instructed her to tell me immediately. "There's a genealogical center there. Maybe they can help. Are you stayin' in Sligo?"

I nodded in surprise.

"There's really nowhere to lodge around here, unless you've rented a room at the manor by the lake, but most people don't even know it's there. They don't advertise," Deirdre explained.

I shook my head, indicating I had not known either, and Deirdre reported this to Maeve.

"The family name is Gallagher." She listened for a moment. "I'll tell her." She pulled the receiver away from her mouth again.

"Maeve wants you to bring her the book about the billionaire and have some tea with her. She says you can tell her about your family, and maybe she'll think of something. She's as old as the hills," Deirdre whispered, muffling the receiver so Maeve wouldn't hear her commentary. "But she remembers everything."

The woman opened the door before I could knock. Her hair was so fine and wispy, it created a gray cloud around her head. Her glasses, rimmed in black and as thick as the palm of my hand, were wider than her face. She peered up at me through them with blinking blue eyes and pursed lips painted fuchsia.

"Maeve?" I realized suddenly I didn't know her last name. "I'm so sorry. Deirdre didn't tell me your full name. Can I call you Maeve?"

"I know you," she said, her brow—already a topographic map of grooves and valleys—wrinkling even further.

"You do?"

"I do."

I stuck out my hand in greeting. "Deirdre sent me."

She didn't take it but stepped back and waved me in. "What was your name, lass? Just because I know your face doesn't mean I remember your name." She turned and tottered away, clearly expecting me to follow. I did, shutting the door behind me, the smell of damp and dust and cat dander wafting around me.

"Anne Gallagher," I said. "I'm Anne Gallagher. I suppose I'm on a roots trip of sorts. My grandfather was born here, in Dromahair. I would really like to find where his parents are buried."

Maeve was heading for a small table set for tea tucked next to a pair of tall windows looking out on an overgrown garden, but when I said my name, she stopped abruptly as though she'd forgotten her destination entirely.

"Eoin," she said.

"Yes! Eoin Gallagher was my grandfather." My heart cantered giddily. I took a few steps, not certain if she wanted me to sit for tea or remain standing. She was perfectly still for several moments, her back to me, her small figure framed by the afternoon light and frozen in remembrance or forgetfulness, I didn't know which. I waited for her to offer instruction or extend an invitation, hoping that she wouldn't forget she'd let a stranger into her home. I cleared my throat gently.

"Maeve?"

"She said you'd come."

"Deirdre? Yes. She also sent your book." I dug it from my purse and took a few more steps.

"Not Deirdre, goose. Anne. Anne said you'd come. I need tea. We'll have tea," she muttered, moving once again. She sat at the table and looked at me expectantly. I debated making my excuses. I suddenly felt like I was caught in a Dickens novel, taking tea with Miss Havisham. I had no desire to eat ancient wedding cake and drink Earl Grey in dusty teacups.

"Oh. That's very kind of you," I hedged, setting the bad-boy billionaire book on the end table nearest me.

"Eoin never came back to Dromahair. Not many do. There's a name for that, you know. They call it an Irish goodbye. But here you are," Maeve said, still staring at me.

I couldn't resist the lure of Eoin's name. I set my bag down next to the chair across from her and slid into the seat. I tried not to look too closely at the little plate of cookies or the flowered plates and teacups. What I didn't know wouldn't hurt me.

"Will you pour?" she asked primly.

"Yes. Yes, I'd be glad to," I stammered, trying to remember a moment when I'd felt more uncomfortably American. I mentally scrambled for the etiquette, trying to remember what came first.

"Strong or weak?" I asked.

"Strong."

My hands shook as I held the little strainer over her cup and filled it three-quarters full. Eoin had always preferred tea. I could serve tea.

"Sugar, lemon, or milk?" I asked.

She sniffed. "Plain."

I bit my lip to hide my gratitude, splashed a little tea in my own cup, and wished for wine.

She raised the tea to her lips and drank with disinterest, and I followed her lead.

"Did you know Eoin well?" I asked after we'd both set our saucers down.

"No. Not really. He was much younger than I. And a little scamp at that."

Eoin was younger than Maeve? Eoin was just shy of eighty-six when he died. I tried to calculate what "much younger" might mean.

"I'm ninety-two," Maeve supplied. "My mother lived to be one hundred and three. My grandmother was ninety-eight. My great-grandmother was so old, no one really knew exactly how old she was. We were glad to see the *auld wan* go."

I hid my snort of laughter in a demure cough.

"Let me look at you," she demanded, and I raised my eyes to hers obediently.

"I can't believe it. You look just like her," she marveled.

"Like Eoin's mother?"

"Like Anne," she agreed. "It's uncanny."

"I've seen pictures. The resemblance is strong. But I'm surprised you remember. You would have been a very little girl when she died."

"No." She shook her head. "Oh no. I knew her well."

"I was told Declan and Anne Gallagher died in 1916. Eoin was raised by his grandmother, Brigid, Declan's mother."

"Nooo," she disagreed, drawing out the word as she shook her head. "Anne came back. Not right away, mind you. I remember how folks talked about her after she returned. There were some rumors . . . speculation about where she'd been. But she came back."

I stared at the old woman, stunned. "M-my grandfather didn't tell me," I stammered.

She considered this, nodding and drinking her tea, her eyes cast down, and I gulped my own, my heart racing from a sense of betrayal.

"Maybe I am confused," she retracted softly. "Don't let the ramblings of an old woman cause you to doubt."

"It was a long time ago," I offered.

"Yes. It was. And memory is a funny thing. It plays tricks on us."

I nodded, relieved that she had withdrawn her assertion so easily. For a moment, she had seemed so sure, and her confidence had made mine crumble.

"They're buried in Ballinagar. That I am sure of."

I rushed to retrieve my little notebook and a pencil from my bag. "How do I get there?"

"Well now. It's a pretty walk from here. Or a short drive. Maybe ten minutes or less. Go south on the main street—just there, see?" She pointed toward the front door. "It'll take you straight out of town. Go about three kilometers. You're going to veer right at the fork and continue for, oh . . . for half a kilometer or so. Then go left. Go a wee bit farther. Then the church—St. Mary's—will be on your left. The cemetery is there too, behind it."

I'd stopped writing after she said to veer right.

"Don't these streets have names?"

"Well, they're not streets, dear. They're roads. And people around here just know. If you get lost, pull over and ask someone. They'll know where the church is. And you can always pray. God always hears our prayers when we're wantin' a church."

15 May 1916

The drive to Dromahair with Declan's body wrapped and secured to the running board of the car was the longest of my life. Brigid would not speak, and the baby was inconsolable, as though he felt the black of our despair. After I dropped them at Garvagh Glebe, I took Declan to Father Darby for burial. We laid him to rest in Ballinagar, next to his father. I purchased a stone that will be laid when the engraving is done. If Anne is dead, as I fear, we will bury her beside Declan, and they will share the stone. It is what they would have wanted.

I returned to Dublin, though getting back into the city proved arduous. The British army had declared martial law, and all the roads were cordoned with armoured vehicles and soldiers. I showed my papers and my medical bag, and they eventually let me pass. The hospitals are full of injured insurgents, soldiers, and civilians. Mostly civilians. The need is great enough so they let me through when others were turned away.

I searched the deadhouses and the hospital morgues—Jervis Street, the Mater, St. Patrick Dun's, even the women's hospital where I'd heard the rebels had gathered on the grass after they surrendered. A temporary field hospital had been assembled at Merrion Square, and I went there as well, though nothing remained but the folks that resided in the homes nearby. They told me the wounded and dead had been taken, and they weren't sure where. Rumours of mass graves of the unidentified dead at the Glasnevin and Deansgrange cemeteries had me begging beleaguered groundsmen for names they couldn't provide. I was too late, they said, adding that the lists of the dead would be compiled and eventually posted in the Irish Times, *though no one knew when.*

I searched the streets, walking down the burned-out shell of once grand buildings on Sackville and trundling through endless ash that was still hot enough in some places to melt my shoes. On Moore Street, where I had found Declan, people moved in and out of the crumbling tenements. One, situated right in the centre, had taken a direct hit. It had collapsed in on itself, and children scrambled over the debris, searching for firewood and things they could sell. Then I saw Anne's shawl, a bright grass-green that matched her eyes. When I saw her last, she'd been wearing it wrapped tightly around her shoulders and tucked into her skirt to keep it out of the way. A young girl wore it now, and it fluttered in the breeze like the tricolour flags we'd raised above the GPO as triumphant conquerors. Those flags were gone now, destroyed. Just like Declan and Anne.

Senseless with fear and fatigue, I ran to the girl and demanded that she tell me where she'd found the shawl. She pointed to the rubble at her feet. She had a blank stare and old eyes, though she couldn't have been more than fifteen.

"It was just here, buried under the bricks. It has a small hole. But I'm keeping it. This was my house. So it's

mine now." She jutted out her chin, as though she thought I'd rip it from her. Maybe I would have. Instead, I spent the rest of the day in the tumbled pile of rock and walls, searching through debris, looking for Anne's body. When the sun set and I had nothing to show for my efforts, the girl removed the shawl and handed it to me.

"I've changed my mind. You can have it. It might be all that's left of your lady." I could not hide my tears, and her eyes were not as ancient when she turned to go.

Tomorrow I'll go back to Dromahair and bury the shawl beside Declan.

T. S.

3

THE STOLEN CHILD

For he comes, the human child,
To the waters and the wild
With a faery, hand in hand,
From a world more full of weeping than he can understand.

—*W. B. Yeats*

With my heart in my throat and my eyes peeled, I repeated Maeve's directions like a Gregorian chant. I found my way to Ballinagar Cemetery and to the church that sat like a guardian over the graves. It was in the middle of empty fields, a parochial house behind it and only the endless stone walls of Ireland and a smattering of cows keeping it company. I pulled into the empty lot in front of the church and stepped out into the tepid June afternoon—if Ireland had a summer, it hadn't arrived—feeling as though I'd found Golgotha and seen Jesus on the cross. With tear-filled eyes and shaking hands, I pushed through the huge wooden doors into the empty chapel, where reverence and memory had seeped into the walls and the wooden pews. The high ceiling echoed with a thousand christenings, countless deaths, and innumerable unions that stretched back beyond the dates on the nearby graves.

I loved churches the way I loved cemeteries and books. All three were markers of humanity, of time, of life. I felt no censure or guilt, no heaviness or dread, inside religious walls. I knew my experience was not widely shared, and perhaps that was because of Eoin. He had always approached religion with respect and humor, an odd combination that valued the good and put the bad into perspective. My relationship with God was equally untroubled. I'd heard once that our view of God has everything to do with those who taught us about Him. Our image of Him often reflected our image of them. Eoin taught me about God, and because I loved and cherished Eoin, I loved and cherished God.

In school, I'd studied Catholicism, learned the catechisms and the history, and absorbed it the way I'd absorbed all my other subjects, cleaving to the things that resonated and setting aside the things that didn't. The nuns complained that religion was not a buffet from which I could select only certain dishes. I politely smiled and quietly disagreed. Life, religion, and learning were exactly that. A series of choices. If I had tried to consume everything that was presented to me all at once, I would have become too full too quickly, and all the flavors would have run together. Nothing would have made any sense in and of itself.

As I sat in the old church where generations of my ancestors may have worshipped, where prayers had been spoken and hearts broken and healed, it *all* made sense for a small moment. Religion made sense, if only to add context to the struggle of life and death. The church was a monument to what had been, a connection to the past that comforted those in the present, and it comforted me.

I climbed the slope beyond the church to where the cemetery stretched. It overlooked the spires and the winding road I'd just traveled. Some of the stones were tipped or sunken; some were so covered with lichen and time that I couldn't make out names or dates. Other plots were new, lined by rocks and filled in with mementos. The newer plots, newer deaths, rimmed the edges of the graveyard, as if death rippled outward like a rock tossed in a lake. Those markers were clean, the marble smooth, the names easily read. Maeve had warned that the cemeteries in much of Ireland were a mix of ancient and recent, the connections familial, even if the relationship was centuries old. In Ballinagar Cemetery, most of the graves, especially those higher up the rise, stood like petrified gnomes and hobbits amid the grass, peeping out at me and drawing me to them.

I found my family beneath a tree on the edge of an older section. The stone was a tall rectangle with the name Gallagher engraved at the base. Just above it were the names Declan and Anne. I stared, incredibly moved, and touched their names. The years, 1892 to 1916, were visible as well, and I felt a flood of relief that Maeve had been wrong after all. Declan and Anne had died together, just as I'd believed. I sank to my knees, light-headed and euphoric, not trusting myself to remain standing. I found myself talking to them, telling them about Eoin, about myself, about how much it meant to me to find them.

When I was talked out, I rose to my feet and touched the stone again, noticing for the first time the graves around it. A smaller stone, also with the name Gallagher, sat to the left. The names Brigid and Peter were visible, but the dates, two sets of them, were not. Peter Gallagher, Declan's father, had died before Declan and Anne, and Brigid had passed away sometime after. Eoin hadn't ever told me. Or maybe I'd never asked. I only knew his grandmother was gone when he left Ireland.

I touched Brigid's and Peter's names too, thanking Brigid for raising Eoin, for molding him into the man who had loved and looked after me with so much care. Surely, she had loved him as intently as he'd loved me. He had to have learned it somewhere.

The clouds were gathering, and the wind nipped at my cheeks, telling me it was time to go. As I turned to leave, a headstone, set back from the Gallaghers, caught my eye, or maybe it was the faded name stretched across the dark stone. It said Smith, the word so close to the ground that the grass obscured part of the lettering. I hesitated, wondering if the grave belonged to Thomas Smith, the somber man in the three-piece suit, the man Eoin had loved like a father.

I felt one raindrop and then another, and the skies split with a groan and a grumble, releasing an angry torrent. I abandoned my curiosity and stumbled down the hill, weaving in and out of the now-glistening monuments and promising the stones that I would be back.

That night, back in my hotel in Sligo, I dug through my suitcase in search of the items from Eoin's locked drawer. I'd thrown the manila envelope into my suitcase on a whim—mostly because Eoin had been so insistent that I read the book—but I'd hardly given it a second thought since his death. I'd been too grief-stricken to concentrate, too frazzled for research, too lost to do anything but search for my bearings. But now that I'd seen the graves of my great-grandparents, I wanted to remember their faces.

I wondered how long it had been since someone had remembered them, and my heart broke again. I'd been fighting tears since Eoin's death, and Ireland had not eased my pain. Still, the emotion was different now. It was laced with joy and gratitude, and though the tears looked the same, they didn't feel the same.

I upended the envelope across the small desk, the way I'd done a month ago at Eoin's bedside. The book, heavier than the other items, slid out first, the pictures fluttering around it like afterthoughts. I tossed the envelope aside, and it fell heavily, making a small thunk as it hit the edge of the desk. I picked it up again, curious, and reached inside. A ring had found its way under the padded lining and was wedged into the corner. I worked it free, finding a delicate band of gold filigree that widened around a pale cameo on an agate background. It was lovely and old—an intoxicating combination for a historian—and I slipped it on my finger, delighted that it fit, wishing Eoin could tell me to whom it had belonged.

It was probably his mother's, and I picked up the old photos to see if she wore it on her hand in any of the shots. Anne's hands were tucked in the pockets of her gray coat in one photo, wrapped around Declan's arm in another, and out of frame or out of sight in the rest.

I thumbed through them all again, touching the faces that had preceded my own. I stopped on Eoin's picture, his unhappy little face and stiffly parted hair making my eyes tear and my heart swell. I could see the old man in the child's expression in the set of his chin and the frown on his lips. Age was the only color in the photo, and I could only guess at the vibrancy of his hair or the blue of his eyes. My grandfather had been snowy-haired as long as I'd known him but claimed he'd had hair as red as his father's before him and my father after him.

I set Eoin's picture aside and studied the others, pausing once more at the picture of Thomas Smith and my grandmother. It hadn't been taken at the same time as the picture with the three of them—Anne, Thomas, and Declan—together. Anne's hair and clothes were different, and Thomas Smith wore a darker suit. He seemed older in the one, though I couldn't think why. The patina was forgiving, his hair dark and uncovered. Maybe it was the set of his shoulders or the solemnity in his stance. The picture was slightly overexposed, leaching the details from Anne's dress and giving their skin the pearly quality so often found in very old photos.

There were pictures in the stack I hadn't seen. Eoin's pain had interrupted my perusal on the night of his death, and I paused over a photo of a grand house with trees clustered around the edges and a glimmer of lake in the distance. I studied the landscape and the stretch of water. It looked like Lough Gill. I should have taken the photos with me to Dromahair. I could have asked Maeve about the house.

In another photo, a group of men I didn't know stood around Thomas and Anne in an ornate ballroom. Declan wasn't in the picture. A big, smirking man with dark hair stood in the center of the shot, one arm slung loosely around Anne's shoulders and his other arm around Thomas. Anne stared at the camera, wonder stamped all over her face.

I recognized that look—it was one often captured on my own face at book signings. It was a look that telegraphed discomfort and disbelief that anyone would want a picture with me in the first place. I'd gotten better at controlling my expressions and pasting on a professional smile, but I made a rule not to look at any of the shots my publicist regularly sent me from such events. What I didn't see wouldn't fill me with insecurity.

I continued to study the picture, suddenly riveted by the man who stood next to Anne.

"No," I gasped. "It can't be." I gazed at it in wonder. "But it is." The man with his arm around Anne's shoulders was Michael Collins, leader of the movement that led to the Treaty with England. Before 1922, there were very few pictures of him. Everyone had heard of Michael Collins and his guerilla tactics, but only his inner circle, men and women who worked alongside him, knew what he looked like, making it harder for the Crown to detain him. But after the Treaty was signed and he began rallying the Irish people for its acceptance, his picture had been taken and saved in the annals of history. I'd seen those shots—one of him midspeech, his arms raised in passion, and one in his commander's uniform the day the British relinquished control of the castle, a symbol of British control in Dublin for the last hundred years.

I stared at the picture a moment longer, marveling, before I set it aside and reached for the book. It was a journal, an old one, the writing neatly slanted, the cursive beautiful in the way old handwriting often was. I thumbed through it without reading, simply checking the dates. The entries ranged from 1916 to 1922 and were often sporadic, with months between them and sometimes years before the record picked up again. The handwriting was the same throughout the entire book. Nothing scribbled or crossed out; no ink stains or torn pages. Each entry had *T. S.* at the bottom of the page and nothing more.

"Thomas Smith?" I said to myself. It was the only thing that fit, but it surprised me that Eoin would have the man's journal. I read the first entry, a date marked May 2, 1916. My horror and amazement grew as I read about the Easter Rising and the death of Declan Gallagher. I thumbed through several more entries and read about Thomas's efforts to find Anne and to come to terms with the loss of his friends. An entry the day Seán Mac Diarmada was executed at Kilmainham Gaol simply said, *Seán died this morning. I thought he might be spared when the executions were halted for several days. But he's been taken too. My only comfort is that I know he welcomed it. He died for the cause of Irish freedom. That's the way he would have seen it. But selfishly, I can only consider it a dreadful shame. I will miss him terribly.*

He wrote of his return to Dromahair after attending medical school at the University College, Dublin, and of trying to set up a practice in Sligo and County Leitrim.

> *The people are so poor, I can't imagine I will make much of a living from the effort, but I have more than sufficient for my needs. It is what I've always planned to do. And here I am, driving from one end of the county to the other, from the north to the south, east to Sligo and west again. I feel like a peddler half the time, and the people can't pay for what I'm offering. I made a house call in Ballinamore yesterday and collected no payment but a sweet song from the oldest daughter. A family of seven in a two-room cottage. The youngest, a girl of six or seven, had been unable to get out of her bed for several days. I discovered she wasn't sick. She was hungry—hungry enough to have no energy to move. The entire family was skin and bones. I have thirty acres at Garvagh Glebe that are not being cultivated and an overseer's house sitting empty on the property. I told the father—a man named O'Toole—that*

I needed someone to farm it and the position was his, if he thought he could do it. It was an impulsive offer. I have no interest in farming or in taking on the responsibility of providing for an entire family. But the man wept and asked if he could start in the morning. I gave him twenty pounds, and we shook hands on it. I left the supper Brigid had packed for me that morning—more food than I needed—and made the little girl eat a piece of bread and butter before I left. Bread and butter. Years of medical training and study, and the child simply needed bread and butter. From now on, I'll bring eggs and flour along with my medical bag on my travels. I think the food is needed more than a doctor. I'm not sure what I'll do when I come across the next family starving in their beds.

I stopped reading, a lump in my throat, and turned the page only to find another sad account of doctoring in Dromahair. He wrote, "One mother seemed more interested in me marrying her daughter than healing her. She pointed out her fine features, rosy cheeks, and bright eyes, which were all due to an advanced case of consumption. She won't live much longer, I'm afraid. But I promised to come back with medicine to ease her cough. The mother was ecstatic. I don't think she understands that I'm not calling on the girl."

He wrote of Brigid Gallagher's anger at the Irish Republican Brotherhood, of which Thomas was still an active member. Brigid blamed the Brotherhood for Declan's death and for the increased presence of the Black and Tans, the British police force, throughout Ireland. Thomas "refused to argue the issue with her. I can't talk her out of her opinions any more than I can ignore my own. I still yearn for liberty and Irish emancipation, though I don't see how we will accomplish it. My guilt is almost as great as my longing. So many of the men who fought in the Rising, men that I consider my friends, are at Frongoch in Wales. And in my heart, I know I should be with them."

He wrote lovingly of Eoin. "He is a light in my life, the glimmer of something better in my days. I've asked Brigid to keep house for me so that I can take care of her and the boy. Anne had no family to call on. She and I were alike in that way. Alone in the world. She has a sister in America. Parents and a brother long dead. Brigid is all the family Eoin has left, but I will be his family, and I will make sure he knows who his parents were and who Ireland is."

He was like a father to me, Eoin had said. I felt a rush of tenderness for the melancholy Thomas Smith and read on. His next entry was months later. He spoke of the O'Tooles, of the efforts of the new overseer, and the satisfaction he felt at the weight the children had gained. He wrote of Eoin's first words and his propensity to run to him, babbling, when he arrived home. "He has begun to call me Da. Brigid was horrified when she realized what he was saying and cried noisily for days. I tried to convince her that Eoin was saying Doc. But she refused to be comforted. I have begun coaching the little lad in the evenings. He says Doc quite clearly now and calls Brigid Nana, which made her smile just a bit."

He wrote of the release, just before Christmas 1916, of the last of the Irish freedom fighters, as he called them. He went to Dublin to see them home and remarked at the welcome, at the change in the people. "When we marched through the streets the day after Easter, with all intentions of staging a rebellion and inciting a confrontation, the people jeered and told us to go fight the Germans. Now they welcome the boys home like they are returning heroes instead of troublemakers. I am glad of it. Maybe the hearts of the people have turned enough that real change is possible. Mick seems to think so."

Mick? Michael Collins was known as Mick among his friends. The picture I'd seen made me think Thomas Smith was well acquainted with him. The journal was a treasure trove, and I wondered why Eoin hadn't given it to me much earlier. He knew I was knee-deep in research about events that Thomas Smith had seemed to know intimately.

My eyes were growing heavy, and my heart had not recovered from the odd emotional toll of my visit to Ballinagar. I moved to set the book aside, and the pages fell forward, revealing the final page. Instead of a journal entry, four stanzas marched across the yellowed paper. No title, no explanation, just a piece of poetry written in Thomas Smith's hand. It sounded like Yeats. It felt like him too, though I'd never seen it before. I wondered if it was possibly the poem about the woman who drowned in the lough, the poem the owner of the candy store had mentioned just that morning. I read the words and read them again. The lines were so filled with longing and trepidation, I couldn't tear my eyes from the page.

I pulled you from the water
And kept you in my bed.
A lost, forsaken daughter
Of a past that isn't dead.

Somehow love from sweet obsession
Branched and broke a heart of stone.
Distrust became confession,
Solemn vows of blood and bone.

But in the wind, I hear the strain,
Pilgrim soul that time has found.
It moans to whisk you back again.
Bid me follow, sweetly drown.

Don't go near the water, love.
Stay away from strand or sea.
You cannot walk on water, love.
The lough will take you far from me.

I turned the page and was met with the leather-bound back of the book. There was nothing else written. *Pilgrim soul that time has found.* Yeats referred to a pilgrim soul in his poem "When You Are Old." But this was not Yeats, I was certain, though it was beautiful. Maybe Thomas Smith had simply loved it and wanted to remember it. Or maybe the words were his.

"Don't go near the water, love. Stay away from strand or sea. You cannot walk on water, love. The lough will take you far from me," I read again.

In the morning, I would take Eoin's ashes to Lough Gill. And the lake would take him. I shut the book softly and turned off the lamp, drawing the spare pillow on the bed to my chest, lonely and alone in a way I'd never been. The tears came then, a deluge, and there was no one to pull me from the water and keep me in his bed. I wept for my grandfather and wept for a past that was dead, and I felt forsaken when the wind refused to whisk me away.

11 July 1916

Eoin turned one today. He is a smiley lad, healthy and content. I find myself watching him, absorbed in his perfect innocence and unblemished spirit. And I mourn for the day when he will grasp what he's lost. He wanted his mother in the days after Dublin and cried for her. He had not yet been weaned from her milk, and he sought a comfort no one else could give. But he doesn't ask for her anymore. I doubt he'll have any memory of them at all, and the tragedy of that truth weighs on me.

There is a rumbling in rural Ireland spurred on by the executions after Easter week. Some men were spared— Eamon de Valera, who was in command at Boland's Mill—while others, Willie Pearse and John MacBride, men on the periphery, were sentenced to death. Instead of the executions and imprisonments tamping down the rebellious undercurrent in the country, it seems to have fed it, contributing to a growing sentiment that another injustice has been done. We simply add it to the centuries-old list every Irishman keeps tucked in the back of his mind and hands on to the next generation.

Regardless of the rumbling, the people are wounded and afraid. We are in no position to fight back now. Not yet. But there will come another day. When Eoin is a man, Ireland will be free. I have promised this to him, whispering the words into his downy hair.

Brigid has begun to mutter about taking Eoin to America. I have not discouraged her or made my feelings known, but I can't bear to lose Eoin too. He has become mine. My stolen child. Brigid worries that I will marry, and then I will not need her to keep house and look after me. On that count, I have reassured her often. She and Eoin will always have a place in my home. I have not told her that when I close my eyes, I see Anne's face. I dream about her, and my heart is unsettled. Brigid would not understand. I'm not sure I do. I didn't love Anne, but she haunts me. If I had found her, maybe it would be different.

But I didn't find her.

T. S.

4

THE MEETING

Hidden by old age awhile
In masker's cloak and hood
Each hating what the other loved,
Face to face we stood.

—*W. B. Yeats*

Deirdre didn't seem especially surprised to see me, and she beamed at me in cheerful welcome when I walked through the library door the next day.

"Maeve sent you to Ballinagar. Any luck?" she asked.

"Yes. I found them—where they are buried, I mean. I'm going to go back tomorrow and put flowers on their graves." The tender feelings I'd had among the grass and the stones welled in me again, and I smiled awkwardly, embarrassed that I was, once more, becoming overly emotional in the librarian's presence. I cleared my throat and retrieved the picture of the house I'd tucked between the pages of Thomas Smith's journal and held it out to Deirdre, brandishing it like a shield.

"I wondered if you could tell me where this is?" I asked.

She took it, looking down through the lower half of her glasses, her chin jutting forward, her eyebrows raised.

"That's Garvagh Glebe," she said, delighted. "This is an old picture, isn't it? Goodness! When was this taken? It really doesn't look all that different. Except for the carpark off to the side. I think there's been some guest cottages added in recent years as well." She squinted at the picture. "You can just see Donnelly's cottage there in the trees. It's been there for longer than the manor. Jim Donnelly fixed it up about ten years ago. He takes tourists out on the lake and out exploring the old caves where smugglers used to store arms during the Black-and-Tan War. My grandfather told me the lough was used to move weapons in and out of this area all through those years."

"Garvagh Glebe," I breathed, stunned. I should have known. "It was owned by a man named Thomas Smith, wasn't it?"

She looked at me blankly. "When would that have been?"

"In 1916," I said, sheepish. "I guess that was a little before your time."

"Just a bit," she laughed. "But I might remember something about that. Well, I don't know. I think so. The house and property are run from a family trust. None of the family live there now. They have grounds-keepers and a staff, and they let out rooms. It's on the Dromahair side of Lough Gill. Some folks call it the manor."

"You mentioned the manor yesterday. I didn't realize."

"Yes. There's a dock there as well, and people rent boats from Jim to fish or just spend the day on the lake. The lake leads to a little inlet. When the tides are high, you can follow the inlet all the way out past the strand in Sligo and into the sea. There are stories of pirate ships in Lough Gill back in the days of O'Rourke, the man who built the castle—they call it Parke's Castle. Have you been?"

I nodded, and she babbled on with barely a pause.

"He built Creevelea Abbey as well. O'Rourke was hung for treason by the English for giving shelter to marooned Spanish sailors of the Spanish Armada. The English king gave O'Rourke's castle to a man named Parke—can you imagine working for twenty years to build something that would survive for centuries and having someone just swoop in and take it away?" She shook her head in disgust.

"I'd like to see Garvagh Glebe. Is the house open to visitors?"

She gave directions much the way Maeve had the day before. "Go left for a bit; go right for a bit more. Pull over and ask if you get lost, but you shouldn't get lost because it's not that far."

I listened intently, scratching notes into the little pad from my purse. "Thank you, Deirdre. And if you talk to Maeve, would you thank her for me as well? It meant a great deal to me to find those graves."

"Maeve O'Toole is a veritable fountain of information. She knows more than all the rest of us put together. I'm not surprised she knew something about your kin."

I turned to leave and stopped, realizing I'd heard the name before. "Maeve's last name is O'Toole?"

"It was her maiden name. It's been McCabe and Colbert and O'Brien. She's outlived three husbands. It got a bit confusing, so most of us just stick with what came first. Why?"

"No reason." I shrugged. If Maeve's family had once lived at Garvagh Glebe, she hadn't mentioned it, and I hadn't read far enough into the journal to know what became of the O'Tooles Thomas had tried to help.

The lane to Garvagh Glebe was gated, and the gate was closed and padlocked. I could see the house through the trees. The photograph come to life, drenched in color but just as unattainable. I pushed a buzzer to the left of the gate and waited impatiently for a response. None came. I climbed back in the car, but instead of going back the way I'd come, I took the fork, following the lane that ran along the lake, hoping to see the house from another angle. Instead, the narrow road ended in a gravel parking lot overlooking a long dock where a handful of canoes and small boats were tied off. The cottage Deirdre had mentioned, which was gleaming white under blue shutters and matching blue trim, was nearest the dock, and I walked toward it, hoping someone was home. A little sign hung from a nail next to the door and declared the establishment open, and I went inside.

The tiny foyer had been converted to a reception area with a narrow wooden counter and a few folding chairs. A little bell had been placed on the counter, and I tapped it reluctantly. One of the nuns in Catholic school had had one just like it on her desk that she pinged constantly and ferociously. The sound had put my teeth on edge ever since. I didn't ring it again, though several minutes passed without a response.

"Mr. Donnelly?" I called. "Hello?"

The door opened behind me, and I turned expectantly. A man with watery eyes and a red nose ambled in with tall waders on his feet, a baker boy cap on his head, and suspenders keeping his pants from falling down. I startled him, and he jerked, wiping at his mouth.

"I'm sorry, miss. I didn't know you were waitin' on me. I saw your car, but I assumed it was someone takin' a stroll or throwin' a line."

I stuck out my hand, and he took it awkwardly. "I'm Anne Gallagher. I was wondering if I could rent a boat for an hour."

"Anne Gallagher?" he asked, his brow furrowed, his voice disbelieving.

"Yes?" I said, drawing out the word. "Is there something wrong?"

He shrugged and shook his head. "Nah. It's nothin'," he grunted. "I can take you out if you want. There're clouds rollin' in, and I don't like people goin' out alone."

I didn't want to tell him I was throwing ashes into his lake, and I really didn't want him with me when I said goodbye to Eoin. "I won't go far. You'll be able to see me the whole time. I'll take a paddleboat or one of those small rowboats I saw on the dock. I'll be fine."

He stewed, eyeing me and peering out the window to the overcast afternoon and the boats bobbing, empty, at his dock.

"I just need a half hour, Mr. Donnelly. I'll pay double," I pressed. Now that I was here, I wanted to be done with the task before me.

"All right. Sign here, then. But stay close and watch the clouds."

I signed his waiver, plunked forty pounds down on the counter, and followed him to the dock.

The boat he chose for me was sturdy enough, though it had clearly seen better days—or a better decade. Two oars and a life jacket completed the package, and I put one on to allay Mr. Donnelly's concerns. One of the straps was broken, but I pretended it was perfectly fine. Mr. Donnelly had offered to put my things in a small locker in the foyer, but I declined. The bag held Eoin's urn, and I wasn't about to pull it out in front of him.

"Your bag will get wet. And you aren't dressed for the lake," he complained, eyeing my clothes and my slim flats. I'd worn a heavy cable-knit sweater, a plain white blouse, and cream slacks. This was the only burial Eoin would receive, and sneakers and jeans were too informal for the occasion.

My thoughts tiptoed back to Ballinagar Cemetery once more, to the stones in the grass I'd visited the day before. I wanted that for Eoin. A monument that he had lived. Something permanent. Something with his name and the span of his life. But that was not what he'd asked for, and leaving a grave in Ballinagar, a grave no one would visit or care about once I returned to the States, seemed wrong too.

I'd made a promise, and with a sigh, I grasped Jim Donnelly's hand, stepped into the swaying skiff, and took up the oars in determination. Mr. Donnelly looked down at me doubtfully before untying the boat and giving it a good shove with his foot.

I dipped the oar into the water to my left and then to my right, experimenting a little, trying to find a rhythm. The boat cooperated, and I began to inch away from the dock. I would just row a little way out. The skies had grown gray, but the water was placid and peaceful. Mr. Donnelly watched me for a while, making sure I had the hang of it before making his way back up the dock toward the beach and his cheery house with the blue roof and the gorse blooming along the walk.

I was pleased with myself, moving smoothly through the water. The stretch and pull of rowing was new to me, but the lake was as calm as bathwater, lapping softly against the boat, and I found I enjoyed the motion. Sitting for hours at my writing desk was not conducive to good health, and I'd found if I forced myself to exercise, it aided me in my writing. I ran and forced myself to do push-ups to keep my arms from wasting away and my back from growing a hump. The sweat, the motion, and the music that blared in my ears all contributed to getting me out of my head for a blessed hour. It shook off the brain fog and got the synapses firing, and I'd made it part of my daily schedule in the last ten years. I knew I was fit enough to row out a way and have some privacy to talk to Eoin before I gave him to the wind.

My oars slid in and out, pulling and displacing the water with hardly a murmur. I wouldn't go far. I could see the dock behind me, and beyond that, the manor tucked back against the roll of the hills, its pale roofline stark against the green. I continued rowing, the bag with the urn at my feet, my gaze drifting away from the shore and up into the sky. It was strange, the gray sky melding with the water. All was quiet, almost otherworldly, and I was lulled by the stillness. I ceased rowing for a time and drifted, the shoreline to my right, the sky all around me.

I picked up the urn and cradled it for a heartbeat, then uncorked it, readying myself for the ceremony only I would attend.

"I brought you back, Eoin. We're here. In Ireland. Dromahair. I'm in the middle of Lough Gill. It's lovely, just like you described, but I'll hold you responsible if I get pulled out to sea." I tried to laugh. We had laughed so much, Eoin and I. What was I going to do without him?

"I'm not ready to let you go, Eoin," I choked, but I knew I had no choice in the matter. The time had come to say my last goodbyes. I said the words he'd said to me a hundred times growing up, words from a poem by Yeats, words that I would have put on his headstone, had he allowed me to bury him as I wished.

"Faeries, come take me out of this dull world,

For I would ride with you upon the wind,

Run on the top of the disheveled tide,

And dance upon the mountains like a flame."

I clutched the urn to my chest a moment more. Then with a silent prayer to the wind and water to forever keep Eoin's story on the breeze, I upended it, flinging my arm in a wide arc, gasping as the white ashes melded completely with the wispy tendrils of mist that had begun to settle around me. It was as though the ash became a wall of white fog, billowing and collecting, and suddenly I could not see beyond the end of my boat. There was no shoreline, no sky—even the water was gone.

I put the urn in my bag and sat that way for a while, hidden in the fog and unable to continue. The boat rocked me as Eoin had once done, and I was a child again, cradled in his lap, consumed by grief and loss.

Someone was whistling. I started, the tune instantly recognizable. "Remember Him Still." Eoin's favorite. I was out in the middle of the lake, and someone was whistling. The whistling shivered through the mist, a cheerful flute in the eerie white, disembodied and disparate, and I couldn't tell from which direction it originated. Then the sound waned, as if the whistler moved away, teasing me with his game of hide-and-seek.

"Hello," I called, lifting my voice into the mist just to make sure I still could. The word didn't echo but sat flatly in the air, cushioned by moisture and curtailed by my own reluctance to break the stillness. I grasped the oars but didn't begin rowing, suddenly uncertain of my direction. I didn't want to come out on the other side of the lake. Best to let the fog lift before attempting to row back to shore.

"Is someone there?" I called. "I think I might be in trouble."

The bow of a barge slid into view, and I was suddenly staring up at three men, who in turn stared down at me, clearly as shocked by my presence as I was by theirs. They wore the peaked caps of a bygone era, the brims pulled low over their foreheads, over eyes that peered at me with obvious alarm.

I stood slowly, beseeching, suddenly fearful that I would be stuck in the fog forever and that these men would be my only chance at rescue.

It wasn't the smartest thing I've ever done, or maybe it saved my life.

The men stiffened as I rose, as if my standing posed a threat, and the man in the middle, his eyes wide with tension and his lips thin with mistrust, jerked his hand from his pocket and pointed a gun at me. His hand shook, and I swayed. With no warning, no demand, no reason at all, he pulled the trigger. The sound was a muted crack, and the sudden and violent shuddering of my skiff felt wholly separate from his action, as if a great, whistling beast had risen from the depths of Lough Gill beneath my boat and tossed me into the drink.

The frigid water stole my breath and didn't give it back. I chased it, floundering, and kicked for the surface, sputtering as my face broke free into the heavy white that was almost as wet and thick as the water I'd fallen into.

I couldn't see anything but white, endless white. No boat. No land. No sky. No men with guns.

I tried to lean back, to force myself to float and stay silent. If I couldn't see them, they couldn't see me, I rationalized. I managed to keep my head above water without a great deal of splashing, listening and peering into the white. Beneath the adrenaline and the clawing cold was a burning fire in my side. I continued treading water, trying to avoid the truth; I'd been shot, and I had to find my boat. If I didn't find my boat, I was going to drown.

I began swimming furiously this way and that, making a wide circle around the area where I'd fallen, trying to find my boat in the mist.

The whistling began again, abruptly, midtune, as if the whistler had been singing whole stanzas in his head while his lips took a ten-minute breather. The sound warbled and broke and came back stronger, and I cried out again, my teeth chattering around my plea, my arms and legs kicking frantically to keep my head above water. If the whistler was one of the men on the barge, I was only alerting them that I was still alive, but somehow the thought did not occur to me at the time.

"Help me! Is someone there?"

The whistling ceased.

"Help! Please! Can you hear me?"

The life vest with the broken strap was gone. My shoes had come free the moment I started kicking my legs. My clothes were heavy, my cable-knit sweater dragging me down even as I tried to swim in the direction of the whistling.

"Is someone there?" I called again, and my panic made my voice shrill, cutting through the dense fog.

A faded red boat, not unlike the one I'd rented from Jim Donnelly, emerged from the mist like a sea serpent and glided toward me. There was a man at the oars, his features obscured by the thick fog, but I heard him curse in surprise. I was too cold to know if I was hallucinating or dying, or maybe both, but the face looking down at me was strangely familiar. I could only pray I wasn't imagining him.

"Can you grab on? I'll pull you in," he urged. I reached for the mirage and felt the sweet answer of solidity. The boat was real, as was the man, but I could only cling to the side, so grateful I began to cry.

"Good God. Where did you come from?" the man asked. His hands gripped mine, encircling my wrists. Then he was pulling me up and into the boat, with no assistance whatsoever from me. I felt the bump and scrape of the side of the boat against my hip and stomach and cried out, drawing his attention to the blood that seeped from my stomach.

"What the hell?" he hissed, and I cried out again. "What happened to you?" The bottom of the boat was a cloud, and I was boneless, so weary I couldn't pull his face into focus. He pulled my arms from the sopping sweater that had made it so hard for me to swim. His hands worked briskly against my skin, rubbing and bringing warmth back into my limbs, and I forced my eyes open so I could whisper my thanks. His face was so close, framed by a peaked cap like the ones the men in the barge wore and set with a pair of blue eyes as pale as the fog. They widened as they met mine.

"Anne?" he asked, the incredulous lift of his voice and the familiarity with which he said my name as odd as my predicament.

"Yes," I whispered, forcing the word between wooden lips. My eyes would not stay open. I thought I heard him ask again, more urgently this time, but my tongue was as heavy as my head, and I didn't respond. I felt hands on my blouse, pulling it from my body and pushing it over my head. I protested by clutching the fabric weakly.

"I need to stop the bleeding, and I need to get you warm," he insisted, and brushed my hands away. He cursed at what he found.

"You've been shot. What the bloody hell!" His brogue was so like Eoin's, so comforting and welcome, it was as if Eoin himself had found me. I nodded weakly. Yes, I'd been shot. I didn't understand it either, and I was tired. So tired.

"Look at me, Anne. Don't go to sleep. Not yet. Keep your eyes open."

I did as he commanded, letting him hold my gaze. In addition to the cap, he wore a tweed coat over a wool vest and brown slacks, as though he'd set out for Mass and decided to go fishing instead. He shrugged out of his jacket and vest and tore at his dress shirt, buttons popping free in his haste. He pulled me up and propped me against him, my head bobbing against his chest, which was now covered only in a long-sleeved undershirt. He smelled of starch, soap, and chimney smoke. He made me feel safe. Then he was wrapping his white shirt around my midsection, making a bandage by tying off the sleeves. He put his jacket around my shoulders, enveloping me in his body heat.

I'm going to bleed on his clothes, I thought wearily as he made quick work of the buttons. Then he was easing me back down to the bottom of the boat, tucking the coat firmly around me and draping something larger over that. I willed my eyes open again and peered up at him beneath drooping lids.

The man was staring at me with shock stamped on his handsome face. It *was* a handsome face, I noted. He was square-jawed with a deep groove in his chin that matched the creases in his cheeks and the slash of his brows. I noted once more that he reminded me of someone. I'd seen him before. I tried to place him, but in my state, the familiarity eluded me.

He slid back into his seat, gripped the oars, and began rowing, digging into the soft swells of the lake as if there was a race to be won, and his urgency reassured me. He knew my name, and I'd been found. For now, that was enough.

I must have slept because all at once I was floating again, lost in the water and the fog, and I moaned in distress, certain the rescue had been nothing but a dream. Then it occurred to me that I wasn't struggling or sinking, and I realized I wasn't floating but being lifted, hoisted from the boat and onto the dock. I felt the slats against my cheek and the brush of damp, worn wood beneath my palms.

"Eamon!" my rescuer shouted, and I heard him scrabble up the dock, his footsteps retreating briskly, the slats vibrating beneath my ear. "Eamon!" he shouted again, though this time from farther off. Two sets of hurried feet returned, pulling a cart that made a *wop-wop* sound against the uneven planks. The man who'd found me on the lake crouched beside me, pushing my hair from my face.

"Do you know who this is, Eamon?" my rescuer asked.

"Annie?" a different voice gasped. "Is that Annie?"

My rescuer cursed, as if the man named Eamon had confirmed something he hadn't quite believed himself.

"What happened to her, Doc? Who did this to her?"

"I don't know what's happened, Eamon. Or what she's gotten herself into. And I need you to be quiet about this until I do."

"I thought she was dead, Doc!" Eamon gasped.

"We all did," Doc murmured.

"How're ya gonna keep this a secret? You can't exactly hide a person," Eamon protested.

"I'm not going to keep *her* a secret . . . but I need to keep *this* a secret until I know where the hell she's been all this time and why someone shot her and dumped her in the lough."

The man named Eamon was silent then, as if something had been communicated without conversation. I wanted to explain, to protest whatever misunderstanding had developed. But the desire was no more than a disintegrating thought, and when they laid me in the cart—a cart that reeked of cabbage and wet dog—it slipped away entirely. I felt their urgency and their fear, but the fog, not unlike the mist that hid the men with guns, stole my questions and my consciousness.

24 February 1917

Michael Collins was campaigning for Count Plunkett in North Roscommon, south of Dromahair, and I went to hear him speak. It's only been two months since he was released from Frongoch, yet he's already in the thick of things.

Mick saw me in the crowd and bounded down the steps when he was finished speaking, grabbing me up in his arms and swinging me around like I was his dearest friend. Mick has that way with people. It is something I have always admired, as it is not a trait I possess.

He asked after Declan and Anne, and I had to tell him the news. He didn't know Anne well, but he knew Declan and admired him.

I took him home to Garvagh Glebe for the night, anxious to hear what was simmering in Brotherhood circles. According to Mick, the public perception is that we're all Sinn Féiners. "But Sinn Féin's core principles vary from my own, Tommy. I believe it will take physical force to rid my country of British rule."

When I asked him what he meant, he refilled his whiskey and sighed like he'd been holding his breath for a month.

"I'm not talking of holing up in buildings and burning down Dublin. That doesn't work. We made a statement in 1916, but statements aren't good enough. It's going to take a different kind of warfare. Stealth. Strikes on the important players.

"We're going to reorganize the Irish Volunteers and invite Sinn Féin and the Irish Republican Brotherhood to join us. All the factions that came together in some form or other during the Rising need to come together again with one goal: getting the British out of Ireland, once and for all. It's the only way we'll ever win a damn thing."

When I asked him how I could help, he laughed and pounded me on the back. He stewed for a minute and asked about my house in Dublin. They needed safe houses all over the city to hide men and stash supplies at a moment's notice.

I agreed immediately, giving him a spare key and promising to contact the old couple who looked after the residence in my absence. He pocketed the key and said mildly, "We're going to need guns too, Tommy."

I was silent, and his dark eyes grew sober.

"I'm setting up networks to smuggle weapons throughout Ireland. I know how you feel about taking a man's life when you're sworn to save them. But we have to be able to fight a war, Doc. And the war is coming."

"I won't run guns for you, Mick."

"That's what I thought you'd say." He sighed. "But maybe there's another way you can help." He eyed me for a moment, and I was certain he'd thrown the idea for arms smuggling out first, knowing I'd say no and that it would be harder to refuse him twice.

He asked if my father was an Englishman.

I told him my father was a farmer. His father was a farmer, and his father before him, back for hundreds of years. I told him the land they farmed now lies fallow since my great-great-grandfather was accused of being a croppy and was dragged away by the yeomanry to be flogged and blinded with pitch. I told him my great-grandfather lost half his family in the famine of 1845. My grandfather lost half his children to emigration. And my father died young, working land that didn't belong to him.

Mick's eyes grew bright, and he clapped me on my back again. "Forgive me, Tommy."

"My stepfather was an Englishman," I admitted, knowing all along it was what Mick meant but feeling the sting of past wrongs that I hadn't righted.

"So I thought. You are well respected, Tommy. And you don't have the taint of Frongoch like the rest of us. You have a position and connections that may be of use to me here and in Dublin."

I nodded my assent, not certain that I really could be of use to him. But Mick said no more, and we began to talk of better days. But even writing of the conversation here, in a book I keep hidden away, makes my heart pound.

T. S.

5

A CRAZED GIRL

That crazed girl improvising her music,
Her poetry, dancing upon the shore,
Her soul in division from itself
Climbing, falling she knew not where.

—*W. B. Yeats*

I awoke to ruddy darkness and dancing shadows. A fire. A log cracked
and fell in the grate, sending splinters hissing and making me jump and
then cry out at the flash of pain along my side. The crack sounded like
a gunshot, and I remembered, though I wasn't sure if it was a memory
or a new story. It was like that for me sometimes. I would become so
immersed in writing that the scenes and characters I created came alive
in my head, fleshed out and independently animated, visiting me as I
slept.

I'd been shot. I'd been pulled from the water by a man who knew
my name. And now I was here in a room that looked a little like
my room at the Great Southern Hotel, though instead of carpet, the
floors were wood and covered with flowered rugs, the paper on the
walls was less purple, and the windows were adorned with long lace
curtains instead of the heavy drapes that allowed the guests to sleep
in darkness at midday. Two lamps with pleated fabric shades trimmed

with drops of glass sat on end tables at each side of the bed. I breathed deeply, trying to determine how badly I was injured. I fingered my abdomen carefully, tiptoeing around the thickest section of bandaging along my right side. It burned and pulled when I moved even slightly, but if the placement of the bandage was any indication, the bullet hadn't done any serious damage. I'd been cared for, I was clean and dry—though completely naked beneath the blankets—and I had no idea where I was.

"Are you leaving again?" The child's voice came from the base of my bed, disembodied and startling. Beyond the bars of the brass footboard, someone stood, peering at me.

I raised my head slowly for a better look and immediately abandoned the effort, the muscles of my abdomen contracting painfully.

"Will you come closer, please?" I asked, breathless.

There was a weighty silence. Then I felt the brush of a little hand at my feet, and the bed shook faintly as if the child hugged the edge and used it as cover. The approach took several long seconds, but curiosity clearly won out over trepidation, and a moment later I found myself eye to eye with a small boy. He wore a white shirt tucked haphazardly into dark pants held up by a pair of suspenders, making him look like a little old man. His hair was a red so deep and warm, it was crimson. He had a fine, pert nose and a missing front tooth, the hole visible behind his parted lips. Even in the flickering light, his eyes were blue. They searched mine frankly, wide and measuring, and I was sure I knew him.

I knew those eyes.

"Are you leaving again?" he repeated.

It took me a moment to separate his accent from his words. "Air ya leavin' agin?" he'd said.

Was I leaving? How could I? I didn't know how I'd even arrived.

"I don't know where I am," I whispered, my words strangely slurred even as I copied his accent. Morphine. "So I don't know where I'll go," I finished.

"You're in Garvagh Glebe," he said simply. "No one ever sleeps in this room. It can be your room now."

"That's very nice of you. My name's Anne. Can you tell me your name?"

"Doncha know?" he asked, his nose wrinkling.

"No," I whispered, though, oddly, the confession seemed like a betrayal.

"Eoin Declan Gallagher," he answered proudly, giving me his full name, the way children sometimes do.

Eoin Declan Gallagher. My grandfather's name.

"Eoin?" My voice rose in wonder, and I reached out to touch him, suddenly certain he wasn't really there at all. He stepped back, his eyes swinging to the door.

I was sleeping. I was sleeping and having an odd, wonderful dream.

"How old are you, Eoin?" my dream-self asked.

"You don't remember?" he responded.

"No. I'm . . . confused. I don't remember very much. Can you tell me? Please?"

"I'm almost six."

"Six?" I marveled. Six. My grandfather was born in 1915, less than a year before the uprising that took his parents' lives. If he was almost six, it was . . . 1921. I was dreaming about 1921. I was hallucinating. I'd been shot, and I'd almost drowned. Maybe I'd died. I didn't *feel* dead. I hurt—despite the pain medication, I hurt. My head. My stomach. But my tongue was working. In dreams, my tongue never worked.

"Your birthday is July the eleventh, isn't it? I remember that," I said.

Eoin nodded enthusiastically, his skinny shoulders crowding his too-big ears, and he smiled as if I'd redeemed myself a little bit. "Yes."

"And . . . what month is it now?"

"It's June!" he squealed. "That's why I am almost six."

"Do you live here, Eoin?"

"Yes. With Doc and Nana," he said impatiently, as if he'd already explained as much.

"With the doctor?" *The good doctor, Thomas Smith. Eoin had said he was like a father to him.* "What's the doctor's name, Eoin?"

"Thomas. But Nana calls him Dr. Smith."

I laughed softly, delighted that my dream was so detailed. No wonder he'd been familiar. He was the man from the pictures, the man with the pale stare and the unsmiling mouth, the one who Eoin said loved Anne. Poor Thomas Smith. He'd been in love with his best friend's wife.

"And who is your nana?" I asked the boy, enjoying the dizzy dream conundrum I found myself in.

"Brigid Gallagher."

"Brigid Gallagher," I breathed. "That's right." Brigid Gallagher. Eoin's grandmother. Declan Gallagher's mother. Anne Gallagher's mother-in-law. Anne Gallagher.

Thomas Smith had called me Anne.

"Thomas says you're my mother. I heard him tell Nana," Eoin said in a rush, and I gasped, the hand I'd raised to touch him falling back to the bed. "Is my da comin' back too?" he pressed, not waiting for my reply.

His father? Oh God. This *was* Eoin. This was *my* Eoin. Just a child. And his mother and father were dead. I was not his mother, and *neither* of them were coming back. I put my hands over my eyes and willed myself to wake up.

"Eoin!" The woman's call came from somewhere else in the house, seeking, searching, and the little boy was gone in a flash, racing to the door and slipping out of the room. The door shut carefully, quietly, and I let myself fall away into another dream, a safe darkness, where grandfathers didn't become little boys with crimson hair and winsome smiles.

When I awoke again, there were hands on my skin, and the bedcovers were pushed aside, baring my abdomen while my bandages were changed.

"It will heal quickly. It made a furrow in your side, but it could have been far worse." It was the man from the pictures again. Thomas Smith. He thought I was someone else. I closed my eyes to keep him away, but he didn't leave. His fingers danced around my denial, steady and sure. I started to panic, my breaths coming in short gasps.

"Are you hurting?"

I whimpered, more afraid than in pain. I was terrified of giving myself away. I was not the woman he thought I was, and more than anything, I was suddenly, desperately afraid to tell him he'd made a terrible mistake.

"You've been asleep so long. You'll have to talk to me sometime, Anne."

If I talked to him, what would I say?

He gave me a spoonful of something clear and syrupy, and I wondered if laudanum was responsible for my hallucinations.

"You saw Eoin?" he asked.

I nodded and swallowed, recalling the image of the little boy with his vivid hair and familiar eyes peeking at me through the brass footboard. My mind had created such a beautiful child.

"I told him not to come in here," he sighed. "But I can't really blame the lad."

"He's exactly the way I pictured him." I said this softly, slowly, concentrating on saying the words the way my grandfather would have said them, the soft burr something I could imitate, something I *had* imitated, all my life. But it felt false, and I winced even as I tried to deceive Thomas Smith with the accent. The words were true. Eoin *was* just as I'd pictured. But I was not his mother, and none of this was real.

When I awoke again, my head was much clearer, and the colors that had swum in deep burgundy and orange in the firelight now remained still, within concrete lines and solid shapes. Light was gathering—or going?—beyond the glass of the two tall windows. The night had faded, but the dream continued.

The fire in the grate and the little boy with my grandfather's name were both gone, but the pain was sharper, and the man with the gentle hands remained. Thomas Smith slumped in a chair, as if he'd fallen asleep watching me. Once, I had studied him in black and white as he stared up at me from an old photograph, and I did so again, telling myself there was no danger in my delusions. The shadows of the room added little color to the man. The hue of his hair—dark—was unchanged from the photograph, but the slicked-back waves from yesteryear had fallen over deep-set eyes I knew to be blue, the only color separate from the fog. His lips were softly parted, and their forgiving shape and gentle slope tempered a chin that was too square, a face that was too thin, and cheekbones that were too sharp.

He wore the clothes of a much older man—high-waisted trousers topped with a fitted vest secured over a flat torso. A pale, collarless dress shirt was buttoned to his throat. His sleeves were rolled to his elbows, and his feet in black wingtips were firmly planted, as though he'd drifted off expecting to be immediately reawakened. He looked long and angular in the high-backed chair, limbs loose and dangling, wrists and fingers pointed toward the floor, an exhausted warrior king asleep on his throne.

I was thirsty, and my bladder was full. I eased to my left and attempted to push myself up, gasping at the fire in my side.

"Careful. You'll reopen your wound," Thomas protested, his voice rough with sleep and soft with Ireland. The chair squeaked as I heard him rise, but I ignored him, feeling the covers fall from my shoulders even as I braced myself and held the sheet to my breasts. Where were my clothes? I was turned away from him, my back was bare to his view, and I heard him approach and stop beside the bed.

He held a glass of water to my lips, and I drank gratefully, shakily. His hand was at my back, warm and solid.

"Where have you been, Anne?"

Where am I now?

71

"I don't know." It was a whisper. I didn't look at him to gauge his reaction. "I don't know. I just know that I'm . . . *here*."

"And how long will you be here?" His voice was so cold that my fear grew, filling my chest and making my limbs numb and my fingertips pulse.

"I don't know that either," I said.

"Did they do this to you?" he asked.

"Who?" The word was a wail in my head but a sigh on my lips.

"The gunrunners, Anne." It was his turn to whisper. "Were you with them?"

"No." I shook my head adamantly, the room swimming with the movement. "I need to use the restroom."

"The restroom?" His voice rose, puzzled.

"The toilet? The loo?" I searched my memory for the Irish terminology.

"Hold on to me," he instructed, leaning over me and sliding his arms beneath me. I grappled with the sheet and didn't hold on to him at all, struggling to remain covered as he straightened, hoisting me as he did.

He carried me from the room, down a narrow hallway, and into a bathroom, setting me down carefully on the toilet. The tank was high on the wall, connected by a long brass pipe to the perfectly round seat. The space was spotless and white; the pedestal sink and claw-foot tub with heavy rounded curves gleaming and proud. I was ridiculously relieved that he hadn't had to traipse through the house and out into the yard to an outhouse or that I hadn't had to squat over a chamber pot. At the moment, squatting was out of the question.

Thomas left without a word, clearly confident I could handle the rest by myself. He was back, tapping softly, a few minutes later, and I opened the door to him, catching our reflections in the little mirror above the basin before he swept me up again, careful, his eyes clashing with mine in the glass. My hair was a curling mess, flatter on one side than the other, and my eyes were hollow beneath the tepid green. I looked terrible, and I was too exhausted to care. I was almost asleep before he laid me back on the bed and pulled the covers over me.

"Five years ago, I found Declan. But I didn't find you," he said, as if he couldn't stay silent any longer. "I thought you and Declan were together. I was evacuating the wounded from the GPO to Jervis Street. Then the fire was too great, and the barricades were up, and I couldn't get back."

I lifted my concrete lids and found him watching me, his expression desolate. He scrubbed at his face as though he could wipe the memory away. "When the fires consumed the GPO, everyone abandoned it. Declan . . ."

"The GPO?" I was so tired, and the question slipped out.

He stared at me, his brow furrowed. "The post office, Anne. Weren't you and Declan with the Volunteers at the post office? Martin said he thought you evacuated with the women, but Min said you turned back. She said you insisted on being with Declan to the end. But you weren't with Declan. Where did you go, Anne?"

I didn't remember, but I suddenly knew. The Easter Rising. He was describing events I'd read about in considerable detail.

"It was a battle we weren't going to win," Thomas murmured. "We all knew it. You and Declan knew it. We talked about what revolution would mean, what it meant to even fight back. There was something glorious about it. Glorious and terrible."

"Glorious and terrible," I whispered, picturing it, wondering again if I'd conjured this scene the way I'd imagined stories as a child, putting myself in the very center of the action and losing myself in my own productions.

"The day after we withdrew from the GPO, the leadership surrendered. I found Declan lying in the street." Thomas gazed at me, watching my face as he spoke of Declan, and I could only stare back helplessly. "He wouldn't have left you in the GPO, and the Anne I knew wouldn't have left him at all."

The Anne I knew.

Fear, sour and hot, churned in my stomach. I didn't like this development in the story. They had never found Eoin's mother. They'd never found her body. They had assumed she was dead, alongside her husband, lost in an insurrection that had ended very badly. And now I was here, raising questions that were long since buried. This was bad. This was very bad.

"We would have known. If you'd been sent to England with the other prisoners, we would have known. They released the other women. Everyone has been released. Years ago. And . . . and you're well!" Thomas insisted. He turned away, shoving his hands into the pockets of his trousers. "Your hair . . . your skin. You look . . . well."

My good health was an accusation, and he threw the words at me, although he never raised his voice. He turned back toward me but didn't approach the bed.

"You look well, Anne. You definitely haven't been wasting away in an English prison."

There was nothing I could say. No explanations I could give. I didn't know what had happened to the Anne Gallagher of 1921. I *didn't* know. The image of the graves in Ballinagar rose in my mind, a tall stone with the name Gallagher at the base. Anne and Declan shared that stone, and the dates had been clear: 1892 to 1916. I'd seen it yesterday. I was dreaming. Only dreaming.

"Anne?" Thomas pressed.

I was a wonderful liar. Not because I was deceitful, but because my mind could immediately conjure variations and plot twists, and any lie became an alternate version of a tale. I didn't especially like that I was so skilled but considered it an occupational hazard. I couldn't lie now.

I didn't know enough to create a convincing story. Not yet. I would go to sleep, and when I woke, this would be over. I gritted my teeth and closed my eyes, blocking it all out.

"I don't know, Thomas." I used his name, a plea to let me be, and turned my head toward the wall, needing the safety of my own thoughts and the space to examine them.

8 September 1917

Garvagh Glebe means "rough place." I've always thought that an interesting name for such a beautiful spot, as the land sits next to the lough, and the trees are tall, the soil rich, and the grass green. The land isn't a rough place. Yet for me, that is exactly what Garvagh Glebe has always represented. A rough place. A hard spot. And I've always struggled between loving her and resenting her. She belongs to me now, but she was not always mine.

She belonged to John Townsend, my stepfather, an English landowner whose family had been granted the land on the lough three hundred years before his birth. John was a kind man. He was good to my mother, good to me, and when he died, I inherited it. An Irishman. For the first time in three hundred years, the land had returned to Irish hands. I'd always believed that Irish land should be owned by Irish men and women, by the people who had lived and died in the soil generation after generation.

But the knowledge did not stir pride or vindication within me. Instead, contemplating Garvagh Glebe and the fates that had smiled on me usually filled me with quiet desperation. To whom much is given, much is expected, and I expected a great deal of myself.

I did not blame John Townsend for his Englishness. I loved him. He had carried no ill opinions or intentions, no biases against the Irish, no hate in his heart. He was simply a man who received what he'd been given. The taint on his inheritance had faded with the centuries. He felt no guilt for the sins of his fathers. And he shouldn't. But the history was not lost on me.

I supposed I was no different than my stepfather. I'd benefitted from his wealth. I'd happily taken what I'd been given. He provided an excellent upbringing and brought in the best doctors and tutors when I was young and ill. He paid for my advanced education when I grew older, for the fine house in Dublin where I'd lived to attend medical school at the University College, Dublin. He'd purchased the car to take me back home when my mother died halfway through my second year. And when my stepfather died six months before the Rising, he left everything he owned to me. I had not made the money I'd invested in the London Stock Exchange. I hadn't worked for the funds that sat in the Royal Bank on Knox Street or the bank notes that filled the safe in the library at Garvagh Glebe. The accounts all bore my name, but it wasn't money I'd earned.

I could have walked away in protest, rejecting John Townsend's wealth and his kindness. But I was not a fool. I was an idealist, a nationalist, a proud Irishman, but I was not a fool. I'd promised myself as a boy of fifteen sitting in a classroom in Wexford, listening to my teacher read Speeches from the Dock, *that I would use my education, position, and good fortune to better Ireland. Those were the days when Declan was always at my side, just as passionate and just as committed to the cause of Irish freedom as I was. John Townsend's money had paid for Declan's education too. My stepfather had wanted me to live among friends, and he had paid Declan's room and board, arranged for his trips back home to see his mother, and years later, when Declan had married Anne, he even paid for the wedding and let the couple live in the over-seer's cottage on Garvagh Glebe, rent-free.*

John Townsend had not approved when Declan and I became involved in the local branch of Sinn Féin or when we joined the Irish Republican Brotherhood. But he'd never withdrawn his funds or his affection. I wonder now that the walls of Garvagh Glebe no longer echo with his voice if we hurt him in our fervor. I wonder if our rhetoric of unjust British rule and bloody Englishmen ever made him wilt and walk away. The thought causes me great remorse. I have had to come to terms with the fact that idealism often rewrites history to suit her narrative. The truth is, the English are not all tyrants, and the Irish are not all saints. Enough blood has been spilt, enough blame has been cast, to condemn us all.

But Ireland deserves her independence. I am not as fiery or fierce as I once was. I am not as naïve or blind. I've seen what revolution costs, and the price is dear. But when I look at Eoin and see his father, I still feel the longing in my belly and the promise in my bones.

T. S.

6

A DREAM OF DEATH

I dreamed that one had died in a strange place
Near no accustomed hand,
And they had nailed the boards above her face,
The peasants of that land.
And left her to the indifferent stars above
Until I carved these words:
She was more beautiful than thy first love,
But now lies under boards.

—*W. B. Yeats*

I'd seen a documentary once on a nightly news program about a woman who had woken up in her own home one morning, clueless as to how she'd gotten there. She didn't know her children or her husband. She didn't know her past or her present. She'd walked through the hallways and the rooms of her home, looking at the pictures of her loved ones and her life and staring at her unfamiliar face in the mirror. And she decided to fake it. For years, she didn't let on that she couldn't remember anything before that day. Her family had never guessed her secret until she'd tearfully confessed years later.

Doctors believed she'd had some sort of aneurism, some health issue that had affected her memory but left her otherwise whole. I had watched the program with great skepticism—doubting not that she'd forgotten but that she'd been able to pull such a thing off without her family realizing something was terribly wrong.

For three days, I lay in discomfort and denial, sleeping when I could and staring at the flowered walls when I could not. I listened to the house and begged it to take me into its confidence, to reveal the secrets I didn't know and to confess the details I should know, the pieces that were scattered like bits of paper in the wind, impossible to recapture. With all the innocent ambivalence of a child, I hadn't thought to ask Eoin about his early life. Growing up, I was immersed in the world he built for me—a world that was filled with all the accoutrements of childhood. I was the center of his universe. I had never thought about the time before, when he had existed separate from me, without me. But he had. And I realized how little I knew of that life.

There were moments I wept in fear, pulling the blankets up over my face to hide and tremble beneath a comforter that should not—did not—really exist. These people—Thomas, Brigid, Eoin—*they* didn't exist. Not anymore. Yet here they were, as alive as I was, flesh and bone and feelings, moving through days that were already past. And then the tears would begin again.

I was half convinced I was dead, that I'd died on the lake and gone to a strange heaven where Eoin existed as a child again. Ultimately, that was the thought that glimmered and grew, a spark that became a flame, warming me and calming the crazed circling of my thoughts. Eoin was here, in this place. In my world, he was gone. Here, we were together again, just like he'd promised we would be. Eoin made me want to stay, if only for a while.

Thomas checked on me frequently, changing my bandages and checking for infection. "You'll be fine, Anne. Sore. But fine. No serious damage was done."

"Where's Eoin?" I asked. The boy had not been in to see me since that first night.

"Brigid has gone to her sister's in Kiltyclogher for a few days."

"Kiltyclogher," I repeated, trying to remember where I'd heard it before. "Seán Mac Diarmada was born in Kiltyclogher," I said, pulling the factoid from the recesses of my mind.

"He was. His mother, Mary, was a McMorrow. She and Brigid are sisters."

"Declan and Seán were cousins?" I marveled.

"They were. Anne, you know this."

I could only shake my head in incredulous denial. Why had Eoin kept so much of his history from me? Such an important family connection, and he'd never divulged it. Brigid *McMorrow* Gallagher. I closed my eyes and tried to clear my head, but not before a little honesty slipped from my lips.

"Brigid wants to keep Eoin from me," I whispered.

"Yes," Thomas answered, unapologetic. "Can you blame her?"

"No." I understood Brigid perfectly. I wouldn't trust me either. But I was not guilty of Anne's sins, whatever they might be. "I'd like a bath. Would that be possible?" I needed a bath. Desperately. My hair was lank and limp against my back, and I smoothed it self-consciously.

"No. Not yet. You need to keep your wound dry."

"Maybe I can just wash a little? With a cloth? Brush my teeth, maybe wash my hair?"

His eyes fell on the tangled mess and quickly looked away. He nodded. "If you feel strong enough, then yes. But the help is gone. Even Brigid is not here to assist you."

I didn't want Brigid to assist me. She'd entered my room once like a frigid wind and left a draft in her wake. She wouldn't look directly at me, not even when she'd helped me into an ancient nightgown that tied at my throat and hung to my ankles.

"I can do it myself, Thomas."

"Not your hair, you can't. You'll pull the stitches from your side. I'll do it," he said stiffly, drawing back the blankets and helping me rise. "Can you walk?"

I nodded, and he held my arm as I shuffled to the bathroom he'd carried me to several times in the last few days. My persistent, ordinary need to pee was one of the things that had convinced me I wasn't dreaming. Or dead.

"Teeth first, please," I said.

Thomas set a small wooden brush with short bristles and a tube, not unlike the toothpaste I was familiar with, on the sink. The bristles were some sort of animal hair, and they were rough. I tried not to think too much about it or the soapy taste of the paste. I scrubbed carefully, finishing with my finger to avoid making myself bleed. Thomas waited for the warm water to gurgle through the pipes, though I caught him watching me, a small furrow between his brows.

When I was finished, Thomas moved a wooden stool of medium height next to the enormous claw-foot tub and eased me down onto it. I wrapped Brigid's ill-fitting old nightgown around me and tried to lean over the edge of the large tub, but the angle made me hiss in pain.

"I don't think I can bend over yet."

"Stand. Hold on to the side, and I'll do the rest."

The angle was better with me on my feet, but I was wobbly and weak, and the weight of my head was uncomfortable. I let it fall against my chest as he began to fill a porcelain pitcher and pour the water over my head, following the lukewarm stream with steady hands.

It felt wonderful, the warmth and his gentle ministrations, but I felt so undignified as I tried to keep the voluminous nightgown from getting wet while I struggled to stay upright that I started to laugh. I felt Thomas become still beside me.

"Am I doing it wrong?" he asked.

"No. You're doing fine. Thank you."

"I'd forgotten what it sounded like."

"What?"

"Your laugh."

I stopped laughing immediately. I was an imposter, and the knowledge was ugly and frightening. The stream of water continued until my head was so heavy with the watery weight, it pulled at my side. I swayed, and Thomas steadied me, wringing the length of my hair with his right hand while he held on to me with his left.

"I need both my hands to wash your hair. If I let go, are you going to fall?"

"No."

"It does no good to say you won't if you will," he chided. Something about the accent, the singsong words chopped with very distinct *T*s, slid beneath my skin. I didn't know if it was simply the sound of my childhood, of Eoin, but it comforted me. Thomas released me slowly, testing the veracity of my claim. When I didn't wobble, he rushed to lather the streaming mass with a chunk of soap. I grimaced, but not from pain. I couldn't imagine what my hair was going to look like when it dried. I used expensive hair products to keep my curls from becoming frizzy and unmanageable.

He was thorough but gentle—working the soap through my hair and rinsing it free, long fingers on my scalp, a steady presence at my side—and his kindness made me weepy. I gritted my teeth to battle the tears that pricked my eyes and told myself I was ridiculous. I must have swayed again because Thomas pulled a towel around my shoulders, squeezed the excess water from my hair, and eased me down to the stool once more.

"Do you have . . . oil . . . or tonic . . . to smooth the hair?" I stammered, trying to use appropriate terms. "Something to ease the tangles?"

Thomas's brows rose, and he pushed back the dark lock of hair that had fallen over his forehead. His shirt was damp, and his sleeves, rolled to the elbows, hadn't fared much better.

I felt like a needy child. "Never mind. I'm sorry. Thank you for helping me."

He pursed his lips, thinking, and turned to the tall cupboard near the door. "My mother used to wash her hair with a well-beaten egg and rinse it with rosemary tea. Maybe next time, eh?" He looked at me with the barest hint of a smile. He took a fine-toothed metal comb and a small glass bottle from the cupboard. A yellow label with "Brilliantine" written above a drawing of a man with deeply parted, slicked-back hair made me think the bottle belonged to him.

"I'll just use a wee dab. It leaves a greasy residue that Brigid complains about. She says I leave spots on the furniture where I rest my head." He sat on the toilet and pulled the stool I was sitting on toward him so that I was situated between his knees, my back to him. I heard him remove the lid of the tonic and rub his hands together. The scent was not unpleasant, as I'd feared. It smelled like Thomas.

"Start at the tips and work your way up," I suggested softly.

"Yes, madam." His tone was droll, and I bit my lip, trying not to laugh. The intimacy of his actions was not lost on me. I couldn't imagine other men of the 1920s caring for their women this way. And I was not his woman.

"No patients to see today?" I asked as he began to do as I'd suggested, working his hands up through the wet strands that hung down my back.

"It's Sunday, Anne. The O'Tooles don't work on Sundays, and I don't see patients, unless it's an emergency. I've missed Mass two weeks in a row. I'm sure Father Darby will be stopping by to ask why and to drink my whiskey."

"It's Sunday," I repeated, trying to remember what day it had been when I'd spread Eoin's ashes on Lough Gill.

"I pulled you out of the lough *last* Sunday. You've been here for a week," he supplied, gathering my hair in his hand and carefully working the stiff comb through the length.

"What's the date?" I asked.

"July third."

"July 3, 1921?"

"Yes, 1921."

I was silent as he continued, carefully picking through the snarls. "They'll call a truce," I murmured.

"What?"

"The British will propose a truce with the Dáil. Both sides will agree on July 11, 1921." The date, unlike many of the others, had stuck in my head, because July 11 was Eoin's birthday.

"And you know this how, exactly?" He didn't believe me, of course. He sounded weary. "De Valera has been trying to convince the British prime minister to accept a truce since December of last year."

"I just do." I closed my eyes, wondering how I would ever tell him, how I would convince him of who I was. I didn't want to pretend I was someone else. But if I wasn't Anne Finnegan Gallagher, would he let me stay? And if I couldn't go home, where would I go?

"There. That should do it," Thomas said, and ran the towel over the freshly combed strands, blotting up the water and excess oil. I touched the sleek length, the ends already starting to curl, and thanked him quietly. He stood and, hands curved around my upper arms, helped me to my feet.

"I'll leave you now. There's a cloth and soap for washing. Stay clear of your bandages. I'll be close. Call to me when you're done. And for heaven's sake, don't faint." He moved toward the door but hesitated as he turned the knob. "Anne?"

"Yes?"

"I'm sorry." The apology rang in the air for several moments before he continued. "I left you behind in Dublin. I looked for you. But I should have kept looking." His voice was very soft, his face averted, his back rigid. I'd read his words, his account of the Rising. I'd felt his anguish. I felt it now, and I wanted to unburden him.

"You have nothing to apologize for," I said, conviction ringing in my voice. "You took care of Eoin. And Brigid. You brought Declan home. You are a good man, Thomas Smith. A very good man."

He shook his head, resistant, and when he spoke again, his voice was strained. "Your name is on his headstone. I buried your shawl beside him—the green one you loved. It was all I could find."

"I know," I soothed.

"You know?" He turned abruptly, and the grief I'd heard in his voice glittered in his eyes. "How do you know?"

"I've seen it. I've seen the grave at Ballinagar."

"What happened to you, Anne?" he pressed, repeating the question he'd asked too many times.

"I can't tell you," I implored.

"Why?" The word was a frustrated cry, and I raised my voice to match it.

"Because I don't know. I don't know how I got here!" I was clinging to the edge of the sink, and there must have been enough truth or desperation in my face because he sighed heavily, running his hand through his now-tousled hair.

"All right," he whispered. "Call to me when you're done." He left without another word, closing the bathroom door behind him, and I washed myself with shaking hands and trembling legs, more afraid than I'd ever been in my entire life.

Eoin and Brigid returned the next day. I heard Eoin scampering up the wide staircase and down again and heard Brigid telling him I was resting and not to disturb me. I'd been to the bathroom twice by myself, moving gingerly but with increasing confidence, brushing my teeth, and combing my own hair. I wanted to get dressed, to see Eoin, to move, but I had nothing to wear but the two borrowed nightgowns I'd been wearing through my convalescence. I was restless and weak, and I spent the day staring at the view beyond my two windows. The room I slept in was on the corner of the house, and I had a clear view of the front drive out one window and a nice view of the lake out the other. When I wasn't staring at the leafy trees and the shimmering lake framed in their boughs, I was watching for Thomas to return down the canopied lane.

The man rarely slept. Someone had summoned him Sunday evening—a baby needed delivering—and I'd spent the night in the big house alone, exploring the main floor. Thomas had come to my room before he left, concerned that I was not well enough to be left by myself. I reassured him that I was fine. I didn't tell him that I'd spent much of my adult life alone, and I didn't need constant companionship.

I didn't explore for long. My shuffling from the formal dining room to the huge kitchen and beyond, to the two rooms Thomas clearly used as an office and clinic, almost did me in. I wobbled to my bed, grateful beyond measure that the room I'd been given didn't require climbing stairs.

The staff returned the next morning, and a young girl in a long, plain dress covered in a white apron, her blond hair braided down her back, came in with a tray of soup and bread at suppertime. She stripped my bed of the sheets and comforter while I ate, making it up again with quiet competence. When she finished, she turned, her eyes curious, her arms full of the soiled bedding.

"Can I do anything else for you, ma'am?" she asked.

"No. Thank you. Please call me Anne. What's your name?"

"I'm Maeve, ma'am. I've just started. My older sisters, Josephine and Eleanor, work in the kitchen. And I'm here to help Moira, my other sister, clean. I'm a hard worker."

"Maeve O'Toole?" My spoon clattered loudly against the porcelain bowl.

"That's right, miss. My dad is the overseer for Dr. Smith. My brothers work outside; we girls work inside. There's ten of us

O'Tooles, though wee Bart is just a baby. Eleven if you count my great-grandmother, though she's a Gillis, not an O'Toole. She's so old, we might have to count her twice!" She laughed. "We live a little farther down the lane, behind the big house."

I stared at the girl—twelve years old at the most—and tried to find the old woman in her features. I couldn't. Time had transformed her so completely there was no obvious resemblance.

"It's lovely to meet you, Maeve," I stammered, trying to cover my shock. She beamed and bobbed her head, as if I were visiting royalty, and left the room.

She came back. Anne came back. That's what Maeve had said. She hadn't forgotten. I'd been a part of her history. Me. Not my great-grandmother. Anne Finnegan Gallagher hadn't come back. I had.

23 May 1918

An anticonscription pledge was waiting for Irish signatures at the doors of every church in Ireland last month. The prime minister of England declared that Britain's boys are in anguish, fighting on a fifty-mile front in France, and the Irish have no real grievance. Forced conscription into the British armed services is the current fear in every Irish home.

The British have begun a cat-and-mouse game of releasing political prisoners only to snatch them up again and rearrest them. They've also started arresting people for participating in any activity seen as promoting Irishism—traditional dancing, language classes, hurling matches—and fomenting anti-British sentiment.

It's only made the pot simmer.

I went to Dublin on 15 May, only to get news of a series of raids that were going to be conducted at homes of prominent members of Sinn Féin the following Friday. My name was not on the list, but Mick was worried. He got the list from one of his inside men in Dublin Castle and warned me not to go home. I spent the night at Vaughan's Hotel with Mick and a few others, waiting out the raiders. De Valera and several others of the council went home despite the warning, and they were picked up and arrested in the sweep. I'm not sure what would make a man doubt Michael Collins when he tells you not to go home, but the British had to be happy with the men they detained. Mick was back at it at dawn, bicycling all over town in his grey suit, right under the noses of the very men who wanted nothing more than to arrest him.

Comforted by the fact that my name was still clear, I made my own rounds to Dublin Castle. The newly appointed general governor of Ireland, Lord John French, is an old friend of my stepfather's. Mick is thrilled by the connection. I met Lord French for tea in his office at his headquarters at the Castle as he listed all his ailments, which people tend to do when they have a doctor's ear. I promised to check in on him once a month with new treatments for his gout. He promised to get me an invitation to the governor's ball held in the fall. I tried not to grimace and was mostly successful.

He also claimed, in strident tones, that his first order of business in his new position was to make a proclamation banning Sinn Féin, the Irish Volunteers, the Gaelic League, and Cumann na mBan. I nodded, contemplating the pot that would soon be a cauldron.

Whenever I go to Dublin, I think of Anne. Sometimes I catch myself looking for her, as though she remained here after the rebellion, just waiting to be found. The list of the casualties of the Easter Rising was finally published in the Irish Times *last year. Declan's name was there. Anne's was not. There were a handful of casualties still listed as unidentified. But at this point, they will never be identified.*

T. S.

7

HOUND VOICE

Some day we shall get up before the dawn
And find our ancient hounds before the door,
And wide awake know that the hunt is on;
Stumbling upon the blood-dark track once more.

—*W. B. Yeats*

Thomas must have arrived home after I'd gone to bed, and he was gone most of the next day. I spent another day in my room, venturing as far as the bathroom and back again and listening to the boiler rumble in the basement—a modern extravagance most rural homes did not enjoy. I'd heard Maeve and another girl—Moira?—marveling about it in the hallway outside my room. It was Maeve's second day in the big house, and she was obviously thrilled by the luxury. Thomas arrived home after dark and knocked softly on my door. When I called out, he stepped partially inside. His blue eyes were bloodshot and red-rimmed. He had a dark smudge on his forehead and his dress shirt was soiled, the button-down collar of his shirt missing.

"How are you feeling?" he asked, hovering at the door. He hadn't gone a day without checking my bandages, and it had now been two, but he didn't approach the bed.

"Better."

"I'll be back to change your bandages after I wash," he said.

"No need. I'm fine. Tomorrow will be soon enough. How's the baby?"

He looked at me blankly for a moment before his eyes cleared in comprehension. "Baby and mother are well. I was hardly needed."

"Why do you look like you've been to war?" I asked gently.

He looked at his hands and the state of his rumpled shirt, and sagged wearily against the door frame. "There was trouble at the Carrigan farm. The . . . constabulary . . . were looking for weapons. When there was resistance, they set the barn and the house on fire and shot the mule. The oldest son, Martin, is dead. He killed one of the constables and wounded another before they brought him down."

"Oh no," I gasped. I knew the history, but it had never been real.

"When I got there, there was nothing left of the barn. The house fared a little better. It will need a new roof. We saved what we could. Mary Carrigan kept trying to pull their belongings out of the cottage while the thatch rained down on her. Her hands are burned, and her hair is half gone."

"What can we do?"

"You can't do anything," he said, and smiled feebly to soften his rejection. "I'll make sure Mary's hands heal. The family will move in with Patrick's kin until the roof is repaired. Then they'll carry on."

"Were there weapons?" I asked.

"They didn't find any," he answered, his eyes holding mine for a moment, considering, before he looked away. "But Martin has—had—a reputation for gun running."

"What are the guns for?"

"What the guns are always for, Anne. We fight the British with flaming balls of shit and homemade grenades. And when we're lucky, we fight them with Mausers too." His voice had grown edgy, and his jaw was tight.

"We?" I ventured.

"We. Once upon a time *we* included you. Does it still?"

I searched his eyes, uncertain and unsettled, and remained silent. I could not answer a question I didn't understand.

When he closed the door, he left a dark handprint behind.

Sometime long after the tall clock in the broad foyer struck one, I came awake to little hands on my cheeks and a small nose pressed to mine.

"Are you sleeping?" Eoin whispered.

I touched his face, overjoyed to see him. "I must be."

"Can I sleep with you?" he asked.

"Does your grandmother know you're here?" I murmured, moving my hand to the soft pelt of crimson hair curling over his brow.

"No. She's asleep. But I'm afraid."

"What are you afraid of?"

"The wind is very loud. What if we don't hear the Tans? What if the house is on fire, and we are all asleep?"

"What are you talking about?" I soothed, stroking his hair.

"They burned down Conor's house. I heard Doc talking to Nana," he explained, his eyes wide, his tone plaintive.

"Eoin?" Thomas stood at the door, washed and changed but not for bed. From the looks of it, he hadn't been sleeping. He wore trousers, a white button-down shirt, and his boots. He clutched a rifle in his right hand.

"Are you watching for the Tans, Doc?" Eoin gasped.

Thomas didn't deny it but propped the gun against the wall and entered the room. He closed the distance to my bed and stretched out his hand to Eoin. "It's the middle of the night, lad. Come."

"My mother is going to tell me a story," Eoin fibbed stubbornly, and my heart groaned in tender protest. "What if you watch from that window and listen with me, Doc?" Eoin pointed, impudent, at the view of the long lane stretching into darkness.

"Anne?" Thomas sighed, clearly seeking reinforcement.

"Please let him stay," I urged. "He's frightened. He can sleep here."

"I can sleep here, Doc!" Eoin warmed to the idea like it was his own, which, after all, it was.

"Careful, Eoin," Thomas warned. "Don't climb over your mother. Go around."

Eoin immediately scurried to the other side of the bed and scrambled up, squirming down in the covers beside me, his body so close to mine, there was room for Thomas to join us. He didn't.

Instead, he moved the chair beside my bed to the window overlooking the lane and sat, eyes trained on the shadows. Eoin had not been wrong; he was keeping watch.

I told Eoin the Irish legend of Fionn and the Salmon of Knowledge and how Fionn came to have a magic thumb. "When Fionn needed to know something, he simply stuck his thumb in his mouth, and the answer would come to him," I said, coming to the end of the tale.

"More, please," Eoin whispered, clearly hoping Thomas wouldn't hear. Thomas sighed but didn't protest.

"Do you know the story of Setanta?" I asked.

"Do I know the story of Setanta, Doc?" Eoin forgot he was being sneaky.

"Yes, Eoin," Thomas answered.

"I can't remember it very well, though. I think I need to hear it again," Eoin implored.

"All right," I agreed. "Setanta was the son of Dechtire, who was sister to Conchobar mac Nessa, the king of Ulster. Setanta was just a young boy, but he wanted very badly to be a warrior like the knights who fought for his uncle. One day, when his mother wasn't looking, Setanta sneaked away and began the long journey to Ulster, determined to join the Knights of the Red Branch. It was a grueling journey, but Setanta did not turn back to the safety of his mother's arms."

"Grueling?" Eoin interrupted, puzzled.

"Very difficult," I supplied.

"Didn't he love his mother?" he asked.

"Yes. But he wanted to be a warrior."

"Oh." Eoin sounded doubtful, as though he didn't really understand. He twined one arm around my neck and laid his head on my chest. "He could have waited," he murmured.

"Yes," I whispered, and closed my eyes against a sudden rise of tears. "But Setanta was ready. When he reached his uncle's court, he did everything he could to impress the king. And even though he was small, he was very fierce and very courageous, and the king said he could train to be a knight. Setanta learned many things. He learned to stay silent when it was wise to be silent. He learned to fight when he must. He learned to listen to the wind and to the earth and to the water so that his enemies would never take him by surprise."

"Did he see his mother again?" Eoin asked, still caught on that one detail.

"Yes. And she was very proud," I whispered.

"Tell me the part about the hound," he demanded.

"You *do* remember this story," I murmured.

Eoin was silent, realizing he'd been caught in a lie. I finished, regaling him with the story of King Conor dining at the house of his smith, Culann, and Setanta killing Culann's savage hound. Setanta had pledged from that day forward to guard the king as the hound had done, forever more being called Cú Chulainn, the hound of Culann.

"You are a very good storyteller," Eoin murmured sweetly, tightening his small arms around me, and the lump in my throat grew so big, it overflowed and spilled down my cheeks.

"Why are you crying? Are you sad Setanta killed the hound?" Eoin asked.

"No," I answered, turning my face into his hair.

"You don't like dogs?" Eoin was shocked, and his voice rose.

"Shh, Eoin. Of course, I do." His dismay made me giggle despite the emotion that clogged my throat.

"Setanta *had* to kill the hound," Eoin reassured me, still convinced the story had made me weep. "Or the hound would have killed him. Doc says killing is wrong, but sometimes it has to be done."

Thomas turned from the window, a flicker of lightning illuminating the angles of his face only to retreat and leave him in darkness again.

"Eoin," he rebuked softly.

"You're just like the hound, Doc. You protect the house." Eoin was undeterred.

"And you are like Fionn. You ask too many questions," Thomas retorted mildly.

"I need a magic thumb like Fionn." Eoin held his hands in the air, curling his fingers and sticking out his thumbs, examining them.

"You will have magic fingers instead. Just like Doc. You will make people well with your steady hands," I said, keeping my voice low. It had to be close to three o'clock in the morning, and Eoin showed no signs of drowsiness. The little boy almost vibrated with energy.

I reached up and wrapped my hands around his, pulling them down to his sides and repositioning the pillow beneath his head.

"It's time to sleep now, Eoin," Thomas said.

"Will you sing to me?" Eoin asked, raising imploring eyes to mine.

"No. But I will tell you a poem. Poems can be like a song. But you need to close your eyes. It is a very, very long poem. More like a story."

"Good," Eoin said, clapping.

"No clapping. No talking. Eyes closed," I said.

Eoin obeyed.

"Are you comfortable?" I whispered.

"Yes," he whispered back, keeping his eyes shut.

I pitched my voice soft and low and began, "I hardly hear the curlew cry, nor the grey rush when the wind is high." I narrated slowly, letting the rhythm and the words lull the boy into slumber. "Baile and Aillinn" had always put Eoin to sleep. He was snoring softly before I reached the end, and I stopped, allowing the story to fade without being finished.

Thomas turned from the window. "That isn't the end."

"No. Eoin's asleep," I murmured.

"But I'd like to hear it," he said quietly.

"Where did I leave off?"

"They come where some huge watcher is, and tremble with their love and kiss," he said, quoting the line perfectly. The words from his mouth sounded erotic and warm, and I picked up the thread eagerly, wanting to please him.

"They know undying things, for they wander where earth withers away," I recited, and I continued softly through the final stanzas, finishing with the words I loved the most. "For never yet has lover lived, but longed to wive, like them that are no more alive."

"For them that are no more alive," he whispered. The room was hushed with the afterglow that a good story always leaves behind, and I closed my eyes and listened to little Eoin breathe, hardly daring to breathe myself, not wanting the moment to pass too soon.

"Why were you crying? You didn't answer him."

I examined my answer briefly, unsure of what to reveal, before settling on the simplest version of my complicated emotions. "My grandfather told me those stories. He told me about the hound of Culann. Now I'm telling Eoin. Someday, he will tell his granddaughter the stories I told him."

I told you. You told me. Only the wind knows which truly comes first.

Thomas turned from the window, framed in the weak light, waiting for me to continue, and I tried to explain the glorious tumult in my chest.

"Lying here next to him. His sweetness. His arms around my neck. I realized how . . . happy . . . I am." The truth was odd, making it seem false. I missed my grandfather. I missed my life. I was afraid. Terrified. Yet a part of me was overcome with gratitude for the little boy beside me and the man who stood guard at my bedroom window.

"You're happy, so you cry?" Thomas questioned.

"I've cried a great deal lately. But this time, they were tears of joy."

"There is little reason for happiness in Ireland these days."

"Eoin is reason enough for me," I answered, and marveled again that it was true.

Thomas was quiet for so long my eyes grew heavy, and sleep crept up on me.

"You are so different, Anne. I hardly know you," Thomas murmured. Sleep fled, frightened off by my pounding heart and the sound of his voice. Sleep didn't return, and Thomas didn't leave. He kept vigil, eyes on the dark trees and the empty lane, watching for a threat that never came.

When dawn peeped through the trees, Thomas lifted the sleepy child, limp and loose, from my arms. I watched them go, Eoin's vivid head on Thomas's shoulder, his little arms dangling over his back.

"I'll put him back in his bed before Brigid wakes. She need never know. Try to sleep now, Anne," Thomas said wearily. "I think we're safe from the Tans for the time being."

I dreamed of pages that whirled around my head. I would capture one and hold it against my chest, only to lose it again when I tried to read it. I chased the fluttering bits of white out into the lake, knowing the water would blur the words I hadn't read. I watched the pages come closer with the waves, taunting me for a moment with the possibility of rescue, only to sink slowly beneath the surface. It was a dream I'd had before. I'd always thought it stemmed from my need to write things down, to preserve them, to give them eternal life, if only on a page. I came awake gasping, remembering. Thomas Smith's journal, the one that ended with a warning to his love, might very well be at the bottom of Lough Gill. It had been in my bag, the picture of Garvagh Glebe tucked between the pages. I'd forgotten about it; it had been lying there beneath the urn with Eoin's ashes.

A wave of sorrow and regret pinned me back against the pillows. I'd been so foolish, so careless. In that book Thomas Smith had lived, and now it was gone. We were specks, bits of glass and dust. We were as numerous as the sands that lined the strand, one unrecognizable from the other. We were born; we lived; we died. And the cycle continued endlessly on. So many lives lived. And when we died, we simply vanished. A few generations would go by. And no one would know we even *were*. No one would remember the color of our eyes or the passion that raged inside us. Eventually, we all became stones in the grass, moss-covered monuments, and sometimes . . . not even that.

Even if I returned to the life I'd lost in the lough, the book would still be gone. Thomas Smith would be gone—the slant of his words, the turn of his phrase, his hopes and his fears. His life. Gone. And the thought was unbearable to me.

19 March 1919

The Great War is over, but Ireland's war is just beginning. An armistice was signed on 11 November, signaling the end of the bloody conflict and the end of conscription fears. Over two hundred thousand Irish boys still fought, even without conscription, and thirty-five thousand of them died for a country that doesn't recognize their right to self-determination.

Maybe that boiling cauldron is finally ready to overflow. In the December general elections, Sinn Féin candidates won seventy-three of the 105 Irish seats in the House of Commons of the United Kingdom. None of the seventy-three will take their seats at Westminster. In accordance with the manifesto signed by each member of Sinn Féin in 1918, Ireland will form her own government, the first Dáil Éireann.

Mick has been organizing breakouts for political prisoners, smuggling in files to cut through bars, throwing rope ladders over walls, and pretending the spoons in their coat pockets were revolvers to scare off the warders. He couldn't stop laughing when he described the Mountjoy jail breakout and the fact that they got twenty prisoners instead of three.

"O'Reilly was waiting outside the jail with three bicycles!" he howled. "He came in here shouting that the whole jail was loose."

Mick broke Eamon de Valera, the newly elected president of the Irish Republic, out of Lincoln Prison in February only to discover de Valera has plans to go to America to raise money and support for Irish independence. No estimates as to how long he'll be there. I've never seen Mick so flabbergasted. He feels abandoned, and I can hardly blame him. The load on his shoulders is enormous. He sleeps even less than I do. He's ready for all-out war, but de Valera says the public is not.

I've had very little time for collecting information. Influenza has broken out all over Europe, and my little corner of Ireland has not been spared. I hardly know what day it is most of the time, and I've tried to stay far away from Eoin and Brigid to protect them from the disease that must cling to my skin and clothes. When I'm able to come home at all, I remove my clothes in the barn and have bathed in the lough more times than I can count.

I've seen Pierce Sheehan and Martin Carrigan on the lake a time or two when I rowed across to check on the O'Briens. I know they're bringing guns from Sligo's docks. Where they go when they leave the lake, I don't know. If they've seen me, they pretend not to; I suppose it's safer that way, for all of us.

Peader and Polly O'Brien's grandson, Willie, passed away from influenza last week. He wasn't much older than Eoin. Eoin will miss the lad. They played together a few times. Peader insisted on spreading the boy's ashes on the lake. Cremation has become preferable to stop the spread of the disease. Peader's boat turned up on the Dromahair side of the lake day before last. Eamon Donnelly found it, but sadly, Peader wasn't in it. He hasn't come home, and we fear the lough has taken him. Now poor Polly is all alone. Too much sadness all around.

T. S.

8

THE MASK

I would but find what's there to find,
Love or deceit.
It was the mask engaged your mind,
And after set your heart to beat,
Not what's behind.

—W. B. Yeats

I wasn't sure if Thomas sent Brigid or if she'd taken it upon herself, but she'd stomped into my room two days later and declared it time I was up and dressed. "When you didn't come back from Dublin, I put your things in the chest there. I kept Declan's belongings." Her voice caught, and she finished in a rush. "I'm sure you'll recognize your clothes. It isn't much. The doctor is seeing patients in Sligo today. He said he'd take you to the shops for the other things you're in need of."

I nodded eagerly, climbing gingerly from my bed. I was healing, but it would be a while before I could move without pain.

"You look like a gypsy with that hair," Brigid snapped, eyeing me. "You'll need to cut it or pin it up. People will think you've escaped from an asylum. But that's what you want them to think, isn't it? If people think you're crazy, you won't have to explain yourself."

I tried to smooth my dark curls, embarrassed. I couldn't imagine myself with the Gibson Girl updo Brigid wore. I didn't know if it was the fashion of the day, but I wouldn't be adhering to it. Anne's hair had been jaw-length in one of her photos, her hair curling softly around her face. I couldn't imagine myself in that style either. My hair was too curly. With no weight from its length to hold it down, it would be enormous. As for Brigid's assertion of craziness, it wasn't a terrible idea. If people thought I was deranged, they *would* keep their distance.

Brigid continued, muttering bitterly as though I weren't in the room. "You turn up out of nowhere—with a gunshot wound, no less—wearing men's clothes, and you expect us to welcome you with open arms."

"I expected no such thing," I answered, but she ignored me, unlocking the chest beneath the front window with a small key she withdrew from her apron pocket. She lifted the top and, satisfied that the chest contained the items she remembered, turned to leave the room.

"I think it would be best if you let Eoin be. He doesn't remember you, and you'll only upset him with your forgetfulness," she demanded, tossing the order over her shoulder.

"I can't do that." I spoke before I realized the words were even on my tongue.

She spun to look at me, her mouth tight, her hands pressed to the apron she wore. "Ya can. And ya will," she insisted, so cold and adamant I almost backed down.

"I won't, Brigid," I said quietly. "I am going to spend as much time with him as I can. Don't attempt to keep him away. Don't do it. I know you love him. But I'm here now. Please don't try to keep us apart."

Her face became granite, her eyes glacial, her lips clamped so tight no softness remained.

"You have loved him so well. He is so beautiful, Brigid. Thank you for all you have done. I will never be able to express the depth of my gratitude," I said, and supplication quivered in my voice. But she turned, seemingly unmoved, and swished from the room.

Her anger was a physical thing, her hurt and resentment as present and real as the wound in my side. I would have to keep reminding myself that her anger, though directed at me, was not my burden.

I padded down the hallway to the bathroom, washed my face, and brushed my teeth and hair before returning to my room and the chest that awaited. I rifled through the contents, eager to be free of the nightgown and to clothe myself and leave the room I'd languished in for ten days.

I stepped into a long dark skirt and tried to fasten it. The waistband was too small, or I was still too swollen. I stepped out of the garment and searched the chest for underthings. The panties I'd been wearing when Thomas pulled me out of the lake were damp from the scrubbing I'd given them the day before in the bathroom sink. The rest of my clothes were folded neatly on the upper shelf of the small wardrobe, the bullet holes expertly mended. I'd considered donning them even before today but knew the oddness of that attire would inspire more scrutiny and encourage questions better left tucked away. I unearthed a thigh-length jacket with a thick band around the waist, a wide collar, and three big buttons marching down the front. A matching ankle-length skirt of the drabbest brown I'd ever seen was beneath it. I found a brown silk hat adorned with a wilted brown ribbon inside a tattered hatbox and guessed the items had all been worn together.

A pair of low-heeled boots, worn in the toes and soles, were wedged beneath the hatbox. I managed to stuff my feet into them, pleased that they fit well enough that I wouldn't be going barefoot. However, bending to lace them was out of the question. I stepped out of the boots and continued exploring.

I pulled out a contraption that could only be a corset; the boning and ties and hanging buckles had me shuddering in horror and fascination. I slipped it around my midsection, where it sat, gaping like a wide bracelet, its ends not quite touching. At the top it widened slightly, providing a ledge for my breasts to rest on, the crumpled clump of ribbon sitting like a rosebud between them.

The corset hung lower in the front and back and rose slightly on the sides, freeing my hips for movement. Clearly the jangling straps in front and back were designed to attach to long stockings. But what did women wear beneath? The juxtaposition of wearing something as old-fashioned and confining as a corset and simultaneously being naked where it counted most was hilarious to me, and I giggled while trying to force the two silk-covered sides together. Most women in Ireland did not have personal maids—I was convinced of that. So how in the world did they fasten the damned things? I succeeded in connecting the top two hooks beneath my breasts before, breathless and aching, I abandoned the contraption. Corsets and gunshot wounds to the abdomen, however minor, did not mix. I turned back to the chest in hopes of finding something I could actually wear.

A white blouse—wide-collared and long-sleeved, horribly wrinkled, and slightly yellowed in places—fit well enough. The sleeves were a hair too short, but the overall style was forgiving and voluminous, and the three-quarter-length sleeve looked almost deliberate. The brown jacket and skirt fit, but the wool smelled of damp places and mothballs, and the thought of wearing the garment for any length of time was distasteful. I looked like Mary Poppins's dowdy sister and wondered why the first Anne Gallagher had picked a color that wouldn't have looked any better on her, considering I was her doppelganger.

I took off the suit and blouse and went on to the next thing.

A white sheath, the neckline square and unadorned except for some bits of lace at the hem and down the center, looked promising. Another piece, embroidered with the same lace, was clearly designed to be worn over the sheath. It had slim elbow-length sleeves and sides that hung open to reveal the dress beneath. A thick sash was banded around the two garments, and I pulled the sheath over my head, donned the thin overdress, and tied the sash loosely around my waist, the bow in back. It needed to be pressed and hung almost to my ankles, but it fit. I stared at my image in the long oval mirror and realized with a start that it was the dress my great-grandmother had worn in the picture with Declan and Thomas. In the photograph, my great-grandmother had worn a round-brimmed white hat wreathed in flowers. The dress was too pretty for everyday wear, but I was relieved to have something I could call my own. I pulled my hair off my face and tried to knot it at my nape.

A soft knock at the door had me abandoning my hair and curling my bare toes nervously against the wood floors.

"Come in," I called, kicking the corset across the floor. It slid under the bed, a buckle peeping out accusingly.

"You found your things, then," Thomas said, his mouth soft and his eyes sad.

It felt like yet another lie to admit to a previous ownership, so I drew attention to the wrinkles in the linen. "It needs to be pressed."

"Yes . . . well, it's been in that chest a long time," he said.

I nodded and smoothed it self-consciously.

"Is there anything else in there you can wear?" he asked, his voice pained.

"A few things," I hedged. I would need to sell my ring and the diamond studs in my ears. I couldn't get by with the contents of the chest. Thomas clearly agreed.

"You'll need more than the dress you were married in. You could wear it to Mass, I suppose," he mused.

"Married in?" I said, too surprised to guard my tongue. I touched my head, thinking of the hat Anne had worn in the picture. It hadn't looked like a wedding photo.

"You don't remember that either?" His voice rose in disbelief, and the softness of fond memories left his eyes when I answered him with a shake of my head. "It was a good day, Anne. You and Declan were so happy."

"I didn't see a . . . veil . . . in the chest," I said inanely.

"You wore Brigid's veil. You didn't like it very much. It was beautiful, a little out of fashion, but you and Brigid . . ." Thomas shrugged as if the poor relationship was old news.

Mystery solved. I breathed deeply and tried to meet Thomas's gaze.

"I'll change into the wool suit," I murmured, looking away, desperate to change the subject.

"I don't know why Brigid saved that. Ugliest thing I've ever seen. But you're right. That dress won't do."

"Brigid says I need to cut my hair," I said. "But I'd rather not. I just need some pins or ties, and I'll make it look presentable. I could also use a little help tying my boots."

"Turn around," Thomas ordered.

I did as he asked, unsure but obedient. I gasped when he took my hair in his hands and began braiding, weaving the strands around each other until he had a long plait. I was so surprised, I remained perfectly still, welcoming the feel of his hands in my hair once more. He tied off the braid and looped the end and then looped it again, piercing the whole thing several times with what felt like hairpins.

"Done!" he exclaimed.

I felt the coiled knot at the base of my skull and turned around. "You are full of surprises, Thomas Smith. You carry hairpins in your pockets?"

His cheeks pinked the slightest bit, a blush so faint I would have missed it if I hadn't been standing so close and looking so intently.

"Brigid told me to give them to you." He cleared his throat. "My mother always had long hair. I watched her wind it up a thousand times. After her stroke, she couldn't do it. Sometimes I would do it for her. I didn't do a bang-up job. But if you wear that ugly hat with that hideous suit, no one will be looking at your hair."

I laughed, and his eyes fell to my smile.

"Sit down," he commanded, pointing to the bed. I obeyed again, and he grabbed the boots.

"No stockings in there?" He tossed his head toward the chest.

I shook my head.

"Well, we'll fix that as soon as we can. But for now, boots." He sank down on his haunches and I pushed my foot into the upheld shoe. He made short work of the hooks and eyes, my foot resting against his chest.

"I can't help you with that," he murmured, his eyes on the corset that was all too visible from his angle.

"I won't be wearing it any time soon. I'm too sore, and no one will be able to tell anyway."

"No. I don't suppose they will." The flush colored his cheeks again, and it puzzled me. He was the one who brought it up. He finished tying my other boot and set it gently on the floor. He didn't rise but clasped his hands between his knees and looked at the floor, his head bowed.

"I don't know what to tell them, Anne," he said. "I can't keep you a secret forever. You've got to help me. You've been dead for five years. It would help if we had an explanation—even if it's pure fiction."

"I've been in America."

His eyes shot to mine. "You left your child, a babe, and went to America?" His voice was so flat I could have built a wall on it. I looked away.

"I was unwell. Mad with grief," I murmured, unable to meet his gaze. I *had* been in America. And when Eoin died, I *was* mad with grief.

He was quiet, and from the corner of my eyes, I could see his slightly stooped shoulders, the stillness in the tilt of his head.

"Brigid says I look like I've escaped from an asylum. Maybe that's what we should tell them," I continued, wincing.

"Jaysus," Thomas whispered.

"I can play the part," I said. "I feel crazy. And God knows I'm lost."

"Why do you have to play a part? Is it true? What's the truth, Anne? That's what I want to know. I want to know the truth. You can lie to the rest of them, but please don't lie to me."

"I'm trying so hard not to," I mumbled.

"What does that mean?" He rose from his haunches and stood, looking down at me.

"The truth will be impossible for you to believe. You *won't* believe it. And you will think I'm lying. I would give you the truth if I thought it would help. But it won't, Thomas."

He stepped back as if I'd slapped him. "You said you didn't know," he hissed.

"I don't know what occurred after the Rising. I don't know how I got here. I don't understand what is happening to me."

"So tell me what you do know."

"I will promise you this. If silence is a lie, I'm guilty. But the things I've told you, the things I've said to you so far, are true. And if I can't tell you the truth, I won't say anything at all."

Thomas shook his head, anger and bewilderment on his face. Then he turned and walked from my room without another word, and I was left to wonder yet again when my predicament would end, when it would all be over, when my life would right itself. I was stronger now, well enough to slip away to the lough. Soon, I would walk out into the water and sink beneath the surface, willing myself home and leaving Eoin and Thomas behind. Soon, but not yet.

"Will they recognize me?" I asked, raising my voice to be heard over the wind and the rumble of the motor. Thomas sat behind the wheel of a car straight out of *The Great Gatsby*, driving us to Sligo. Eoin was perched between us, neatly dressed in a little vest and jacket, his bony knees sticking out between the hem of his long shorts and the tops of his tall dark socks. He wore the same type of peaked hat he'd worn all his life, the thin brim pulled low over his blue eyes. The car had an open top—a hazard in rainy Ireland—but the sky was clear, the breeze gentle, and the trip pleasant. I had not been outside since the day on the lake, and my eyes were glued to the familiar landscape. The population in Ireland had not grown in a hundred years, leaving the scenery mostly unchanged generation after generation.

"Are you worried someone *might* recognize you?" Thomas answered, his tone quizzical.

"I am," I admitted, meeting his eyes briefly.

"You aren't from Sligo. Few will know you. And those who do . . ." He shrugged, not finishing his sentence, his eyes shifting away from me in contemplation. Thomas Smith didn't bite his lip or wrinkle his brow when he stewed. His face was perfectly still, as though he thought so deeply, no echoes crossed his face or marred his features. It was odd, really, that in a matter of days, I'd come to recognize his posture, the way he stooped with his head slightly bowed and his features quiet. Had Eoin learned his ways? Was that why I knew Thomas Smith so well? Had Eoin absorbed the habits of the man who had stepped into his life and raised the boy Declan had left fatherless? I recognized little similarities—the wide stance, the downcast eyes, the outward calm, and the unruffled ruminations. The resemblances made me long for my grandfather.

Without thinking, I reached for Eoin's hand. His blue eyes shot to mine, and his hand tightened and trembled. Then he smiled, a toothy revelation that eased one longing and gave rise to another.

"I'm a little afraid to go shopping," I whispered near his ear. "If you hold my hand, it will help me be brave."

"Nana loves the shops. Don't you?"

I did. Usually. But the fear in my belly, magnified by the thought of corsets with hanging straps, strange clothes, and my complete dependence on Thomas grew as Sligo appeared in the distance. I looked around me in wonder, trying to find the cathedral to orient myself. My chest began to burn.

"I have earrings . . . and a ring. I think both would sell for a good price," I blurted and then thought better of my statement. I really knew nothing about the ring. I pushed the thought from my head and tried again.

"I have some jewelry. I'd like to sell it so that I have some money of my own. Could you help me with that, Thomas?"

"Don't worry your head about money," Thomas clipped, eyes forward.

A country doctor paid in chickens and piglets or bags of potatoes couldn't be completely unconcerned with money, and the worry coiled deeper.

"I want money of my own," I insisted. "I'll need to find employment too." Employment. Dear God. I'd never had a job. I'd been writing stories from the moment I could form a sentence. And writing wasn't a job. Not for me.

"You can assist me," Thomas said, his jaw still tight, eyes on the road.

"I'm not a nurse!" Was I? Was *she*?

"No. But you're capable of following directions and giving me a spare set of hands every now and again. That's all I need."

"I want money of my own, Thomas. I will buy my own clothes."

"Nana says you should call Thomas Dr. Smith," Eoin said, inserting himself into the conversation. "And she says he should call you Mrs. Gallagher."

We were silent. I had no idea what to say.

"But your nana is Mrs. Gallagher too. That would be confusing, wouldn't it?" Thomas replied. "Plus, Anne was my friend before she was Mrs. Gallagher. Do you call your friend Miriam Miss McHugh?"

Eoin covered his mouth, but a snort of laughter gurgled out. "Miriam isn't a miss! She's a pest," he crowed.

"Yes . . . well, so is Anne." Thomas looked at me and looked away, but his eyebrows quirked, softening his words.

"Is there a jeweler or a pawnbroker in Sligo?" I insisted, not willing to let the matter go, pest or not. Were they even called pawnbrokers in 1921? The hysteria continued to build inside me.

Thomas sighed, and we bounced down the deeply rutted road. "I have three patients to see. None of the stops will take me long, but I will drop you and Eoin—stay close to your mother, Eoin, and help her—on lower Knox Street. There's a pawnbroker next to the Royal Bank. Daniel Kelly. He'll be fair with you. When you're done, walk up to Lyons department store. You should be able to get everything you need there."

Eoin was bouncing on the seat between us, obviously thrilled at the mention of the department store.

"I will meet you there when I'm finished," Thomas promised.

We crossed the River Garavogue on Hyde Bridge—a bridge I'd walked across less than two weeks before—and I gaped in wonder. The countryside had not changed, but the times certainly had. The streets, unpaved and free of the traffic and congestion of 2001, seemed much larger and the buildings much newer. The Yeats Memorial Museum sat on the corner, but it wasn't a museum any longer. The words *Royal Bank* were written in bold across the side. A few cars and a delivery van rumbled along the street, most of them black, all of them antique, but horse-pulled carts were just as common. The bulk of the traffic was pedestrian, the clothing smart, the steps brisk. Something about the apparel—the formality of suits and ties, vests and pocket watches, dresses and heels, and hats and long coats—gave everything a decorum that contributed to my sense of the surreal. It was a movie set, and we were actors on a stage.

"Anne?" Thomas prodded gently. I tore my eyes away from the storefronts, from the wide footpaths and lampposts, from the old cars and the wagons, from the people who were all . . . long . . . dead.

We were parked in front of a small establishment just two doors down from the stately Royal Bank. Three golden balls were suspended from an ornate wrought-iron pole, and "Kelly & Co." was written across the glass in a baroque font no one used anymore. Eoin squirmed impatiently beside me, anxious to get out of the car. I reached for the door handle, my palms damp, my breath shallow.

"You said he'd be fair. But I have no idea what that might be, Thomas," I blurted, stalling.

"Don't take less than a hundred pounds, Anne. I don't know where you got diamonds, but those earbobs are worth a lot more than that. Don't sell your ring. As for the department store, I have an account at Lyons. Use it. They know Eoin is mine." Thomas immediately amended his statement. "They know Eoin lives with me, and they won't ask any questions. Put your purchases on my account, Anne," he repeated firmly. "Buy the boy an ice cream cone, and save the rest of your money."

30 November 1919

Several months ago, on a quick trip to Dublin, I spent a harrowing night on Great Brunswick Street, locked in detective headquarters and going through the files that laid out the Castle's secret intelligence operation and named their informants—known as G-Men— in Ireland. One of Mick's inside men, a detective who worked at the Castle but fed information to Sinn Féin, got Mick inside the records division, and Mick brought me along, "just for the craic." He didn't need me for courage, but he seemed to want company. Between the two of us, in a matter of hours, we were able to get a fairly clear picture of how the information flowed in the G Division and who it flowed through.

Mick found the file compiled about him and had a good laugh at the grainy photo and the halfhearted compliments made to his acumen.

"But there's no file here for you, Tommy," he'd said. "Clean as a whistle, boyo. But not if they catch us here."

We got a good scare when a window of the room we were locked in was broken, causing us to hide behind the shelves, praying no one would come to investigate. We could hear the drunken song of the vandal outside and a policeman shooing him away. After a moment, when it seemed we were in the clear, Mick began to whisper, not about what we'd learned or the contents of the files, but about life and love and women. I knew then he was trying to distract me, and I let him, trying to return the favour.

"Why haven't you settled down, Doc? Married a pretty girl from County Leitrim and made a few blue-eyed babies?" he said.

"Why haven't you, Mick? We're roughly the same age. The ladies love you. You love them," I responded.

"And you don't?" he scoffed.

"Yes. I love you too."

He laughed, a great happy sound, and I flinched at his boisterous disregard for our situation.

"Quiet, ya big oaf!" I shushed him.

"Yer a good friend, Tommy." His broad Cork accent was more pronounced in a whisper. "We make time for what's important. There's got to be someone you can't stop thinkin' about."

I thought of Anne then. I thought of her more than I should. In truth, I thought of her constantly and was quick to deny it. "I haven't found her yet. I doubt I ever will."

"Ha! Says the man who shunned advances from one of the most beautiful women in London," Mick teased.

"She was married, Mick. And she was more interested in you," I said, knowing he spoke of Moya Llewelyn-Davies, who was indeed beautiful and very married. I'd met her when I'd accompanied Mick to London when he'd been trying to write up a proposal to the American president. He was hoping President Wilson would pledge his support and shine a light on the Irish question. Irish

born, Moya had become interested in the Anglo-Irish conflict and the excitement and intrigue surrounding it. She'd offered her estate near Dublin—Furry Park—to Mick to use as a safe house, and he'd taken her up on it.

"Not in the beginning, boyo. She said I was pasty and loud, and I smoked too much. She liked your looks. It was obvious. She only turned her attentions on me when she realised I was Michael Collins and you were just a country doctor," Mick teased, and grabbed me, wrestling and roughhousing the way he was wont to do when the tension got to be too much.

"And what exactly is a country doctor doing, hiding in this dust hole with a wanted man?" I asked, my throat itching from said dust and my arms aching from trying to keep Mick from biting my ear, which was what he always did if he managed to wrestle you to the ground.

"He's doing his duty for Ireland. For love of country. And for a bit of fun," Mick wheezed, narrowly avoiding upending a stack of files.

It was fun, and I escaped unscathed, even my ears. Mick's man, Ned Broy, had come for us before dawn, and we'd been spirited out, with no one the wiser. Except Mick. That night, Michael Collins grew much wiser. I finished my business in Dublin and returned to Dromahair, to Eoin and Brigid and to the people who needed me to be a country doctor more than a soldier in Mick's army. I'd had no idea then what that night meant in his war. In our war.

It was in those files that Mick devised his own plan to destroy British intelligence in Ireland from the inside out. Not long after our night in the records division, Mick formed his own elite militarized squad. A group of very *young men—younger than Mick or me—all incredibly loyal, all completely committed to the cause. Some call them the twelve apostles. Some call them murderers. And I suppose they are both. They follow Mick. They do as he tells them. And their orders are ruthless.*

There are things I don't think Mick wants to discuss with me and things I don't want to know, but I was there that night on Great Brunswick Street, and I saw the names in those files. When the targeted killing of G-Men began happening in Dublin, I knew why. The rumours are that the targets are warned before they're taken out. They're told to back off. To step down. To quit working against the IRA—the Irish Republican Army—which is what the Irish resistance is now being called. It's no longer the Volunteers or the IRB or Sinn Féin. We're the Irish Republican Army. Mick shrugs and says it's about damned time we're seen as one. Some of the G-Men listen to the warnings. Some don't. And some die. I don't like it. But I understand it. It isn't vengeance. It's strategy. It's war.

T. S.

9

HIS BARGAIN

Who talks of Plato's spindle;
What set it whirling round?
Eternity may dwindle,
Time is unwound.

—*W. B. Yeats*

With Eoin's hand clutched in mine, I pushed through the pawnbroker's door, the bell tinkling over my head, and found myself inside a treasure box with the quaint and the curious, the valuable and the varied: tea sets and toy trains, guns and golden gadgets, and everything in between. Eoin and I stopped, stunned, and gaped at the trove. The room was long and narrow, and at the far end, a man stood patiently at the wooden counter, his white shirt crisp. His dark tie was tucked into his neatly buttoned dark-colored vest, a pair of tiny gold-rimmed glasses on his nose. He had a thick head of wavy gray hair, and a tidy beard and mustache covered his lower face.

"Good afternoon, madam," he called. "Are you looking for something in particular?"

"Uh, no, sir," I stammered, pulling my eyes away from the walls of intricate oddities, promising myself and Eoin that we would come back one day, just to look. Eoin was reluctant to budge, his eyes glued to a model car that looked just like Thomas's.

"Good day, Eoin. Where's the doctor today?" the pawnbroker asked, demanding Eoin's attention. Eoin sighed gustily and let me propel him toward the counter.

"Good day, Mr. Kelly. He had patients to visit," Eoin replied, sounding so grown up, I was reassured. At least one of us wasn't terrified.

"He works too hard," the pawnbroker commented, but his eyes were on me, curious and considering. He extended his hand, clearly expecting me to take it. I did, though he didn't shake it like I expected. He grasped my fingers and pulled me forward, ever so slightly, and brought my knuckles to his bristly lips, setting a small kiss there before releasing me.

"We have not had the pleasure, madam."

"This is my mother," Eoin crowed, his small hands gripping the edge of the counter, bouncing on his toes, gleeful.

"Your mother?" Mr. Kelly repeated, confusion furrowing his brow.

"I'm Anne Gallagher. Pleasure to meet you, sir," I said, but offered no other explanation. I could see the wheels turn behind the small glasses, the questions that begged to be asked. He stroked his beard once, twice, and then again before setting both hands on the counter and clearing his throat.

"How can I be of service, Mrs. Gallagher?"

I didn't correct him but slipped the ring from my finger. The cameo against the dark agate was pale and lovely, the gold band delicate, the filigree finely detailed. I couldn't help but think my grandfather would understand my predicament.

"I would like to sell my jewelry and was told you would treat me fairly."

The man produced a jeweler's loupe and made a great show of examining the ring before he stroked his beard once more.

"You said jewelry," he hedged, not quoting a price. "Do you have something else you'd like to show me?"

"Yes. I thought I might sell my . . . earbobs." I used the word Thomas had used and pulled the diamond studs from my ears, setting them on the counter between us.

His furry brows jumped, and he raised the jeweler's loupe again. He took a moment longer on the earrings, saying nothing. They were each two carats and set in platinum. They had cost me almost ten thousand dollars in 1995.

"I cannot give you what they're worth," the man sighed, and it was my turn for surprise.

"What *can* you give me?" I pressed gently.

"I can give you one hundred fifty pounds. But I'll be able to sell those in London for a great deal more. You will have six months to repay the loan before I do so," he explained. "It would be wise to keep them, madam."

"One hundred fifty pounds is more than satisfactory, Mr. Kelly," I said, ignoring his suggestion. The earrings meant nothing to me, and I needed money. The thought had hysteria burbling in my throat. I needed money. I had millions of dollars in a time and place that did not yet exist. I took a deep breath, steadying myself, and focused on the task before me. "And the ring?" I asked firmly.

The pawnbroker fingered the cameo again. When he hesitated too long, Eoin reached into his pocket and placed his own treasure on the counter. His eyes barely cleared the edge, and he pinned the pawnbroker with a hopeful gaze.

"What'll ya give me for my button, Mr. Kelly?"

Mr. Kelly smiled and picked up the button, eyeing it through the loupe as though it were of great value. I was slow to make the connection and had just begun to protest when the jeweler frowned.

"*S McD,*" he read. "What's this, Eoin?"

"It's very valuable," Eoin said.

"Eoin!" I rebuked softly. "I'm sorry, Mr. Kelly. We won't be selling that button. I didn't realize Eoin had it with him."

"I heard Seán Mac Diarmada scratched his name in a few buttons and coins. Is this one of them?" Mr. Kelly asked, still studying the little brass bauble.

"I don't know about that, Mr. Kelly. But the button is a keepsake. Will you excuse us for a moment?"

Mr. Kelly inclined his head and turned his back, busying himself with the cases behind him. We stepped away from the counter, and I knelt in front of Eoin.

"Eoin, do you know what that button is?"

"Yes. It was Doc's. His friend gave it to him, and Doc gave it to me. I like to carry it in my pocket for good luck."

"Why would you want to sell something so precious?"

"Because . . . you need the money," Eoin explained, his eyes wide and pleading.

"Yes. But that button is more important than money."

"Nana said you are penniless. She said you are a beggar with no home and no shame," he quoted. "I don't want you to be a beggar." His eyes grew shiny, and his lips quivered. I swallowed the angry lump in my throat and reminded myself again that Brigid was my great-great-grandmother.

"You must never, ever, part with that button, Eoin. It is the kind of treasure that no amount of money can replace because it represents the lives of people who are gone, people who mattered and are missed. Do you understand?"

"Yes," Eoin said, nodding. "But I missed *you*. And I would give up my button to keep you."

My eyes swam, and my lips trembled in concert with his. "Someone very wise told me that we keep the people we love in our hearts. We never lose them as long as we can remember how it felt to be loved by them." I pulled him to me, embracing his small body so tightly that he squirmed and giggled. I released him and wiped at the tear that had escaped and was clinging to my nose.

"Promise me you will stop carrying that button in your pocket. Put it somewhere very safe and treasure it," I said, infusing as much sternness into my voice as I could muster.

"I promise," Eoin said simply. I rose, and we walked back to the counter to the man who was pretending not to watch us. "My mother won't let me sell the button, Mr. Kelly."

"I think that's wise, young man."

"Dr. Smith told my mother not to sell her ring either."

"Eoin," I whispered, embarrassed.

"Did he, now?" Mr. Kelly asked.

"Yes, sir," Eoin said, nodding.

Mr. Kelly raised his eyes to mine. "Well, then. I suppose he's right. Mrs. Gallagher, I will give you a hundred sixty pounds for the diamonds. And you must keep your ring. I remember a young man coming in here quite a few years ago and buying this piece." He rubbed his thumb over the cameo, reflective. "It was more than he could afford, but he was determined to have it. He told me it was for the girl he wanted to marry. We made a deal—his pocket watch for this ring." He placed the ring in my hand and folded my fingers over it. "The watch wasn't worth much, but he was a great negotiator."

I stared at Mr. Kelly in stunned remorse. No wonder Thomas had been so adamant. I had tried to sell Anne's wedding ring.

"Thank you, Mr. Kelly. I have never heard that story," I whispered.

"Well, now you have," he answered kindly. A memory skittered across his features, and his lips pursed in reflection. "You know . . . I might still have that pocket watch. It stopped ticking shortly after the trade. I set it aside, thinking it might just need tinkering." He pulled open drawers and unlocked curios. A moment later, he cried out in triumph, pulling a long chain attached to a simple gold timepiece from a velvet-lined drawer.

My heart caught, and I pressed a trembling palm to my mouth to muffle my surprise. It was the timepiece Eoin had worn most of his life. It had always made him look old-fashioned—the drooping chain and the golden locket—but he'd never abandoned it for a newer model.

"See this, lad?" Mr. Kelly showed Eoin how to release the latch on the cover, revealing the clock face beneath. Eoin nodded happily, and the pawnbroker stared down at the watch with a frown.

"Well, look at that!" Mr. Kelly marveled. "It's ticking after all." He checked his own watch, which was hanging from the little pocket in his vest. With a little tool, he adjusted the time on Declan Gallagher's watch and studied the tiny hands as they ticked. He grunted in satisfaction.

"I think you should have it, lad," Mr. Kelly said, pushing the time-piece across the counter until it was within Eoin's reach. "After all, it belonged to your father."

Little Eoin and I left the pawnshop with much more than we'd arrived with. In addition to one hundred sixty pounds and Declan's pocket watch—which Eoin clutched tightly in his hand, even though I'd pinned the chain to his vest—a pair of agate earrings with tiny dangling cameos were clamped to my lobes. I realized belatedly that most women probably didn't have holes in their ears in 1921. Mr. Kelly insisted the earrings matched my ring so well that I should have them. He was being so kind and generous, I suspected I'd given him a very good deal indeed. But I still wore Anne's ring, and I could never repay him for that. The pawnbroker had saved me from making a terrible blunder, and he'd told me a story even more precious than the ring itself.

I found myself puzzling over the dizzying ramifications of Declan's timepiece. If I had not gone into the pawnbroker with Eoin, would Mr. Kelly have ever given Eoin the watch? Eoin had had the watch all the years I'd known him. Was I changing history, or had I always been part of it? And how had Eoin gotten Anne's ring? If she'd died and was never found, wouldn't she have been wearing it?

I realized suddenly that I had no idea where I was going. I was clutching the money pouch in my right hand and Eoin's hand in my left, letting him lead me along, my mind eighty miles—or years—away.

"Eoin, do you know where the department store is?" I asked sheepishly.

He laughed and let go of my hand. "Right there, goose!"

We were standing across the street from a row of huge glass windows—at least six of them—shaded by a deep-red awning that boasted the store's name, "Henry Lyons & Co. Ltd., The Sligo Warehouse" in pale lettering. Behind the glass, hats and shoes were displayed on pedestals, and dresses and suits were modeled by pale-faced mannequins. Relief swelled for seconds before fear regained dominance.

"I will simply ask for help," I encouraged myself out loud, and Eoin nodded.

"Nana's friend Mrs. Geraldine Cummins works here. She's very helpful."

My heart sank so low it rubbed the bottom of my belly, and I thought for a moment I would be sick. Brigid's friend would surely know about Anne Gallagher. The real Anne Gallagher. The original Anne Gallagher. I braced myself as Eoin pulled me forward, clearly eager for the wonders of the huge store.

A group of men were gathered around the large set of windows just right of the entrance. Their backs were to the road, their arms folded as they stared at something on the other side of the pane. I craned my neck, trying to see what had drawn the crowd. As I neared, one man abandoned his spot, giving me a clear view of the window before the hole closed with someone else. They were reading a newspaper. Someone had taped the *Irish Times* to the inside of the department store window, the pages open and spread to allow passersby to read through the glass.

I slowed, curious and predictably drawn to the words, but Eoin surged ahead. I was propelled through the door being patiently held open by a man who tipped his hat as I passed. All thoughts of newsprint and words were replaced by wonder and dread as I looked around at the high shelves and wide aisles, the displays, and the décor and tried to ascertain exactly where to start. There was no canned music being piped into the store and no fluorescent lighting. Lamps were suspended overhead, spilling warm light on the highly buffed wood floors, and I turned in a complete circle to get my bearings. I was in the men's department and would need to explore.

"Clothes, stockings, a pair of new boots, a pair of shoes, a hat, a coat, and a dozen—two dozen—other things," I murmured, trying to make a list that would keep me from crying in a corner. I had no idea how far my money would take me. I peeked at the price tag on the overcoat hanging to my right. Sixteen pounds. I started doing mental calculations and gave up immediately. I would simply buy as much as I could for one hundred pounds. That would be my limit. The other sixty would be my emergency money until I could earn more or until I woke up. Whichever came first.

"Nana always goes up the stairs where the dresses are," Eoin prodded, and I let him lead the way once more. We climbed a broad staircase, which opened up to the second floor, revealing elaborate hats, colorful fabrics, and perfumed air.

"Hello, Mrs. Geraldine Cummins," Eoin cried, waving at a woman about Brigid's age who was standing behind a nearby glass display. "This is my mother. She needs help."

Another woman shushed him loudly as though we were in a library and not standing amid racks of clothes. Geraldine Cummins moved out from behind the glass and walked toward us, her posture regal, her figure plump.

"Hello, Mr. Eoin Gallagher," she greeted sedately. She was well coiffed in a navy dress with a loose sash, her enormous bosom covered with a drooping bow of the same shade, her sleeves elbow-length, and her flowing skirt brushing just above her ankles. Her hair was a tidy gray cap of shellacked waves hugging her round face, and she met my gaze unblinking, hands clasped in front of her, heels together like a soldier at attention.

She didn't seem surprised the way Mr. Kelly had, and I wondered if Brigid had made a trip to Sligo while I was recovering. I decided it didn't matter as long as the woman could help me and as long as I didn't have to answer any questions.

"How can I help you, Mrs. Anne Gallagher?" she said, wasting no time on polite introductions and small talk.

I began to rattle off my list, hoping she would fill in the blanks.

She raised one hand in the air, summoning a young woman standing next to a huge rack of hats. "I will take Mr. Eoin Gallagher with me. Miss Beatrice Barnes will personally assist you."

I realized that Eoin called Geraldine Cummins by her full name because she called everyone else by theirs, title included. Beatrice Barnes was hurrying toward us, a helpful smile pasted on her pretty face.

"Miss Beatrice Barnes, this is Mrs. Anne Gallagher. You will assist her. I trust you to be prudent."

Beatrice nodded emphatically, and Geraldine turned away, extending a hand toward Eoin.

"W-where will you take him?" I asked, certain good parents did not just hand their children over to complete strangers. Eoin knew her, but I did not.

"The toy department upstairs, of course. And then we will go to Ferguson's drugstore for a treat." She smiled down at Eoin, two deep dimples appearing on her powdered cheeks. When she met my gaze again, her smile was gone. "My shift is over. I'll bring him back at half past the hour. That should give you plenty of time to see to your purchases without the lad underfoot."

Eoin bounced on his toes, clasping her hand in excitement before his face fell and his shoulders slumped. "Thank you, Mrs. Geraldine Cummins," he said, "but Doc said I must stay close to my mother and help her."

"And you will help your mother most by coming with me," Mrs. Cummins said briskly.

Eoin looked at me, hope and doubt in his smile.

"Go ahead, Eoin. Enjoy yourself. I'll be fine," I lied.

I watched Eoin walk away, his hand in the older woman's grasp, and desperately wanted to call him back. He was already showing her his pocket watch, babbling about our recent adventure at the pawnshop.

"Shall we get started, Mrs. Gallagher?" Beatrice said, her voice high, her eyes bright.

I nodded, insisting she call me Anne, and stammered through my list of needs once more, eyeing the prices as we walked, pointing out the things I liked and the colors I preferred. The average dress was around seven pounds, and the way Beatrice was prattling about dinner dresses and house frocks and winter wear and summer clothes, not to mention hats, shoes, and handbags, made me start to feel faint.

"You will need slips, corsets, knickers, and stockings as well?" she asked discreetly, though there was no one near us.

"Yes, please," I said, deciding it was time to lie a little if I was going to accomplish anything. "I've been ill for a long time, you see. And I'm afraid it's been so long since I purchased clothing that I don't know what size I am or what's in fashion. I'm not even sure what a lady needs," I said, and it wasn't hard to make my eyes well up pathetically. "I hope you'll be able to give me some advice, bearing in mind that a whole new wardrobe could get expensive. I need the basics, nothing more."

"Of course!" she said, patting my shoulder. "I am going to take you to a dressing room, and we will begin. I have a good eye for sizes. This is going to be great fun."

When she returned, her arms were filled with white frills.

"We have some lovely artificial silk just in from London and knickers that fall above the knee," she purred. "We also have some new corsets that lace up in the front and are quite comfortable." An image of me at my writing desk wearing drawstring cotton pants and a ribbed tank flitted through my mind, and I swallowed the bubble of panic that wanted to break free.

The "artificial silk" felt like rayon, and I wondered how well it would launder, but I did my best to wiggle into the corset, appreciating the relative ease of the front laces and the long ruffle that fell halfway down my thighs. It was designed to wear over the chemise, which fit like a square-necked slip and provided little lift or support to my breasts but was soft and comfortable. I slipped on the knickers Beatrice had whispered about and decided it could be worse.

I tried on a deep-blue dress with a square neckline and sheer elbow-length sleeves. The lines were straight and simple, with a bit more volume at the hem of the skirt so it swished softly a few inches above my ankles. A sash gave the dress some shape, and Beatrice studied me, her lips pursed.

"The color is good. The style too. You have a lovely neck, and you could wear this with jewels and dress it up for dinner or wear it plain with just a hat for Mass. We'll add the rose-colored one just like it to the stack."

Two cotton blouses, one pink and one green, with lapels that created a wide *V* above three buttons could be worn with the long gray skirt Beatrice insisted was a staple. I tried on two "housedresses" next: one peach, the other white with tiny brown dots. Both had deep, thigh-high pockets and long, straight sleeves that ended in thick cuffs. They were simply styled with round necklines that skirted the collarbones and a pleated waistband that separated the bodice from the shin-length skirt. Beatrice set a wide-brimmed white straw hat decorated in peach flowers and lace on my head and declared me perfect. She added two shawls to my purchases, one a soft green and one white, and scolded me when I tried to tell her no.

"You were born in Ireland, yes? You've lived here all your life. You know you must have shawls!"

Beatrice brought me a long wool coat and a matching charcoal hat decorated with a spray of black roses and a black silk ribbon. She called it a cloche hat. Instead of the stiff circular brim and round dome of the straw hat, the cloche hat was snug and flared around my face coquettishly, following the line of my head. I loved it and left it on while I moved on to the next thing.

I started making a pile. In addition to the underthings and clothes, I would need four pairs of stockings, a pair of brown kid pumps, a pair of medium-heeled black T-strap shoes, and a pair of black boots for the colder months. I could also use Anne's old boots for long walks or chores. I mentally balked at the thought of chores, wondering what kind of chores a woman in 1921 was typically tasked with. Thomas had servants, but he'd said he wanted me to assist him with his patients. I reassured myself that the boots would suffice for that as well.

I'd been keeping a tally in my head—stockings four for a pound, shoes and shawls three pounds apiece. The cotton dresses were five pounds each, the boots and the linen dresses were seven, the chemises and knickers were a pound apiece, and the skirt was four. The blouses were two and a half pounds, the corset a little more, the hats as much as the cotton dresses, and the wool coat fifteen pounds all by itself. I had to be getting close to ninety pounds, and I still needed to buy toiletries.

"You need a dress or two for parties. The doctor is often invited to the homes of the well-to-do," Beatrice insisted, a frown curving between her brows. "And do you have jewelry? We have some beautiful costume jewelry that looks almost real."

I showed her my ring and earrings and indicated that was the extent of it. She nodded, biting her lip.

"You also need a handbag. But that can wait, I suppose. When winter comes, you'll wish you had another wool suit," she added, eyeing the ugly, outdated suit I'd worn coming into the department store. "That's not the . . . loveliest . . . suit I've ever seen. But it will be warm."

"I won't be going to any parties with the doctor," I protested. "And this suit will have to do. I'll have my shawls and my coat. I'll be fine."

She sighed as if she'd failed me but nodded her assent. "All right. I'll have your purchases wrapped and boxed up while you finish dressing."

26 October 1920

Black and Tans and Auxiliaries—forces pumped into Ireland from Great Britain—are everywhere, and they don't seem to answer to anyone. Barbed wire and barricades, armoured vehicles, and soldiers with fixed bayonets patrolling the streets are all commonplace now. It's quieter in Dromahair than in Dublin, but we still feel it here. All of Ireland is feeling it. In little Balbriggan, just last month, the Tans and the Auxies set half the town on fire. Homes, businesses, factories, and whole sections of town were burned to the ground. Crown forces said it was a reprisal for the death of two Tans, but the reprisals are always excessive and are always completely indiscriminate. They want to break us. So many of us are already broken.

This past April, the Mountjoy jail was full of Sinn Féin members whose only crime was political association. The political prisoners were mixed in among the regular criminals, and in protest of their incarceration, several of them began a hunger strike. In 1917, a political prisoner, a member of the IRB, went on strike and was force-fed. The brutal way in which he was "fed" cost him his life. As the crowds outside Mountjoy Prison grew, the national attention grew as well, until Prime Minister Lloyd George, still feeling the sting of worldwide outrage from the hunger strike of 1917, capitulated to their demands, gave the men prisoner-of-war status, and moved them to the hospital to recover. I was able to see them at the Mater Hospital in an official capacity, as a medical representative appointed by Lord French himself. I volunteered. The men were weak and thin, but it was a battle won, and they all knew it.

The Dáil, Ireland's newly formed government made up of the elected leaders who refused to take their seats at Westminster, has been outlawed by the British administration. Mick and the other councilmembers—those who aren't in jail—have continued to carry on in secret, establishing a working government and doing their best to create a system under which an independent Ireland can function. But local mayors, officials, and judges who work in a more public capacity can't hide as easily as the Dáil officials can. One by one, they have been arrested or murdered. The lord mayor of Cork, Thomas MacCurtain, was shot in his house and his elected replacement, Terence MacSwiney, was arrested during a raid on Cork City Hall not too long after he took office. Mayor MacSwiney, along with the ten men he was arrested with, decided to go on a hunger strike to denounce the continued unlawful imprisonment of public officials. Their strike, just like the one in April, has attracted national attention. But not because it ended well. Terence MacSwiney died yesterday in England at a Brixton jail, seventy-four days after he began his hunger strike.

Every day it's another terrible story, another unforgiveable event. The whole country is under immense strain, yet there is an odd hopefulness mixed with the fear. It's as if all of Ireland is coming awake and our eyes are fixed on the same horizon.

T. S.

10

THE THREE BEGGARS

You that have wandered far and wide
Can ravel out what's in my head.
Do men who least desire get most,
Or get the most who most desire?

—*W. B. Yeats*

Beatrice was waiting for me when I emerged from the dressing room, my hair a little disheveled. I was wearing one of the cotton dresses and a new hat that covered the worst of my hair. Beatrice left the brown kid pumps, as she called them, for me to wear out of the store as well, saving me from having to lace Anne's boots by myself. Beatrice had taken Anne's old brown suit, hat, and boots to be boxed with the rest of my purchases. I looked much better than I had when I arrived, but my side ached, and my head pounded from overexertion. I was glad the adventure was almost over.

Beatrice prattled on beside me, inquiring over my toilette. I told her I needed a shampoo for my hair and something to smooth the curl. She nodded as if shampoo was a known term. "I need products for my . . . menses?" It was the most old-fashioned word I knew to describe a woman's period. But Beatrice nodded again, clearly understanding.

"We have sanitary napkins and menstruation belts on a discreet display with a little money box beside them so that women don't have to purchase them publicly. Most ladies are more comfortable with that. But I'll put them in your box while no one is looking and add them to your total," she murmured. I thought it better not to ask what a menstruation belt was. I would figure it out.

The two most important things tackled, I followed her to the cosmetics department on the lower floor, scouring the products stacked and displayed and pointing gleefully at names I recognized—Vaseline, Ivory soap, and Pond's Cold Cream. Beatrice began making a receipt, writing the items in a neat row and adding my selections to a pale-pink box that reminded me of something from a bakery. Beatrice added Pond's Vanishing Cream to my purchases.

"Cold cream at night, vanishing cream in the morning," she instructed. "It won't make you shine, and it works well under powder. Do you need powder?"

I shrugged, and she pursed her lips, studying my skin. "Flesh, white, pink, or cream?" she asked.

"What do you think?" I hedged.

"Flesh," she said confidently. "LaBlache is my favorite face powder. It's a bit more expensive, but worth the extra. And maybe a soft pink rouge?" She took a small tub from behind the glass and unscrewed the metal lid. "See?"

The color was a little too pink for my taste, but she reassured me. "It will be the softest blush on your cheeks and lips, and no one will even know you are wearing it. And if they do, never admit it."

That seemed to be the goal, to look like you weren't wearing any "paint," which suited me fine.

"There's a new lash cream—we always used Vaseline and ash growing up. Well, not anymore." She unscrewed another small container, no bigger than a lip balm, and showed me the black grease inside. It didn't resemble any mascara I'd ever seen.

"How is it applied?" I asked.

Beatrice closed the distance between us, told me to hold still, and dabbed her pointer finger in the goo and then against her thumb. With absolute confidence, she rubbed the ends of my lashes between the pads of her blackened fingertips.

"Perfect. Your lashes are already so long and dark, you hardly need it. But they're more noticeable now."

She winked and tossed it into the box. She added some coconut-oil shampoo that she swore would make my hair luxurious, as well as some talcum powder to "keep me fresh" and a little glass spritzer of a perfume that didn't make me sneeze. I added a tube of toothpaste, a toothbrush, a little box of silk "tooth floss" as well as a comb-and-brush set. When I asked where I could settle my bill, Beatrice gave me an odd look. "It's already settled, Anne. The doctor is waiting for you at the entrance. Your purchases are there as well. I thought you were simply being frugal."

"I would really like to pay for these things on my own, Beatrice," I insisted.

"But . . . it's done, Mrs. Gallagher," she stammered. "Your bill has been added to his account. I don't want to cause a stir."

I didn't want to cause a stir either, but embarrassment welled in my chest. I took a deep breath to tamp it down.

"These things have not been added to his tab." I raised the pink box in my arms. "I will pay for my toiletries," I insisted.

She looked as though she wanted to argue, but nodded, veering to the cash register near the entrance and the mustached clerk who waited there. She handed him the receipt for my toiletries.

"Mrs. Gallagher needs to purchase these things, Mr. Barry," she explained, taking the box from my hands so I could pull out the thick paper money pouch Mr. Kelly had given me.

"Dr. Smith said for me to add Mrs. Gallagher's purchases to his account," Mr. Barry said, frowning.

"I understand. But I will be paying for these items," I said firmly, matching his frown with one of my own.

The clerk looked from me to the door and back again. I followed his gaze to where Thomas stood watching me, his head tilted slightly, one hand holding Eoin's and the other shoved into his trouser pocket.

Eoin's cheek bulged with the round end of a lollipop, the stick protruding from his puckered lips.

"What is the total, please?" I said, turning my attention back to the clerk.

The man grunted in disapproval, but he entered the items into the cash register, a happy dinging signaling each new total.

"That will be ten pounds, madam," he huffed, and I took what appeared to be two five-pound notes from my stash. I would have to examine the bills when I had more privacy to do so.

"We've just finished boxing your other purchases," Mr. Barry said, taking my notes and putting them in his till. He indicated the stack of parcels behind him and beckoned to a boy who scrambled to his side and began piling boxes in his arms. "After you, Mrs. Gallagher," Mr. Barry said, pointing to the door.

I turned and walked toward Thomas. I felt flushed and uncomfortable, the "beggar with no shame" leading a royal procession. Beatrice tottered behind me, carrying my toiletries and two hatboxes, while the boy and Mr. Barry juggled the rest of the parcels between them.

Thomas held the door and nodded to his car parked next to the sidewalk.

"Put the parcels on the back seat," Thomas instructed, but his eyes were on four men walking swiftly down the street toward the store. They wore khaki uniforms and tall boots with black belts and glengarry hats. The hats made me think of Scottish men and bagpipes, but these men weren't carrying bagpipes. They had guns.

"You look like a beautiful queen, Mother!" Eoin cried, reaching for the skirt of my dress with sticky fingers. I sidestepped his attempt and grabbed his hand instead, ignoring the way his palm stuck to mine. Thomas began hustling us into the car, his eyes never leaving the approaching soldiers.

When Mr. Barry saw the men, he shoved the packages in the rear seat and urged Beatrice and the boy to go back in the store.

Thomas shut the door behind me and strode around to the front of the car. With one swift pull on the crank, the car, clearly already warm and primed, roared to life. Thomas slid behind the wheel and pulled his door shut just as the men stopped in front of the large window that featured the open pages of the *Irish Times*. With the backs of their rifles, they began to hit the huge window, shattering it and causing the newspaper to flutter and fall amid the broken glass. One soldier leaned down and lit the pages with a flick of a match. People on either side of the street had stopped walking, watching the vandalism.

"What are you doing?" Mr. Barry pushed through the door, his mouth gaping and his cheeks red.

"Tell Mr. Lyons he's fomenting rebellion and violence against the Royal Irish Constabulary and the Crown. Next time he displays the paper, we'll break all the windows," one of the men said, his Cockney voice raised so the growing crowd across the street could hear. With a final kick at the smoldering pages, the men continued down the street, toward Hyde Bridge.

Thomas was frozen, both hands on the wheel, the car rumbling impatiently. His jaw was clenched so tight a muscle danced near his ear. People started to rush across the street to view the damage and talk among themselves, and Mr. Barry started organizing the cleanup.

"Thomas?" I whispered. Eoin's eyes were huge, his lower lip trembling. His sucker had fallen from his mouth, and it lay forgotten beside his feet.

"Doc? Why did the Tans do that?" Eoin asked, tears threatening. Thomas patted Eoin's leg, released the choke, and adjusted the levers by the wheel, and we eased away from the department store, leaving the destruction behind us.

"What was that about, Thomas?" I asked. He hadn't answered Eoin, and his mouth was still tight, his eyes bleak. We'd crossed Hyde Bridge behind four constables and headed out of Sligo, back toward Dromahair. The farther away from town we moved, the more Thomas relaxed. He sighed and cast a quick glance my way before settling his gaze back on the road before us.

"Henry Lyons sends a driver to Dublin every day to get a paper. He puts it up in the store window so the people know what is happening in Dublin. The action is in Dublin. The battle for all of Ireland is being fought in Dublin. And people want to know about it. The Tans and the Auxies don't like him posting the paper."

"The Auxies?"

"The Auxiliaries, Anne. They're a separate command from the regular constabulary. They're all ex-officers of the British army and navy who have nothing to do now that the Great War is over. Their one job is to crush the IRA."

I remembered that much from my research.

"They weren't Tans?" Eoin asked.

"No, lad. The Auxiliaries are even worse than the Tans. You'll always know an Auxie from his hat—and his gun belt. You saw their hats, didn't you, Eoin?" Thomas pressed.

Eoin nodded so emphatically, his teeth chattered.

"Stay far away from the Auxies, Eoin. And the Tans. Stay the hell away from all of 'em."

We were quiet then. Eoin was biting his lips and picking the dirt from his reclaimed sucker, clearly needing the comfort of it back in his mouth.

"We'll wash it off when we get home, Eoin. You'll see. It will be good again. Why don't you show Thomas your watch and tell him the story Mr. Kelly told us?" I urged, trying to distract him, to distract us all.

Eoin unreeled the long chain from his pocket, extending the swinging timepiece in front of Thomas's face so he was sure to see it.

"Mr. Kelly gave it to me, Doc. He said it was my dad's. Now it's mine. And it still ticks!"

Thomas lifted his left hand from the wheel and took the watch in his palm, surprise and sorrow twisting his lips.

"Mr. Kelly had it in a drawer. He forgot all about it until we came into the shop," Eoin added.

Thomas's eyes met mine, and I felt certain he already knew the story of the ring.

"I got my father's watch, and my mother got to keep her ring, see?" Eoin patted my hand.

"Yes. I see. You'll have to take very good care of this watch. Put it with your button somewhere safe," Thomas said.

Eoin looked at me, a guilty expression on his sticky face. He wondered if I was going to tell Doc about his attempt to sell his treasure; I could see the dread wrinkling his nose. I helped him put the watch back into his pocket, meeting his eyes with a smile, reassuring him.

"Do you know how to tell time, Eoin?" I asked.

He shook his head.

"Then I will teach you so that you can use the watch."

"Who taught *you* how to tell time?" he asked.

"My grandfather," I said softly. There must have been sadness in my face because the little boy patted my cheek with his grubby fingers, comforting me.

"Do you miss him?"

"Not anymore," I said, and my voice quaked.

"Why?" He was shocked the way I had been once, long ago.

"Because he is still with me," I whispered, repeating the words my grandfather had said to me as he'd rocked me in his arms. And suddenly the world shifted and the light dawned, and I wondered if my grandfather had known who I was all along.

I helped Eoin wash his hands, and together we tidied ourselves before dinner. My hair had lost its pins, and curls hung loose around my face and down my back. I set it all free, wet my fingers, and tamed each curl as best I could before pulling the bulk of it back into a loose ponytail with a piece of ribbon I'd found in Anne's chest. I wanted nothing more than to fall, face-first, into my bed. My side screamed, my hands shook, and I had no appetite, but for the first time, I sat down at the table with the family.

Brigid sat in stony silence at dinner, her back stiff. She chewed miniscule bites of food that barely moved her jaw. Her eyes had grown wide and then narrowed to slits when she'd watched us traipse inside, arms full of parcels, shoeboxes, and hatboxes that were taken to my room. She didn't respond to Eoin's excited recounting of the smashed store windows or the lollipop Mrs. Geraldine Cummins had purchased for him or the wondrous toys he'd seen on the shelves. Brigid had placed the boy next to her at the table, with Thomas as the head and me on the opposite side, across from Eoin, an empty space between Thomas and me. It was an odd placement, but it saved Brigid from having to look at me and kept me as far away from Eoin and Thomas as possible.

Eleanor, Maeve's older sister, hovered near the kitchen door, standing by in case something was needed. I smiled at her and complimented her on the fare. I didn't have much appetite, but the food was delicious.

"That will be all, Eleanor. Run along home. Anne can clear the table and clean up when we are finished," Brigid commanded.

After the girl excused herself, Thomas eyed Brigid with raised brows. "Reassigning chores, Mrs. Gallagher?" he asked.

"I'm happy to do it," I interjected. "I need to contribute."

"You are exhausted," Thomas said, "and Eleanor is going to worry all the way home that she's done something wrong and displeased Brigid because she always cleans up after dinner and takes the leftovers home to her family."

"I simply think Anne owes you a great debt that she should begin repaying as soon as possible," Brigid shot back, her color high, her voice elevated.

"I will handle my debts and those who are indebted to me, Brigid," Thomas said, his tone quiet but clipped. Brigid flinched, and Thomas sighed.

"First two beggars and now three?" Brigid sniffed. "Is that what we are?"

"Mother isn't a beggar with no shame, Nana. Not anymore. She sold her earbobs. Now she's rich," Eoin said happily.

Brigid pushed back her chair and stood abruptly. "Come, Eoin. It's time for a bath and bed. Say good night to the doctor."

Eoin began to protest, though his plate was empty and had been for some time. "I want Mother to tell me about the hound of Culann," he wheedled.

"Not tonight, Eoin," Thomas said. "It's been a long day. Go with your nana."

"Good night, Doc," Eoin said sadly. "Good night, Mother."

"Good night, Eoin," Thomas said.

"Good night, sweet boy," I added, blowing him a kiss. It made him smile, and he kissed his own palm and blew it back to me, as if it was the first time he'd ever done such a thing.

"Eoin," Brigid demanded.

He followed his grandmother from the room, his shoulders drooping and his head low.

"Go to bed, Anne," Thomas ordered when the sound of their footsteps faded. "You're about to fall asleep in your soup. I'll take care of this."

I ignored him and stood, stacking the dishes around me. "Brigid's right. You've taken me in. No questions—" I began.

"No questions?" he interrupted wryly. "I've asked several, if I recall."

"No demands," I adjusted. "And when I'm not terrified, I'm incredibly grateful."

He stood and took the plates. "I'll do the heavy lifting. You can wash."

We worked quietly, neither of us especially comfortable in the kitchen—though I suspected our reasons were different. I didn't know where anything belonged, and Thomas wasn't much help. I wondered if he'd ever washed a dish or prepared a meal.

I was surprised by the luxury—a huge icebox, a large sink, two recessed ovens, eight electric burners, and a pantry—Thomas called it a larder—the size of the dining room. The counter space was vast, each surface clean and well cared for. I already knew the home, and the comforts weren't typical of average homes in 1920, especially in rural Ireland. I'd read Thomas's journal entry about Garvagh Glebe, about his stepfather, about the wealth he'd inherited and the responsibility he felt because of it.

I collected all the food from the plates and put it into a bowl, afraid to throw it away. Didn't pigs eat scraps? I knew Thomas had pigs and sheep and chickens and horses that the O'Tooles looked after. I rinsed the plates and saucers, stacking them on top of each other in one basin, unable to locate anything that resembled dish soap. Thomas cleared the dining room table, shoved the leftovers into the icebox, and put the bread and butter in the larder. I wiped off the counters, admiring the heavy wood surfaces worn and well used by hands more able than mine. I was sure Brigid would be down to check my work, but until I had some practical instruction, it was the best I could do.

"Why are you afraid?" Thomas asked quietly, watching me finish.

I turned off the water and blotted my hands dry, satisfied that we'd cleaned up enough to keep the mice away.

"You said when you're not terrified, you're incredibly grateful. Why are you terrified?" he pressed.

"Because everything is very . . . uncertain."

"Brigid is afraid you will take Eoin and leave. That is why she is behaving so badly," Thomas said.

"I won't. I would never . . . where would I go?" I stammered.

"That depends. Where have you been?" he asked, and I pivoted away from the question he persisted in asking.

"I would never do that to Eoin, to Brigid, or to you. This is Eoin's home," I said.

"And you are his mother."

I wanted to confess that I was not, that I had no claim on him beyond love. But I didn't. To confess would be to sever my access to the only thing I cared about. So I confessed the only truth I could. "I love him so much, Thomas."

"I know you do. If I know nothing else, I know that." Thomas sighed.

"I promise you, I will not take Eoin from Garvagh Glebe," I pledged, meeting his gaze.

"But can you promise that *you* won't leave?" Thomas said, finding the chink in my armor.

"No," I whispered, shaking my head. "I can't."

"Then maybe you should go, Anne. If you're going to go, go now, before more damage is done."

He wasn't angry or accusatory. His eyes were grim and his voice was soft, and when tears rose in my throat and welled in my eyes, he drew me to him gently and embraced me, stroking my hair and patting my back as though I were a child. But I did not relax against him or let my tears fall. My stomach roiled, and my skin felt too tight. I pulled away, afraid that the panic scratching at my heels and oozing out the palms of my hands would break free in his presence. I turned and walked from the kitchen as swiftly as I was able, holding the stitch in my side, focused only on the safety of a closed door.

"Anne. Wait," Thomas called behind me, but a door slammed, and excited voices filled the kitchen as a worn couple, their clothes tidy but a little tattered, crowded around Thomas, keeping him from pursuing me as I slipped down the hallway toward my bedroom.

"Our Eleanor says Mrs. Gallagher dismissed her, Doctor! She cried all the way home, and I'm beside myself. If there's a problem, you'll tell me, won't you, Dr. Smith?" the woman cried.

"You've always been fair with us, Doctor. More than fair, but if the girl doesn't know what she's done wrong, how can she fix it?" the man joined in. The O'Tooles had interpreted Eleanor's early night exactly as Thomas said they would.

Poor Thomas. It must be hard always being right. He was right about so many things. If I was going to go, I *should* go now. He was right about that too.

I just didn't know how.

28 November 1920

I sat with Mick in Dublin last Saturday, eating eggs and rashers at a place on Grafton Street called the Café Cairo. Mick always eats like it's a race, shoveling food into his mouth, his eyes on his plate, focused on the task of refilling so he can keep moving. It never fails to amaze me how freely he moves about the city. He usually wears a neat grey suit and a bowler hat, rides his bike as often as not, and smiles and waves and makes small talk with the very people who are hunting him. He hides in plain sight, and runs circles, literally and figuratively, around everyone else.

But he was fidgety last Saturday, impatient. And at one point he shoved his plate aside and leaned across the table towards me until our faces were mere inches apart.

"Ya see the Cocks at the back tables, Tommy? Don't look right now. Wait a bit and drop your napkin."

I took a deep pull of the black coffee in front of me and knocked my napkin to the floor as I set my cup back down. As I retrieved the napkin, I let my eyes trip across the half-filled tables along the far wall. I knew instantly which men he was referring to. They wore three-piece suits and ties, not uniforms. Their hats were pulled lower on the right than the left, demanding your gaze, while their eyes warned you to quickly look away. I didn't know if they were Cockneys, but they were Brits. There were five at one table and a few more at the next. Maybe it was the way they surveyed the room or talked around their cigarettes, but they were together, and they were trouble.

"That's not all of 'em. But they'll be gone tomorrow," Mick said.

I didn't ask what he meant. His eyes were flat, his mouth turned down.

"Who are they?" I asked.

"They call them the Cairo Gang, 'cause they always meet here. Lloyd George sent them to Dublin to take me out."

"If you know who they are, isn't it possible they know who you are, and you and I are about to get pumped full of lead?" I murmured around the rim of my cup. I had to set it down again. My hands were shaking. Not from fear. At least not for myself. For him. And I was angry at the risk he'd taken.

"I had to see them off," Mick said mildly, shrugging. His jitters were gone. He'd passed them on to me. He put his hat on his head and stood, counting out a few coins for our breakfast. Neither of us looked back as we walked out of the café.

The next morning, in the early hours before dawn, fourteen men were gunned down across Dublin, many of them members of the special unit sent in to deal with Michael Collins and his squad.

By afternoon, the Crown forces were in an uproar. Reeling from the blow to their officers, they sent armoured cars and military lorries to Croke Park, where Dublin was playing Tipperary in a football match. When the ticket sellers saw the armoured cars and the packed lorries, they ran inside the park. The Tans chased them down, claiming they thought the ticket sellers were IRA men. Once inside the park, the Black and Tans opened fire into the crowd of spectators.

People were trampled. Others were shot. Sixty injured. Thirteen dead. I spent the evening offering my services to the wounded, riddled with guilt at my part in the mayhem, seething with anger that it had come to this, and filled with longing for it all to end.

T. S.

11

BEFORE THE WORLD WAS MADE

If I make the lashes dark,
And the eyes more bright
And the lips more scarlet,
Or ask if all be right
From mirror after mirror,
No vanity's displayed;
I'm looking for the face I had
Before the world was made.

—*W. B. Yeats*

Thomas knocked on my door after the O'Tooles, clearly reassured that all was well, left. I watched the couple walk past my window, their arms laden with loaves of bread and the mutton, potatoes, and gravy Eleanor had prepared for dinner.

I was burrowed in my covers, my face hidden and the light extinguished. The door was not locked, and after a moment, Thomas opened it carefully.

"Anne, I want to check your wound," he said, coming no farther than the threshold.

I feigned sleep, keeping my swollen eyes shut, my face buried, and after a moment he left, closing the door softly behind him. He'd said I should go. I considered pulling on the clothes that sat on my top shelf, dressing myself for the life I'd lost, and tiptoeing out to the lough. I would steal a boat and sail home.

I pictured the morning dawning as I sat in a stolen boat on the lough, waiting to return to 2001. What if nothing happened? What if Thomas had to rescue me again, me dressed in my odd clothes with nowhere to go? He would think I was truly crazy. He wouldn't want me near Eoin. I moaned, the thought snatching my nerve and quickening my heartbeat. But what if it worked? What if I could go home?

Did I really want that?

The thought brought me up short. I had a beautiful apartment in Manhattan. I had enough money to comfortably last a lifetime. I had respect. Acclaim. My publicist would worry. My editor would fret. My agent might even grieve. *Would anyone else?*

I had thousands of devoted readers and no close friends. I had hundreds of acquaintances in dozens of cities. I'd dated a handful of men a handful of times. I'd even slept with two of them. Two lovers, and I was thirty years old. The term *lovers* made me wince. There had been no love involved. I had always been married to my work, in love with my stories, and committed to my characters, and I'd never wanted anyone or anything else. Eoin had been my island in a very lonely sea. A sea I'd chosen. A sea I'd loved.

But Eoin was gone, and I found I had no desire to cross the waters if he wasn't waiting for me on the other side.

Thomas had left before I rose the next day and was home again after I retired that night. I changed my bandages with very little trouble, confident that Thomas wouldn't have to tend them again, but he obviously didn't agree. When he knocked the following night, I had not yet extinguished my light and was sitting at the small desk. Feigning sleep would not be possible.

I knew Eoin's birthday was coming on Monday, and I wanted to make something for him. I'd found paper in the drawer in Thomas's office, along with a few pencils and a fountain pen that I had no idea how to use. Maeve had helped me put a long, fat stitch down the center of a thick stack of paper, binding the pages and making a spine. Eoin had danced around, knowing it was going to be for him, and I'd let him help me spread glue on the stitches to strengthen and harden them. When it dried, I'd folded the pages in half over the seam. Now I had to create a story just for him. He wouldn't see the finished product until Monday, which was only three days away.

Now Thomas was at my door, and I didn't want to see him. The memory of his words made my chest burn. I had not gone like he'd asked, and I'd been dreading the moment when I had to face him again, with no answers, no explanations, and no invitation to remain under his roof.

I wore the sweater and trousers I'd worn the day Thomas pulled me out of the lake. I hadn't expected company, and I had no pajamas other than the voluminous nightgowns that tangled around my body and strangled me in the night. I was still flirting with the future, with going home. Plus, wearing the clothes made me feel more like myself, and I needed to be Anne Gallagher, the writer, to create a special story for a perfect little boy.

Thomas knocked again and gently turned the knob.

"May I come in?" he asked. He had his medical bag in his hand, the dutiful doctor till the end.

I nodded, not looking up from the small stack of paper I was using to jot down my ideas before I committed them to the pages that waited.

He drew up behind me, a warm presence at my back. "What's this?"

"I'm making Eoin a book for his birthday. Writing him a story that's never been told before. Something just for him."

"You're writing it?" There was something in his voice that made my heart quicken.

"Yes."

"You always made Declan read to you. You said the letters moved when you tried to read them. I assumed writing would be difficult as well," he said slowly.

"No. I don't struggle with reading or writing," I whispered, setting the pencil down.

"And you're left-handed," Thomas said, surprised.

I nodded hesitantly.

"I guess I never knew that. Declan was left-handed. Eoin is too."

Thomas was silent for several seconds, musing. I waited, afraid to resume my writing for fear he'd notice something else.

"I need to check your wound, Anne. It should be sufficiently healed to remove the stitches."

I rose obediently.

His brow furrowed as his eyes traveled down my clothing and back up to my unbound hair.

"Countess Markievicz wears trousers," I blurted, defensive. Constance Markievicz was a leading figure in Irish politics, a woman born to wealth but more interested in revolution. She'd been imprisoned after the Rising and enjoyed a certain notoriety and respect among the people, especially those sympathetic to the cause of Irish independence. The fact that she'd married a Polish Count only made her more fascinating.

"Yes. So I hear. Did she give you those?" he countered, a sardonic twist to his lips. I ignored him, walking to the bed and stretching out carefully on the crisp spread. I'd caught Maeve pressing it. She'd then given me a quick lesson in using the iron, though she'd insisted I wouldn't need to press my own clothes. They'd already been ironed and hung in the huge wooden wardrobe in the corner.

I raised the hem of my sweater to uncover the bandages, folding the bottom over my breasts, but the waistline of the trousers still covered the edge of the bandage. I unbuttoned them and eased them down an inch, my eyes fixed on the ceiling. Thomas had seen me in less. Much less. But baring my skin this way felt different, like I was engaging in a strip tease, and when he cleared his throat, his discomfort magnified my own. He pulled the chair from the desk to the side of my bed and sat, removing a small pair of scissors, some tweezers, and a vial of iodine from his bag. He removed the bandage I'd applied the day before, swabbed the area, and with steady hands, began to pluck the neat stitches from my side.

"Beatrice Barnes informed me when we were at the department store that there were several things you still need. Since you had to resort to wearing Countess Markievicz's trousers, I am inclined to believe her."

"I didn't intend for you to pay for my clothes," I said.

"And I didn't intend for you to think I wanted you to leave," he countered softly, slowly, making sure I understood him.

I swallowed, determined not to cry, but felt a traitorous tear scurry down the side of my face and disappear into the whorl of my ear. I had never cried much in my life before Eoin died. Now I cried constantly.

"My car is filled with parcels. I'll bring them in when I am finished here. Beatrice has reassured me that you now have everything you need."

"Thomas . . ."

"Anne," he responded in the same tone, raising his blue eyes to mine briefly before he continued his careful snipping. I could feel his soft breath on my skin, and I closed my eyes against the flutter in my belly and the curling of my bare toes. I liked his touch. I liked his head bowed over my body. I liked him.

Thomas Smith was the kind of man who could quietly slip into and out of a room without drawing much attention. He was handsome if one stopped to contemplate each feature—deep-set blue eyes, more glum than glittering. Long grooves in his cheeks when he flashed a brief smile. Straight white teeth behind well-formed lips that perched above a dimpled chin at the apex of a clean-cut jaw. Yet he had a slight stoop to his shoulders and an air of melancholia that had folks respecting his space and his solitude, even as they sought him out. His hair was dark, more black than brown, though the glint of stubble he removed from his cheeks each morning was decidedly ruddy. He was lean, his ropey muscles giving his spare frame girth. He wasn't tall. He wasn't short. He wasn't a big man. He wasn't a small man. He wasn't loud or obtrusive even as he moved and acted with an innate confidence. He was simply Thomas Smith, as ordinary as his name, and yet . . . not ordinary at all.

I could have written stories about him.

He would be the character that grew on the reader, making them love him simply because he was good. Decent. Dependable. Maybe I *would* write stories about him. Maybe I would . . . someday.

I liked him. And it would be easy to love him.

The knowledge was sudden, a fleeting thought that settled on me with butterfly wings. I had never met someone like Thomas. I'd never once been intrigued by a man, even the men I'd temporarily let into my life. I'd never felt that pull, that pressure, that desire to discover and be discovered in return. Not until now, not until Thomas. Now, I felt all those things.

"Tell me the story," Thomas murmured.

"Hmm?"

"The story you are planning for Eoin's book. I'd like to hear it."

"Oh." I thought for a moment, putting the threads of my ideas into sentences. "Well . . . it is about a boy who travels through time. He has a little boat—a little red boat—and he takes it out on the water . . . on Lough Gill. The boat is just a child's toy, but when he sets it in the water, it becomes big enough for him to climb inside. He rows across the lake, but when he reaches the other side, he is always somewhere else. America during the revolution, France with Napoleon, China when the Great Wall was being built. When he wants to go home, he simply finds the nearest lake or stream, sets his little boat in the water, and climbs inside."

"And he finds himself back on the lough," Thomas finished, a smile in his voice.

"Yes. Home again," I said.

"Eoin will love that."

"I thought I would write the first story, the first adventure, and then we can continue to add more, depending on what he is most interested in."

"What if you give him the book you've already made, the one with empty pages, for that purpose, and I help you construct another?" Thomas straightened, drawing my sweater down over my stomach and tucking his tools away, the operation completed. "I'm a decent artist. I can certainly draw a picture of a wee boy in a red boat."

"I'll write the words, and you'll draw the pictures?" I asked, pleased.

"Yes. It will be easier to do that on loose pages. When we're done, we'll organize the words and pictures so they correspond. Stitching and gluing will be last."

"We don't have much time."

"Then we should get started, Countess."

Thomas and I worked deep into the early morning hours on Friday and Saturday—how he managed to work all day and make a child's book most of the night was beyond me. He created a system so that the pictures and text would align once we bound them, and I began to craft the tale, keeping it pithy, limiting the narrative to a small paragraph per page. Thomas added simple pencil sketches beneath the words, interspersing a full-page picture here and there to make it more fun. He gave me a fountain pen with a little well at the top that was big enough to insert ink tablets and a few drops of water. I had to hold the pen just so to keep it from dripping all over the page. I was so inept I resorted to writing in pencil, and Thomas traced my words in ink, his tongue between his teeth, his shoulder hunched over the page.

Brigid, Eoin, Thomas, and I went to Mass on Sunday; Thomas said missing Mass three Sundays in a row would cause almost as big a stir as coming back from the dead. Which was what I had done. I found myself eager to see the chapel at Ballinagar again but was filled with dread at the attention I would get. I took extra care with my appearance, knowing I would be judged by it. I decided I would wear the deep-rose dress with the cream-colored cloche hat Beatrice had sent home with Thomas. She had also sent a box of baubles, earrings that worked with several outfits, several pairs of gloves, and a charcoal-gray handbag that was neutral enough to carry with anything.

Beatrice had tucked a shaving kit in the parcels as well, one that was identical to Thomas's—a little box of blades and a thick handle with a wide head, all kept in a small tin box with an eagle emblazoned on the cover. I wondered if Thomas had noticed that I'd borrowed his a few times and purchased another so that I would stop. The razor was bulky and unwieldy compared to what I was used to, but with care and attention, it worked. I didn't know if women of the era shaved, but if Thomas had provided me with a razor of my own, it couldn't be completely unheard of.

I experimented with the cosmetics, smoothing on the vanishing cream, following it with the powder, the rouge, and the eyelash tint, and was pleasantly surprised by the effect. I looked fresh-faced and appealing, and Beatrice had been correct about the shade of pink on my cheeks and lips—subtle yet becoming.

My hair continued to be the most difficult part of the costume, and I wrangled it into a French braid, weaving the curls into place and wrapping the tail of the braid into a knot at my nape. I stuck the knot with a few long pins and willed it to stay put. I wore a corset for the first time, attaching my stockings to the long straps, and I was so tired and winded after dressing, I pledged to never wear it again.

Brigid sniffed when I climbed into the rear seat of the car with Eoin, leaving the front seat to her, but Eoin's countenance brightened considerably.

"Mass is very long, Mother," he whispered, warning me. "And Nana won't let me sit by my friends. But if you sit by me, maybe it won't be so boring."

"Someday, you will like it. It can be very peaceful being surrounded by people you care about and who care about you. That is really what church is for. It's a chance to just sit still and think about all the wonderful things God has made and count all the blessings we have."

"I am a good counter," Eoin said hopefully.

"Then you won't be a bit bored."

We drove through Dromahair and into the fields, following the same road—albeit an unpaved one—I'd taken with Maeve O'Toole's instructions ringing in my ears. When I saw the church, it was like glimpsing a familiar face, and I found myself smiling despite my apprehensions. We rumbled to a stop among cars of a similar shape and style, and Thomas opened his door and stepped out, lifting Eoin from the back seat and helping Brigid alight before doing the same for me.

"Brigid, take Eoin and go inside. I need to talk to Anne for a moment," Thomas instructed. Eoin and Brigid frowned in tandem, but Brigid took the little boy's hand and started across the grass to the open doors that welcomed the stream of congregants arriving in cars, delivery trucks, and the occasional horse-drawn wagon.

"I saw Father Darby early this morning. He was giving last rites to Sarah Gillis, Mrs. O'Toole's grandmother."

"Oh no!"

"The woman was so old, she was praying to go," he said. "She was a hundred years if she was a day. Her passing is a blessing on the family."

I nodded, thinking of Maeve and the longevity she would inherit.

"But that's not why I needed to speak to you. I asked Father Darby to make an announcement today from the lectern. He makes announcements every week—church picnics, death notices, birth notices, pleas for help for this parishioner or that parishioner. You know the kind," Thomas explained. He took off his hat and placed it on his head again.

"I asked him to announce that you've returned home after a long illness, and that you are residing at Garvagh Glebe with your son. I thought it would be easier than trying to tell people one at a time. And no one can follow up Father Darby's announcement with questions, although they will try when Mass is over."

I nodded slowly, both nervous and relieved. "What now?"

"Now . . . we have to go inside," he said with a wry smile.

I balked, and Thomas tipped my chin to meet my gaze beneath the brim of my hat.

"People will talk, Anne. They'll talk, and they'll speculate about where you've been and what—and who—you've been doing it with. What they don't know, they might fabricate. But in the end, none of that really matters. You're here, impossible as it seems. And no one can dispute that."

"I'm here. As impossible as it seems," I repeated, nodding.

"What you say to fill in the blanks—or not—is entirely up to you. I'll be beside you, and eventually . . . they'll lose interest."

I nodded again, more firmly, and linked my arm through his. "Thank you, Thomas." My words were paltry, considering how much he'd done for me, but he let me hold on to him, and we entered the church together.

8 July 1921

She is the same. But not the same at all.

 Her skin has the same luster, her eyes the same tilt. Her nose, her chin, and the shape of the fine bones of her face are all unchanged. Her hair has grown so long that it brushes the middle of her back. But it is still dark, and it still curls. She is as slight as I remember and not especially tall. Her laugh made me want to weep—a memory come to life, the sound of a sweeter time, of an old friend and new pain. New pain because she has returned, and I'd given up on her. I didn't find her. She found us, and oddly, she isn't angry. She isn't broken. It's almost as if she isn't Anne.

 Her voice is the same, musical and low, but she speaks slowly now, almost gently, like she's not sure of herself. And the stories she tells, the poetry that trips so effortlessly from her lips! I could listen for hours, but it's so unlike the girl I knew. The old Anne used to spit out her words like she couldn't release them fast enough; she was fiery and full of ideas. She could never sit still. Declan would laugh and kiss her to slow her down. She would try to kiss him back while finishing her point.

 Anne has a quiet about her now, an inner calm that is very different—like a contented Madonna, though I wonder if it's because she has been reunited with Eoin.

She watches him with such love and devotion, such fascination, that I am ashamed for doubting her. Her joy in him makes me angry at the years she lost. She should be angry too. She should be sorrowful. She should be scarred. But she's not. The only visible scar is the gunshot wound on her side, and that, she won't explain.

She refuses to tell me where she's been or what has happened to her. I've tried to imagine plausible scenarios, and I can't. Was she wounded in the Rising? Did someone find her and care for her? Did she lose her memory only to regain it five years later? Was she really in America? Is she a British spy? Did she have a lover? Or did Declan's death send her over the edge? The possibilities—or lack thereof—will drive me mad. When I press her for answers, she seems truly afraid. Then her terror makes her mouth tremble and her hands shake, and she struggles to meet my gaze. And I give up and give in and postpone the questions that must be answered. Eventually.

She has holes in her ears—and diamonds, until she sold them—but no gap between her front teeth. I noticed it when she begged to clean them the first time, and I don't know what to make of it. Maybe my memory's flawed, but the straight white row of perfect teeth seems wrong.

When I pulled her from the lake, she answered immediately to her name, yet she didn't call me by mine. I shudder to think what would have happened had I not been there. I'd been returning from checking on Polly O'Brien across the lough, the first time I'd been there in ages. A complete fluke that I was there at all. I heard a crack, unmistakable, and nothing more. Minutes later, she called out, leading me to her. She has been leading me by the nose ever since, and I have no idea what to do about it.

When she is out of my sight, I don't breathe easy until I see her again. Brigid thinks Anne will take Eoin and run if given the chance. I'm afraid of that too, and though I am drawn to her like never before, I don't trust her. It's made leaving much harder. For Eoin's sake, I don't want to frighten Anne off. And if I'm being honest, I can't bear to see her go.

I went to Dublin in June, making rounds to Dublin's jails, using my medical credentials to check on the political prisoners Mick was negotiating to get released. Lord French has resigned from his duties, but the clearance he gave me during the hunger strikes still got me in almost everywhere. I was denied visits with a few prisoners, which most likely meant the prisoners were in rough shape, too rough for an official inspection. I threatened and waved my papers around, insisting I be allowed to do my job, which got me in a few more doors but not all. I made special note of where the men were being kept, gathered as much information as I could from their jailers, and made sure Mick knew which prisoners were in the greatest danger of not making it out again.

It took me three days to make my rounds, write up my reports, and draw my diagrams. Mick was already putting plans in motion for several breakouts when I left. I haven't been back again. But with rumours of a truce—a truce Anne predicted would come—I need to see where Mick's head is. He was shut out of the negotiations between de Valera and Lloyd George, though Mick ran the government and the war while de Valera sat in America for eighteen months, raising money, tucked away from the hell that is Ireland, from the front lines of a war fought without him.

T. S.

12

A FIRST CONFESSION

Why those questioning eyes
That are fixed upon me?
What can they do but shun me
If empty night replies?

—*W. B. Yeats*

"You're very good, you know. These illustrations are delightful," I said on Sunday evening, after Eoin had been coaxed into bed.

"When I was a boy, I was sick a lot. When I wasn't reading, I was sketching," Thomas replied, his eyes on the picture he was creating, a picture of a man looking out onto a lake where a tiny boat floated in the distance. The book was finished, but Thomas was still drawing. I had already stitched the finished pages together and glued the thick seam into the spine of a cloth-bound cover Thomas had removed from an old ledger. The cover was a plain blue cloth, which served our purposes perfectly. Thomas had written *The Adventures of Eoin Gallagher* across the front in his ornate hand and drawn a small sailboat beneath the title. We'd created three different voyages for Eoin to take—one back to the days of the dinosaurs, one to the building of the pyramids, and one to the future when man walked on the moon. Eoin's boat had to sail through the Milky Way to return home, and Thomas was quite impressed with my imagination. With my input, his sketches of a rocket ship and a space traveler were unsurprisingly prescient.

"Did you live in this house?" I asked. I stood and began to tidy the space so I could wrap our gift.

"I did. My father died before I was born." His eyes shot to mine, gauging whether he was telling me things I already knew.

"And your mother remarried an Englishman," I provided.

"Yes. He owned this house. This land. My mother and I became part of the landed class." His tone was wry. "I spent most of my child-hood days staring out the window in the room where you now sleep. I couldn't play or run or go outside. It would make me cough and wheeze, and a few times I even stopped breathing."

"Asthma?" I asked absentmindedly.

"Yes," he said, surprised. "How did you know? It isn't a well-known term. My doctors called it bronchospasms, but I came across an article in a medical journal published in 1892 that introduced the term. It comes from the Greek word *aazein*, which means to pant, or breathe with an open mouth."

I didn't comment. I waited, hoping he would continue. "I thought if I learned enough, I could heal myself, since no one else seemed able to. I dreamed of running down the lane, running and running and never stopping. I dreamed of hurling and wrestling. I dreamed of a body that wouldn't grow tired before I did. My mother was afraid to let me go to school, but she didn't argue with me or dictate what I read or studied. She even asked Dr. Mostyn if I could look at his anatomy books when I showed an interest. I read them and then read them again. And sometimes the doctor would come and sit with me and answer my questions. My stepfather hired a tutor, and the tutor humored me too. He sent away for medical journals, and in between sketching and read-ing Wolfe Tone and Robert Emmet, I became a bit of a medical expert."

"You're not sick anymore."

"No. I like to think I cured myself with regular doses of black coffee, which eased the symptoms immensely. But besides staying away from things that seemed to exacerbate it, like hay, certain plants, or cigar smoke, I think I mostly outgrew it. By the time I was fifteen, my health was good enough for me to go to St. Peter's College in Wexford for boarding school. And you know the rest of that story."

I didn't. Not really. But I remained quiet, wrapping Eoin's book in brown paper and tying it securely with a long piece of twine.

"What did you think of Father Darby's announcement this morning?" Thomas asked, his tone perfectly measured. I knew he wasn't talking about the announcement that had caused every head to turn and neck to crane toward me. I'd kept my eyes focused on my lap when Father Darby had welcomed me home as Thomas had asked him to do. Eoin had wiggled and waved beside me, enjoying the attention, and Brigid, sitting on his other side, had pinched his leg sharply, reining him in. I'd glared up at her, angered by the nasty welt she'd raised on his leg. Her cheeks had been bright with embarrassment, her jaw tight, and my anger had fizzled into despair. Brigid was suffering. Through the announcement, her eyes had never strayed from the stained-glass depiction of the crucifixion, but her discomfort was as great as my own. She'd relaxed slightly when Father Darby had moved on to political matters and captured the congregation's attention with the news of a truce that had been brokered between the newly formed Dáil, Ireland's unrecognized parliament, and the British government.

"My dear brothers and sisters, word has spread that tomorrow, July 11, Eamon de Valera, president of the Irish Republic and the Dáil Éireann, and Lloyd George, prime minister of England, will sign a truce between our two countries, ending these long years of violence and ushering in a period of peace and negotiation. Let us pray for our leaders and for our countrymen, that order can be maintained and freedom in Ireland can finally be achieved."

Cries and exclamations rang out, and for a moment Father Darby was silent, letting the news settle on his jubilant flock. I peeked up at Thomas, praying he'd forgotten my prediction. He was staring down at me, his face carefully blank, his pale eyes shuttered.

I held his gaze for a heartbeat, then looked away, breathless and repentant. I had no idea how I was going to explain myself.

He'd said nothing about it after Mass. Nothing at dinner, discussing the news benignly with Brigid and later with several men who stopped by to speak with him. They'd argued in the parlor about what the truce really meant, about Partition, and about every member of the IRA having a target on his back. They talked so loudly and so long, puffing cigarettes that made Thomas wheeze, that he finally suggested they move to the rear terrace where the air was cold and fresh, and their conversation would not keep the rest of the house from retiring. Brigid and I had not been invited to join the discussion, and eventually, I helped Eoin get ready for bed. I spent a long time in his room, telling him stories and reciting Yeats, until he finally drifted off to "Baile and Aillinn," the only story he cared nothing about.

When I'd sneaked down to my room to finish Eoin's book, the men were gone, and Thomas was already there, sitting at my desk, waiting for me. And even then, we spoke of easy things.

Now he looked up at me, weary. His fingers were smudged with lead, and he smelled of cigarettes he didn't smoke. His expression was no longer mild, the conversation no longer easy.

"I know you aren't Declan's Anne," Thomas said quietly. I was silent, heart quaking, waiting for recriminations. He stood, moved around the desk, and stopped in front of me, still an arm's length away. I wanted to step into him. I wanted to be closer. Being near him made my belly flutter and my breasts tighten. He made me feel things I hadn't felt before. And even though I feared what he would say next, I wanted to move toward him.

"I know you aren't Declan's Anne—not anymore—because Declan's Anne never looked at me the way you do." The last words were said so simply, I wasn't certain I'd heard him right. Our eyes clashed and held, and I swallowed, trying to dislodge the hook from my throat. But I was caught as surely as I'd been when he pulled me out of the lake.

"And if you keep looking at me that way, Anne, I'll kiss you. I don't know if I trust you. I don't even know who you are half the time. But damn if I can resist you when you look at me like that."

I wanted him to. I wanted him to kiss me, but he didn't close the distance between us, and his lips didn't press into mine.

"Can't I just be Anne?" I asked, almost pleading.

"If you aren't Declan's Anne, who are you?" he whispered, as if he hadn't heard me at all.

I sighed, my shoulders drooping, my eyes falling away. "Maybe I'm Eoin's Anne," I said simply. I had always been Eoin's Anne.

He nodded and smiled sadly. "Yes. Maybe you are. Finally."

"Were you in love . . . with . . . me, Thomas?" I ventured, suddenly brave. My shamelessness made me wince, but I needed to know how he'd felt about Declan's Anne.

His eyebrows rose in slow surprise, and he stepped back from me, distancing himself farther, and I felt the loss even as I filled my lungs in relief.

"No. I wasn't. You were Declan's, always. Always," Thomas said. "And I loved Declan."

"And if I hadn't been . . . Declan's . . . would you have wanted . . . me to be yours?" I pressed, trying not to slip and use the wrong pronoun.

Thomas shook his head as he spoke, almost denying the words as he said them. "You were wild. You burned so hot that none of us could help but draw closer, just to bask in your warmth. And you were—you are—so beautiful. But no. I had no wish to be consumed by you. I had no desire to be burned."

I didn't know what to feel, relief or despair. I didn't want Thomas to love her, but I *did* want him to care about me. And the two were suddenly intertwined.

"Declan could withstand the heat," Thomas continued. "He loved it. He loved you. So much. You lit him up inside, and I always thought you felt the same way about him."

To not come to Anne's defense would be wrong. I couldn't let Thomas doubt her, not even to save myself.

"I'm sure she did. I'm sure Anne Finnegan Gallagher felt the exact same way," I said, head bowed.

He was quiet, but I felt his turmoil even as I refused to meet his gaze.

"I don't understand. You speak as if you are two different people," he pressed.

"We are," I choked, struggling for my composure.

He took one step, and then another, drawing close enough to lift my chin and search my eyes, his fingers soft on my face. I saw my emotions—grief, loss, fear, uncertainty—reflected in his gaze.

"None of us are the same, Anne. Some days I hardly recognize myself in the mirror. It's not my face that has changed; it's the way I see the world. I've seen things that have permanently altered me. I've done things that have distorted my vision. I've crossed lines and tried to find them again, only to discover that all my lines have disappeared. And without lines, everything blurs together."

His voice was so heartsick, his words so heavy, that I could only gaze back at him, moved to tears and silenced by his sadness.

"But when I look at you, I still see Anne," he whispered. "Your lines are sharp and clean. The faces around you are faded and dull—they've been faded and dull for years now—but you . . . you are perfectly clear."

"I am not her, Thomas," I said, needing him to believe me and not daring to make him understand. "Right now, I almost wish I were. But I am not that Anne."

"No. You're right. You've changed. You don't burn my eyes like you once did. Now, I don't have to look away."

My breath caught at his confession—the sound ricocheted between us—and he leaned in to gently free it, brushing my mouth with his. His lips were so soft and shy, they slipped away without letting me greet them. I followed, frantic to call them back, and he hesitated, forehead pressed to mine, hands on my shoulders, letting my bated breath extend an invitation before he accepted it and returned. His hands slid around to my back as his mouth lowered and stayed, letting me feel the warmth and the press of his kiss, so real, so present, so impossible.

Our mouths moved in a halo of swollen caresses, a brush and a slide, a nudge and a pause, reveling in the weight of lips against lips. Over and over, and then again. Plying and persuading, urging and unraveling, until the pounding of my heart trembled in my mouth and quivered in my belly. *Need, need, need,* it panted. *More, more, more,* it roared. The hound of Culann, baying a warning at the door. We both drew back in breathless wonder, eyes wide, hands clinging, lips parted.

For a moment we simply stared at one another, inches apart, our bodies charged and howling. And then we widened the distance, releasing each other. The clanging in my chest and the rushing of my blood was slower to ebb.

"Good night, Countess," Thomas murmured.

"Good night, Setanta," I said, and a smile ghosted past his lips as he turned and left my room. I was drifting off to sleep when I realized he'd never demanded an explanation about the truce.

The next few weeks, I moved in a sort of haze, straddling reality and an existence that was both illogical and absolutely undeniable. I stopped questioning what had happened to me—what would happen to me—and accepted each day as it came. When one dreams terrible dreams, part of the unconscious mind reassures that wakefulness will summon reality and banish the nightmare. But it was not a terrible dream. It had become a sweet sanctuary. And though that stubborn voice still whispered that I would wake, I stopped caring if I slept. I accepted my predicament with the imagination of my childhood, lost in a world I had created and fearful that the story *would* come to an end and that I would return to my previous life, where Eoin and Ireland and Thomas Smith no longer existed.

Thomas had not kissed me again, and I had not given him any indication that I wanted to be kissed. We'd established something that we were not ready to explore. Declan was gone, and Anne was gone. At least the Anne he thought I'd been. But Thomas was still caught between the memory of them and the prospect of me, and I was snagged between a future that was my past, and a past that might be my future. So we settled into an ever-narrowing circle of discovery, talking of nothing and everything, of this and that, of now and then. I asked questions, and he freely answered. He asked questions, and I tried not to lie. I was happy in a way that made no sense, content in a manner that called into question my sanity and surrounded by people who made me glad to be alive, if alive is what I was.

Thomas took me with him once or twice a week or when he thought he would need an extra set of hands, and I'd done my best to provide them. I'd been raised by a doctor; I knew basic first aid, and I wasn't prone to freak-outs or fainting at the sight of blood, which was about all I had going for me. But Thomas seemed to think it was enough. When he could, he left me home to spend time with Eoin, who would be starting school in the fall. Eoin introduced me to all the animals at Garvagh Glebe and told me their names—the pigs, the chickens, the sheep, and the pretty brown mare who was expecting a foal. We began taking long walks along the shore and down the lane, over the green hills and across the low rock walls. I was traipsing over Leitrim's fields with Eoin babbling at my side. Ireland was gray and green, shot with the yellow of the gorse that grew wildly on the hills and in the valleys, and I wanted to know her intimately.

Sometimes Brigid came too, first because she feared Eoin and I would disappear together and then because she seemed to enjoy the exercise. She started to soften toward me, infinitesimally, and sometimes she could be coaxed to talk of the days when she was a girl living in Kiltyclogher in northern Leitrim, giving me a glimpse into her life. It seemed to surprise her that I listened so intently, that I cared to hear her stories, that I wanted to know her at all. I discovered she had two sons and a daughter, all older than Declan, and a little girl buried in Ballinagar. I hadn't seen a stone and wondered if the child's marker was just a plot of grass with a heavy rock to mark her resting place.

Her oldest daughter was in America, in New Haven, Connecticut. Her name was Mary, and she'd married a man named John Bannon. They had three children, grandchildren Brigid had never seen, cousins Eoin had never told me about. Brigid's two sons were unmarried. One, Ben, was a train conductor in Dublin, and the other, Liam, worked on the docks in Sligo. Since I'd been at Garvagh Glebe, neither had come to visit. I listened to Brigid provide updates on each one of her children, and I hung on her words, trying to absorb things I should have known, things Anne *would* have known, and doing my best to bluff my way through the rest.

"You are kind to her, to Brigid," Thomas remarked one day, when we returned from our walk to find him already at home. "She has never been especially kind to you."

Maybe the difference between the "real" Anne Gallagher and me was that Brigid was her mother-in-law and Brigid was *my* great-great-grandmother. Brigid's blood ran in my veins. She was part of me—how big a part, only my DNA would tell, but she belonged to me, and I wanted to know her. The first Anne might not have felt the same sense of belonging.

Thomas went to Dublin for a few days in the middle of August. He wanted to bring me along, and Eoin too, but changed his mind in the end. He seemed reluctant to leave and anxious to go, but he made me promise, as he stuck his medical bag and a small suitcase in the back seat of his Model T, that I would still be at Garvagh Glebe when he returned.

"Don't leave, Anne," he said, his hat in his hands, fear in his eyes. "Promise me you'll stay close. Promise me so I can do what I need to do in Dublin without my head running back here."

I had nodded with only a flicker of fear. If I hadn't gone home yet, it was doubtful I ever would again. Maybe Thomas saw the flicker in my eyes, faint as it was, for he pulled in a sigh and held it, weighing it, considering it, before he released it with a gust of submission.

"I won't go," he said. "I'll wait a bit longer."

"Thomas, go. I'll be here when you get back. I promise."

He looked for a moment at my mouth, as if he wanted to kiss it, to taste it for the truth, but Eoin rushed out of the house and threw himself at Thomas, demanding affection and wheedling a prize from Dublin if he was very good while Thomas was away. Thomas lifted him easily and hugged him close before extracting his own promises.

"I'll bring you back a present if you mind your nana and look after your mother. And don't let her go near the lough," he said to Eoin, raising his pale-blue eyes to mine as he set the boy back on the ground.

My heart lurched, and a memory flooded back, bringing with it an odd sense of déjà vu and a line tripping through my mind.

"Don't go near the water, love, the lough will take you far from me," I murmured, and Thomas cocked his head.

"What?" he asked.

"Nothing. Just something I read once."

"Why can't Mother go near the lough?" Eoin asked, confused. "We go there all the time. We walk on the shore and skip rocks. Mother showed me how."

Eoin had taught me how to skip rocks, once upon a time. Yet another dizzying circle of what came first.

Thomas frowned, ignoring Eoin's question, and sighed again, as if his head and stomach were at war with one another.

"Thomas, go. All will be well while you are gone," I said firmly.

22 August 1921

I drove to Dublin with both hands on the wheel and my heart in my throat. I'd had little contact with Mick since de Valera had returned and Lord French had been replaced as general governor. I wasn't much help to Mick in the scheme of things. I was nothing but a sounding board. A friend. A financial backer and a secret keeper who did what I could, where I could. But still, I'd been away too long, and despite the truce, I was worried.

I met Mick and Joe O'Reilly, Mick's personal assistant, at Devlin's Pub. They were huddled in the back room Mick had been given for an office. The door was left ajar so he could see trouble coming. The rear exit provided a quick escape. Mick was at Devlin's more than he was at his own apartment. He rarely stayed in one place too long, and if it weren't for the loyalty of average citizens, who knew exactly who he was and never said a word despite the reward on his head, he would have been captured long ago. His reputation had grown to epic proportions, and I was afraid much of the rub with the president of the Dáil was due to Mick's popularity. I became alarmed when he told me Dev (de Valera) was considering sending him to America to "get him out of the fight."

I couldn't believe what I was hearing. Mick is the fight, and I told him as much. Without him, our Irish rebellion is all symbolism and suffering with no results— just like every other Irish rebellion over the last several hundred years has been.

Joe O'Reilly agreed with me, and I wondered for the first time how old Joe O'Reilly was. Young. He had to be younger than me. But the man was worn thin. Mick was too. His stomach had been bothering him, the pain so intense I suspected ulcers and made him promise to adjust his diet.

"Dev won't send me away—he can't get any support for it. But he might send me to London, Doc. He's making noise about sending me to negotiate the terms of a treaty," Mick said.

I told Mick I thought that was good news, until he told me de Valera wanted to stay behind, in Dublin.

Mick said, "He's been meeting with Lloyd George for months over the truce, yet now he wants to stand back when it's time to negotiate a treaty? Dev isn't stupid. He's wily. He's playing puppet master."

"So you're the scapegoat." It wasn't a hard conclusion to arrive at.

"I am. He wants me to take the fall when it fails. We won't get everything we want. We might not get anything we want. And we sure as hell won't get an Irish Republic with no partition between the north and south. Dev knows this. He knows England has the power to crush us in a head-to-head conflict. We have three, maybe four thousand fighting men. That's it. He knows nothing about the strategy we've engaged in."

Mick's heels dug into the floor with agitation, and I could only listen as he paced and talked through his fears. "We've fought dirty and we've fought lean. We've relied on the Irish people to hide us, to shelter us, to feed us, and to keep their mouths shut. And they have. Goddammit, they have! Even when farms were burned in Cork last year, and businesses were torched in every county. When reprisals were being carried out in Sligo and priests were being shot in the head by Auxies for refusing to point fingers at their parishioners. When young men who had nothing to do with Bloody Sunday were being tortured and hung because someone had to pay, nobody talked, nobody turned."

Mick fell into a chair and took a deep swallow of the stout in front of him, wiping at his mouth before he continued.

"All we're asking—all we've been asking for centuries—is for them to leave. To let us govern ourselves. Lloyd George knows that to declare all-out war on the Irish people will not go over well in the world court. The Catholic Church has made a statement of condemnation against Britain's tactics. They've begged George to consider an Irish solution. America has even gotten involved. And that is our linchpin. But we can't continue on this way. Ireland can't."

Ireland can't. And Mick can't. Joe O'Reilly can't either. Something has to give.

"Will you go?" I asked Mick, and he nodded.

"I don't see any other way. I'll do my best. Whatever that is. I'm not a statesman."

"Thank God for that," Joe O'Reilly said, clapping him on the back.

"Dev's surely not sending you alone. You know Lloyd George will have a team of lawyers and negotiators," I worried.

"He wants to send Arthur too. He belongs there, and he'll represent us well. There will be a few more, I'm sure."

"I'll be there too. In London. If you need me," I said. "They won't let me sit at the negotiating table, but you'll have my ear if you need it."

He nodded and sighed heavily, as if talking through it had already helped. His eyes were clearer, his posture less agitated. And he suddenly smiled, a wicked twist of his lips that put me immediately on edge.

"I heard through my network of spies that you have a woman living in your house, Doc. A beautiful woman you've made no mention of in your letters. Is she the reason you've stayed away from Dublin so long? Has the mighty Thomas Smith been smitten at last?"

When I told him it was Anne—Declan's Anne—his mouth fell open, and he had nothing to say for a good stretch. Joe hadn't known Declan or Anne and sipped his stout quietly, waiting for me to explain, though he probably welcomed the silence. I didn't suppose Joe or Mick ever sat for long. Joe rode his bike all over Dublin, delivering Mick's dispatches and keeping the cogs oiled.

"She's been alive all this time . . . and she never sent word?" Mick whispered.

I told him how I'd found her in the lough, a gunshot wound in her side, and he stared at me, dumbfounded.

"Oh, Tommy. Be careful, my friend. Be very, very careful. There are forces at work you can't even begin to understand. Spies come in all shapes and sizes. You don't *know where she's been or who's gotten to her. I don't like the sound of this at all."*

I nodded wordlessly, knowing he was right. I've been telling myself the very same things from the moment I pulled her from the water. I didn't tell Mick she knew about the truce before it even happened. And I didn't tell him that I'm already in love with her.

T. S.

13

HER TRIUMPH

I did the dragon's will until you came
Because I had fancied love a casual
Improvisation, or a settled game.

And then you stood among the dragon-rings.
I mocked, being crazy, but you mastered it
And broke the chain and set my ankles free.

—*W. B. Yeats*

I promised Thomas everything would be all right while he was gone, but it was a promise I was unable to keep. Two days after he left, long after the house had grown quiet and the night had grown black, Maeve, in her nightgown and a shawl, woke me with frantic whispering.

"Miss Anne, wake up! There's trouble in the barn. Dr. Smith isn't here, and I know you help him sometimes. We need bandages and medicine. Da says we might need whiskey too."

I got out of bed, pulling on the deep-blue robe Beatrice had picked out for me and Thomas had purchased in spite of me, and hurried to Thomas's clinic, filling Maeve's arms with bandages and whatever else seemed useful before visiting the liquor cabinet and helping myself to three bottles of Irish whiskey, taking a quick pull off one for courage.

I didn't let myself think about what was waiting for me or if I'd be able to do a damn thing about it. Instead, I ran out the back door, across the veranda, and through the heavy rain that had begun sometime after I'd gone to bed.

The stables and the large barn were separated from the house by a wide lawn rimmed in trees, and the grass was cold and wet against my bare feet. A lantern flickered through the trees, beckoning us, and Maeve ran ahead, trailing bandages that wouldn't do much good if they were drenched.

A young man, unconscious and soaking wet, lay on the barn floor, surrounded by a handful of men who weren't much older or dryer. One held a lantern high over the body of the wounded man, and when I entered behind Maeve, every head turned and every weapon was raised.

"Doc is still in Dublin, Da. Miss Anne is all we've got." Her voice was fearful, as though she worried she might have made a mistake. I rushed past her to where Maeve's father was doing his best to mop up the blood from the young man's head with his shirt, begging sweet Mary, mother of God, to intercede for his son.

"What happened?" I demanded, sinking down beside the boy.

"His head. Robbie's eye is gone," Daniel O'Toole stammered.

"A bullet, ma'am. The boy took a bullet," someone said from the circle standing watch above us.

"Let me see, Mr. O'Toole," I demanded. He pulled his dirty, smeared shirt away from his son's face. Robbie's right eye was a bubbling mess. Miraculously, he moaned as I turned his head toward the light, letting me know he still lived. Another hole, black and jagged, gaped at his temple just an inch from his eye socket, as if the bullet had skimmed past his eye at an extreme angle and taken a chunk off the side of his head. I didn't know enough about head wounds or the brain to make a better guess, but if the bullet had come out again, that seemed positive.

I knew there was nothing I could do but try to stop the bleeding and keep him alive until Thomas got home. I shouted for Maeve to bring me the bandages and pressed a thick section of gauze to Robbie's eye and another to the exit wound. His father kept the gauze in place as I began to wrap the boy's head as securely as I dared, layering another round of gauze as I went until his entire head from his eyes up was swaddled tightly.

"We need blankets, Maeve. You know where to find them," I instructed. Maeve nodded and was out the door in a flash, running back toward the house before I finished speaking.

"Should we try to bring him home, Ma'am?" Daniel O'Toole asked. "Where his mother can look after him?"

"The less we move him, the better, Mr. O'Toole. He needs to be kept warm, and we need the bleeding to stop. That's the best we can do until the doctor returns," I answered.

"What about the guns?" someone murmured, and I was reminded of the dripping audience looking down on me.

"How many guns are we talking about?" I asked.

"The less you know, the better," a man argued from the shadows, and I nodded.

"We can hide them below the floor. I'll show ye," Daniel O'Toole offered, unable to meet my gaze.

"We might have Tans on our tail. They were all over the shore. We couldn't get to the caves without leading them right to the rest of the stash."

"Shut up, Paddy," someone snapped.

"How did Robbie get shot?" I asked, my voice level, my hands shaking.

"One of the Tans riddled the trees, hoping to spook us out. Robbie didn't even cry out. He kept moving until we were all inside."

Maeve was back, her arms full, but her face was white.

"Miss Anne, there are Tans coming down the lane. Two lorries. Mrs. Gallagher is awake, and Eoin too. And they're afraid. Eoin's asking for you."

"If they come out here and see Robbie, they'll know. Even if we hide the guns in the loft and the rest of us scatter, they'll know. They'll search this place—maybe torch it—and they'll take Robbie," the man with the lantern said.

"Take Robbie back into the tack room," I said. "There's a bed back there. Douse him in what's left of the whiskey in this bottle and put the bottle on the floor by his bed. Then cover him well and warmly. Cover his head too, leaving his lower face exposed like he's fallen asleep with the pillow over his head. Mr. O'Toole, get the mare, the one who's pregnant. Lay her down and fuss over her, like she's close to delivering. The rest of you, hide the guns, hide yourselves. I'll keep them out as long as I can. Maeve, come with me," I directed, and streaked back across the grass, the girl at my heels. I raced through the house, pulling off my bloodied robe and the nightgown beneath it, stuffing them under my bed and putting on the dress I'd worn the day before, pausing to spritz myself with perfume and run a hand over my loose braid.

"Miss, you've blood on your face and your hands!" Maeve cried as I met her in the hall, and I tumbled toward the kitchen sink, scrubbing at my hands and face as a sharp rap echoed through the house. Soldiers at the door.

"Go to Brigid and Eoin. Tell them to stay upstairs. Stay with them, Maeve. I'll be all right."

She nodded and was gone again, flying soundlessly up the huge staircase as I walked to the door, a character in my own story, my head flying with plotlines and possible scenarios before I opened the door with a fluttering hand and greeted the stony-faced men standing in the rain like I was Scarlett O'Hara entertaining a dozen callers.

"Oh my!" I said, abandoning the Irish accent I'd worn like armor since waking up at Garvagh Glebe. "You all scared me! It's miserable out there. I was just outside myself. In the barn. We have a foal coming. Our girl is suffering. I had to sit with her for a while. Do any of you know any husbandry?" I laughed, like I'd told a joke. "I mean animal husbandry, of course," I prattled, allowing the rain to soak the front of my dress and wet the curls around my face before moving back and swinging my arm wide, inviting them in.

"What can I do for you? The doctor is gone, I'm afraid. I hope none of you are in need of medical attention."

"We're going to need to search the house, ma'am. And the grounds," the man in charge said, though he made no move to enter. He wore a glengarry cap and tall boots, and I remembered what Thomas had said about the Auxiliaries. They didn't answer to anyone.

"All right," I said, frowning. "But whatever for?"

"We have reason to believe there are gun smugglers in the woods around this house."

"Oh my," I said again, and the fear in my voice was very real. "Well, you may certainly search the house, Captain. Can I call you Captain?" I stepped aside, out of his way. "It's awfully wet for being outside. And I was just in the barn. I didn't see anyone. And if you all go tromping through the barn, our poor mare is likely to lose her foal. Could I just escort a few of you to peep inside so we don't upset her?"

"Who else is in the house, ma'am?" the Auxie asked, dismissing my request.

"For goodness' sake, Captain!" I insisted, stamping my foot. "I'm getting absolutely soaked to the skin." The man's eyes dropped to my chest and rose again. "All of you, please come inside if you're going to come inside."

The captain—he hadn't argued with the rank I'd assigned him— barked orders for six of the men to circle the house and wait for further instructions and the rest to come inside with him. There were ten men in total, and four of them eagerly stepped into the foyer and let me close the door behind them.

"Can I take your coats and hats, gentlemen?" I asked, knowing they wouldn't comply.

"How many in the house, ma'am?" the captain asked again, his eyes roving up the stairs. A lamp from the upper corridor and the light I'd left on in the kitchen were the only lights on in the house. I flicked on the chandelier overhead, flooding the men in light.

"My son—he's six and he's sleeping, so please search quietly—my mother-in-law, and a servant girl. The doctor is in Dublin. Our overseer is in the barn with the mare. His son is probably with him too, though he might have given up and gone to bed."

"They were there when you left?"

"Yes, Captain. But I left them with a bottle of whiskey, so they weren't too unhappy about waiting up with the mare." I smiled conspiratorially.

"You're an American, ma'am?" one of the other men asked, and I realized I recognized him from Sligo. He was one of the men who broke the windows of Lyons department store.

"Yes, I am. I haven't mastered the brogue, I'm afraid."

"No loss there," the man said, and his captain pointed up the stairs. "Barrett, you and Ross search the rooms upstairs. Walters and I will search down here."

"Do be mindful, please, Officers Barrett and Ross," I pled sweetly. "My mother-in-law is quite crotchety. I wouldn't want either of you to be struck with a poker."

They blanched and hesitated before traipsing up the stairs. I wavered, not knowing which men I should shadow, hoping Brigid would keep her head and help Eoin keep his. I had no doubt Maeve would be fine.

"Could I get you something to warm you—some tea or brandy, Captain?" I asked lightly.

"No, ma'am," the captain said, striding through the foyer. I stayed with him, making inane conversation, and he ignored me, searching my room, the bathroom, and the kitchen before the man named Walters called out to him.

"Captain? What do you make of this?"

My heart thundered as I accompanied the captain to the back of the house, where Walters was standing in Thomas's clinic, staring at the open cupboards and drawers, which had clearly been rummaged through.

"Ma'am?"

"Yes, Captain?" I said innocently.

"The rest of the house is as neat as a pin. Who needed medical attention?"

"The mare, Captain!" I laughed. "I was looking for laudanum. The doctor hides it from me. He worries that I like it too much. But my father told me that if you put a little on a horse's tongue, it'll calm them right down. Have you ever tried putting laudanum on a horse's tongue, Captain?"

He looked at me doubtfully.

"I can see you haven't. It's easier said than done."

"Did you find any?" he queried.

"No. I didn't. But I made a mess, didn't I?"

"I think we need to go see that mare, ma'am."

"Yes, sir. Let me grab my shawl, please."

I walked through the house, breathing through my nose to stay calm, smiling as the two constables came down the stairs. There'd been no commotion, and I prayed Eoin had stayed asleep through it all.

I pulled a shawl from my wardrobe and stuffed my feet into Anne's old boots, tying them as swiftly as I could. I didn't want the captain searching without me. I wanted his eyes to see the picture I had already painted. I just prayed the men in the barn and the guns were long gone.

We walked through the drizzle, some cadets walking to the edge of the lawn, looking into the trees, and some remaining back at the house. A lantern still flickered from the barn, and I stumbled purposefully, reaching for the captain. He slowed, and I took his arm with a grateful smile.

"Well, we've had an adventure, haven't we?" I said. "The doctor will be all ears when he gets home. And hopefully we'll have a new foal as well."

"When do you expect the doctor, Mrs. . . . ?"

"Gallagher," I supplied. "Tomorrow or the next day. He used to go to Dublin a great deal more when Lord French was governor general. The doctor's late father was a friend of Lord and Lady French. Do you know Lord French, Captain?"

"I haven't had the pleasure, Mrs. Gallagher," the captain replied, but I heard a softening in his tone. Thomas might not have wanted me to share that information, but under the circumstance, a friendship with a British loyalist could only reassure the captain.

When we walked into the barn, Daniel O'Toole was leading the sweat-slicked mare around in circles, stopping every now and again to murmur to her before he began walking again. His shirt was still covered in blood, and his one arm, his shirtsleeves rolled above his elbows, was streaked with it.

He jerked in surprise upon seeing us—a convincing act, though I doubted the fear in his face was anything but genuine.

"How's the mare, Mr. O'Toole?" I said brightly, as if the men around me were simply special visitors. Daniel's eyes snapped to mine, noting the American accent.

"I'm walking her for a bit, Mrs. Gallagher. Sometimes it helps."

"You're covered in blood, man," the captain snapped.

"Oh, I am that, sir!" Mr. O'Toole agreed heartily. "It looks worse than 'tis. Her waters broke when I checked her. But I felt the wee wan's head, I did. Two little front hooves too."

"Are you the only one here, Mr. O'Toole?" the captain barked, clearly not interested in the grittier details of birthing a foal.

"My son Robbie is in the bunk in back. He's sleepin' now. Had a little too much to drink, he did. But it's almost dawn, Captain. We've been up with the mare all night."

The captain was unimpressed, and he walked the length of the barn, directing some of his men to climb to the loft and another to search the back room. I held my breath, afraid for Robbie. His bandages could give us away. But the man returned minutes later, wiping his mouth. I had an image of an open bottle of fine Irish whiskey sitting ever so innocently where a tired, wet constable could help himself.

"It's just as the man says, Captain," he said amiably.

"Mrs. Gallagher, we will be scouring the fields and the shore over the next few hours. I would recommend that you keep your servants and your family inside. I will check back sometime tomorrow."

"Are you sure I can't offer you something to drink, Captain? I will have a full staff at dawn, and my cook could prepare a large breakfast for you and your men."

He hesitated, and I wondered if I had gone too far. The sooner they left, the better.

"No. Thank you, madam." The captain sighed. His men began filing out, and just before the captain turned to go, he cocked his head. "Mr. O'Toole, have you ever heard of giving laudanum to a mare in labor?"

Daniel frowned, and my heart sank. "I've never had any to spare, Captain, but iffen I did, I don't see how it could hurt."

"Huh. Mrs. Gallagher seems convinced of it."

"Well, the lady would know, Captain. She's very clever." Daniel nodded, not even looking at the man. Hysterical laughter bubbled in my throat, and I followed the captain from the barn.

The rain stopped just after dawn, and the sun rose on Garvagh Glebe as though the night before had been one of peaceful slumber. Robbie O'Toole gave us all a fright when he staggered out onto the lawn, disoriented and howling in pain. His legs and his lungs worked fine. We spirited him into the house and into my room. I was afraid of infection setting in but didn't dare remove his bandages to check the ugly wound. The bleeding had stopped, and he had no fever, so I dosed him with the same syrup Thomas had given me, and he fell into a deep—and mercifully quiet—sleep.

The men with Robbie had dispersed into the night, the guns hidden in a cellar located directly below where Daniel O'Toole had paced with the pregnant mare—she wasn't even close to delivering, which presented another concern if the Tans came back. But for now, we'd escaped the worst of it, and the O'Tooles, except for Robbie, congregated in the kitchen at Garvagh Glebe. Maggie, the mother of the crew, kept vigil over her oldest son, and I did my best to keep her brood inside, just as the captain had instructed. He came back at sundown, reporting that a patrol would continue in the area. I thanked him as though he and his men were keeping us all safe and waved him off like he was an old friend.

I had questions for Daniel, and I knew he had questions for me, but we both stayed quiet, going about the day as best we could, eyes and ears peeled for Thomas's return. At dusk, Daniel took his children home, as exhausted as I after a night with no sleep, and Maggie remained at Garvagh Glebe to sit with Robbie. Brigid cornered me briefly, hissing a stream of questions about the Tans, what they'd wanted, and why Robert O'Toole was lying wounded in my bed. I didn't tell her about the men in the barn or the weapons they were hiding. I pled innocent and told her none of us knew what had happened. Robbie had been hit by a stray bullet, and we were taking care of him.

She complained mightily, cursing the English and the IRA, grumbling about truces that weren't truces, doctors who weren't ever home, and women who kept dangerous secrets. I ignored the last bit and prayed harder for Thomas to return. I had been sleeping in his empty bed in the room beside Eoin's because I'd been ousted from my own.

Thomas returned in the early morning hours, four days after he'd left. Maggie O'Toole had intercepted him as soon as he entered the house, and he'd removed Robbie's bandages, sterilized and irrigated the wound as best he could, and wrapped it up again, telling Maggie that Robbie had the luck of the Irish. He might not have a working right eye, but he would still have a life. Daniel O'Toole had come in not long after Thomas, and he'd filled Thomas in on the excitement he'd missed. The O'Tooles had failed to mention I was asleep in his bed, and Thomas had come in and lain down beside me, waking me and surprising us both.

"Jaysus, Anne!" he said, gasping. "I didn't even see you there. I thought it odd that my bed wasn't made, but I figured with all the commotion, it had been missed. I thought you were in Eoin's room."

"How's Robbie?" I said, so relieved to see him I felt like crying.

Thomas told me what he'd told Maggie and Daniel, adding that if it could be kept from infection, it would heal, and the young man would recover.

We were silent for a moment, our thoughts heavy with what might lie ahead.

"Daniel told me you hatched the whole plan," Thomas said softly. "He said Liam and Robbie and the rest of the boys would have been sunk without you. Not to mention Garvagh Glebe. The Tans have torched homes for less, Anne."

"I find I am a very good actress," I mumbled, embarrassed and pleased by his praise.

"Daniel said the same thing. He also said you sounded like a lady all the way from America." He brooded for a moment. "Why America?"

"I did everything I could to make them think I wasn't a threat. Everything I could to distract them. If I wasn't Irish, why would I care about the Irish Republican Army? I let them in without protest, chatted like a mindless girl, and made it all up as I went. I thought I was done for when they found the clinic had been rummaged through."

"The laudanum?" Thomas asked, his lips twitching.

"Yes. The laudanum. Daniel O'Toole's not a bad fibber either."

"What made you think of the mare? It was really quite brilliant. The blood, the distraction, all of it."

"I once . . . read . . . a story about a family in Louisville, Kentucky, in the mid-1800s, who raised and sold horses to the wealthiest people in America." I was lying again, but it was a white lie. I hadn't read a book like that. I'd written one. Thomas gazed at me, his eyes heavy with fatigue, waiting for me to continue. "There was a scene where the family used the birth of a foal to distract the authorities . . . only it wasn't guns they were hiding but slaves. The family was part of the Underground Railroad."

"That . . . is . . . amazing," he whispered.

"The book was based on a true story too," I said.

"No, Anne. You. You are amazing."

"And you are exhausted," I whispered, watching as his eyes closed and his face relaxed. We lay, turned toward each other on the big bed, like old friends at a sleepover.

"I knew I shouldn't leave. I could feel it the whole time I was gone. I left Dublin at two o'clock in the morning. Gave my report to the Big Fella and drove straight here," Thomas mumbled.

"Rest, Setanta," I said, wanting to smooth the hair on his forehead, to touch his face, but I contented myself with watching him sleep instead.

25 August 1921

Liam Gallagher, Declan's older brother by several years, was the one who decided to bring the guns to Garvagh Glebe. I'd known for some time that Mick was using Liam's access on the docks at Sligo to move cargo around under the noses of the Tans. When the tide was high, they moved down the long canal from the sea to the lough and hid weapons in the caves on the shore, distributing them inland from there. Ben Gallagher, the oldest of Brigid's boys, is a conductor on the route from Cavan to Dublin, and I have no doubt there are frequently guns stowed on his train. Mick talked a while back about a shipment of Thompson guns that would give the IRA another level of firepower, but so far, the shipment hasn't materialized.

The guns Liam and his boys brought to Garvagh Glebe are now stacked in a ten-by-ten space beneath the wooden slats that make up the barn floor. Daniel and I carved out the space and lined it in rock years ago. It's hard to find the trap door unless you know it's there; a little spring-lock mechanism on the inner corners makes a handle unnecessary.

Ben and Liam have kept their distance over the years. I suspect that it's guilt and helplessness more than anything else. They were relieved when their mother moved to Garvagh Glebe with Eoin. Neither of them are in any position to support her or the boy. Two groups of people exist in Ireland—farmers with huge families and single adults. With emigration one of the only viable options to find work, men and women who don't want to leave Ireland are waiting longer than ever to marry, the fear of being unable to provide for a family keeping men from committing to anything but their own survival and women from welcoming a man to their beds.

Brigid talks about her children. She misses them. She writes them letters and begs her sons to come to Garvagh Glebe to visit. They don't come often. Since Anne has returned, I haven't seen or heard from either of them. Until now.

Liam visited his mother this evening. He ate dinner with us, made small talk with his mother, and roundly avoided conversing with Anne, though his eyes were continually returning to her. She seemed just as uncomfortable with him, sitting silently beside Eoin, her eyes on her plate. I wonder if it's his resemblance to Declan that pains her or the unanswered questions hanging over her head. She's won Daniel over, though. He is convinced she saved them all. Liam doesn't seem so sure.

When dinner was through, Liam asked for a private word, and we walked to the barn, our voices low and our eyes wide as we scanned the darkness for eavesdropping shadows.

"I'll wait for the Tans and the Auxies to suspend the patrol," he told me. "They're supposed to be pulling back, though we all know the truce is just an excuse for them to double down. We're not twiddling our thumbs either, Doc. We're stockpiling. Planning. Preparing for it to ramp

up again. In three days, the guns will be moved, and I'll do my best not to put you in this position again."

"It could have ended very badly, Liam," I said, not to reprimand but to remind.

He nodded glumly, his shoulders hunched, his hands stuffed in his pockets. "It could have, Doc. And it still might."

"How so, Liam?"

"I don't trust Anne, Thomas. Not at all. She turns up, and suddenly the Tans are on to us. We've been running guns through here for three years. The day you dragged her out of the lough, we had to ditch the weapons in the west shore caves instead of unloading them on O'Brien's dock like we've done every other time. We had two dozen Tans waiting for us on the dock. If the fog hadn't rolled in, we would have been sunk."

"Who told you I dragged her out of the lough, Liam?" I kept my voice level, but alarm bells were ringing in my head.

"Eamon Donnelly. He thought I should know, being family and all," he answered, defensive.

"Huh. The way Daniel tells it, if Anne was working with the Tans, you wouldn't have survived the night," I said.

"That woman isn't Anne," Liam hissed. "I don't know who she is. But that's not our Annie." He scrubbed at his eyes like he wanted to erase her, and when he spoke again, weariness had replaced his adamancy. "You've taken care of my mother and my nephew. You take care of a lot of people, Thomas. Everyone knows it. And none of us will ever be able to repay you. But you don't owe

Anne anything. None of us do. You've got to get rid of her.
The sooner the better."

Liam left without saying goodbye to Brigid. Anne
took Eoin to his room without saying good night to me.
I've moved Robbie onto a cot in the clinic so Anne doesn't
have to sleep in my bed. The thought tightens my body
and loosens my mind. From my desk, I can hear her in
the next room, telling Eoin the legend of Niamh and
Oisín and the Land of the Young.

I stop writing to listen, entranced once again by her
voice and her stories.

I am no longer haunted by Anne but enchanted.

Liam says she isn't Anne. He's lost his mind. But deep
down I am half convinced he's right, which makes me just
as daft as he.

T. S.

14

I AM OF IRELAND

'I am of Ireland,
And the Holy Land of Ireland,
And time runs on,' cried she.
'Come out of charity,
Come dance with me in Ireland.'

—*W. B. Yeats*

Liam Gallagher, Declan Gallagher's brother and Brigid's son, was the man who shot me on the lough. He was one of the men on the riverboat. The one who raised his arm, pointed a gun at me, and pulled the trigger.

Part of me had believed that I'd fallen through time and into 1921 as an odd way of saving myself from something in 2001. But Liam Gallagher was as real in 1921 as he'd been on the lake that day, before I'd even realized where I was. I'd rowed away from the shores of 2001 and into another world. And in that world, Liam Gallagher had tried to kill me.

He must have been among the men in the barn, the men who brought the guns. But my attention had been riveted on Robbie, my fear and apprehension focused on the threat to Garvagh Glebe and the people she sheltered, and I hadn't looked at any of the men closely. But

Liam had been there, and he'd seen me. And tonight, he came back again, sitting down to a supper of roast beef, potatoes, and carrots in a caramelized sauce as though the day on the lough never happened.

Maybe it didn't.

I considered for the umpteenth time that I might be mistaken, that the trauma of my trip through time had skewed my vision and altered events. But there was a thick pink scar on my side as evidence to the contrary. And Liam Gallagher was a gunrunner.

He'd already been seated at the table when I'd walked into the dining room that evening. He and Brigid had ignored me, and Eoin had patted the chair next to him, excited that I would be sitting by him for the first time. I'd almost fallen into the chair, sick and shocked. Thomas had come in a few moments later, and he'd been drawn into conversation with Liam, leaving me to shrink in petrified silence.

I'd excused myself as quickly as I could, but Eoin had slipped his hand in mine and begged me to give him his bath and a story. Brigid had agreed eagerly, clearly wanting to spend time with her son. Now I sit in Eoin's room in the dark, watching him sleep, afraid to be alone, afraid to move at all.

I will have to tell Thomas. I will have to tell him Liam shot me. But he will want to know why I'd said nothing before. If I was Anne Gallagher, I would have recognized Liam. And Liam would have recognized Anne. Yet he'd tried to kill her. Me. Us.

A terrified moan slipped through my lips, and Eoin stirred. I pressed my hand over my mouth to muffle my distress. Liam hadn't been afraid. He'd sat across the table from me and made small talk with Thomas and his mother, eating everything on his plate and asking for seconds. He must feel safe; I'd been at Garvagh Glebe for almost two months, and I hadn't made a single accusation.

If I did, it was my word against his, and I was the one with the most to explain.

I spent the night sitting in the chair in Eoin's room, too afraid to return to my own. Thomas found me there early the next morning. I was curled in an unnatural position, my neck stiff and my dress rumpled. He leaned over the chair and touched my cheek. I came awake gasping and flailing, and he shushed me, putting a hand to my mouth.

"Your bed hadn't been slept in. I was worried," Thomas said softly. "I thought—" He straightened, not finishing his sentence.

"What's wrong?" I asked. I wasn't the only one still dressed in the clothes from the night before.

"Robbie's taken a turn for the worse. He needs a hospital. I think he's got some swelling—maybe bone fragments—in his brain. I don't have the facilities or the expertise to do what needs to be done. I'm taking him to Dublin."

"Can I come with you?" I asked. I didn't want to be left behind again. Not yet. Not with Liam Gallagher still lurking around. When the guns were gone, maybe he would go too, and I would have nothing to fear.

My question surprised Thomas. "You want to come with me to Dublin?"

"You drive, and I'll do my best to take care of Robbie."

He nodded slowly, as if considering.

"I wanna come too," Eoin mumbled from his bed. "I'll help take care of Robbie."

"Not this time, Eoin," Thomas soothed, sitting on Eoin's bed and pulling him close for a quick embrace. "I miss you, lad. I would like nothing better than to bring you with me everywhere I go. But Robbie's very sick. This won't be an outing you would enjoy."

"But Mother will enjoy it?" Eoin asked doubtfully.

"No. She won't enjoy it either. But I might need her help."

"But we're working on our book," Eoin protested. "She's writing a new adventure for Eoin Gallagher."

The book for his birthday had been a great hit. I'd written another and was working on a third, and Eoin had already asked for adventures in Japan and New York and Timbuktu.

"Are you leaving room for pictures?" Thomas asked.

Eoin nodded. "At the bottom. You'll never catch up, Doc," he said sadly.

"I promise I will. And you might want to try drawing some of the pictures too," Thomas suggested. "Your drawings always make me smile."

Eoin yawned and nodded. Rejected and still sleepy, he rolled over, and Thomas pulled the covers over his shoulders. I kissed Eoin's cheek and whispered my devotion, and we crept out.

"We need to leave as quickly as possible. I'll have Daniel help me get Robbie to the car. Can you be ready in fifteen minutes?" Thomas asked.

I nodded eagerly and started down the hall, making a mental list.

"Anne?"

"Yes?"

"You'll need to pack a nice dress. The red one. There's a suitcase in the closet beneath the stairs."

I nodded, not questioning him, and raced to my room.

The drive between Dublin and Dromahair took much longer than it had in 2001. Dirt roads, lower speeds, and a patient in the rear seat all contributed to a stressful ride. However, traffic was minimal, and I was not the one behind the wheel dodging oncoming traffic and praying for deliverance like I'd done a lifetime ago. We stopped once for gas—petrol—and I had to disembark because the gas tank, much to my surprise, was located under the front seat. Thomas noted my surprise and frowned, asking, "Where else would it be?"

Three and a half hours after we left Dromahair, we arrived in Dublin. I should have been prepared for the clothes and the cars, the streets and the sounds, but I wasn't. Thomas remarked with relief at the absence of checkpoints—the most glaring sign of the truce. I could only nod and stare, trying to take it all in. It was nine on a Friday morning, and Dublin was dingy, dilapidated, and completely unrecognizable until we neared the center of the city. The old pictures I'd studied were suddenly bustling backdrops; the black-and-white photos were now drenched in life and color. Sackville had been renamed O'Connell Street—I remembered that much—and Nelson's Pillar had not yet been blown up. The post office was a burned-out shell, and my eyes clung to its skeletal remains. From what I remembered of the maps of 1916 Dublin—one of which was still pinned to my office wall—I didn't think we were taking the most direct route to the Mater Hospital. I suspected Thomas wanted to gauge my reaction to the war zone. If my wonder confused him, he kept it hidden.

We drove past a row of tidy, connected brownstone-style homes, and Thomas nodded toward them. "I sold the old house on Mountjoy and bought another, three houses down. No bad memories there."

I nodded, grateful that I wouldn't be expected to remember a home Anne Gallagher would have been familiar with. We pulled in front of the Mater, the soaring columns and stately entrance not unlike the pictures of the GPO before the Rising. I stayed in the car with Robbie, parked at the front entrance, while Thomas ran inside for a gurney and assistance.

He was back within minutes, along with a nun in a white habit accompanied by two men and a stretcher. Thomas gave a brief explanation of Robbie's condition, as well as a request for a particular surgeon, and the nun nodded, telling him they would do the best they could. She seemed to know him, referring to him as Dr. Smith, and clucked her tongue and shot instructions to the orderlies. We parked the car, and I spent the rest of the day walking the halls and waiting for news.

Nurses in long white pinafores and pert hats strode through halls, pushing patients in ancient chairs and rolling beds, and though medicine had improved dramatically in eighty years, the atmosphere of a working hospital had not. There was the same sense of frantic competence, of sadness layered with relief, and most of all, the sharp tang of tragic endings. Eoin had spent his entire adult life in a hospital. I suddenly understood why he hadn't wanted to die in one.

Thomas was able to observe the surgery, and at six p.m., he joined me in the hospital mess hall, where I'd purchased us both some bread and soup that had long ago grown cold.

I'd eaten my portion huddled over the pages of a new story for Eoin. I'd decided I should plant the seed of Brooklyn in his little head. In this episode, Eoin Gallagher crossed Lough Gill and found himself in New York harbor, looking up at Lady Liberty. He walked across the Brooklyn Bridge on one page, walked to the corner of Jackson Street and Kingsland Avenue on another, and strolled through the halls of old Greenpoint Hospital, built in 1914, where my grandfather had worked until it closed in the early eighties. I included a page where the young adventurer watched the Dodgers play at Ebbets Field, sitting in the upper deck that hung over left field, listening to Hilda Chester ring her cowbell when Gladys Gooding wasn't playing her organ. I described the brick arches and the flagpole and the Abe Stark advertisement on the bottom of the scoreboard that said, "Hit Sign, Win Suit."

I'd never been to Ebbets Field. It was demolished in 1960. But Eoin had loved it, and he'd described it to me in great detail. Eoin said baseball was never the same after the Dodgers left Brooklyn. But he'd always said it with a nostalgic smile, the kind of smile that said, "I'm just glad I got to be there."

I sketched a small picture of Coney Island with little Eoin eating a hot dog and staring up at the Ferris wheel, another thing my grandfather had loved. It wasn't as good as Thomas's renderings, but it would do.

When Thomas sat down beside me, a cup of black coffee in his hands and declaring Robbie's surgery a success, I read the story to him. He listened, his eyes far away, his hair tousled.

"Baseball and Brooklyn, huh?" he murmured.

"Eoin said he wanted an adventure in New York," I said. Ebbets Field was completed before 1921. I knew I was safe with my dates, but his attention made me squirm.

"Eoin wants an adventure in New York. But do you want an adventure in Dublin, Anne?" he asked softly.

"What did you have in mind, Dr. Smith?"

He set his coffee down and took a chunk of the hard bread and dipped it into the cold soup. He chewed slowly, his eyes still on me, considering. When he swallowed, he took another swig of his coffee and sighed as if he'd come to a decision.

"There's someone I'd like you to meet."

Beatrice Barnes, the pretty sales clerk at Lyons department store, had chosen a red figure-skimming dress with a boat neckline, cap sleeves, and a slight dropped waist. It swished around my lower legs, making me feel like I should break into the Charleston like a flapper girl—which I wouldn't be doing—but I could not fault her taste or her eye. It fit me perfectly, and the color made my skin glow and my eyes sparkle. She'd included a red rouge and a matching pair of silk gloves that enveloped my arms past my elbows, leaving only my upper arms uncovered. I put them on and immediately pulled them off again. August, even in Ireland, was too hot for full-length silk gloves, whatever the fashion. I parted my hair deeply on the side, wrapped it into a loose knot low on my neck, and gently pulled a few curls free to brush my collarbones. Powder, lash tint, and the red rouge on my lips made me look like I'd made an effort, and I stepped back from the mirror, hoping I would please him. Thomas rapped on the door, and I called out for him to come in. He stepped inside, freshly shaved, his hair slicked back in sooty waves. He was wearing a black three-piece suit and tie over a crisp white shirt, a long black duster over his arm.

"It's damp out. You'll want a coat over that dress," he suggested, walking to the wardrobe where I'd hung my things. The room was well appointed in rich tones and dark furniture—nothing ostentatious yet nothing inexpensive. The whole house was furnished in the same manner, timeless and unassuming, welcoming yet slightly aloof, like a gracious butler. Like Thomas himself.

"There's no curfew. Dublin's celebrating the truce," he said, his eyes soft on my face, and I had to mentally amend my description. He was not always aloof. I smiled, welcoming the warmth of his gaze.

"Are *we* celebrating?" I asked.

"I suppose we are. Do you mind walking? It's not too far."

"Not at all."

He escorted me to the door, helped me with my coat, and offered his arm. But instead of taking it, I threaded my fingers through his. His breath hitched, and his eyes flared ever so slightly, making my pulse quicken and my heart quiver. We stepped out into the night and made our way down the street, hand in hand, our footsteps echoing in clicking syncopation.

The mist hung low, making the streetlamps look like candles behind a cloth, smeared and tepid. Thomas didn't stroll; he strode, his long black coat making him blend oddly into the fog, just another shape melding in and out. The stockings, secured to my legs by the corset straps I couldn't get used to, were little protection against the damp, but the air felt good against my skin. I'd left my hat behind, not wanting to flatten my hair, but Thomas had pulled on his peaked hat, the style he seemed to favor, the kind Eoin had worn his entire life. It sat above Thomas's deep-set blue eyes, a hat jaunty and boyish, so unlike the man. I noticed many men wore a bowler hat, the hat of a more genteel set.

But Thomas rarely wore one. It was as though he liked the statement the peaked hat made: "I'm just a regular fellow. Nothing to see here."

"We're going to the Gresham Hotel. A friend of mine was married today. Since we're in town, I thought we should attend the celebration. We missed the ceremony at St. Patrick's, but the party is just beginning."

"Is this friend the someone you'd like me to meet?"

"No," he said, and his hand tightened around mine. "Dermot Murphy is a helluva guy. But he'll only have eyes for Sinead tonight. You might remember Sinead."

I was certain I would not remember Sinead, and I swallowed back my nerves. We turned off Parnell and onto O'Connell, and the Gresham loomed, overlooking the street. It was the matriarch of the city center, well lit and lively, her occupants spilling out into the misty evening only to turn back again for another go.

We were greeted like royalty, our coats checked with swift efficiency, and we were directed up a set of wide stairs to a private ballroom. Lights twinkled and music trickled, luring us into the wide expanse where a band played and people danced on a floor rimmed by small tables filled with men and women in their wedding finery. A huge bar ringed by stools and hanging lamps sat just beyond the dance floor, and Thomas paused to survey the room, his hand at the small of my back.

"Tommy!" someone yelled, and a few voices joined in, creating a chorus from the back left corner.

He looked down at me and grimaced a little, and I ducked my head, trying not to smile. He removed his hand from my arm and squared his shoulder.

"He always calls me Tommy. And then everyone else thinks they can too. Do I look like a Tommy to you?"

A flashbulb went off suddenly, blinding us, and Thomas and I winced, stepping back. We'd paused in just the right place, and the photographer, set up in front of the entrance to capture guests as they arrived, stuck his head out from behind a camera that looked more like a one-eyed accordion and gave us a smile.

"You'll like how that one turns out, folks. It's not often I get such a candid shot."

Seconds later, we were swarmed by several men clapping Thomas on the back and greeting him with cries of welcome at his surprise appearance.

"I thought you'd gone back home, Doc!" was the gleeful refrain, until the men parted and someone else joined the fray.

"Introduce us to the lady, Tommy," the man said, and I looked up into the speculative gaze of Michael Collins. His hands were shoved in his pockets; his weight was on his heels, his head tipped to the side. He was young. I knew his story, the history, the basic details of his life and his death. But his youth shook me all the same.

I stuck out my hand, doing my best not to tremble and squeal like a fan at a rock concert, but the significance of the moment, the weight of the past, and the measure of the man made my heart quake and my eyes shimmer.

"I'm Anne Gallagher. It's an honor to meet you, Mr. Collins."

"Feckin' Anne Gallagher," he said, each syllable deliberate. Then he whistled long and slow.

"Mick," Thomas rebuked.

Michael Collins looked slightly chagrined and bobbed his head in apology at his language, but he continued to study me, holding my hand in his.

"What do you think of our Tommy, Anne Gallagher?"

I started to answer, but he squeezed my hand and shook his head slightly, warning me, "If you lie to me, I'll know."

"Mick," Thomas cautioned again.

"Tommy. Quiet," he murmured, his gaze locked on mine. "Do ya love him?"

I breathed deeply, unable to look away from the dark eyes of a man who wouldn't live to make his own wedding vows, who wouldn't see his thirty-second birthday, who wouldn't ever know how truly remarkable he was.

"He's easy to love," I answered softly, each word like an anchor mooring me to a time and place that weren't my own.

Collins whooped and swung me up in his arms, as if I'd just made him a very happy man. "Did you hear that, Tommy? She loves you. If she'd said no, I was going to wrestle you for her. Let's get a picture!" he demanded, pointing at the smiling photographer. "We need to mark this occasion. Tommy has a lass."

I couldn't look at Thomas, couldn't breathe, but Michael Collins was in charge, and he drew us around him and slung an arm over my shoulder, smirking at the camera as though he'd just bested the Brits. I was flooded with the feeling that I'd seen and done this all before. The bulb flashed and realization dawned. I remembered the picture I'd seen of Anne standing in a group beside Michael Collins and the picture of Thomas and Anne, the suggestion of intimacy in the line of their bodies and the angle of their gazes. Those weren't photos of my great-grandmother at all.

They were pictures of me.

"Was Thomas in love with Anne?" I'd asked my grandfather.

"Yes and no," Eoin had answered.

"Oh wow. There's a story there," I'd crowed.

"Yes. There is," he'd whispered. "A wonderful story."

And now I understood.

26 August 1921

I'll never forget this day. Anne has gone to bed, and still I sit, watching the fire as though it holds a different, better set of answers. Anne told me everything. And yet . . . I know nothing.

I called Garvagh Glebe before we left for the Gresham Hotel, knowing the O'Tooles would be hovering, waiting for word on Robbie's condition. There are two telephones in all of Dromahair, and Garvagh Glebe boasts one. I'd rationalized the expense of phone lines; a doctor needed to be easily accessible. But no one else had telephones in rural Ireland. They didn't call me; they fetched me. The only calls I ever received were from Dublin.

Maggie was waiting breathlessly on the end of the line as the operator patched me through, and I could hear her tears when I told her "my patient" had come through surgery well and that the swelling had receded substantially. She was crying the Rosary as she handed the telephone to Daniel, who thanked me profusely, though he knew better than to specify what for, and then, oddly, he gave me an update on the foal that wasn't due for another two weeks.

"We went in to check on her this afternoon, Doc . . . and the foal was gone," Daniel said, his voice slow and heavy with meaning.

It took me a moment to understand.

"Someone's been in the barn, Doc. It's gone. Nobody knows where. Liam's been by to see Brigid, and I had to tell him. He's upset. He had plans for the foal, as you know. Now, with her being gone . . . we need to figure out who took her. Tell Miss Anne, will you, Doc? Liam is certain she already knows. But I don't imagine how."

I was silent, reeling. The guns were gone, and Liam was blaming Anne. Daniel was quiet for a moment too, letting me process his metaphor. I told him we would inquire further when I returned from Dublin. He agreed, and we signed off.

I almost told Anne we weren't going to the Gresham after all, but when I stepped into her room and saw her, lithe and lovely, her curling mass of hair loosely bound, her eyes warm, and her smile eager, I changed my mind once more.

She held my hand, and I walked, half numb and wholly unprepared for the risk I was taking. All I knew was I wanted Mick to meet her. To reassure me. To absolve me. It was madness, bringing Anne to see him. I don't know what compelled me to do it or what compelled him to draw a confession from her red lips. It was his way; I knew that well enough by now. He was completely unconventional, but he never failed to surprise me.

He asked her what she thought of me, asked her if she loved me, and with only a small hesitation, the kind that comes from admitting personal things publicly, she said she did. The world spun, my heart leapt, and I wanted to *pull her back out into the night where I could keep Mick safe and kiss her silly.*

Her colour was high, her eyes were bright, and she couldn't meet my gaze. She seemed as dazed and dazzled as I, though Mick has that effect on people. He insisted we pose for a picture, then coaxed her onto the dance floor, despite her protestations. "I can't dance, Mr. Collins!" I heard her say, though she'd always been a frenetic dancer, dragging Declan to his feet whenever there was music.

Mick made up for whatever skill she thought she lacked by tucking her close and doing a simple two-step to the ragtime rhythm that mostly kept them in the same spot. And he talked to her, eyes boring down into hers like he wanted to know all her secrets. I understood the desire. I watched her shake her head and answer him with great seriousness. It was all I could do not to cut in, to save him, to save her, to save myself. It was all madness.

I was pulled towards the corner table, Joe O'Reilly at my side. Tom Cullen put a drink in my hand while the newly released Sean MacEoin, who I had seen and administered to in Mountjoy jail in June, pushed me into a chair. They were ebullient, the calm of the truce and the cessation in hiding and fighting making them loud and loose in their conversation and celebration. I could only marvel. How long had it been since they could sit at the wedding of a friend and not have guards stationed at the doors, watching for patrols, for raids, for arrests?

Mick brought Anne back to the corner table as well, and she fell into a seat beside me and took a long pull from my drink, wincing as she set it down.

"Dance with the woman, Tommy. I've monopolized her long enough," Mick ordered. His eyes were shadowed,

and his mood was not nearly as jubilant as his men. They had been relieved, temporarily, of their burdens. He had not, and his nomination to attend the Treaty talks, to play the dancing puppet, was not sitting well on him.

I stood and extended my hand to Anne. She didn't refuse me but begged patience with her abilities, just like she'd done with Mick.

She was light in my arms, her curls brushing my cheeks, her breath tickling my neck. I am an accomplished dancer. Not from any desire to be so. It is actually the opposite. I feel no pressure to impress, no desire to be noticed, and I approached dancing with the same attitude I have approached most everything else in my life. Dancing was just a skill to be learned and, in the case of traditional Irish dance, an act of defiance.

Anne followed along, stepping as little as possible, swaying against me, her pulse thrumming, her lip caught between her teeth in concentration. I reached up and set it free with the pad of my thumb, and her eyes found mine, looking at me in that very un-Anne-like way. We didn't speak of her confession, of the growing feelings between us. I didn't mention the missing guns at Garvagh Glebe.

Then something cracked, and someone screamed, and I pushed Anne behind me. Laughter ensued immediately. It wasn't a gun; it was champagne. It bubbled and overflowed from a newly uncorked bottle, and Dermot Murphy raised his glass and made a traditional toast about death in Ireland. Death in Ireland meant a life in Ireland, not a life as an immigrant somewhere else.

Glasses were raised in agreement, but Anne had grown still.

"What day is it?" she asked, a note of panic in her voice.

I answered that it was Friday, the twenty-sixth of August.

She began to mumble, as if trying to remember something important. "Friday the twenty-sixth, 1921. August 26, 1921. The Gresham Hotel. Something happens at the Gresham Hotel. A wedding party. Who is getting married? Their names, again?"

"Dermot Murphy and Sinead McGowan," I answered.

"Murphy and McGowan, wedding party. Gresham Hotel." She gasped. "You need to get Michael Collins out of here, Thomas. Right now."

"Anne—"

"Right now!" she demanded. "And then we have to figure out how to get everyone else out as well."

"Why?"

"Tell him it's Thorpe. I think that was the name. A fire is set, and the door is barricaded so no one can get out."

I didn't ask her how she knew. I simply turned, grabbing her hand, and strode to the corner where Mick was drinking and laughing with hooded eyes.

I leaned over and spoke in his ear, Anne hovering behind me. I told him there was a threat of arson from a man named Thorpe—I had no idea who he was—and the room needed to be cleared immediately.

Michael turned his head and met my gaze with an expression so weary I felt my own bones quake. Then he snapped to attention, and the weariness fell away.

"I need a man at every exit, boys. Right now. We might have some fire starters on the premises." The

table cleared at once; glasses were emptied and slammed down again, and hair was smoothed back as if vigilance demanded a certain appearance. The men scattered, moving towards the doors, but Mick stayed at my side, waiting for a verdict. A moment later, a shout rose up. Gearóid O'Sullivan was kicking at the main entrance door, which appeared to be barricaded. Just like Anne had said.

Mick met my gaze, and then his gaze touched on Anne briefly, his brow furrowed, his eyes troubled.

"This one's open," Tom Cullen cried from behind the bar.

The bartender stammered, "You can't go out that way!"

Cullen just shouted over him. "Everybody needs to file out! Let's go. Girls first, gents! We're okay. Just a little precaution to make sure the Gresham isn't on fire . . . again." The Gresham, sitting in Dublin's city centre, has seen more than its fair share of havoc in its hundred years. Mick was already striding towards the exit, hat in his hand; Joe was at his side, loping to keep up.

There was some nervous chuckling, but the wedding party made haste, filing out the door into the damp darkness of the August night. Even the bartender decided staying was foolish. I was the last to go, pushing Anne and O'Sullivan—who had abandoned his efforts to break down the other door—out before I scanned the room once more, making sure we'd left no one behind. Smoke had begun to billow through the vents.

T. S.

15

ERE TIME TRANSFIGURED ME

Although I shelter from the rain
Under a broken tree,
My chair was nearest to the fire
In every company
That talked of love or politics,
Ere Time transfigured me.

—*W. B. Yeats*

It was the groom's toast—death in Ireland—that had triggered my memory. I'd read about an attack on a wedding party when I'd researched the Gresham Hotel. I'd planned to stay there when I returned to Dublin after my pilgrimage to Dromahair. I'd chosen the Gresham for its history and for its central location to the Rising of 1916 and the tumultuous years that followed. I'd seen pictures of Michael Collins standing at her entrance, meeting contacts in her restaurant, and drinking in her pub. I'd read about Moya Llewelyn-Davies, one of the women who'd been in love with him, staying at the Gresham after she'd been released from jail.

The Gresham plot—yet another attempt on Michael Collins's life—was just one of many. But the fact that it had come after the truce and that so many people had been targeted made it notable. The British government had vehemently denied any knowledge or responsibility in the conspiracy. Some believed it was an attempt to undermine the peace process and was ordered by people who profited from conflict. A British double agent known only by the name Thorpe was also suspected. Michael Collins fingered him in his personal accounts. But no one ever knew for sure.

I didn't know if I'd saved lives or simply incriminated myself. I didn't know if I'd changed history or just modified it by sounding the alarm. For all I knew, I'd been part of the history all along. Regardless, I'd planted myself firmly in the middle of it. And, however innocent, my foreknowledge of the fire was still impossible to explain.

As I ran beside Thomas, my pulse pounding, lifting my skirts so I could keep up, I knew I'd only made things worse for myself. Michael Collins had leaned down and spoken in my ear as we'd stood waiting for his men to check the doors.

"I don't want to kill you, Anne Gallagher. But I will. You know that, don't you?" he'd said.

I had nodded. Oddly, I wasn't frightened. I'd simply turned my head and met his gaze.

"I am not a good man," he'd said grimly. "I've done terrible things I will have to answer for. But I've always done them for good reason."

"I am no threat to you or to Ireland, Mr. Collins. I give you my word."

He'd replied, "Only time will tell, Mrs. Gallagher. Only time will tell."

Michael Collins was right. Only time *would* tell. Only time *could* tell. And time would not defend me.

The members of the wedding party moved up the alley toward O'Connell, joining the guests now streaming from the front entrance. The fog and smoke were mating and recreating, distorting the shapes and the shrieks of the guilty and the guileless. And no one knew which was which. Michael Collins and his entourage disappeared into the night, piling into cars that came out of nowhere and screeched away.

Clanging fire trucks and emergency personnel approached from two directions, and Thomas began moving among the people, creating triage across the street from the hotel, checking guests for smoke inhalation, sending those who seemed the worse for wear away in the St. John ambulances that had arrived on the scene, and releasing others to secure new lodgings. As I tried to stay out of the way and keep Thomas in my sights, the rain began to fall, aiding the efforts of the firemen. Curious onlookers and the milling crowd scurried for cover, effectively clearing the area. Our coats were still inside the Gresham and were as good as gone, at least for the time being. My dress was soaked, my hair streaming. Thomas took off his suit coat and slung it over my shoulders, and he found me waiting for him, huddled beneath it, as the last ambulance pulled away from the hotel.

"There's nothing more I can do here. Let's go," he said. His shirt was plastered to his skin, and he swept his hair back from his face, running his hands over his soot-streaked cheeks, removing the water only to have it replaced again.

The water streamed from the eaves, running from the wrath of sodden skies, finding shelter in the cracks and crevices, and covering the streets and buildings in a wet blanket.

He held my hand as we rushed through the streets, steadying me on the red heels that slowed us down and made me slip, but I felt his tension against my palm, radiating from his tight fingers and sculpting the line of his jaw.

We had entered his neighborhood when Thomas stopped suddenly, cursing. He pulled me into an alcove, out of the rain, and began searching his pockets.

"My house key is in my coat," he said.

I reached into the pocket of his suit jacket I was wearing before realizing he was talking about the overcoat still hanging in the Gresham Hotel's cloakroom.

"Let's go back. Maybe someone can get us into the cloakroom or retrieve it for us," I offered, bouncing in place to keep warm. The alcove shielded us from the worst of the downpour but not from the cold, and we couldn't stay there all night.

Thomas shook his head slowly, his lips pursed, his face pensive.

"One of the firemen I treated said the fire was started in the coatroom, Anne. All the coats were doused in petrol. The door was locked and the vents opened. It's right next to the ballroom where the wedding party was gathered. Or didn't you know that part of the plot?" He looked down at me and then away, water dripping from the lock of hair on his forehead, his expression as dark as the shadows where we stood. His voice was quiet, perfectly level but infused with bleak expectation.

I had no way to defend myself. Nothing I could say would make things any better, so I said nothing. We stood silently under the overhang, staring out at the storm. I stepped closer to him so our bodies were pressed together along my right side. I was cold. Miserable. And I knew his misery exceeded my own. He stiffened, and my eyes shot to his face, catching on the clean line of his jaw. It was clenched, a muscle ticking like a clock, warning me I had seconds to start talking.

I didn't. I turned my head with a sigh and peered out into the deluge, wondering if the mist could take me home again, like the mist on the lake had brought me here.

"I talked to Daniel earlier this evening," Thomas continued, his tone brittle. "He said the guns are gone, Anne. Liam thinks you might know something about that too. In fact, he's convinced you aren't Anne Gallagher at all."

"Why?" I gasped, caught completely off guard. "Why would I know anything about Liam's guns?" I latched on to the accusation that wasn't true.

"Because you know all kinds of things you have no business knowing," Thomas shot back. "Jaysus, woman! I don't know what to think anymore."

"I didn't have anything to do with the guns or their disappearance. I didn't have anything to do with the fire at the Gresham or anything else," I said, trying to maintain my composure. I stepped out of the alcove and began walking again, moving toward his house in the square. We were almost there, and I didn't know what else to do.

"Anne!" Thomas shouted, and I could hear his desperate frustration. His distrust was the hardest thing to bear. I understood it, even sympathized with it. But it was corrosive and exhausting, and I was dangerously close to falling apart. I didn't want to hurt Thomas. I didn't want to lie to him. And I didn't know how to tell him the truth. In that moment, I wanted nothing more than to escape, to close the book on this impossible tale.

"I want to go home."

"Wait until the rain eases," Thomas said. "I'll figure something out."

I hadn't realized I'd spoken out loud, but I didn't slow. "I can't live like this." Again, I spoke without meaning to.

"Like what?" Thomas scoffed, incredulous, matching his steps to mine.

"Like this," I mourned, letting the rain disguise the tears that had begun to streak down my cheeks. "Pretending to be someone that I'm not. Being punished for things I can't explain and blamed for things I know nothing about."

Thomas grabbed my arm, but I pulled free, stumbling and warding him off. I didn't want him to touch me. I didn't want to love him. I didn't want to need him. I wanted to go home.

"I am not the Anne Gallagher you think I am," I insisted. "I am not her!"

"Who are you, then? Huh? Don't play games, Annie," he said, moving around me, heading me off. "You ask me things you should know.

You never speak of Declan. You never speak of Ireland! Not like we used to. You seem lost half the time, and you're so different, so changed, that I feel like I'm seeing you for the first time. And dammit if I don't like what I see. I like you!" He ran an impatient hand over his face, wiping the rain from his eyes. "And you love Eoin. You love the boy. And every time I'm convinced you really are someone else, I see the way you look at him, the way you watch him, and I feel like a feckin' lunatic for doubting you. But something has happened to you. You aren't the same. And you won't tell me anything."

"I'm sorry, Thomas," I cried. "You're right. I'm not the same Anne. She's gone."

"Stop it. Stop saying that," he begged. He raised his face to the sky, as if begging God for patience. Hands fisted in his hair, he took a few steps toward the long row of homes along the square, putting distance between us. The lights of his house beckoned weakly, taunting us. A shadow moved behind the drapes, and Thomas froze, watching the dark silhouette against the tepid smear of light.

"Someone's already here," Thomas said. "Someone's in the house." He cursed and supplicated the heavens once more. "Why now, Mick?" he said under his breath, but I heard the words. Thomas turned back to me, pulling me into his side, keeping me close in spite of it all. My control broke.

I wrapped my arms around him, burying my face in his chest, clinging to him—and the impossibility of us—before our time ran out. The rain drummed against the pavement, counting off the seconds, and Thomas welcomed me into his body, his lips pressing against my hair, his arms encircling me, even as he groaned my name.

"Anne. Ah, lass. What am I going to do with you?"

"I love you, Thomas. You'll remember that, won't you? When this is over?" I said. "I've never known a better man." I needed him to believe that, if nothing else.

I felt a tremor shake him, but his arms tightened around me, a vise of desperation that spoke of his turmoil. For a moment more, I embraced him; then I let my arms fall as I pulled back. But Thomas didn't release me, not completely.

"It'll be Mick. Inside. He's going to demand answers, Anne," Thomas warned, his voice weary. "What do you want to do?"

"If I answer every one of your questions, will you promise to believe me?" I begged, looking up at him through my tears.

"I don't know," Thomas confessed, and I watched his frustration disintegrate, washed away in the downpour, leaving resignation in its wake. "But I can promise you this. Whatever you tell me, I'll do my best to protect you. And I won't turn you away."

"Liam was the one who shot me on the lough," I blurted. It was the truth I was most afraid of, the truth that pertained to this time and place, and the truth Thomas might be able to explain, even understand.

Thomas froze. Then his hands rose from my arms to cradle my face as if he needed to keep me still while he examined my eyes for veracity. He must have been satisfied with what he saw because he nodded slowly, his mouth grim. He didn't ask why or how or when. He didn't seek clarification at all.

"You'll tell me everything? Mick too?" he asked.

"Yes," I breathed, surrendering. "But it's a long . . . impossible . . . story, and it will take me a while to tell it."

"Then let's get out of this rain." He tucked me against his body, and we moved toward his house, toward the soft light that glimmered in the windows.

"Wait," he commanded and climbed the stairs to the front stoop without me. He knocked on his own door, rapping a rhythm that was clearly preestablished, and the door swung open.

Michael Collins took one look at the two of us and pointed to the stairs.

"We'll talk when you're dry. Joe made a fire. Mrs. Cleary left bread and meat pies in the larder. Joe and I helped ourselves, but there's plenty left. Go. It's been a helluva night."

Mrs. Cleary was Thomas's Dublin housekeeper. Joe O'Reilly, Mick's righthand man, looked on sheepishly. The fact that it was Thomas's home and Michael Collins was giving orders was clearly not lost on him, but I didn't need any further encouragement. I climbed the stairs, my shoes squelching and my teeth chattering, and stumbled into the room Thomas had assigned to me, peeling off his suit coat and my red dress, hoping Mrs. O'Toole could rehabilitate the clothing like she'd saved my bloodstained blue robe. Our clothes were covered in a layer of soot, and they reeked of smoke, just like my hair and skin. I wrapped my robe around me, gathered my things, and took a hot bath. If Michael Collins objected to the time I was taking, too bad. I scrubbed my hair and skin, rinsed it, and scrubbed it all once more. When I finally made my way downstairs, my hair was still wet, but the rest of me was clean and dry. The three men were huddled around the kitchen table, speaking in voices that quieted when they heard my footfalls.

Thomas stood, his face scrubbed free of the grime but not the concern. He wore clean, dry trousers and a white shirt. He hadn't bothered to button on a collar, and his sleeves were rolled up, revealing the wiry strength of his forearms and the tension in his shoulders.

"Have a seat, Anne. Right here." Michael Collins patted the empty place beside him. The kitchen table was perfectly square, with a chair on each side. "Can I call you Anne?" he asked. He stood, shoved his hands into his pockets and sat down again, agitated.

I sat next to him obediently, the sense of an ending all around, like I was caught in a dream I was about to wake from. Joe O'Reilly sat on my right. Collins sat on my left. Thomas sat directly across from me, his blue eyes troubled and oddly tender, his teeth clenched against the realization that he could not save me from what was about to go down.

I wanted to reassure him and tried to smile. He swallowed and shook his head once, as if apologizing for his failure to return my offering.

"Tell me something, Anne," Michael Collins said. "How did you know what was going to happen tonight at the Gresham? Tommy here tried to pretend it wasn't you who tipped him off. But Tommy's a terrible liar. It's the reason I like him."

"Do you know the story of Oisín and Niamh, Mr. Collins?" I asked softly, letting my mouth find comfort in the sound of their names—*usheen* and *neev*. I'd learned the story in Gaelic, speaking the language before I'd learned to write it.

I'd startled Michael Collins. He'd expected an answer, and I'd asked a question instead. An odd one.

"I know it," he said.

I fixed my gaze on Thomas's pale eyes, on the promise he'd made not to turn me away. I'd thought of Oisín and Niamh more than once since I'd fallen through time; the similarities of our stories were not lost on me.

I began to recite the tale the way I'd learned it, in Gaelic, letting the Irish words lull the table into a hushed silence. I told them how Niamh, Princess of Tír na nÓg, the Land of the Young, had found Oisín, son of the great Fionn, on the banks of Loch Leane, not so different from the way Thomas had found me. Collins snorted and O'Reilly shifted, but Thomas was still, holding my gaze as I wove the ancient tale in a language every bit as old.

"Niamh loved Oisín. She asked him to go with her. To trust her. And she promised to do all in her power to make him happy," I said.

"This is an odd way of answering my question, Anne Gallagher," Michael Collins murmured, but there was a softness in his tone, as if my Gaelic had calmed his suspicions. Surely one who spoke the language of the Irish could never work for the Crown. He did not stop me as I continued with the legend.

"Oisín believed Niamh when she described her kingdom, a place that existed separate from his own world, and he went with her there, leaving his land behind. Oisín and Niamh were very happy for several years, but Oisín missed his family and his friends. He missed the green fields and the loch. He begged Niamh to let him return, if only for a visit. Niamh knew what would happen if she let him go back, and her heart broke because she knew Oisín would not understand unless he saw the truth for himself." My throat ached, and I paused, closing my eyes against the blue of Thomas's steady gaze to gather my courage. I needed Thomas to believe me but didn't want to see the moment when he stopped.

"Niamh told Oisín he could go but to stay on Moonshadow, her horse, and to not let his foot touch Irish soil. And she begged him to return to her," I said.

"Poor Oisín. Poor Niamh," Joe O'Reilly whispered, knowing what came next.

"Oisín traveled for several days until he returned to the lands of his father. But everything had changed. His family was gone. His home too. The people had changed. Gone were the castles and the great warriors of the past," I said. "Oisín stepped down from Moonshadow, forgetting, in his shock, what Niamh had begged him to remember. When his foot touched the ground, he became a very old man. Time in Tír na nÓg was very different from time in Éire. Moonshadow ran from him, leaving him behind. Oisín never returned to Niamh or the Land of the Young. Instead, he told his story to whomever would listen, so the people would know their history, so they would know they descended from giants, from warriors."

"I always wondered why he couldn't return, why Niamh never came for him. Was it his age? Maybe the fair princess didn't want an old man," Collins mused, locking his hands behind his head, completely serious.

"Cád atá á rá agat a Aine?" Thomas murmured in Gaelic, and I met his gaze again, my stomach trembling, my palms damp. He wanted to know what I was *really* trying to say.

"Just like Oisín, there are things you won't understand unless you experience them for yourself," I urged.

Joe rubbed his brow wearily. "Can we speak English? My Irish isn't as good as yours, Anne. A story I already know is one thing. Conversation is another. And I want to understand."

"When Michael was a child, his father predicted he would do great things for Ireland. His uncle predicted something very similar. How could either of them possibly know such a thing?" I asked, reverting to English once more.

"An dara sealladh," Michael murmured, his eyes narrowed on my face. "Second sight. Some say there's a touch of it in my family. I think it was just the pride of a father in his young son."

"But time has proven your father right," Thomas said, and Joe nodded, his face filled with devotion.

"I cannot explain what I know. You want me to give explanations that will make no sense. I will sound crazy, and you'll be afraid of me. I told you I was no threat to you or Ireland. And that is the only reassurance I can give you. I cannot explain *how* I know, but I will tell you *what* I know, if it will help. I knew that the doors would be barred and a fire would be started only moments before it happened. When Murphy made his toast . . . I just . . . knew. I also knew the truce would be signed before it was. I knew the date, and I told Thomas, though even he had no knowledge of an agreement."

Thomas nodded slowly. "She did, Mick."

"I know that in October, you will be sent to London to negotiate terms of a treaty with England, Mr. Collins. Mr. de Valera will stay behind. And when you return with a signed agreement, the people of Ireland will overwhelmingly support it. But de Valera and some members of the Dáil—those loyal to him—will not. Before long, Ireland will not be fighting England anymore. We will be fighting each other."

Michael Collins, his eyes full of tears, pressed a fist to his lips. He rose slowly, burying his hands in his hair, his anguish terrible to watch. Then, with violent emotion, he picked up his saucer and teacup and smashed them against the wall. Thomas handed him another, and it shared the same fate. The dish that held a single slice of meat pie followed, raining bits of potato and crust across the kitchen. I could not lift my eyes from his empty chair as he made short work of anything that would shatter. The shaking in my belly had moved to my legs, and beneath the table, my knees bounced uncontrollably. When he sat back down, his emotion was banked, and his eyes were hard.

"What else can you tell me?" he asked.

26 August 1921
(continued)

If I had not seen it, not heard it, I wouldn't have believed it. Anne entered the lion's den and calmed the beast with nothing but a tale delivered in perfect Irish and a well of knowledge that should have condemned her, not saved her.

Ireland has long since abandoned her heathen roots, but my Anne has druid blood. I'm convinced of it. It's in her soft eyes and her purring voice, in the magic she weaves with her words. She's not a countess; she's a witch. But there's no evil in her, no ill intent. Maybe that, in the end, is what won Mick over.

He asked her a dozen questions, and she answered him without hesitation when she could and with calm denial when she claimed she couldn't. I watched her— amazed, stricken, proud. Mick didn't want to know where she'd been or how she'd come to be in the lake— those were my questions. He wanted to know if Ireland would survive, if Lloyd George would uphold his end of the Treaty, if Partition would be defeated, and if the British would actually leave Irish soil, once and for all. It was only when Mick asked if his days were numbered that she hesitated at all.

"Time will not forget you, Mr. Collins, nor will Ireland," she said. "That is all I can tell you." I don't think he believed her, but he didn't press her. And for that, I was grateful.

When Mick and Joe finally left, slipping out the back and into a waiting car, she wilted in relief, laying her head down on the kitchen table and clinging to the edge. Her shoulders shook, but she cried silently. I tried to draw her up, to comfort her, but her legs wobbled, and she swayed. I picked her up instead, carrying her from the kitchen to the rocking chair by the fire, to the place where Mrs. Cleary knitted on nights when I asked her to keep watch for men or materials.

Anne curled into me, letting me hold her. I held my breath, fearful I would startle her, that she would bolt. Or that I would. She tucked her legs beneath her and turned her face until it was resting against my shoulder. Her breath was warm against my shirt and her tears wet, making me long to hold her tighter, to draw her even closer, to be nearer. My rough exhalation stirred her hair—the breath I'd been holding—and I tightened my arms and dug in my heels. Our combined weight deepened the sound of the swaying chair against the wood floor, echoing the beat of my heart in my chest, reminding me I was alive, mind and body, and so was she. My hand mimicked the rhythm of the chair, stroking her back as we rocked to and fro. We didn't speak, but there was a conversation happening between us.

The window closest to the fire rattled suddenly, making her breath catch and her head lift infinitesimally.

"Shh," I soothed. "'Tis just the wind."

"What story is it trying to tell?" she murmured, her voice rough with spent emotion. "The wind knows every story."

"You tell me, Anne," I whispered. "You tell me."

"I had a teacher who told me fiction is the future. Nonfiction is the past. One can be shaped and created. One cannot," she said.

"Sometimes they are the same thing. It all depends on who is telling the story," I said. And suddenly I didn't care anymore. I didn't care where she'd been or what secrets she guarded. I just wanted her to stay.

"My name is Anne Gallagher. I was not born in Ireland, but Ireland has always been inside of me," she began, as though she were simply reciting another poem, telling another tale. Our eyes clung to the fire, her body clung to mine, and I let her words take me away once more. It was the legend of Oisín and Niamh, where time was not flat and linear but layered and interconnected, a circle that retraced its path again and again, generation after generation, sharing the same space if not the same sphere.

"I was born in America in 1970 to Declan Gallagher—named after his paternal grandfather—and Hannah Keefe, a girl from Cork who spent a summer in New York and never went home again. Or maybe she did. Maybe Ireland claimed her when the wind and water took them away," she whispered. "I hardly remember them at all. I was six, just like Eoin is now."

"In 1970?" I asked, but she didn't answer. She just continued, not rushing, the lilt and flow of her voice quieting my questions even as my head rebelled against my heart.

"We've traded places, Eoin and I," she said, inexplicably. "Who is the parent, and who is the child?" For a moment, she was silent, contemplative, and I continued rocking, staying in one place while my thoughts went in all directions.

"My grandfather recently passed away. He was raised in Dromahair, but he left as a young man and never went back. I don't know why . . . but I'm starting to believe he did it for me. That he knew this story, the story we're living now, before I was even born."

"What was your grandfather's name?" I asked, dread coating my mouth.

"Eoin. His name was Eoin Declan Gallagher, and I loved him so much." Her voice broke, and I prayed that her account would turn from parable to confession, that she would abandon the storyteller and just be the woman in my arms. But she pressed on, her agitation growing with every word.

"He made me promise I would bring his ashes back to Ireland, to Lough Gill. So that's what I did. I came to Ireland, to Dromahair, and I rowed out onto the lake. I said my goodbyes, and I spread his ashes in the water. But the fog grew so thick I couldn't make my way back. I couldn't see the shore anymore. Everything was white, like I'd died without knowing I'd passed. A riverboat appeared out of nowhere, and there were three men on board. I called out to them, alerting them and asking for help. The next thing I knew, one was shooting, and I was in the water."

"Anne," I pled. I needed her to stop. I didn't want to hear any more. "Please. Shh," I soothed. I buried my face in her hair, muffling my moan. I could feel her heart *pounding against mine; the softness of her breasts couldn't mask her terror. She believed what she was telling me, every impossible word.*

"Then you came, Thomas. You found me. You called me by my name, and I thought I was saved, that it was all over. But it was just beginning. Now I'm here, it's 1921, and I don't know how to go back home," she cried.

I could only stroke her hair and rock back and forth, desperate to forget everything she'd just said. She didn't take it back or laugh it off, but her tension slowly ebbed the longer we sat, lulled by the movement and lost in our private thoughts.

"I've crossed the lough, and I can't go back, can I?" she murmured, and her meaning was all too clear. Words spoken could not be unheard.

"I stopped believing in fairies long ago, Anne." My voice was heavy, like a death knell in the quiet.

She was still curled in my lap, but she pushed herself up from my chest so she could look me in the eyes, the waving strands of her hair creating a soft riot around her beautiful face. I wanted to sink my hands into that hair and pull her mouth to mine to kiss away the madness and the misery, the doubt and the disillusionment.

"I don't expect you to believe in fairies, Thomas."

"No?" My voice was sharper than I intended, but I had to get away from her before I ignored the howling in my heart and the warning in my veins. I could not kiss her. Not now. Not after all that had been said. I rose and set her gently on her feet. Her eyes were steady as she gazed up at me, their green warming to gold in the firelight.

"No," she answered softly. "But will you try to believe . . . in me?"

I touched her cheek, unable to lie but unwilling to wound. But my silence was answer enough. She stood and walked up the stairs, bidding me a soft good night. And now I sit, staring at the fire, writing it all down in this book. Anne has confessed all . . . and still, I know nothing.

T. S.

16

TOM THE LUNATIC

Sang old Tom the lunatic
That sleeps under the canopy:
What change has put my thoughts astray
And eyes that had so keen a sight:
What has turned to smoking wick
Nature's pure unchanging light.

—W. B. Yeats

I read somewhere that a person will never know who they really are unless they prioritize what they love. I had always loved two things above everything else, and from those two things, I had formed my identity. One identity grew from what my grandfather had taught me. It was wrapped around his love for me, our love for each other, and the life we'd had together. My other identity was formed from my love of storytelling. I became an author, obsessed with earning money, making bestseller lists, and coming up with the next novel. I had lost one identity when I'd lost my grandfather, and now I'd lost the other. I was no longer Anne Gallagher, *New York Times* bestselling author. I was Anne Gallagher, born in Dublin, widowed wife of Declan, mother of Eoin, friend of Thomas. I had assumed several identities that were not my own, and they had begun to chafe and rub, even when I did my best to wear them well.

In the weeks after Dublin, Thomas kept his distance, avoiding me when it was possible, remaining politely aloof when it was not. He treated me like Declan's Anne again, though he knew I was not. I'd told him a truth he could not accept, so he wrapped me tightly in her role, refusing to cast me in another. Sometimes I caught him staring at me like I was dying from an incurable illness, his countenance stricken and sad.

Thomas returned to Dublin and brought a healing Robbie O'Toole back to Garvagh Glebe. He had a jaunty patch over his missing eye, an angry scar on the side of his head, and a mild weakness on his left side. He moved slowly, a young man grown old, his days of smuggling arms and ambushing Tans behind him.

No one spoke of Liam or the missing guns, but the foal was finally born, making honest men of us all. Thankfully, the Auxiliary captain did not return to Garvagh Glebe either, and whatever suspicions and accusations had been leveled against me were quietly shelved. Still, I slept with a knife beneath my pillow and asked Daniel O'Toole to put a lock on my bedroom door. Liam Gallagher might feel safe from me, but I didn't feel safe from him. There would be a point of reckoning, I had no doubt. The worry made me weary, and the wondering stole my sleep.

I thought about the lough relentlessly, pictured myself pushing a boat out onto the waves and never coming back. Each day I walked along the shore, considering. And each day I turned away, unwilling to try. Unwilling to leave Eoin. To leave Thomas. To leave myself, this new Anne, behind. I ached for my grandfather—the man, not the boy. I mourned for my life—the author, not the woman. But the choice was easy to make. Here, I loved. And, in the end, I wanted to love more than I wanted to return.

The years ahead, years that would come and go—years that, for me, had already come and gone—weighed heavily on me as well. I knew what was to come for Ireland. Not every twist and bend or every turn and tumble. But I knew the rocky destinations. The conflicts. The never-ending fighting and turmoil. And I wondered what it was all for. The death and the suffering. There was a time to fight, but there was a time to stop fighting too. Time had not proven especially helpful—not in Ireland's case—in ironing it all out.

Eoin was the light in the continually darkening tunnel that was closing around me. But even that joy was dimmed by the truth. Loving him didn't excuse lying to him. I was an imposter, and all my devotion didn't change reality. My only defense was that I had not set out to harm or deceive. I was a victim of circumstance—improbable, impossible, inescapable—and I could only make the best of it.

Eoin and I had filled several books with expeditions and adventures to far-off places. Thomas had made the connection between my confession in Dublin and Eoin's stories; I had climbed into a boat on Lough Gill and found myself in another world, just like the little boy in Eoin's tales. Thomas had stared at the words and then looked at me, realization flooding his face like a black cloud. He'd made himself scarce after that, adding pictures to the stories after Eoin and I had gone to bed.

When we weren't writing stories, I'd begun to teach Eoin how to tell time and how to read and write. He was left-handed, like me. Or maybe I was left-handed like him. I showed him how to hold his pencil and form his letters in neat little rows so he would be ready when he started school, which came sooner than either of us would have liked. The last Monday in September, Thomas, Eoin, and I walked in silence to the schoolhouse, Eoin dragging his feet, unhappy about our destination.

"Can't you teach me at home, Mother?" Eoin whined softly. "I would like that so much better."

"I need your mother to help me on my rounds, Eoin. And you will be with friends. Your father and I met when we were boys. You might miss a chance at making a lifelong friend if you are tutored at home," Thomas said.

Eoin looked skeptical. Eoin already had a few good friends and probably figured he could see them without attending school. Plus, Thomas hadn't been taking me on his rounds since we returned from Dublin; he didn't want to be alone with me.

Seeing that Eoin was unconvinced, Thomas pointed at a little cottage peeking out of the trees in a small clearing, a cottage I'd seen before but never thought much about. It was clearly abandoned, and the foliage had begun to overwhelm it.

"Do you see that cottage, Eoin?" Thomas asked.

Eoin nodded, but Thomas kept walking, moving us along. There was rain in the air.

"A family once lived in that cottage. A family like us. But then the potato blight came, and the family was hungry. Some of them died. Some of them went to America to find work so they could eat. There are abandoned homes all over Ireland. You must go to school to learn how to make Ireland better for her people, so that families don't die. So our friends don't have to leave."

"Wasn't there *any* food, Doc?" Eoin asked.

"There was food, just no potatoes," Thomas answered, his eyes on the landscape as if he could still see the blight that had ravaged the country seventy years earlier.

"Couldn't they eat somethin' else?" Eoin asked, and I could have kissed him for his curiosity. I really didn't know the answer, and I was expected to. I should know these stories better than I did. The research I'd done had been centered on the Irish Civil War and not the decades that preceded it. I listened intently, turning back to look at the little cottage, which was falling down and forlorn.

"The potatoes wouldn't grow," Thomas explained. "There was a sickness in the crop. People were used to feeding their families all year long with the potatoes they grew in their little gardens. When the potatoes wouldn't grow, they didn't have anything to eat instead. Most families had a pig, but without the potatoes, they couldn't feed their pigs the slops. So the pigs died, or they were eaten before they got too thin. Then the families had nothing.

"Grain still grew in the fields of the English landowners, but that grain was sold and shipped out of Ireland. The families didn't have money to buy the grain or enough land or even the means to grow sufficient grain of their own. There were cattle and sheep, but very few people owned either. The cows and the sheep got fat on the grain, and they too were shipped out of the country. The beef and mutton and wool were sold to other nations, while the poorest people—most of the people in Ireland—got hungrier and hungrier and more and more desperate."

"Couldn't the people steal it?" Eoin offered hesitantly. "I would steal food if Nana was hungry."

"That's because you love your grandmother, and you wouldn't want to see her suffer. But stealing wasn't the answer."

"What *was* the answer?" I asked quietly, as if the question was a philosophical one, a challenge and not a true inquiry.

Thomas's eyes were on me as he spoke, as though willing me to remember, to take up the cause that had once burned so brightly in Anne Gallagher.

"For centuries, the Irish have been scattered in the wind—Tasmania, the West Indies, America—bought and sold and bred and enslaved. The population of Ireland was cut in half by the indentured servitude. During the famine, another million people died on this island. Here in Leitrim, my mother's family survived because the landlord took pity on his tenant farmers and suspended the rents through the worst of the blight. My grandmother worked for the landowner—a maid in his house—and she ate in the kitchen once a day and brought home the scraps to her brothers and sisters. Half of her family emigrated. Two million Irish emigrated during the famine. The British government didn't care. England is only a stone's throw away. It's easy enough to send their own labor over when we leave or starve. We were truly—*are* truly—replaceable." Thomas didn't sound bitter. He sounded sad.

"How do we fight them?" Eoin asked, his face flushed by the seriousness of the story, the heartbreak of it all.

"We learn how to read. We think. We learn. We become better and stronger, and we stand together and say, 'No more. You can't treat us this way,'" Thomas said softly.

"That's why I go to school," Eoin said, serious.

"Yes. That's why you go to school," Thomas agreed.

Emotion clogged my throat and threatened to spill out of my eyes, and I fought it back.

"Your dad wanted to teach school, Eoin. Did you know that? He knew how important it was. But he couldn't sit still. Neither could your mother," Thomas added, his eyes finding mine.

I had no response; sitting still had always been easy for me. I could sit and dream, my mind taking me away until I was no longer inside myself but away on a journey. The differences between the other Anne and me were piling up every day.

"I want to be a doctor like you, Thomas." Eoin tugged on Thomas's hand, peering up earnestly, past the brim of his peaked hat.

"You will, Eoin. That is exactly what you will be," I reassured him, finding my voice. "You will be one of the best doctors in the world. And people will love you because you are wise and kind, and you make their lives better."

"Will I make Ireland better?" Eoin asked.

"You make Ireland better for me. Every single day," I said, kneeling down so I could squeeze him before he entered the schoolyard. He threw his little arms around me and hugged me tightly, kissing my cheek before he repeated the action with Thomas. Then we watched as he ran to the cluster of boys in the yard, tossing his hat and his little satchel aside and forgetting us almost immediately.

"Why do you tell him things that might not come to pass?" Thomas asked.

"He will be a doctor. And he will be wise and kind. He grows up to be a wonderful man," I said softly, my emotion rising again.

"Ah, Countess," Thomas sighed, and my heart leapt at the endearment. He turned and started back down the road, away from the school, and with one last look at the little school and Eoin's bright hair, I followed him.

"It's not hard to believe he will be such a man. He is Declan's son, after all," Thomas remarked as we walked.

"He's more your son than Declan's. He may have Declan's blood, but he has your heart and your soul."

"Don't say that," Thomas protested, as if the notion was a betrayal.

"It's the truth. Eoin is so much like you, Thomas. His mannerisms, his goodness, the way he approaches a problem. He is yours."

Thomas shook his head again, resisting, his loyalty demanding that he take no credit. "Have you forgotten what Declan was like, Anne? He was light personified. Just like Eoin."

"I can't forget what I never knew, Thomas," I reminded him softly. I felt him flinch, and I swallowed back the frustration in my chest. For several minutes we strode in silence, his hands shoved in his pockets, his eyes on the ground. I kept my arms folded, my gaze forward, but I was aware of every step he took and every word he wanted to say. When he finally spoke, it was as if a dam burst.

"You say you can't forget what you never knew. But you *are* Irish, Anne. You have Anne Gallagher's laugh. You have her courage. You have her dark curly hair and her green eyes. You speak the language of Ireland and know the legends and stories of her people. So you can tell me you are someone else, but I *know* who you are."

I could see the lake through the trees. The skies had grown dark and heavy with rain, chasing the clouds until they cowered on the water, caught between the waves and the wind. My eyes stinging and my chest tight, I turned from him and started down the path toward the lough. The grass whispered his words, *"I know who you are."*

"Anne, wait."

I whirled on him. "I look just like her, I know! I've seen the pictures. We are almost identical. Her clothes fit me, and her shoes too. But we are different people, Thomas. Surely you see that."

He began to shake his head, to deny, deny, deny.

"Look at me! I know it's hard to believe. I don't believe it half the time. I keep trying to wake up. But I'm afraid to wake up too because when I do, you'll be gone. Eoin will be gone. And I will be alone again."

"Why are you doing this?" he groaned, closing his eyes.

"Why won't you look at me?" I begged. "Why won't you see me?"

Thomas raised his head, studying me. We stood in the grass on the side of the road, our eyes clinging, our wills clashing. Then he sighed heavily and ran his hands through his hair, turning once and coming back to me, closer than before, as though he wanted to kiss me and shake me and make me give in.

I felt the same way.

"Your eyes are different than I remember—a different green. The green of the sea instead of the green of the grass. And your teeth are straighter," he whispered.

My great-grandmother hadn't had the luxury of expensive braces. Thomas's gaze slid to my mouth, and he swallowed. He touched my top lip and moved his hand immediately. When he spoke again, his voice was softer, begrudging, like he was admitting something painful.

"Declan's Anne had a gap between her front teeth. I noticed when I watched you brush your teeth that the gap was missing. You used to whistle through that gap. You claimed it was your only musical talent."

I laughed, releasing some of the infuriating feelings swelling in my chest. "I definitely can't whistle through my teeth." I shrugged as if it didn't really matter. But it mattered so much I could hardly draw breath.

"You have the same laugh. Eoin's laugh," Thomas continued. "But you have Declan's steadiness too. It's uncanny, really. It's as if they've both come back . . . in you."

"They have, Thomas. Don't you understand?"

His face shuddered with emotion, and he shook his head again, like it was all too much, too hard to believe, and he couldn't grasp it. But he kept on, his voice low, almost talking to himself. "You look enough like the old Anne"—he winced like he couldn't believe he was actually differentiating between us—"that no one would ever doubt you are her. But she was . . . much . . . sharper." He latched upon the word as if he couldn't think of a better one, but I flinched, and I felt my face grow hot.

"I'm plenty intelligent."

"Are ya, now?" His lips actually twitched, humor chasing the strain from his face.

Outrage bubbled in my throat. Was he laughing at me?

"I'm not talking about your intelligence, Anne. The old Anne was all sharp edges. She didn't have your tranquility. She was . . . intense. Forceful. Passionate and, frankly, tiresome. Maybe it was because she felt she had to be. But your softness is beautiful. Soft eyes. Soft curls. A soft voice. A warm, soft smile. Don't be ashamed of it. There's very little softness left in Ireland anymore. It's one of the reasons Eoin loves you so much."

My anger deflated, and my breast swelled with a different feeling entirely.

"You're good, you know," he mused. "Your accent. You sound like one of us. You sound like the same Anne. But sometimes you slip. You forget . . . and then you sound like the girl you claim to be."

"The girl I claim to be," I muttered. I had hoped, just for a moment, that we'd moved past disbelief. But maybe not. "Whether you believe it or not doesn't make it less true, Thomas. I need you to pretend that I am exactly who I say I am. Can you do that? Because regardless of whether you believe me or not, regardless of whether you think I'm lying or deranged or sick, I know things that haven't happened yet, and I don't know half of the things you think I should. I am not Anne Finnegan Gallagher. And you know it. Deep down, you do. I don't know the names of your neighbors or the shopkeepers in town. Or how to style my hair or how to wear these infernal stockings or cook or sew or Riverdance, for God's sake." I yanked at the corset strap beneath my skirt and it snapped against my leg.

Thomas was silent for several long breaths, considering, his eyes on mine. Then his lips quirked all over again, and he began to laugh, his hand hovering near his mouth like he wanted to stop but couldn't. "What the hell is Riverdance?" he wheezed.

"Irish dancing. You know." Keeping my arms straight to my sides, I began kicking up my heels and shuffling in a very poor imitation of *The Lord of the Dance*.

"Riverdance, eh?" he chortled.

He began to kick up his heels too, stepping and tapping, his hands on his hips, laughing as I tried to copy him. But I couldn't copy him. He was wonderful, exuberant, dancing down the lane toward the house as though he heard fiddles in his head. Gone was the morose doctor, the doubting Thomas, and as the thunder cracked and the rain started to fall around us, we were transported back to Dublin, to the rain and the rocking chair, and the intimacy I'd shattered with impossible truths.

We didn't go back to the house. Brigid would be there and so would at least four O'Tooles. Thomas pulled me into the barn, to the scent of clean hay and the chuff and whinny of the mare and her new baby. He bolted the door behind us, backed me up against the wall, and tucked his mouth close to my ear.

"If you're crazy, then so am I. I'll be Tom the Lunatic, and you can be Crazy Jane," he said. I smiled at his Yeats references even as my pulse pounded, and my fingers curled in his shirt.

"The truth is, I *feel* crazy. For the last month I've been slowly going insane," he panted. His breath stirred my hair and tickled the whorl of my ear. "I don't know the right or wrong of it. I can't see beyond tomorrow or next week. Part of me is still convinced that you're Declan's Anne, and it seems all sorts of wrong to feel the way I do."

"I'm not Declan's Anne," I said, urgently, but he continued, the words spilling from his lips, lips so close that I turned my face so they could trail across my cheek.

"I can't fathom where you'll go or where you've been. But I'm afraid for you and terrified for myself and for Eoin. So if you tell me to stop, Anne, I will. I'll back away, and I'll do my best to be what you need. And when . . . if . . . you go, I'll do my damnedest to explain it all to Eoin."

I pressed my mouth to the veiny ridge of his throat and pulled the smooth skin between my lips, wanting to mark him, to absorb the pulse that throbbed below his ear. His heart pounded beneath my hands where they pressed against his chest, and something within me crystallized, as though in that moment a choice was made, and I stepped into a past that would be my future.

Then his mouth was on mine, his hands gripping my face with a zeal that caused my head to thump against the wall and my toes to curl and flex, drawing me up onto the balls of my feet so I could more firmly align my body with his. For long moments, it was the clash and slide of mouths learning to dance again, of tongues teasing hidden corners and frenzy giving way to quiet fervor. His lips left mine to nuzzle the base of my throat; he slid his cheek along the neckline of my blouse before he dropped to his knees, his hands gripping my hips the way he'd held my face moments before, demanding my attention. He knelt there, his face to the most intimate part of me, pressing kisses over my clothes, creating a wet heat that coiled and crooned and called out to him.

I made a sound that would echo in my head long after the moment had passed, a keening that begged for permanence or completion, and he pulled me to the ground, his hands climbing my hips, wrapping around my ribcage until I was prone beneath him. He gathered my skirts in his hands as I clenched my fists in the rumpled waves of his hair and brought his tongue to mine, the heat spreading from my belly to the press of our mouths and the mingling of our breath.

Then he was moving against me, rocking into me like the waves licking at the shores of Lough Gill, persistent and smooth, rolling and retreating and coming again until I could only feel the liquid lapping and the lengthening tide. My mouth forgot how to kiss, my heart forgot when to beat, my lungs forgot why they needed breath. Thomas forgot nothing, lifting me up and into him, breathing life into my kiss, coaxing my heart to pound with his, reminding my lips to form his name. He stroked my hair, and his body stilled as the wave receded and left me breathless, all the forgotten things remembered.

1 October 1921

I've often wondered whether the Irish would be who we are if the English would have simply been more humane. If they would have been reasonable. If they would have allowed us to prosper. We were stripped of every right and schooled only in derision. They treated us like animals, and yet we didn't yield. Since the days of Cromwell, we have been under England's boot, and still we are Irish. Our language was forbidden, and yet we speak it. Our religion was stamped out at every turn, yet we still practise it. When the rest of the world experienced a reformation of sorts, abandoning Catholicism for a new school of thought and science, we dug in our heels. Why? Because that would mean the English won. We are Catholic because they told us we couldn't be. What you try to take away from a man, he will want all the more. What you tell him he can't have, he'll set his heart on. The only rebellion we have is our identity.

Anne's identity is its own kind of rebellion, and she refuses to relinquish it. For a month I found myself in constant argument with my heart, with my head—with her—although I hardly said a word. I silently cajoled, begged, pleaded, and persuaded, and she stood firm, insistent in her absurdity.

I told my heart I could not have her, and the Irish dissident in my blood rose up and said she was mine. The moment I surrendered, embracing the impossible, fate tried once more to take her away. Or maybe destiny simply pulled the veil from my eyes.

Anne was playing with Eoin by the lake, running in and out of the lazy surf, her skirts hiked up in a way that would have shocked Brigid had Brigid called them in to supper herself. I drew up, wanting only to look at her for a moment, to enjoy the flash of her pale legs against the grey-green backdrop of the lough. She made my heart ache in the best way, and I watched her dance with Eoin as they laughed in the fading light, her curls tumbling and her coltish limbs kicking up water. Then Eoin, his arms wrapped around the red ball he'd received from the O'Tooles on his birthday, tripped and fell, scraping his knees on the pebbled sand and losing his ball. Anne scooped him up as I started down the embankment, my reverie broken by his tears. But Eoin was less worried about his scrapes and more worried about the ball that was floating away. He squalled, pointing, and immediately Anne set him down and raced to retrieve it before it was beyond rescue.

She ran into the lough, knees high, holding her skirts from the inevitable. The ball bobbed out of reach. Anne moved out a little farther, straining for it, and the ball lured her deeper. I began to run, filled with an irrational terror, shouting for her to let the ball go. She surged forward, releasing her skirts and immersing herself from the waist down, wading towards the bobbing red sphere.

I was too far away. I yelled at her to come back as I raced across the shore, and for a moment her image wavered, a mirage on the lough. It was like looking through glass, the white of her dress becoming a tendril of mist; the darkness of her hair becoming evening shadows.

Eoin started to scream.

The sound echoed in my head as I splashed towards her fading form, shouting for her to turn back, to stay. The red ball continued to slink away like the sun on the horizon, and I threw myself across the water, to the place where she had been, reaching for the pale suggestion of Anne that still remained. My arms came away empty. I bellowed her name and lunged again, insistent, and my fingers passed through a whisper of cloth. I closed my fist around the folds, drawing them to me like salvation, end over end, until my hands were filled with Anne's dress.

I couldn't see the shore or tell the water from the sky. I was caught between now and then, my feet on shifting sand, and I was enveloped totally in white. I could feel her, the line of her back and the length of her legs, but I could not see her. I wrapped my arms around the shape of her, refusing to relinquish my claim, and began to walk towards Eoin's cries—a siren in the fog—drawing her back with me. Then I heard her say my name, a murmur in the mist, and as the white began to dissipate, the shore began to show herself, and Anne became whole in my arms. I held her body high against my chest, keeping her from the grasping water and the hands of time. When we fell to the pebbled sand, arms locked around each other, Eoin tumbled into the cradle of our bodies, clinging to Anne as she clung to me.

"Where did you go, Mother?" he cried. "You left me! Doc left me too!"

"Shh, Eoin," Anne soothed. "We're all right. We're here." But she did not deny what the boy had witnessed.

We lay in a panting pile—limbs and clothes and reassurances—until our hearts began to quiet and a sense of reality returned. Eoin sat up, his fear already forgotten, and pointed happily at the innocent red ball that had found its way back to shore.

He untangled himself, freeing us from his clinging arms and unanswered questions. Then he was off, scooping up his ball and heading towards the embankment. Brigid had grown tired of waiting for supper and was calling to us from the trees that separated the house from the shore. But she would have to wait a bit longer.

"You were there, walking into the water," I whispered. "And then you grew faint . . . like a reflection in thick glass, and I knew you were going to disappear. You were going to leave, and I would never see you again." I had come to terms with the impossible. I had joined Anne's rebellion.

Anne lifted her face, pale and solemn, and found my eyes in the twilight. She searched my expression for the baptismal glow of the new believer, and I proceeded to bear testimony.

"You really aren't Anne Finnegan, are you?"

"No, Thomas." Anne shook her head, her gaze locked on mine. "No. I'm not. Anne Finnegan Gallagher was my great-grandmother, and I'm a long, long way from home."

"Jaysus, lass. I'm so sorry." I brushed my mouth over her forehead and down her cheeks, following the rivulets that still clung to her skin and trickled towards her mouth. Then I was kissing her softly, chastely, afraid I would break her, the paper doll in the lough in danger of disintegrating.

T. S.

17

A TERRIBLE BEAUTY IS BORN

He, too, has resigned his part
In the casual comedy;
He, too, has been changed in turn,
Transformed utterly:
A terrible beauty is born.

—*W. B. Yeats*

Like the sun coming out from behind the clouds, everything changed the moment I was believed. The storm receded, the darkness lifted, and I shrugged off the heavy layers I'd been cowering behind, warmed by sudden acceptance.

Thomas had been freed as well, liberated by his own eyes, and he began to shoulder my secrets with me, taking their weight onto his back without complaint. He had a million questions but no doubts. Most nights, when the house was quiet, he would slip into my room, crawl into my bed, and with hushed voices and clasped hands, we would talk of impossible things.

"You said you were born in 1970. What month? What day?"

"October twentieth. I will be thirty-one. Although . . . technically I can't age if I don't even exist yet." I smiled and waggled my eyebrows.

"That's the day after tomorrow, Anne," he scolded. "Were you going to tell me it was your birthday?"

I shrugged. It wasn't something I was going to announce. For all I knew, Brigid had known the "real" Anne's birthday, and I doubted they were the same.

"You're older than me," he said, smirking, as though my advanced age was my punishment for withholding information from him.

"I am?"

"Yes. I turn thirty-one on Christmas Day."

"You were born in 1890. I was born in 1970. You've got me by eighty years, *auld wan*," I teased.

"I have been on the earth for two months less than you have, Countess. You are older."

I laughed and shook my head, and he propped himself up on his elbow, staring down at me.

"What did you do? What did the Anne of 2001 do?" He said "2001" with carefully enunciated awe, like he couldn't believe such a time would ever exist.

"I told stories," I said. "I wrote books."

"Yes. Of course. Of course you did," he breathed, his wonder making me smile. "I should have guessed. What kind of stories did you write?"

"Stories about love. Magic. History."

"And now you are living it."

"The love or the magic?" I whispered.

"The history," he murmured, but his eyes were bright and soft on my face, and he leaned in and kissed me lightly before pulling back. We had discovered that kissing halted conversation, and we were both as hungry for the exchange of words as we were for each other. The words made the kisses mean more when we finally circled back to them.

"What do you miss?" he asked, his breath tickling my mouth, making my stomach shiver and my breasts ache.

"Music. I miss music. I write while listening to classical music. It is the only thing that sounds like stories feel. And it never gets in the way. Writing is about emotion. There is no magic without it."

"How did you write to music? Do you know many musicians?" he asked, confused.

"No," I giggled. "I don't know any. Music is easily recorded and reproduced, and you can play it anytime you want."

"Like a gramophone?"

"Yes. Like a gramophone. But much, much better."

"Which composers?"

"Claude Debussy, Erik Satie, and Maurice Ravel are my favorites."

"Ah, you like the French men," he teased.

"No. I like the piano. The period. Their music was beautiful and deceptively uncomplicated."

"What else?" he asked.

"I miss the clothing. It's much more comfortable. Especially the underwear."

He grew quiet in the darkness, and I wondered if I'd embarrassed him. He surprised me every once in a while. He was passionate but private, ardent but reserved. I wasn't sure if it was just Thomas or if he was simply a man of the times, where a certain dignity and decorum were still de rigueur.

"It's a great deal smaller too," he murmured, clearing his throat.

"You noticed." The sweet ache began again.

"I tried not to. Your clothes and the holes in your ears and a million other little things were easy to rationalize and ignore when your very presence was so unbelievable."

"We believe what makes the most sense. Who I am doesn't make sense," I said.

"Tell me more. What is the world like in eighty years?" he asked.

"The world is full of convenience. Fast food, fast music, fast travel. And because of it, the world is a much smaller place. Information is easily shared. Science and innovation grow by leaps and bounds in the next century. Medical advances are staggering; you would be in heaven, Thomas. Discoveries are made with inoculations and antibiotics that are almost as miraculous as time travel. Almost."

"But people still read," he murmured.

"Yes. Thankfully. They still read books." I laughed. "'There is no frigate like a book to take us lands away,'" I quoted.

"Emily Dickinson," he supplied.

"She's one of my favorites."

"You love Yeats too."

"I love Yeats most of all. Do you think I might meet him sometime?" I was half kidding, half serious. The thought that I might meet William Butler Yeats had only just occurred to me. If I could meet Michael Collins, surely I could meet Yeats, the man whose words had made me want to be a writer.

"It might be arranged," Thomas murmured. The shadows in my room were mellow and moonlit, softening but not obscuring his expression. His brows were furrowed, and I smoothed the small groove between his eyes, encouraging him to release the worrisome thought that perched there.

"Is there someone waiting for you, Anne? Someone in America who loves *you* most of all? A man?" he whispered.

Ah. So that was the fear. I began shaking my head before the words even left my lips.

"No. There is no one. Maybe it was ambition. Maybe self-absorption. But I was never able to give anyone the kind of energy and focus I gave to my work. The person who loved me most in the world no longer exists in 2001. He is here."

"Eoin," Thomas said.

"Yes."

"That might be the hardest thing to imagine . . . my little lad, grown and gone." He sighed. "I don't like to think of it."

"Before he died, he told me that he loved you almost as much as he loved me. He said you were like a father to him, and I never knew. He kept you a secret, Thomas. I knew nothing about you until that final night. He showed me pictures of you and me. I didn't understand. I thought they were pictures of my great-grandmother. He also gave me a book. Your journal. I've read the first few entries. I read about the Rising. About Declan and Anne. About how you tried to find her. I wish now that I'd read everything."

"Maybe it is better that you haven't," he murmured.

"Why?"

"Because you would know things that I haven't even written yet. Some things are better left to discover. Some paths are better left unknown."

"Your journal ended in 1922. I can't remember the exact date. The book was full, all the way to the last page," I confessed in a rush. It was something that had bothered me . . . that date. The end of the journal felt like it was the end of our story.

"Then there will be another book. I've kept a diary since I was a small boy. I have a shelf of them. Fascinating reads, all," he said, his expression wry.

"But you gave that one to Eoin. That was the only one he had," I argued.

"Or maybe that was the only one you needed to read, Anne," he offered.

"But I didn't read it. Not all of it. Not even close. I didn't read any entries past 1918."

"Then maybe it was the one *Eoin* needed to read," he reasoned slowly.

"When I was a girl, I begged him to take me to Ireland. He wouldn't. He told me it wasn't safe," I said. Thinking of my grandfather made my chest ache. It was like that, his loss. Out of the blue, his memory would tiptoe past, reminding me he was gone and I would never be with him again. At least . . . not the way he was, not the way *we* were.

"Can you blame him, Anne? The boy saw you disappear into the lough." We were both quiet, the memory of the white space between places making us move closer and cling unconsciously. I laid my head on his chest, and his arms tightened around me.

"Will I be like Oisín?" I murmured. "Will I lose you, just like he lost Niamh? Will I try to return to my old life and discover that I can't, that three hundred years have passed? Maybe my old life is already gone—my stories, my work. Everything I've accomplished. Maybe I am one of the vanished," I said.

"The vanished?" Thomas asked.

"We all vanish. Time takes us away, eventually."

"Do you *want* to go back, Anne?" Thomas asked. His voice was gentle, but I could feel his tension in the weight of his arms.

"Do you think I get to choose, Thomas? I didn't choose to come. So what if I can't choose whether or not I go?" My voice was timorous and small; I didn't want to wake time or fate with my musings.

"Don't go in the lough," he begged. "If you stay out of the lough . . ." His voice trailed off. "Your life could be here, Anne. If you want it to be, your life could be here." I could hear the strain in his voice, his reluctance to ask me to stay, even though I was sure it was what he wanted.

"One of the best things about being a writer, about being a storyteller, is that it can be done in any time and in any place," I whispered. "I just need a pencil and some paper."

"Ah, lass," he murmured, protesting my capitulation, even as his heart quickened against my cheek. "I love you, Manhattan Annie. I do. I'm afraid that love will only bring us pain, but it doesn't change the truth now, does it?" he said.

"And I love you, Tommy Dromahair," I replied, glib and unwilling to talk of pain or hard truths.

His chest rumbled with laughter. "Tommy Dromahair. That I am. And I'll never be anything else."

"Niamh was a fool, Thomas. She should have told poor Oisín what would happen if he set foot on Irish soil." His hands rose to my hair, and he began to loosen my braid. I tried not to purr as he separated my curls, spreading them over my shoulders.

"Maybe she wanted him to choose," Thomas argued, and I knew it was what he expected me to do, without pressure from him.

"Then maybe she should have let him know what was at stake, so he could," I chided, rubbing my lips across his throat. Thomas's breath hitched, and I repeated the action, enjoying his response.

"We're arguing about a fairy tale, Countess," he whispered, his hands tightening in my hair.

"No, Thomas. We're living in one."

He rolled me beneath him abruptly, and the fairy tale took on new life and new wonder. Thomas kissed me until I began to float up, up, up before drifting down, down, down, sinking into him as he welcomed me home.

"Thomas?" I moaned into his mouth.

"Yes?" he murmured, his body thrumming beneath my hands.

"I want to stay," I panted.

"Anne," he demanded, swallowing my sighs and caressing my cares away.

"Yes?"

"Please don't go."

October 20, 1921, fell on a Thursday, and Thomas brought home presents—a gramophone with a wind-up crank and several classical recordings, a long coat to replace the one I'd lost in Dublin, and a newly published book of Yeats poetry. Hot off the presses. He quietly put the gifts in my room, probably worried that I would be uncomfortable with his generosity, but he instructed Eleanor to make an apple cake with custard sauce and invited the O'Tooles to dinner, making the meal a celebration. Brigid obviously didn't remember when her daughter-in-law's birthday had been, and she didn't balk at all when Thomas insisted on a party.

Eoin was more excited for me than he'd been for his own birthday, and he asked if Thomas was going to hold me upside down and administer my "birthday bumps," knocking my head against the floor for every year of my life and once more for the year to come. Thomas laughed and said birthday bumps were for laddies and lassies, and Brigid scolded Eoin for his impertinence. I whispered to Eoin that he could give me thirty-one kisses instead and a tight squeeze for the year to come, and he climbed up into my lap and dutifully complied.

The O'Tooles didn't bring gifts, thankfully, but they each offered a blessing and took a turn bestowing them on me after the meal was consumed, with their cups raised high.

"May you live a hundred years with an extra year to repent," Daniel O'Toole quipped.

"May angels linger at your door. May your troubles be less, and your blessings be more," Maggie added.

"May your face remain bonny and your arse never grow bony," was a blessing bestowed by Robbie, who hadn't yet regained a sense of what was appropriate. I laughed into the handkerchief Brigid had adorned with the letter A, and a new blessing was hastily offered by another member of the family. My favorite blessing, the one offered by young Maeve, was that I would grow old in Ireland.

My eyes found Thomas's, my arms tightened around Eoin, and I silently prayed for that blessing with all my might, willing the wind and the water to make it so.

"It's your turn, Doc!" Eoin cried. "What is your birthday blessing?"

Thomas shifted uncomfortably, and a bit of color touched his cheeks. "Anne loves the poet William Butler Yeats. So maybe instead of a blessing I will recite one of his poems to entertain our guests. A perfect birthday poem called 'When You Are Old.'"

Everyone chortled, and Eoin looked confused.

"Are you old, Mother?" he asked.

"No, darling boy. I'm ageless," I answered.

Everyone laughed again, but the O'Toole sisters urged Thomas on, pleading for the poem.

Thomas stood, and with his hands in his pockets and his shoulders slightly hunched, he began.

"When you are old and grey and full of sleep . . ." Thomas enunciated "old and grey," and everyone tittered again, but I knew the poem well, knew every word, and my heart had turned to liquid in my chest.

"When you are old and grey and full of sleep," he repeated over the chuckling, "and nodding by the fire, take down this book, and slowly read, and dream of the soft look your eyes had once, and of their shadows deep; how many loved your moments of glad grace, and loved your beauty with love false or true, but one man loved the pilgrim soul in you, and loved the sorrows of your changing face."

The room had grown quiet, and Maggie's lips trembled, the soft sweetness of memory gleaming in her eyes. It was the kind of poem that made old women remember how it felt to be young.

As he spoke, Thomas looked at everyone in turn, but the poem was for me; I was the pilgrim soul with a changing face. He finished, reflecting on how love fled and "paced upon the mountains overhead and hid his face amid a crowd of stars." Everyone clapped and stamped their feet, and Thomas bowed jauntily, accepting the praise. But he met my gaze before taking his seat. When I dragged my eyes away, I found Brigid watching me, her expression speculative, her back stiff.

"When I was growing up, my grandfather—whose name was Eoin too—wouldn't ask me for a blessing on his birthday, he would ask me for a story," I offered hesitantly, eager for a distraction. "It was our special tradition."

Eoin clapped in delight. "I love your stories!" he yelled. Everyone laughed at his exuberance, but it was all I could do not to bury my face in his red mop and weep. Eoin's love for my stories was where it had all begun, and somehow time and fate had given us another birthday together.

"Tell us the story about Donal and the king with the donkey ears," Eoin requested, and with the encouragement of everyone else, that is exactly what I did, keeping the tradition alive.

Thomas couldn't find Liam. He'd quit his job at the docks right after he claimed the guns went missing, and the men he'd worked with didn't seem especially concerned about his whereabouts. Brigid said he'd gone to Cork, to the seaport town of Youghal, but she only had a hastily written letter, just a few lines and a promise to write, with his name signed across the bottom. Brigid speculated that he'd found a better position on busier docks, but his abrupt departure didn't sit well with anyone. I didn't know what Brigid knew of Liam's activities, but I gave her the benefit of the doubt. He was her son, and she loved him. I would not hold his deeds against her. I was just relieved he was gone, but Thomas was worried about what it all meant.

"I can't protect you from a threat I don't understand," he stewed one evening after we'd said good night to Eoin. We went for a walk in the autumn air, crunching through newly fallen leaves and avoiding the shore. Neither of us wanted to visit the lough.

"Do you really think I need to be protected?"

"Liam wasn't the only one on the barge."

"No. There were two others as well."

"What did they look like? Can you describe them?"

"They all wore the same caps, the same style of clothes. They were roughly the same height and age. I think one had a paler complexion—blue eyes and a few days' growth on his jaw. The other was heavier, I think. He had fuller, red cheeks. I couldn't see his hair color . . . and I was focused on Liam, on the gun."

"That's something, I suppose. Though it doesn't bring anyone immediately to mind," he worried.

"Liam was so shocked to see me. Do you think it was just surprise or . . . fear . . . that made him shoot?" I mused.

"I was shocked to see you too, Anne. But shooting you never crossed my mind," Thomas muttered. "You can lay low, you can keep quiet, but they all know you saw them, and you are not safe. Liam thinks you're a spy. He sounded a bit crazed when he told me you weren't Anne. But seeing as he was right, it only makes me more nervous and more desperate to find him. Mick is from Cork. Maybe he'll have someone who can ask around for me. I would feel better if I knew for sure Liam was in Youghal."

"Do you think he took the guns, Thomas?" I asked, voicing a suspicion that I'd had from the beginning. Divining plots was my specialty.

"They were his to take—at least, his responsibility. Why would he lie about them being gone?"

"To cast suspicion on me. He knows what he did, Thomas. He knows he tried to kill me on the lough. Maybe he wants to make me look crazy . . . or maybe he knows if he paints me as a traitor, a spy, no one will listen if I point the finger of blame at him. All he had to do was move the guns when no one was around—just as he'd intended to do—and then tell Daniel they were missing. Daniel wouldn't know any different. You wouldn't know any different. His accusation did exactly what it was designed to do. It made you wary—warier—of me."

"That makes as much sense as anything else." Thomas was silent, considering, and then he sat down wearily on the low rock wall that divided the grass from the trees, resting his head in his hands. When he spoke again, his voice was tentative, as if he feared my response.

"What happened to her, Anne? To Declan's Anne? You know so many things. Did something happen that you're afraid to tell me?"

I sat down beside him and reached for his hand. "I don't know what happened, Thomas. I would tell you if I did. I didn't even know Declan had older brothers and a sister. I suppose I'm like every other Irish man or woman. I have cousins in America too. I thought Eoin and I were the last of the Gallaghers. Your journal . . . the description of the Rising and their part in it, was the most complete picture I've ever had of my great-grandparents. Eoin never spoke of them. For him, they didn't exist beyond a few facts and photographs. I grew up believing Anne died in the Rising, alongside Declan. It was never even a question. In 2001, their grave looks the same as it does now, minus the lichen. Their names are on the stone, side by side. The dates are unchanged."

He was quiet for a long time, contemplating what it all meant.

"The sad truth is that when people leave Ireland, they rarely come back." Thomas sighed. "And we never know what happens to them. Death or emigration. The result is the same. I'm beginning to think only the wind knows what happened to Anne."

"*Aithníonn an gaoithe.* The wind knows everything," I agreed softly. "That's what Eoin told me when I was small. Maybe he learned it from you."

"I learned it from Mick. But he says the wind is a gossipy wench, and if you don't want anyone knowing your secrets, you're better off telling a rock. He says that's why we have so many rocks in Ireland. Rocks soak up every word, every sound, and they never tell a soul. It's a good thing because the Irish love to blather."

I laughed. It reminded me of the story Eoin had requested on my birthday about Donal and the king with the donkey ears. Donal told the king's secret to a tree because he'd been desperate to tell someone, anyone. Sometime later, that tree was cut down and used to make a harp. When the harp was played, the king's secret sang from the strings.

There were several morals to the old tale, but one of them was that secrets never stay hidden. Thomas didn't blather. I doubted Michael Collins blathered either, but the truth had a way of revealing itself, and some truths got people killed.

27 November 1921

I received a letter from Mick today. He's in London, along with Arthur Griffith and a handful of others who were handpicked to take part in the Treaty negotiations. Half of the Irish delegates resent the other half, and each thinks they have the right of it. The divisions in the group were built in by de Valera and are being exploited by Prime Minister Lloyd George, and Mick is acutely aware of it.

The prime minister has assembled a formidable British team to represent England's interests; Winston Churchill is among them, and we Irish know what Churchill thinks of the lot of us. He was against home rule and free trade, but he supported the use of the Auxiliaries to keep us in line. It's easy for a soldier like Churchill, with a history of military might behind him, to expect and tout a certain kind of warfare, and he has no respect for Mick's methods. To him, the Irish question is little more than a peasant uprising; we are a rabid mob with pitchforks and flaming torches. Churchill also knows world opinion is a tool that can be used against the British, and he is incredibly shrewd in blunting its effectiveness. However, Mick says the one thing Churchill understands is love of country, and if he can recognize the same love in the Irish delegation, a narrow bridge might be forged.

Mick confirmed that peace talks had indeed commenced on 11 October, noting the date and asking me to bring Anne to London—or Dublin—when I could. He said, "I will be travelling to Dublin on the weekends as often as I can, trying to keep the leaders in the Dáil updated on the negotiations. I don't want to be accused of keeping information from Dev or any of the others. I will do everything I can to make sure Anne's prediction doesn't come true. But she's been right so far, Tommy. In a way, she's prepared me. There's a small measure of confidence and poise that comes when a man knows he is doomed. I have little expectation of a good outcome, and I think because of it, I am seeing things as they are and not as I wish they were. Bring her, Tommy. Maybe she'll know what I should do next. God knows I'm in over my head. I don't know what is best for my country. Men have died, men that I admired. They died for an idea, for a cause, and I believed in them. I believed in the dream of an independent Ireland. But ideas are easy. Dreams are even easier. They don't require application.

"The British delegates are comfortable in their halls of power and confident in their position; Downing Street and the Houses of Parliament smell of authority and ages-old domination, neither of which the Irish have ever enjoyed. Lloyd George and his team go home at night and meet in their private studies, plotting how to divide and conquer the delegation here and the Irish leadership back home. Meeting after meeting, conference after subconference, we go round and round.

"It's all a game, Tommy. To us, it is life and death; to the Brits, it is simply political maneuvering. They talk of diplomacy when we know diplomacy means dominion. Regardless, I know that my usefulness is expired. The way I've waged war over these last years won't be possible after I return to Ireland. I am a known entity now. I've been undermined, and my methods of hide-and-seek, attack and retreat will no longer suffice. My picture has now been spread across the papers in England and in Ireland. If the talks break down, I will be lucky to make it safely out of London. Either this little ragtag Irish delegation comes to an agreement, or England and Ireland will descend into all-out war. We don't have the men, the means, the weapons, or the will for that. Not among the regular folks. They want freedom. They've sacrificed a great deal for it. But they don't want to be slaughtered. And I can't, in good conscience, be the man that condemns them to that fate."

The letter made me weep—crying for my friend, my country, and for a future that seems incredibly dim. I've gone to Sligo each day to read the Irish Times taped to the window of Lyons department store, but Anne has not pressed me or asked me about the proceedings. It's as if she's simply waiting, calm and resigned. She already knows what happens next, and her knowledge is a burden she has tried to bear silently.

When I told Anne that Mick asked for her, she readily agreed to help where she could, though I had to show her his letter before she believed it. She's still half convinced he wants her dead. She shed tears when she read his melancholy summary, just as I did, and I had no words to console her. She stepped into my arms and comforted me instead.

I love her with an intensity I didn't think myself capable of. Yeats writes about being changed utterly. I am changed utterly. Irrevocably. And though love is indeed a terrible beauty, especially given the circumstances, I can only revel in all its gory gloriousness.

When I'm not worrying over the fate of Ireland, I'm plotting a future that revolves around her. I'm thinking of her white breasts and the high arches in her small feet, of the way her hips flare and how her skin is like silk behind her ears and on the insides of her thighs. I'm thinking of the way she abandons the Irish inflections when we're alone, and how her flattened vowels and softened Ts create an honesty between us that wasn't there before.

Her American accent suits her. Then I begin thinking about how motherhood suits her as well and how her belly would look swollen with our child—someone for Eoin to love and look after. He needs a sibling. I imagine the stories she'll tell the children, the stories she's written and the stories she'll write, and the people all over the world who will read them.

Then I start to think about changing her name. Soon.

T. S.

18

HIS CONFIDENCE

I broke my heart in two
So hard I struck.
What matter? For I know
That out of rock,
Out of desolate source,
Love leaps upon its course.

—*W. B. Yeats*

The boat Michael Collins was on was hours late docking at Dún Laoghaire; they'd hit a trawler in the Irish Sea and arrived a mere forty-five minutes before the eleven o'clock cabinet meeting with the Dáil. Michael had called Garvagh Glebe from London on December second and asked Thomas and me to meet him in Dublin. We'd driven through the night only to wait on the quay in the Model T for four hours, dozing and shivering while we watched for the boat's arrival. Dublin was crawling with Black-and-Tan patrols and Auxiliaries again. It was as if Lloyd George had given them the signal to come out in force, a final visual reminder of what Ireland would be like indefinitely if an agreement wasn't reached. We'd been stopped and searched twice, once as we arrived in Dublin and once when we'd parked on the wharf at Dún Laoghaire, waiting patiently as they shined their flashlights in our faces and down our bodies, inside the car, and through Thomas's medical bag. I didn't have papers, but I was a pretty female in the company of a doctor with a government stamp on his documents. They let us go without any trouble.

Michael made the journey back to Dublin with Erskine Childers, secretary to the delegation. He was a slim man with fine features and an erudite manner. I knew from my research that he had an American wife and wouldn't, in the end, support the Treaty. But he was only a messenger, not a delegate, and his signature would not be required to forge an agreement with England. He greeted Thomas and me with a tired handshake, but he had his own car waiting, giving us a moment with Michael before he had to be delivered to the Mansion House, where the meeting would take place.

"We'll talk as you drive, Thomas. There might not be another opportunity," Michael instructed, and the three of us slid into the front seat of the car, with Thomas behind the wheel and me in the middle. Michael looked like he hadn't slept in weeks. He shook out his coat and combed his hair while Thomas drove.

"Tell me, Annie," Michael demanded. "What happens next? What possible good can come of this hellish trip?"

I'd spent the night trying to remember the intricate details of the timeline and could only remember the overall back-and-forth that occurred between the commencement of the talks on October 11 and the subsequent signing of the Treaty, or the Articles of Association as they were sometimes called, in the early days of December. This meeting today at the Mansion House didn't ring in my memory as productive or pivotal. There'd been little information on it at all, except when it was referred to in subsequent debates. It was the beginning of the end, but the squabbling would only intensify in the weeks to come.

"Specifics are difficult," I began, "but there will be anger over the oath of allegiance to the Crown that Lloyd George is demanding. De

Valera will insist on external association instead of dominion status, as the articles now read—"

"External association was shot down," Michael interrupted. "We tried that, and it was roundly rejected. Dominion status with an oath that declares the Crown as the head of a collection of individual states—Ireland being one of them—is the closest we can get to a republic. We are a small nation, and England is an empire. Dominion status is the best we are going to get. I see it as one step closer to greater independence down the road. We can get a foothold or we can go to war. Those are the choices," Michael snapped.

I nodded, and Thomas reached over and squeezed my hand, encouraging me to continue. Michael Collins wasn't mad at me. He was weary, and he'd had all these same arguments a hundred times over the previous weeks.

"All I can tell you, Michael, is that those who hated you before, hate you still. There is little you'll be able to say to change their minds."

"Cathal Brugha and Austin Stack," Michael sighed, naming his fiercest adversaries in the Irish cabinet. "Dev doesn't hate me . . . or maybe he does." Michael rubbed at his face. "De Valera's name carries weight throughout Ireland, and he's the president of the Dáil. He has a great deal of political capital to spend. But I can't figure him out. It's as though he wants to dictate the direction the country takes, but he doesn't want to be the one in the driver's seat, steering the vehicle, in case we go off a cliff."

"He will compare himself to a captain whose crew rushed in before the tide and almost sank the ship."

"Will he, now?" Michael said, his countenance darkening. "A captain of a ship who didn't bother to set sail with his crew."

"I believe you say something in one of the debates about him trying to sail the ship from dry land," I murmured.

"Ah. That's even more apt," Michael retorted.

"The people will be with you, Mick. If the Treaty is good enough for you, it's good enough for us," Thomas spoke up.

"It's not good enough for me, Tommy. Not nearly good enough. But it's a start. It's more than Ireland's ever had." He brooded for a moment before asking me his final questions. "So I'll be going back to London, then?"

"You will," I said firmly.

"Will de Valera go to London with us?"

"No."

Collins nodded as if he'd expected as much.

"Will the others sign the Treaty? I know Arthur will sign, but what about the rest of the Irish delegation?"

"They will all sign. Barton will be the hardest to convince. But the prime minister will tell him it will be war in three days if he doesn't." Lloyd George had likely been bluffing about the timeframe, according to historians, but Barton had believed him. They all had. And the Treaty was signed.

Michael sighed heavily. "Then there is little I need to say today. I'm too tired to argue anyway." He yawned widely, his jaw cracking with the action. "When are you going to marry this girl, Tommy?"

Thomas smiled at me but said nothing.

"If you don't marry her, I will." Michael yawned again.

"You already have too many women to juggle, Mr. Collins. Princess Mary, Kitty Kiernan, Hazel Lavery, Moya Llewelyn-Davies . . . am I missing any?" I asked.

His eyebrows shot up. "Good God, woman. You're frightening," he whispered. "Maybe it's time Kitty and I set a date." He was quiet for ten seconds. "Princess Mary?" he asked, brow furrowed in confusion.

"I believe Countess Markievicz accuses you of having an affair with Princess Mary during the Treaty negotiations," I said, chuckling.

"Jaysus," he groaned. "As if I had the time. Thanks for the warning."

We pulled up in front of the Dublin Mansion House, the head-quarters for the Irish parliament. It was a handsome, rectangular edifice with stately windows marching across the pale exterior and lining either side of a canopied entrance. A crowd had formed. Men lined the wall to the left of the building and shimmied up the lampposts to get a better view. The place was teeming with the curious and the well connected.

Michael Collins put his hat firmly on his head and stepped out of the car. We watched the press swarm and the crowds cry out when he was spotted, but he didn't slow and he didn't smile as he crossed the cobbled courtyard toward the steps, several of his men falling in behind him, acting as bodyguards. I recognized Tom Cullen and Gearóid O'Sullivan from the wedding at the Gresham. They'd also been waiting at Dún Laoghaire and had followed closely behind us as we'd driven to the Mansion House. Joe O'Reilly waved at us before they were all swallowed up in the throng.

Michael Collins went back to London, and Thomas and I stayed in Dublin, knowing the delegation would be back soon. Mick returned on December 7; the poor man had been on a boat and a train more hours than he'd been off in the last week. He and the others were greeted by a press release in all the papers stating that President de Valera had called an emergency meeting of the full cabinet in "view of the nature of the proposed Treaty with Great Britain," signaling to the people that peace was uncertain and the agreement they'd all just signed didn't have his support. Like he had only days before, Mick arrived at Dún Laoghaire and stepped into another series of meetings—this time with a divided Irish government—no rest, no respite, no break.

After long arguments in closed session, and after the cabinet had voted four to three in support of uniting behind the Treaty, de Valera issued another statement to the press stating the terms of the Treaty conflicted with the wishes of the nation—a nation that hadn't yet been consulted—and he could not recommend its acceptance. And that was only the beginning.

On December 8, Mick showed up on Thomas's doorstep in Mountjoy Square looking lost and shell-shocked. Thomas urged him to come in, but he just stood there. He could hardly lift his head, as though he thought the recriminations made by de Valera and other members of the cabinet had spilled over and contaminated his reputation, even among his friends.

"I had a woman spit on me, Tommy, outside of Devlin's Pub. She told me I'd betrayed my country. She said because of me, they died for nothing. Seán Mac Diarmada, Tom Clarke, James Connolly, and all the rest died for nothing. She said I betrayed them and everyone else when I signed the Treaty."

I joined Thomas at the door and tried to get Michael to come inside, reassuring him that he'd done all he could, but he turned and collapsed on the top step instead. Darkness had already fallen, and the streetlamps were lit, but the night was cold. I brought a blanket and laid it across his shoulders, and Thomas and I sat on the steps beside him, holding a silent vigil over his broken heart. When he suddenly crumpled in exhaustion and distress, laying his head in his arms like a defeated child, we stayed with him. He didn't ask me for answers or predictions. He didn't want to know what came next or what he should do. He simply cried, his shoulders shaking and his back bowed. After a while, he wiped his eyes, rose wearily, and climbed on his bicycle.

Thomas followed him, begging him to come to Garvagh Glebe for Christmas if he couldn't go home to Cork or to Garland to see Kitty. Michael thanked him quietly and nodded at me, making no promises. Then he rode off into the night, saying only that there was work to be done.

I awoke to screaming, and for a moment I was back in Manhattan, hearing the wail of police vehicles and ambulances, sounds commonplace to city life. The shadowy shapes in the room and the sounds of Garvagh Glebe brought me out of sleep's haze and into awareness, and I jerked upright, heart pounding, limbs shaking. We'd arrived home from Dublin after supper, and Thomas had been immediately summoned to a sick patient. Eoin had been irritable, Brigid had been weary, and I'd put the boy to bed with a story and some bribery. Then I'd fallen into bed myself, worrying as I drifted off about Thomas and his never-ending schedule.

I stumbled out of my room and up the stairs to Eoin, identifying him as the source of the shrieking. Brigid met me in the hallway, and she hesitated, letting me take the lead.

Eoin was thrashing in his bed, his arms flailing, his face wet with tears.

"Eoin!" I said, sitting beside him. "Wake up! You're having a bad dream." He was stiff and hard to hold, his small body pressed and stretched between sleep and reality, and I shook him, saying his name, patting his icy cheeks. His whole body was cold. I began rubbing my hands briskly up his shivering limbs, trying to warm and wake him.

"He used to do this when he was very small," Brigid fretted. "Most of the time, we couldn't wake him. He would toss about, and Dr. Smith would just hold him until he settled."

Eoin let out another blood-curdling cry, and Brigid stepped back, her hands over her ears.

"Eoin," I urged. "Eoin, where are you? Can you hear me?"

His eyes fluttered open. "It's dark," he wailed.

"Turn on the lamp, Brigid. Please."

She rushed to do as I asked.

"Doc!" Eoin cried, his blue eyes searching the room for Thomas. "Doc, where are you?"

"Shh, Eoin," I soothed. "Thomas isn't back yet."

"Where's Doc?" he wept. He wasn't whimpering. He was crying, the raw wails making my own eyes fill and spill over.

"He'll be home soon, Eoin. Nana is here. I'm here. Everything is all right."

"He's in the water," he moaned. "He's in the water!"

"No, Eoin. No," I said, even as my heart grew cold and heavy in my chest. I was to blame for Eoin's nightmare this time. He hadn't just seen me disappear; he'd seen Thomas disappear too.

After several minutes, Eoin's body grew more pliant, but his tears continued as he sobbed with brokenhearted conviction.

I held him close, rubbing his back and stroking his hair.

"Would you like a story, Eoin?" I whispered, trying to coax him back from the edges of the nightmare and into the comfort of waking.

"I want Doc," he cried. Brigid sat down on Eoin's bed. She wore a ruffled nightcap that made her look like Mrs. Claus, and her face was creased and careworn in the meager light. She didn't reach for Eoin but clasped her hands together as if she wished someone would hold her too.

"What if you tell me what Doc does to make you feel better when you have a bad dream?" I suggested.

Eoin continued to cry as if Thomas were never coming back.

"He sings to you, Eoin," Brigid murmured. "Should I sing to you?"

Eoin shook his head, turning his face into my chest.

"He tamed the waters, tamed the wind, He saved a dying world from sin, they can't forget, they never will, the wind and waves remember Him still," Brigid warbled tentatively.

"He healed the sick, the blind, the lame, the poor in heart cry out His name. We can't forget, we never will, the wind and waves remember Him still," she continued.

"I don't like that song, Nana," Eoin said, his voice hitching with the sobs that still shuddered through him.

"Why not?" she asked.

"Because it's about Jesus, and Jesus died."

Brigid looked a little shocked, and I felt inappropriate laughter bubbling in my chest.

"It's not a sad song, though. It's a song about remembering," she protested.

"I don't like remembering that Jesus died," Eoin insisted, his voice rising. Brigid's shoulders fell, and I patted her hand. She was trying, and Eoin wasn't being especially receptive.

"Remember Him, remember when, remember that He'll come again, when all the hope and love is lost, remember that He paid the cost," Thomas sang softly from the doorway. "They can't forget, they never will, the wind and waves remember Him still."

Thomas's pale eyes had dark circles, and his clothes were rumpled, but he walked forward and lifted Eoin from my arms. Eoin clung to him, burrowing his face in Thomas's neck. His sobs rose again, gut-wrenching and unrelenting.

"What's wrong, little man?" Thomas sighed. I stood, vacating my spot so Thomas could tuck Eoin back in his bed. Brigid stood as well, and with a soft good night, she walked quickly from the room. I followed, leaving Eoin in Thomas's capable hands.

"Brigid?"

She turned toward me, her face tragic, her mouth tight.

"Are you all right?" I asked. She nodded briskly, but I could see that she was struggling for her composure.

"When my children were small, sometimes they would cry in their sleep like that," she said. She paused, tangled in a memory. "My husband—Declan's father—he wasn't gentle the way Thomas is. He was bitter and tired. Anger was the only thing that kept him going. He worked himself into the ground; he worked *us* into the ground. And he had no patience for our tears."

I listened, not commenting. It was almost as if she wasn't talking to me at all, and I didn't want to startle her.

"I wouldn't let Eoin call Thomas Daddy. I couldn't bear it. And Thomas has never complained. Now Eoin calls him Doc. I shouldn't have done that, Anne. Thomas deserves more," Brigid whispered. Her eyes found mine then, and there was a look of pleading in them that begged for absolution. I gave it to her, gladly.

"Thomas wants Eoin to know who his father was. He's very protective of Declan," I soothed.

She nodded. "Yes. He is. He looked after Declan the way he looks after everyone else." Her eyes skittered away again. "My children . . . especially my sons . . . inherited their father's temper. I know that Declan—Declan wasn't always gentle with you, Anne. I want you to know . . . I don't blame you for leaving when you had the chance. And I don't blame you now for falling in love with Thomas. Any wise woman would."

I stared at my great-great-grandmother, shocked beyond speech.

"You are in love with Thomas, aren't you?" she asked, misinterpreting my stunned expression.

I didn't answer. I wanted to defend Declan. To tell Brigid that Anne hadn't left, that her beloved Declan hadn't raised a hand to his wife or scared her away. But I didn't know what was true.

"I think I've outlived my usefulness, Anne," Brigid said, her tone brittle. "I'm making plans to go to America to live with my daughter. It's time. Eoin has you. He has Thomas. And like my dear, departed husband, I'm no good with tears anymore."

Emotion swelled in my chest. "Oh no," I mourned.

"No?" she scoffed, but I could hear the emotion in her throat.

"Brigid, please don't. I don't want you to go."

"Why?" Her voice sounded like a child's, like Eoin's, plaintive and disbelieving. "There is nothing for me here. My children are scattered. I am getting older. I am . . . alone. And I am not"—she stopped, searching for the right words—"needed anymore."

I thought of the grave in Ballinagar, the one that bore her name in the years to come, and I pled with her gently. "Someday . . . someday your great-great-grandchildren will come here, to Dromahair, and they will walk up the hill behind the church where your children were baptized, where your children were married and laid to rest, and they will sit by the stones in Ballinagar that bear the Gallagher name, and they will know that this was your home, and because it was your home, it is theirs as well. That is what Ireland does. It calls her children home. If you don't stay in Ireland, who will they come home to?"

Her lips had begun to tremble, and she raised her hand toward me. I took it. She didn't pull me closer or seek my embrace, but the distance between us had been bridged. Her hand felt small and frail in my own, and I held it carefully, grief sitting heavy on my shoulders. Brigid was not an old woman, but her hand felt old, and I inwardly raged at time for taking her away—taking us all away—layer by layer.

"Thank you, Anne," she whispered, and after a moment she released my hand. She walked to her room and softly shut the door behind her.

22 December 1921

The debates continued in the Dáil for hours on end, day after day. The press seems to be firmly on the side of the Treaty, but the early debates were closed to the public, against Mick's wishes. He wants the people to know what the disagreements are, to know what is at stake and what is being argued. But he was overruled, at least in the beginning.

Public debates began on the afternoon of the nineteenth and recessed today for Christmas. Last year on Christmas Eve, Mick came within a hair's breadth of being arrested. He got drunk and loud and careless, drawing too much attention, and we ended up crawling out a second-story window at Vaughan's Hotel only seconds before the Auxies arrived. That's what happens when you carry the weight of the world on your shoulders; sometimes you lose your head. And Mick lost his last year.

This year, getting arrested won't be a problem, though I think he'd gladly exchange the troubles of the past for the troubles he's now facing. He's a man being torn in two, stretched between allegiance and responsibility, between practicality and patriotism, by people he would rather die for than fight with. His stomach is bothering him again. I rattled off the same instructions, the remedies and restrictions, but he brushed me off.

"I gave my official remarks today, Tommy. I didn't say half the things I should have said, and what I did say wasn't delivered well. Arthur (Griffith) said it was convincing, but he's generous that way. He referred to me as the 'man who won the war,' but I might be the man who lost the country after today."

Mick wanted me to ask Anne how she thought the vote would go in the end. I tucked her beneath my arm so she could share the receiver with me and speak into the transmitter on the upright, which I held clutched in my hand. I found myself immediately distracted by the smell of her hair and the feel of her pressed against me.

"Careful, Anne," I whispered in her ear. I didn't like that others could be listening, wondering at Mick's interest in her opinions. Anne wisely told Mick she "believed" the pro-Treaty faction of the Dáil would prevail.

"The margin will be slim, Michael, but I'm confident it will pass," she said.

He sighed so loudly that it rattled through the wires, and Anne and I both withdrew from the receiver to avoid the whistling static.

"If you're confident, then I will try to be confident too," Mick said. "Tell me this, Annie, if I come for Christmas, will you tell me another one of your stories? Perhaps Niamh and Oisín? I'd like to hear that one again. I'll recite something too, something that'll burn your ears and make you laugh, and we'll make Tommy dance. Did you know Tommy can dance, Annie? If he loves like he dances, you're a lucky lady."

"Mick," I chided, but Anne laughed. The sound was warm and rolling, and I kissed the side of her neck, unable to help myself, grateful that Mick was laughing too, his tension falling away for a moment.

Anne promised Mick if he came there would indeed be stories, food, rest, and dancing. She pinched me as she said dancing. I'd shown her my dancing skills one day in the rain. And then I kissed her senseless in the barn.

"Can I bring Joe O'Reilly?" Mick asked. "And maybe a man to watch my back so poor Joe can relax a bit?"

Anne assured him that he could bring anyone he liked, even Princess Mary. He laughed again, but he hesitated before signing off.

"Tommy, I appreciate this," he murmured. "I would go home, but . . . you know Woodfield is gone. And I need to leave Dublin for a while."

"I know, Mick. And how long have I been begging you to come?"

Last year, Mick didn't dare go to Cork for Christmas. It would have been too easy for the Tans to watch his family and swoop in and arrest him. This year, he no longer had a home to go home to.

Eight months ago, the Tans burned Woodfield, Mick's childhood home, to the ground and threw his brother Johnny in jail. The Collins farm is now a burned-out husk, Johnny's health has deteriorated, and the rest of the family is scattered across Clonakilty in County Cork. Mick carries that burden too.

Anne became very still at the mention of Cork and Mick's home. When I hung up the receiver, her smile was bent and misshapen, though she tried her best to keep it *in place. Her green eyes were shimmering like she wanted to cry but didn't want me to see. She hurried from the room, muttering an excuse about bedtime and Eoin, and I let her go, but I see through her. I see through her now the way I saw through her on the lake, the day everything became clear.*

There are things she isn't telling me. She's shielding me from the things she knows. I should insist that she tell me everything, just so I can help her carry the weight of what's to come. But God help me, I don't want to know.

T. S.

19

A NEEDLE'S EYE

All the stream that's roaring by
Came out of a needle's eye;
Things unborn, things that are gone,
From needle's eye still goad it on.

—W. B. Yeats

Michael Collins and Joe O'Reilly arrived early on Christmas Eve with a bodyguard named Fergus in tow, and they took the three empty rooms in the west wing of the house. Thomas had ordered three new beds from Lyons department store, hauling the frames and mattresses up the stairs to the freshly scrubbed rooms where Maggie and Maeve covered them with new linens and plump pillows. Thomas claimed Michael wouldn't know what to do with a big bed in a room of his own, having slept so often wherever his head landed and never staying in one place for too long. The O'Tooles were beside themselves with excitement, preparing the rooms as though ancient King Conor himself were coming to visit.

Eoin was frantic as he waited for them, running from one window to the next, watching for them to arrive. He had a secret he was bursting to share. We had created a new adventure in the Eoin sagas, a story where Eoin and Michael Collins rowed the little red boat across the lough and into an Ireland of the future. The Ireland in our story slept under the tricolor flag, no longer ruled by the Crown, the troubles and tribulations of past centuries long behind her. I told the story in rhyme, plotting each page, and Thomas sketched little Eoin and the "Big Fella" sitting atop the Cliffs of Moher, kissing the Blarney stone, and driving along the Giant's Causeway in Antrim. On one page, the mismatched pair saw the wildflowers and braced themselves against the winds on Clare Island. On another, they witnessed the winter solstice at Newgrange in County Meath. The story hadn't begun as a gift for Michael, but by the time we were finished, it was agreed that it needed to be.

It was a beautiful little book, full of Irish whimsy and hopeful pining, with two Irish lads, one big and one small, traipsing across the Emerald Isle. I knew that Ireland wouldn't know the peace found in the pages of our book for a long, long time. But peace would come. It would come in layers, in pieces, in chapters, just like in a story. And Ireland—the Ireland of the green hills and abundant stone, of the rocky history and the turbulent emotions—would endure.

We wrapped the story in paper and twine and placed it beneath the tree with Michael's name on it, adding it to the parcels that were already there—gifts for each of the O'Tooles and new hats and socks for all the men. Father Christmas would be visiting after Eoin went to sleep. I'd purchased the replica of the Model T Eoin had obsessed over at Kelly's pawnshop, and Thomas had built him a toy sailboat and painted it red, just like the one in our stories.

The photographer from the wedding at the Gresham Hotel had mailed us copies of the pictures he'd taken. I'd managed to intercept the package without anyone else seeing it. I'd put the picture of Thomas and me—the one Eoin would keep all his life—inside a heavy gold frame. It wasn't an exciting gift for a small boy, but it was a precious one. I'd placed the other picture from the wedding, the one with Michael grinning in the center, in another frame to give to Thomas. That was the night when I'd first admitted my feelings, the night when I'd confessed everything, and the memory of those moments and the significance of the history took my breath away every time I looked at the photo.

Garvagh Glebe had been turned into a glittering, glowing wonderland of warm smells and gleaming surfaces, of spice and shine and fragrant trees tied with ribbon and decorated with berries and candles. I wasn't surprised to learn that Thomas opened his doors every year to his neighbors, hiring musicians and supplying enough food to fill a thousand bellies. The festivities always began in the late afternoon and would continue until the party moved to St. Mary's for midnight Mass or home to sleep off the day's excesses.

Just after five o'clock, wagons and rattling farm trucks, cars, and carts began making their way down the lane toward the manor, which was aflame with light and sound. The ballroom that was empty year-round had been dusted and decorated, mopped and waxed, and long tables were laden with pies and cakes, turkey and spiced meat, and potatoes and bread prepared a dozen ways. It wouldn't stay hot, but no one complained, feasting as they milled about, laughing and visiting, their cares set aside for a few hours. Some swarmed Michael Collins while others steered clear; the lines were already being drawn between those who thought he'd brought peace to Ireland with his Treaty and those who believed he'd brought civil war. The news that he was at Garvagh Glebe spread like wildfire, and some stayed away because of it. The Carrigans, the family who had lost their son and their home because of the Tans last July, had refused to take part in the festivities. Mary's burned hands had healed, but her heart hadn't. Patrick and Mary Carrigan didn't want peace with England. They wanted justice for their son.

Thomas had gone to extend a personal invitation and to see how they were faring. He was thanked and turned away with their warning ringing in his ears. "We won't bow down to England, and we won't break bread with any man who will."

Thomas had worried that Michael wouldn't find respite or reprieve, even in Dromahair, and began circulating a warning of his own among the townsfolk. There would be no political debate or even discussion allowed at Garvagh Glebe that Christmas. Those who came to partake of his hospitality would do so with peace in their hearts, in the spirit of the season, or they were not welcome. So far, the people had cooperated, and those who could not had stayed away.

Thomas asked if I would entertain his guests with the story of the holy birth and light the candles in the ballroom windows. The candles were a tradition, a signal to Mary and Joseph that there was room for them inside. In Penal times, when priests were forbidden to perform Mass, the candle in the window was a symbol of the believer, a sign that the inhabitants of the house would also welcome the priests.

There were tight lips and glistening eyes as I spun the tale and lit the wicks. A few people shot withering looks toward poor Michael, condemnation in their gazes, as if he had forgotten all the pain and persecution that had come before. He stood with a glass in his hand, a lock of dark hair falling over his brow. Joe was on one side and the man he had introduced only as Fergus on his other. Fergus had carrot-colored hair, a wiry build, and a gun strapped to his back beneath his suit coat. He didn't look like he'd be much in a fight, but his flat eyes never stopped moving. Thomas had explained to the O'Tooles that Fergus should be allowed unfettered access to the house and grounds and that he was there to keep Michael safe, even in tiny Dromahair.

Then the musicians began to play, the center of the room cleared, and the dancing commenced. The singer's voice was theatrical and warbling, as if he was trying to mimic a style that he wasn't suited for, but the band was eager and spirits were high, and couples paired off and whirled, only to pair off again. The children wound their way through the couples, dancing and chasing each other, and Eoin's cheeks were flushed and his enthusiasm contagious as Maeve and Moira tried to corral him and his playmates and organize a game.

"You made me love you. I didn't want to do it. I didn't want to do it," the singer mourned unconvincingly, and I stared down at the spiced punch in my hand and wished fleetingly for crushed ice.

"Dance with me again, Annie." I knew the speaker before I turned my head.

"I'm afraid I'm not very good, Mr. Collins."

"That's not how I remember it. I never knew you well, but I saw you dancing with Declan once. You were wonderful. And stop calling me Mr. Collins, Annie. We're long past that."

I sighed as he pulled me toward the swirling couples. Of course the other Anne Gallagher could dance. Our differences just kept mounting. I thought of my awkward relationship with rhythm, of dancing in my tiny kitchen in big Manhattan, grateful no one could see, all disjointed limbs and stubbed toes, feeling the music with all my heart but incapable of converting it into grace. Eoin always said I felt too much to dance well. *The music is overflowing in you, Annie. Anyone can see that.*

I believed him, but that didn't make me feel any better about my lack of ability.

"I think I've forgotten how," I protested but Michael was undeterred. But the music suddenly changed, and the singer gave up his attempts at modernity, slipping into something far more traditional. The violin shimmied and whined, and clapping and stomping commenced. The pace was frenetic, the steps far too fast for me to fake, and I stubbornly refused to accompany Michael anymore. But Michael had forgotten me altogether. He was watching Thomas, who'd been pushed into the center of the dancers.

"Go, Tommy!" Michael yelled. "Show us how it's done."

Thomas was grinning, and his feet flew as the onlookers cheered him on. I could only stare, thoroughly caught. The fiddle cried, and his feet followed, stomping and kicking, an Irish folk hero come to life. Then he was pulling Michael, who could hardly contain himself, into the circle with him, sharing the stage. Thomas was laughing, his hair falling into his face, and I couldn't look away. I was dizzy with love and faint with hopelessness.

I was thirty-one years old. Not a girl. Not an innocent. I'd never been a giggling fan or a female obsessed with actors or musicians, with men I couldn't have and didn't know. But I knew Thomas Smith. I knew him, and I loved him. Desperately. But loving him—knowing him—was as implausible as loving a face on a screen. We were impossible. In a moment, in a breath, it could all be over. He was a dream I could easily wake up from, and I knew all too well that once awake, I wouldn't be able to call the dream back.

All at once, the futility and fear that had shadowed me from the moment Thomas pulled me from the lough crashed over me, dark and heavy, and I gulped the punch in my glass, trying to relieve the pressure. My heartbeat thrummed in my head, the pulse swelling into a gong. I left the ballroom at a brisk walk, but by the time I reached the front door, I was running from the reverberations. I hurtled from the house and out into the cover of the trees. Panic clawed at me, and I pressed my hands against the scaly bark of a towering oak, clawing back.

The night was clear and cold, and I pulled the crisp air into my lungs, battling the ringing in my skull, willing the clanging beneath my skin to quiet and slow. The rough reality of the tree anchored me, and I lifted my chin to the breeze, closed my eyes, and held tight to the trunk.

It wasn't long before I heard his voice behind me.

"Anne?" Thomas was still breathless, his shirtsleeves rolled to his elbows, his hair tousled, his suit coat discarded. "Brigid said you shot out of the house like your skirts were on fire. What's wrong, lass?"

I didn't answer him, not because I was contrary, but because I was close to tears, my throat tight and my heart so swollen and sore I couldn't speak around it. The lough beckoned, and I suddenly wanted to walk along it, to taunt it and reject it, just to reassure myself that I could. I released the tree and moved toward it, desperate. Defiant.

"Anne," Thomas said, reaching for my arm, stopping me. "Where are you going?" I heard the fear in his voice, and I hated it. Hated myself for causing it. "You're afraid. I can feel it. Tell me what's wrong."

I looked up at him and tried to smile, lifting my hands to his cheeks and my thumbs to the indentation on his chin. He grasped my wrists and turned his face, kissing the center of my palm.

"You're acting as if you're saying goodbye, Countess. I don't like it."

"No. Not goodbye. Never that," I protested, vehement.

"Then what?" he whispered, his hands moving from my wrists to my waist, drawing me to him.

I took a deep breath and thought how to best explain the persistent whisper of the lough that was always lapping at the edge of my happiness. In the darkness, feelings were harder to ignore and easier to unleash.

"I don't want you to disappear," I whispered.

"What are you talking about?" Thomas murmured.

"If I go back, *you* will disappear. I will still exist, wherever I am, but you will be gone. You will be gone, Eoin will be gone, and I can't bear it." The gong swelled again, and I leaned into him, resting my forehead against his shoulder. I breathed deeply, holding him in my lungs before I let him go again.

"So don't go back, Annie," he said gently, his lips in my hair. "Stay with me." I wanted to argue, to demand he acknowledge the fallibility of his suggestion. But I embraced him instead, comforted by his faith. Maybe it really was that simple. Maybe it was a choice.

I lifted my face, needing his eyes and his steadiness, needing him to know that if it *was* a choice, I'd already made it.

"I love you, Thomas. I think I loved you when you were simply words on a page, a face in an old photo. When my grandfather showed me your picture and said your name, I felt something. Something shifted inside me."

Thomas didn't interrupt or profess his own love. He just listened, staring down at me, his gaze soft, his mouth softer, his touch against my back the softest of all. But I needed something to hold on to, and I curled my hands into his shirt the way I'd clung to the tree. His skin was warm from dancing, and his heart drummed beneath my clenched fists, reminding me that in that moment, he was mine.

"Then the words on the page and the face in the photos became a man. Real. Tangible. Perfect." I swallowed, trying not to cry. "I fell so fast, so hard, and so completely. Not because love is blind, but because . . . it's *not*. Love isn't blind, it's *blinding*. Glaring. I looked at you, and from the very first day, I knew you. Your faith and your friendship, your goodness and your devotion. I saw it all, and I fell so hard. And the feeling continues to grow. My love is so big and full and brimming that I can't breathe around it. It's terrifying to love so much, knowing how fragile our existence really is. You're going to have to hold on to me, or I'll burst . . . or maybe I'll just float away. Up into the sky, out into the lough."

I felt a tremor run through him from his gentle hands to his forgiving eyes, and then his lips were smiling and pressed to mine, once, twice, and again. His sigh tickled my tongue, and my grasping hands flattened against him, yielding. Then he was murmuring into my seeking lips, kissing me even as he spoke.

"Marry me, Anne. I'll shackle you to me so you can't float away, so we won't ever have to be apart. Plus, it's time you had a new name. It's damn confusing to keep calling you Anne Gallagher."

Of all the things I'd thought he'd suggest, marriage was not one of them. I pulled back, my jaw slack, and I laughed in disbelief. For a moment, I forgot about Thomas's lips and searched his eyes instead. They were pale and guileless beneath the sheltering boughs and the light of the winter moon.

"Anne Smith is almost as ordinary as Thomas Smith," he murmured. "But when you're a time-traveling countess, the name isn't all that important." His teasing tone was at odds with his very serious proposition.

"Can we do that? Can we really get married?" I breathed.

"Who's to stop us?"

"I can't prove that I'm . . . me."

"Who needs proof? I know. You know. God knows." Thomas kissed my forehead, my nose, and each cheek before pausing at my mouth, waiting for me to answer.

"But . . . what will people say?" What would Brigid say?

"I hope they will congratulate us." He pressed a kiss to my upper lip, then to the lower one, tugging it softly, urging me to follow his lead.

"What will Michael say?" I panted, pulling back so I could converse. I could picture Michael Collins congratulating Thomas while he whispered warnings in my ears.

"Mick will say something rough and irreverent, I'm sure. And then he'll burst into noisy tears because he loves as intensely as he hates."

"What—" I began again.

"Anne." Thomas pressed his thumbs to my lips, cradling my face and quieting my stream of questions. "I love you. Desperately. I want to bind us together in every way possible. Today, tomorrow, and for every day after that. Do you want to marry me or not?"

There was nothing I wanted more in the world. Not a single, solitary thing.

I nodded, smiling against the pads of his thumbs, submitting completely. He moved his hands, replacing them with his mouth once more.

For a moment, I reveled in the possibility of permanence, in the clean, all-consuming taste of him. Promise sang between us, and I let myself hum along.

Then the wind shifted and the moonlight winked; a branch cracked and a match flickered. A tendril of cigarette smoke hung in the air, alerting us that we were not alone seconds before a voice rose out of the darkness.

"So it's true, eh? You two. Mother said it was like this. I didn't want to believe it." I spun in Thomas's arms, swallowing a gasp, and his arm snaked around me, steadying me as he stepped toward the stranger.

I thought it was Liam. His build and height were similar in the darkness, and the timbre of his voice was almost identical. But Thomas, cool and composed, greeted the man by another name, and I realized my mistake with a flood of relief. This was Ben Gallagher, Declan's oldest brother, the one I'd not yet met.

"Anne," Ben greeted stiffly, inclining his head. "You look well." His voice was stilted, uncomfortable, his expression shrouded by his cap. He took a deep pull on his cigarette before he turned to Thomas.

"Collins is here," he clipped. "I guess that tells me all I need to know about where your loyalties lie, Doc. Though judging from the way you were kissing my brother's wife, I'm not sure loyalty is your strong suit."

"Mick is my friend. You know that," Thomas said, ignoring the jibe. Declan had been gone for five years, and I was not his wife. "Michael Collins was your friend too, Ben. Once."

"Once we had a common cause. Not anymore," Ben muttered.

"And what cause is that, Ben?" Thomas asked, his tone so soft it was hard to detect the venom, but I heard it. Ben heard it too, and his temper flared instantly.

"Feckin' Irish freedom, Doc," he snapped, tossing his cigarette aside. "Have you grown so comfortable in your big house with your powerful friends and your best friend's woman that you've forgotten seven hundred years of suffering?"

"Michael Collins has done more for Irish freedom, for Irish independence, than you or I will ever do," Thomas countered, conviction ringing in his voice.

"Well, it isn't enough! This Treaty isn't what we've bled for. We're almost there, and we can't stop now! Collins caved. When he signed that agreement, it was a knife in every Irish back."

"Don't do that, Ben. Don't let them take that too," Thomas warned.

"Take what?"

"The English have left their imprint everywhere. But don't let them divide us. Don't let them destroy families and friendships. If we fight each other, we will have nothing left. They will have truly destroyed the Irish. And we will have done the wet work for them."

"So it was all for nothing, then? The men who died in '16 and the men who've died since? They died for nothing?" Ben cried.

"If we turn on each other, then they died for nothing," Thomas replied, and Ben immediately began shaking his head, disagreeing.

"The fight isn't over, Thomas. If we don't fight for Ireland, who will?"

"So our loyalty is to Ireland and Irishmen unless they disagree with us, then we mow them down? That's not the way it's supposed to work," Thomas insisted, incredulous.

"You remember how it was, Thomas. The people weren't behind us in '16 either. You remember how they hollered and hissed and threw things at us when the Tans marched us through the streets after we surrendered. But the people came round. You saw the uproar when they started hanging our leaders. You saw the crowds cheering when the prisoners came home from England eight months later. The people want freedom. They're ready for war, if that's what it takes. We can't give up the fight now. Look how far we've come!"

"I watched men die. I watched Declan die. I'm not going to start shooting at the friends I have left. I won't do it. Convictions are all fine and good until they become excuses to go to war with people you once fought with," Thomas said.

"Who *are* you, Doc?" Ben was aghast. "Seán Mac Diarmada must be rolling in his grave."

"I'm an Irishman. And I won't be raising arms against you or any other Irishman, Treaty or no Treaty."

"You're weak, Thomas. Anne comes back—where the hell have you been, anyway?" he hissed, turning on me in fury before shifting his gaze back to Thomas, resuming his argument. "She comes back, and suddenly you've lost your fire. What would Declan think of the both of ya?" Ben spit at our feet, the sound wet and thick, before he turned and waved toward Thomas, dismissing him, dismissing us.

"Your mother will be glad to see you, Ben. It's been too long. Eat. Drink. Rest. Spend Christmas with us," Thomas said, refusing to react.

"With him?" Ben pointed to the row of windows along the east side of the house that revealed the party in full swing. Michael stood near one, outlined in light, conversing with Daniel O'Toole. "Someone needs to tell the Big Fella not to stand in front of the windows. You never know who's hiding in the trees."

Thomas stiffened at the veiled threat, his hand tightening on my body, and I was grateful for the support when a voice spoke up from the shadows, accompanied by the unmistakable snick of a pistol being cocked.

"No, you never do," Fergus intoned, moving toward us. A cigarette hung from the bodyguard's lips, giving him a casual air completely at odds with the weapon he wielded.

Ben flinched, and his hands fluttered at his sides.

"Don't do it," Fergus warned quietly. "You'll ruin Christmas for a lot of good people."

Ben's hands stilled.

"If you're going to go inside, I'll need that gun you're thinking about pulling," Fergus insisted calmly. "If you're not going inside, I'll still take it, just to make sure you live through the night. Then I'll need you to start walking toward Dublin." He let his cigarette fall, and without lowering his eyes, ground the butt into the dirt with the toe of his shoe. He approached Ben and without fanfare, searched him for weapons, removing a knife from his boot and a gun from his waistband.

"His mother is inside. His nephew too. He's family," Thomas murmured.

Fergus nodded once, a quick jerk of his head. "I heard. So why is he out here in the trees, watching the house?"

"I came to see my mother. To see my sister-in-law, back from the dead. To see Eoin and you, Doc. I've come here for Christmas for the last five years. I didn't expect Collins to be here. I hadn't decided if I was going to stay," Ben reasoned, affronted.

"And Liam? Is Liam here too?" I asked. I heard the tremor in my voice, and Thomas grew rigid beside me.

"Liam's in Youghal, down in Cork. He won't be coming home this year. Too much work to do. There's a war on," Ben ground out.

"Not here, Ben. There's no war here. Not tonight. Not now," Thomas said.

Ben nodded, his jaw clenched, but his expression was one of disgust, and his eyes condemned us all. "I want to see my mother and the boy. I'll stay the night in the barn. Then I'll be on my way."

"Go on inside, then," Fergus ordered. He prodded Ben forward, not lowering his gun. "But stay away from Mr. Collins."

24 December 1921

Something changed in Ireland around the turn of the century. There was a cultural revival of sorts. We sang the old songs and heard the old stories—things we'd heard many times before—but they were taught with an intensity that was new. We looked at ourselves and at each other, and there was a sense of anticipation. There was pride, even reverence, for who we were, what we could aspire to, and those we had descended from. I was taught to love Ireland. Mick was taught to love Ireland. I have no doubt Ben and Liam and Declan were taught to love her too. But for the first time in my life, I'm not sure what that means.

After our confrontation with Ben Gallagher, Anne and I stood beneath the trees, shaken by the event.

"I don't like this world, Thomas," Anne whispered. "This world is something the other Anne clearly understood and something I will never understand."

"What world, Countess?" I asked her, though I already knew.

"The world of Ben Gallagher and Michael Collins, of shifting lines and changing sides. And the worst part is . . . I know how it ends. I know the ending, and I still don't understand it."

"Why? Why can't you understand it?"

"Because I haven't lived it," she confessed. "Not like you have. The Ireland I know is one of songs and stories and dreams. It is Eoin's version—we all have one—and yet even that version is softened and reshaped because he left it behind. I don't know the Ireland of oppression and revolution. I haven't been taught to hate."

"We weren't taught to hate, Anne."

"You were."

"We were taught to love."

"Love what?"

"Freedom. Identity. Possibility. Ireland," I argued.

"And what will you do with that love?" she pressed. When I didn't answer, she answered for me. "I'll tell you what you will do. You will turn on each other because you don't love Ireland. You love the idea of Ireland. And each man has his own idea of what that is."

I could only shake my head, wounded, resistant. Outrage for Ireland—for every injustice—burned in my chest, and I didn't want to look at her. She'd reduced my devotion to an impossible dream. A moment later, she drew my face to hers and kissed my mouth, quietly begging my forgiveness.

"I'm sorry, Thomas. I say I don't understand and then lecture you as though I do."

We spoke no more of Ireland, marriage, or Ben Gallagher. But her words kept repeating in my head all evening, drowning out everything else. "And what will you do with that love?"

I sat at midnight Mass with Mick on one side, Anne on the other, and Eoin asleep in my arms. He'd started yawning during the entrance procession and was asleep

291

before the first reading. He snored softly through Father Darby's recitation of the prophecy of Isaiah, oblivious to all care, ignorant of the strain that bowed Mick's head and furrowed Anne's brow. His freckled cheek lay against my chest, against my aching heart, and I was envious of his innocence, his faith, and his trust. When Mick turned to me at the sign of peace, his voice soft, his face earnest, I could only nod and repeat the blessing, "Peace be with you," though peace was the furthest thing from my heart.

Father Darby said in his homily that it is easier for a camel to pass through the eye of a needle than for a rich man to enter the kingdom of God. It might also be said that it is easier for a camel to pass through the eye of a needle than for an Irishman to stop fighting.

I was taught to love Ireland, but love should not be this hard. Duty, yes. But not love. Maybe that's my answer. A man won't suffer or sacrifice for something he doesn't love. In the end, I suppose it all amounts to what we love the most.

T. S.

20

THE WHITE BIRDS

I am haunted by numberless islands, and many a Danaan
shore,
    Where Time would surely forget us, and Sorrow come near
us no more;
    Soon far from the rose and the lily and fret of the flames
would we be
    Were we only white birds, my beloved, buoyed out on the
foam of the sea!

—*W. B. Yeats*

I came awake suddenly, unsure of the reason. I listened, thinking Eoin
had awakened because he was eager to see if Saint Nick had visited in
the night, but instead heard sounds I couldn't identify.

We'd arrived home from midnight Mass in the early morning hours,
everyone subdued and saddled with their private thoughts. Thomas had
carried Eoin to his bed, and I'd trailed after them, helping Eoin into
a nightshirt, though he swayed, half asleep, through the process. He
was deeply asleep again before I pulled the covers around his shoulders. Brigid had not attended Mass but stayed behind to visit with her
son without a houseful of guests. When we'd arrived home, she was in

bed, and Ben was either gone or in the barn. I didn't inquire after his whereabouts.

I'd wished Thomas a soft Merry Christmas and happy birthday, and I could tell I'd caught him by surprise, as though he'd forgotten himself or had not expected me to remember. I had gifts for him and a cake in the larder but would wait until later in the day to call attention to his birthday.

He had drawn me into his room and shut the door behind us, pulling me to him with quiet vehemence, ravenous yet reverent, kissing me like he'd thought about kissing me all night and didn't know when he'd kiss me again. Thomas was not a ladies' man. In fact, I had the distinct impression he'd never been serious about anyone before me, but he kissed with a confidence born of commitment, holding nothing back and demanding everything in return. Michael Collins had joked that if Thomas loved like he danced, I was a very lucky lady. Thomas loved like he danced, like he doctored, like he did everything else—with total commitment and careful attention to detail. We were both breathless and panting when I extricated myself and tiptoed down the stairs to my room.

Thomas, Michael, and Joe O'Reilly had spent much of the night in the library, the rumble of their voices and the occasional burst of laughter warming me as I drifted off to sleep.

Now dawn had broken, though the sun in the winter months was sluggish and slow, the sky shifting on a gradient of gray before finally finding daylight. I pulled on the deep-blue robe I'd left on the end of my bed, stuffed my feet into a pair of wool socks, and slipped out of my room and into the parlor, expecting to find Eoin inspecting packages beneath the tree. I found Maeve stoking the fire instead, her tongue between her teeth, a smudge of soot on her nose.

"Are you and I the first ones up?" I whispered, feeling like a giddy child.

"Oh no, miss. Eleanor, Moira, and Mam are in the kitchen. Dr. Smith, Mr. Collins, my brothers, and a dozen others are in the yard."

"In the yard?" I hurried to the window, peering through the clinging mist and halfhearted dawn. "Why?"

"Hurling, ma'am! They've got quite a match going. My brothers were so excited they didn't sleep a wink. Last Christmas, Doc gave them hurling sticks of their own and promised them they could play with the grown-ups this year. He had a wee stick made for Eoin too. He's out there now, probably making a nuisance of himself," she grumbled, and I was reminded of the old woman she would become, the Maeve with thick glasses who said she knew Anne well and who called Eoin a scamp.

"Eoin's outside?"

She nodded and sat back on her heels, dusting her hands on her apron.

"Maeve?"

"Yes, miss?"

"I have something for you."

She smiled, the fire forgotten. "For me?"

I went to the tree and took a heavy wooden box from beneath it. It was lined and quilted to protect the fragile items inside. I handed it to Maeve, who held it reverently.

"It's from Dr. Smith and me. Open it," I urged, smiling. I'd seen a tea set displayed in Kelly's pawnshop and had recognized the delicate rose pattern. When I told Thomas the story, he had insisted on buying the entire set, complete with saucers, a pitcher, and a sugar bowl with a spoon.

Maeve gingerly opened the box, prolonging the anticipation for as long as she could. When she saw the little teacups nestled in pink satin, she gasped, sounding like the young lady she was becoming.

"If you would like a hurling stick of your own, I can arrange that too," I murmured. "We girls shouldn't miss the fun, just because we're ladies."

"Oh no, miss. Oh no. These are so much better than a silly stick!" She was panting in delight, touching the petals with soot-stained fingers.

"Someday, years from now, when you are grown, a woman from America, a woman named Anne, just like me, will come to Dromahair, looking for her family. She'll come to your house for tea, and you will help her. I thought you might need a tea service of your own for when that day finally comes."

Maeve stared at me, her mouth forming a perfect *O*, her blue eyes so wide they filled her thin face.

She crossed herself as if my predictions had frightened her. "Do you have the sight, miss?" she whispered. "Is that why you're so clever? My da says you are the smartest lass he's ever met."

I shook my head. "I don't have the sight . . . not exactly. I am just a storyteller. And some stories come true."

She nodded slowly, her eyes clinging to mine. "Do you know my story, miss?"

"Your story is a very long one, Maeve," I said, smiling.

"I like the big books best of all," she whispered. "The ones with dozens of chapters."

"Your story will have a thousand chapters," I reassured.

"Will I fall in love?"

"Many times."

"Many times?" she squeaked, thrilled.

"Many times."

"I'll never forget you, Miss Anne."

"I know you won't, Maeve. And I won't ever forget you."

I dressed quickly, loosely braiding my hair and pulling on a dress, my boots, and a shawl, not wanting to miss a chance to watch the match. I'd been raised by an Irishman but had never seen hurling even once in my life. They wielded sticks, their faces fierce in the morning mist. They darted and dashed, driving a small ball from one end of the grass to the other. Eoin wielded his own stick, though he was relegated to the sidelines with a small ball that he hit and then chased over and over again. He ran to me when he saw me exit the house; his nose was as red as his hair. Thankfully he wore a coat and a cap, though his hands were icy when I reached down to clasp them.

"Merry Christmas, Mother!" he crowed.

"Nollaig shona dhuit," I answered, kissing his cherry cheeks. "Tell me, who's winning?"

He wrinkled his nose at the men roaring and trampling over one another, their shirtsleeves rolled, their collars unbuttoned. He was clearly impervious to the cold and shrugged. "Mr. Collins and Doc keep pushing each other down, and Mr. O'Toole can't run, so he keeps getting knocked over."

I giggled, watching as Thomas smacked the ball to Fergus, who deftly sidestepped a charging Michael Collins, his mouth moving as fast as his legs. Some things had not, and seemingly would not, change through the decades. Trash talking was clearly part of the game. Two teams of ten players each had been cobbled together from among the neighboring families. Eamon Donnelly, the man who had supplied the cart the day Thomas pulled me out of the lough, had joined in the competition, and he waved at me merrily before taking a swing at the ball. I watched, fascinated, cheering for everyone and no one in particular, though I winced every time Thomas skidded across the grass and held my breath when sticks clashed and legs tangled. Somehow everyone survived without serious injury, and Michael proclaimed his team the victors after two hours of intense play.

Everyone tumbled into the kitchen for refreshment—coffee and tea, ham and eggs, and rolls so sticky and sweet I was full after two bites. The neighbors were quick to disperse, heading home to their families and traditions, and after Thomas, Michael, Joe, and Fergus washed up and rejoined us in the parlor, we gathered around the tree and exchanged gifts. Michael pulled Eoin into his lap, and together they read the story we'd written. Michael's voice was low and soft, the burr of his West Cork brogue around the words making my heart ache and my eyes smart. Thomas laced his fingers in mine, stroking my thumb in quiet commiseration.

When the story was finished, Michael looked down at Eoin, his eyes bright, his throat working. "Can you keep this for me, Eoin? Can you keep it here at Garvagh Glebe so we can read it together whenever I come to visit?"

"You don't want to bring it to your house to show your mother?" Eoin asked.

"I don't have a house, Eoin. And my mother is with the angels."

"And your da too?"

"And my da too. I was six, just like you are now, when my father died," Michael said.

"Maybe your mother will come back like mine did," Eoin mused. "You just have to wish very hard."

"Is that what you did?"

"Yes." Eoin nodded soberly. "Doc and I found a clover with four leaves. Four-leaf clovers are magic, you know. Doc told me to make a wish, so I did."

Michael's brows rose. "You wished for a mother?"

"I wished for a whole family," Eoin whispered, but everyone heard him. Thomas's hand tightened around mine.

"Do you know, Eoin, if your mother were to marry Doc, then he would be your dad," Michael suggested oh-so-innocently.

"Why can't you ever hold your tongue, Mick?" Thomas sighed.

"Fergus said he overheard a proposal last night," Michael hinted, his grin wicked.

Fergus grunted, but he didn't defend himself or reproach Michael.

"There's a small box tucked back on that branch there. Do you see it?" Thomas directed Eoin. Eoin hopped off Michael's lap and peered into the dense foliage where Thomas was pointing.

"Is it for me?" Eoin chirruped.

"I suppose it is, in a way. Can you fetch it and bring it to me?" Thomas asked.

Eoin retrieved the hidden treasure and brought it to Thomas.

"Would it be all right if your mother opened it, lad?"

Eoin nodded emphatically and watched as I lifted the lid on the tiny velvet box. Inside were two gold bands, one larger than the other. Eoin looked up at Thomas, waiting for an explanation.

"These belonged to my parents. To my father, who died before I was born, and my mother, who married again and gave me another father, a father who was good and kind and loved me even though I was not his son in truth."

"Just like me and you," Eoin said.

"Yes. Just like us. I want to marry your mother, Eoin. How do you feel about that?"

"Today?" Eoin said, delighted.

"No," Thomas began amid laughter all around.

"Why not, Tommy?" Michael pressed, all teasing aside. "Why wait? None of us know what tomorrow will bring. Marry Annie and give the lad his family."

Brigid's eyes met mine, and she tried to smile, but her lips were trembling, and she pressed her fingers to her mouth to cover her emotion. I wondered if she was thinking of her own family, and I said a silent prayer for her sons.

Thomas pulled the ring free of the box and held it out to Eoin, who took it and studied the simple band before turning to me.

"Will you marry Doc, Mother?" he asked, extending the ring toward me. I'd always worn Anne's cameo ring on my right hand—for me it was an heirloom, not a wedding band—and I was grateful that I could slip Thomas's mother's ring on my left without any awkwardness.

"It fits," I said. "Perfectly. I guess that means the answer is yes."

Eoin cheered and Michael crowed, grabbing the small boy and tossing him in the air.

"Now all we need is Father Darby," I murmured.

Thomas cleared his throat. "We should set a date."

"I spoke to him last night after Mass, Thomas," Mick said, smiling.

"You did?" Thomas gasped.

"I did. I asked him if he was available tomorrow. He said a nuptial Mass could be arranged. We're all gathered for Christmas. Why not extend the celebration?" Mick urged.

"Yes, why not?" I blurted. The room fell silent, and I felt my face heat.

"Why not, indeed?" Thomas said slowly, stunned. Then a smile, white and blinding, creased his face, and I suddenly couldn't catch my breath. He tipped my chin and kissed me once, sealing the deal.

"Tomorrow it is, Countess," Thomas whispered.

Then Eoin was squealing, Michael was stomping, and Joe was pounding Thomas on the back. Fergus ducked out of the room, embarrassed by the display and his part in it, but Brigid sat quietly knitting, her gaze warm and her smile genuine. The O'Tooles would be back for Christmas dinner in the evening, and we would break the news to them then, but I was already counting the hours until I became Anne Smith.

I'd come across a personal account describing an occasion where Michael Collins, Joe O'Reilly, and several others were dining at the Llewelyn-Davies estate in Dublin. The name of the estate—Furry Park—brought to mind a forest full of stuffed animals reminiscent of Christopher Robin and Winnie the Pooh, and I'd wondered at its origins. The whimsy of the tale had ended there, however. It was purported that a man had climbed the trees at Furry Park and attempted to shoot Michael Collins through the dining room windows. Michael Collins's bodyguard, a man not named in the account, had discovered the sniper, marched him at gunpoint down into the bog, a short distance from the manor, and killed him.

There were conflicting accounts; Michael Collins was reported to have been somewhere else entirely. But the details of the story were strangely similar to what transpired that evening at Christmas dinner.

A shot, muffled and distant, interrupted the blessing being offered over the meal, and our heads rose as one, the prayer forgotten.

"Where's Fergus?" Michael frowned.

Brigid's teacup crashed to the floor, and without a word, she was out of her seat, skirts in hand, running for the door.

"Stay here. All of you," Thomas ordered as Mick jumped to his feet. "I'll go after Brigid."

"I'll go too, Doc." Robbie O'Toole had risen to his feet, his good eye flat, his blind eye covered.

"Robbie," Maggie protested, overly protective of her grown son. She'd almost lost him and wasn't eager for him to take another bullet.

"I know all the lads round here, Mam, and where their loyalties lie. Maybe I can help sort it out."

We waited in tense silence, staring at our plates. Eoin crawled into my lap and hid his face in my shoulder.

"It's nothing. Don't fret now. Let's eat." Maggie O'Toole clapped her hands, urging her family to fill their plates. After a quick look at me, they obeyed, digging into the feast with the appreciation of those who had once known hunger. I filled Eoin's plate as well, urging him back to his own chair. The chatter rose among the young people, but the adults ate in silence, listening for the men to return, anxious for reassurance.

"Why would she run like that, Anne?" Michael asked me, his voice pitched low.

"I can think of only one reason," I murmured. "She must think her son is involved."

"Fergus would only fire if he had to, Anne," Joe protested.

"He might have had to," I muttered, my heart in my throat.

"Jaysus wept," Joe muttered.

"The Gallagher boys aren't with us, then?" Michael sighed. "They aren't the only ones." I figured if Fergus had told Michael about the proposal the previous evening, he'd also told him about Ben Gallagher's presence and his displeasure at discovering Michael Collins at Garvagh Glebe, but apparently not.

Brigid came back inside, pale but poised, and apologized for her hasty exit. "I worried over nothing," she said quietly, but she offered no further explanation.

We finished dinner and still Thomas and Robbie had not returned. Eoin was drawn into a game of charades with the O'Tooles, and Michael, Joe, and I slipped out the front door and into the twilight, unable to wait any longer. We were met by Thomas and Robbie coming through the trees where the marsh met the lake on the east side of Lough Gill. Their clothes were wet to their hips from walking through the bog, and they were shivering and tight-lipped.

"What happened?" Michael asked. "Where's Fergus?"

"He'll be along shortly," Thomas answered and tried to herd us toward the house.

"Who did he shoot, Tommy?" Michael demanded, refusing to budge, his voice grim.

"Nobody from Dromahair, thank God. There won't be any locals missing a father or a son," Thomas muttered. Reluctance and regret bracketed his mouth, and he rubbed at his eyes wearily. "Fergus said the man had a rifle, long range, aimed at the house. He'd been dug in for a while, waiting for his shot from the looks of it."

"Waitin' for me?" Michael asked, his voice flat.

Robbie's good eye shifted nervously in his head, and he shivered violently. "I recognized him, Mr. Collins. He was a gunrunner for the Volunteers. I saw him a few times with Liam Gallagher. They called him Brody, though I don't know if that was his first or last name. Liam's runners haven't fared especially well."

"How's that?" Michael asked.

"Martin Carrigan was killed by the Tans last July, and now Brody's got himself killed too. They weren't with our column, but they were on our side," Robbie protested, shaking his head as though he couldn't make sense of it.

"The sides are shifting, lad," Michael said. "And every man is feeling caught in the middle."

"Martin Carrigan was bearded, Anne, and blond," Thomas said, his eyes holding mine. "I think he may have been one of the men on the riverboat on the lough last June. Brody matches your description of the third man. I didn't put it together until Robbie told me they were Liam's boys."

"What are you saying, Tommy? What riverboat?" Michael wasn't following. Robbie didn't answer, and Thomas was silent, waiting for me to put the pieces together.

"What he's saying, Michael, is the man Fergus shot this evening wasn't necessarily here to kill you," I said, reeling.

"What?" Joe O'Reilly cried, completely flummoxed.

"He may have been trying to kill me," I said.

26 December 1921

*I married Anne today. For all their physical similarities,
she no longer reminds me of Declan's Anne. She is my
Anne, and that is all I see. She wore Brigid's veil and Anne
Finnegan's dress, a Christmas angel all in white. When I
remarked on her choice, she simply smiled and said, "How
many women get to wear their great-grandmother's dress
and their great-great-grandmother's veil?" She carried a
cluster of holly, the red berries vivid in her pale hands, and
wore her dark hair down. It curled around her shoulders
beneath the veil. She looked so beautiful.*

*The church was cold, and the wedding party was
subdued and sleepy after two days of merriment and
mayhem. I thought Anne would want to postpone our
marriage after the events of last night, but when I'd
suggested it, she shook her head, claiming if Michael
Collins could carry on amid the chaos, so could we. She
was calm and clear-eyed as I took her hand to enter the
chapel. She refused to cover the dress in a coat or shawl,
and she knelt, shivering, at the altar as Father Darby
led us through the nuptial Mass, the liturgy falling from
his lips in a quiet cadence that was answered by all in*

attendance. I trembled too, watching her, but it was not from the cold.

I clung to every word, desperate to savor the ceremony, to miss nothing. Yet in the years to come, it will be the memory of Anne, her gaze steady, her back straight, her promises sure, that I will cherish most. She was as solemn and serene as the stained-glass Madonna looking down on us as the rites were performed.

When Anne said her vows, she abandoned her Irish accent, as if the pledge she made was too sacred for disguises. If Father Darby wondered at her Yankee inflections, he made no sound or indication. If there was confusion amid the congregants, I would never know; our eyes were locked as she promised me a lifetime, however it unfolded.

When it was my turn, my voice echoed in the near-empty church and reverberated in my chest. "I, Thomas, take you, Anne, for my lawful wife; to have and to hold; for better, for worse; for richer, for poorer; in sickness and health; until death do us part."

Father Darby joined us in marriage, and in ringing tones asked that the Lord, in His goodness, strengthen our consent and fill us both with His blessings. "What God has joined together, let no man put asunder," he boomed, and Mick called out a hearty "Amen," which was echoed by Eoin, his little voice adamant and uninhibited by the solemnity of the occasion.

Anne produced the two rings I'd given her Christmas morning, and Father Darby blessed the bands. I was struck again by the symbol of the circle. Faith, fidelity, forever. If time was an eternal round, then it never had to end. With cold hands and hopeful defiance, Anne slid the ring on my finger, and I claimed her in return.

The rest of the Mass—the prayers, the communion, the blessings, and the recessional—occurred distantly, separate from the two of us, as though we'd slipped into a realm of muted sounds and subtleties where only we existed, and time was liquid all around us.

Then we were walking from the church next to Ballinagar, death on the hill behind us, our whole lives in front of us, the past and the present all dusted in white. Snow had begun to fall, the flakes like feathers floating around us, winged and wondrous, white birds circling above our heads. I tipped my face to the sky and watched them come, laughing with Eoin, who raised his arms to greet them while trying to catch one on his tongue.

"The heavens have sent doves," Mick cried, pulling his hat from his head and embracing the sky, letting the softly falling snow rest on his hair and his clothes, adorning him in ice. Anne wasn't looking at the skies, but up at me, her smile wide, and her face radiant. I brought her cold fingers to my lips, kissing her knuckles before I pulled her close, wrapping her in the pale-green shawl Maggie O'Toole had held during the ceremony.

"How often does it snow in Dromahair?" Anne breathed, her voice full of wonder.

"Almost never," I confessed. "But then again . . . it's been a year of miracles, Anne Smith."

She beamed up at me, stealing my breath, and I leaned down to kiss her smiling mouth, not caring at all that we had an audience.

"I think God is blessing your union, Mr. and Mrs. Smith!" Mick shouted, and swooping Eoin up in

his arms, he began to waltz and spin around us. The O'Tooles followed suit, pairing up and kicking up their heels. Joe O'Reilly bowed gallantly in front of a giggling Eleanor, and Maeve convinced a stern Fergus to take a turn around the churchyard. Even Brigid and Father Darby joined in the dancing. In the wintery dusk, our heads wreathed in snowflakes, we swayed, wedded to the moment, to each other, and to a Christmas that will forever live in my memory.

Anne is asleep now, curled on her side, and I can only watch her, my heart so swollen in my chest that I'll suffocate if I don't stay upright. The light of the lamp touches her freely, boldly even, brushing her hair and tracing the dip of her waist and the swell of her hip, and I am irrationally jealous of the caress.

I can't imagine all men love their women the way I love Anne. If they did, the streets would be empty, and the fields would grow fallow. Industry would rumble to a halt and markets would tumble as men bowed at the feet of their wives, unable to need or notice anything but her. If all men loved their wives the way I love Anne, we would be a useless lot. Or maybe the world would know peace. Maybe the wars would end, and the strife would cease as we centred our lives on loving and being loved.

Our marriage is only hours old, and our courtship is not much older than that. I know the novelty will wear off, and life will intrude before long. But it is not the newness of her, the newness of us, that has captured me. It is the opposite. It is as if we always were and always will be, as though our love and our lives sprang from the same source and will return to that source in the end, intertwined and indistinguishable. We are ancient. Prehistoric and predestined.

I laugh at myself and my romantic musings, grateful no one will read these words. I am a man besotted, looking at his slumbering wife, who is soft and naked and well loved, and it's made me silly and sentimental. I reach out and stroke her skin, drawing a finger down the slope of her arm from her shoulder to the top of her hand. Goose bumps rise, but she doesn't stir, and I watch, mesmerized, as her skin becomes smooth once more, my touch forgotten. I've left a smudge in the crook of her arm. There is ink on my fingers. I like the way it looks, my thumbprint on her skin. If I were a better artist, I would paint her in thumbprints, leaving my mark in all my favourite places, a testament to my devotion.

She opens her eyes and smiles at me, heavy lidded and pink lipped, and I am panting and pathetic all over again. Useless. But completely convinced.

No one has ever loved the way I love Anne.

"Come to bed, Thomas," she whispers, and I no longer want to write or paint or even wash my hands.

T. S.

21

PARTING

Dear, I must be gone
While night shuts the eyes
Of the household spies;
That song announces dawn.

—*W. B. Yeats*

The Treaty debates in the Dáil resumed in early January, and Thomas and I planned to travel to Dublin to attend the public sessions. I wanted to bring Brigid and Eoin with us, but Brigid urged us to go alone.

"It might be the only honeymoon you get," she pressed. "And Eoin and I will be fine here with the O'Tooles."

I'd begged him not to tell her that Liam had shot me—the details were too complicated, and making that accusation would require us to explain my presence on the lough, something I couldn't do. The relationship was already so fraught with tension and turmoil, I couldn't see how telling her would help matters.

"Do you trust her to protect you from them?" he'd asked, incredulous.

"I trust her to keep Eoin safe," I argued. "That is my only concern."

"That is your only concern?" Thomas cried, his volume rising with every word. "Well, it isn't mine! Good God, Anne. Liam tried to kill you. For all I know, Ben tried to kill you too. I'm bloody relieved that poor Martin Carrigan and the unfortunate Brody are dead because now I only have the feckin' Gallagher brothers to worry about."

Thomas never yelled, and his vehemence surprised me. When I stared at him, dumbstruck, he gripped my shoulders, pressed his forehead to mine, and groaned my name.

"Anne, you have to listen to me. I know you care about Brigid, but you feel a loyalty to her that she does not return. Her loyalty is to her sons, and I don't trust her where they are concerned."

"So what do we do?" I asked.

"She has to know that I will no longer allow them anywhere near you or Eoin."

"She will blame me," I mourned. "She will think she has to choose between us."

"She does have to choose, Countess. Ben and Liam have always been trouble. Declan was the youngest, but of the three, he had the best head on his shoulders and the biggest heart in his chest."

"Did Declan ever strike Anne?" I asked softly.

Thomas reared back in surprise. "Why do you ask?"

"Brigid told me that she understood why I—why Anne—left when she had the chance. She insinuated that Declan wasn't always gentle, that he and his brothers had inherited their father's temper."

Thomas gaped at me. "Declan never raised his hand to Anne. She would have hit him right back. She slapped his brothers around enough. I know Liam bloodied her lip once, but that was after she'd hit him over the head with a shovel, and he went in swinging, trying to take it away."

"So why would Brigid think Declan was violent?"

"Declan was always covering for Ben and Liam. I know he took the blame, more than once, for things they'd done. He paid their debts, smoothed things over when they got into trouble, and helped them find work."

"And you think Brigid will try to cover for them now." I sighed.

"I know she will."

And with that belief, Thomas sat Brigid down soon after we were married and questioned her on the whereabouts and the activities of her sons. When she'd been reticent to speak about them at all, he told her, in no uncertain terms, that Liam and Ben were not welcome at Garvagh Glebe any longer.

"You are in this fight up to your eyebrows, Dr. Smith. You have been for years. You are not innocent. You are no better than my boys. I hold my tongue. I keep your secrets, what little I know. And it's precious little! Nobody tells me anything." Her chin began to tremble, and she looked at me, her eyes filled with questions and accusations. Thomas regarded her soberly, his face devoid of emotion.

"I'm afraid Liam and Ben will hurt Anne," Thomas said, his voice low, his eyes holding hers. "Do I have reason to be afraid?"

She began to shake her head, to babble something incoherent.

"Brigid?" he interrupted, and she fell silent immediately, her back stiffening, her expression growing stony.

"They don't trust her," Brigid bit out.

"I don't care," he snarled, and for a moment, I saw the Thomas Smith who had carried Declan on his back through the streets of Dublin, who had infiltrated the Castle and the prisons for Michael Collins, who faced death daily with flat eyes and steady hands. He was a little frightening.

Brigid saw him too. She blanched and looked away, her hands clasped in her lap.

"I'm afraid Liam and Ben will harm Anne," he repeated. "I can't allow that."

Brigid's chin fell to her chest.

"I will tell them to stay away," she whispered.

Thomas held my hand tightly in his as we maneuvered through the crowd and into the packed chamber of the Mansion House. Michael had assured us there would be seats reserved for us, and we slid between nervous congregants, who were smoking and shifting and making the room smell like ashtrays and armpits. I pressed my face into Thomas's shoulder, into his clean solidity, and prayed for Ireland, though I already knew how she would fare.

Thomas was greeted and hailed, and even Countess Markievicz, her beauty faded by the ravages of imprisonment and revolution, extended her hand to him with a slight smile.

"Countess Markievicz, may I introduce my wife, Anne Smith. She shares your passion for trousers," Thomas murmured, tipping his hat. She laughed, her hand covering her mouth and her broken and missing teeth. Vanity was not easily relinquished, even among those who eschewed it.

"But does she share my passion for Ireland?" she asked, her brows quirked beneath her black hat.

"I doubt one passion is identical to another. After all, she married me," Thomas whispered, conspiratorial.

She laughed again, charmed, and turned away to greet someone else, releasing me from her thrall.

"Breathe, Anne," Thomas murmured, and I did my best to comply as we found our seats and the session was called to order. Before it was all said and done, Constance Markievicz would call Michael Collins a coward and an oath-breaker, and my loyalty was firmly with him. But I couldn't help but be a little awestruck by her presence.

I'd often wondered, absorbed in piles of research, if the magic of history would be lost if we could go back and live it. Did we varnish the past and make heroes of average men and imagine beauty and valor where there was only dirge and desperation? Or like the old man looking back on his youth, remembering only the things he'd seen, did the angle of our gaze sometimes cause us to miss the bigger picture? I didn't think time offered clarity so much as time stripped away the emotion that colored memories. The Irish Civil War had happened eighty years before I'd traveled to Ireland. Not so far that the people had forgotten it, but enough time had passed that more—or maybe less—cynical eyes could pull the details apart and look at them for what they were.

But sitting in the crowded session, seeing men and women who had lived only in pictures and in print, hearing their voices raised in argument, in protest, in passion, I was the furthest thing from objective and detached; I was overcome. Eamon de Valera, the president of Dáil, towered over everyone else. Hook-nosed, thin-faced, and dark, he clothed his height and his spare frame with unrelenting black. Born in America, he was the son of an Irish mother and a Spanish father and had been sadly neglected and abandoned by both. Above all else, Eamon de Valera was a survivor. His American citizenship had saved him from execution after the Rising, and when Michael Collins, Arthur Griffith, and a dozen others fell under the swath of civil war, Eamon de Valera would still be standing. There was greatness in him, and I was not immune. His political longevity and personal tenacity would be his legacy in Ireland.

He spoke more than everyone else combined, interrupting and interjecting, shifting and sidestepping every idea but his own. He'd introduced a new document he'd drafted during the break, an amendment that wasn't much different from the Treaty, and insisted on its adoption. When it was rejected on the grounds that it was not the document that had been debated in private session, he threatened to resign as president, further muddying the question at hand. I knew my feelings about him were colored by my research, but I had to remind myself that he had not known how it would all play out. I had the advantage of hindsight, where history had already unfolded and pointed the finger of blame. The committee clearly held him in high regard; their respect was evident in their deference and in their attempts to appease him. But where de Valera was venerated, Michael Collins was loved.

Whenever Michael spoke, the people strained to hear, barely breathing so they wouldn't miss it. It was as though our heartbeats synchronized, an inaudible drumbeat reverberating through the assembly, and it was like nothing I'd ever felt before. I'd read about some of Michael's speeches, and

I'd even seen a picture a photographer had snagged from a window above the crowd assembled to hear him speak in College Green in the spring of 1922. The picture had shown a small stage surrounded by a sea of hats, giving the appearance of pale, bobbing balls, every head covered, nothing else visible. The numbers were fewer in the chamber, but the effect was the same; his energy and conviction commanded attention.

The public debates droned on. Arthur Griffith, gray-faced and ailing—he reminded me of a slimmer Theodore Roosevelt with his handlebar mustache and circular glasses—was the most adept at holding de Valera accountable, and when he came to Michael's defense after a particularly nasty attack by Cathal Brugha, the minister for defense, the entire room erupted in applause that didn't end for several minutes.

I'd been wrong about one thing. These were not average men and women. Time had not given them a gloss they had not earned. Even those I wanted to loathe, based on my own research and conclusions, conducted themselves with fervor and honest conviction. These weren't posing politicians. They were patriots whose blood and sacrifice deserved history's pardon and Ireland's compassion.

"History really doesn't do them justice. It doesn't do any of you justice," I murmured to Thomas, who regarded me with ancient eyes.

"Will we make Ireland better? In the end, will we have accomplished that?" he asked quietly.

I didn't think Ireland would ever improve upon the likes of Arthur Griffith, Michael Collins, and Thomas Smith. She would never know better men, but she would know better days. "You will make her freer."

"That's enough for me," he whispered.

In the last hour of the final day of debates, Michael Collins closed the proceedings and asked the Dáil for a vote to accept the Treaty or to reject it.

De Valera, though he'd already had his time on the floor, sought the last word, warning the Dáil that the Treaty would "rise up in judgment against them." His attempt at a final oratorical flourish was cut off.

"Let the Irish nation judge us now and in future years," Michael said, silencing him, and I felt the pangs of doubt and the weight of a nation pressing on every person in attendance. One by one, the elected representatives from every constituency cast their votes. The result was sixty-four in favor of the Treaty, fifty-seven against.

Like distant thunder, a cheer rose up in the streets when the result was announced, but within the chamber there was no gloating or gleeful celebration. The collective heartbeat stuttered and slowed, and one by one, became a cacophony of disparate rhythms.

"I wish to resign immediately," de Valera intoned amid the emotional chaos.

Michael rose and, with his hands planted on the table in front of him, begged the room for calm. "In every transition from war to peace or peace to war, there is chaos and confusion. Please, let us make a plan, form a committee here and now to preserve order in the government and in the country. We must hold ourselves together. We must be unified," he urged, and for a moment there was a hopeful pause, an indrawn breath, a possibility to defy destiny.

"This is a betrayal," a voice cried out from the gallery, and all heads swiveled to the slight female in the front row who stood, hands clenched and mouth quivering, before the assembly. She was a suffering specter of Ireland's not-so-distant past.

"Mary MacSwiney," I whispered, close to tears. Terence MacSwiney, Mary's brother, was the Cork mayor who had gone on a hunger strike and died in a British prison. Mary's words would smash all hope of a united front.

"My brother died for Ireland. He starved himself to death to call attention to the oppression of his countrymen. There can be no union between those who have sold their souls for the fleshpots of the Empire and those of us who won't rest until Ireland is a republic."

Collins tried again amid the calls of support and cries for revolt. "Please don't do this," he begged.

De Valera interrupted him, raising his voice like a southern preacher. "My last words as your president are these. We have had a glorious run. I call on all of you who support Mary in her sentiments to meet with me tomorrow to discuss how we will go forward. We cannot turn away from the fight now. The world is watching." His voice broke, and he could not continue. The room dissolved into weeping. Men. Women. Former friends and new foes. And war returned to Ireland.

I awoke to voices and shadows and lay listening, drowsy and drifting, alone in Thomas's Dublin bed. We'd left the Mansion House in the swell of reveling crowds; the mood in the chamber was not reflected on the streets, and the people were ebullient, rejoicing in the birth of the Free State. A few of Mick's men had embraced Thomas as we exited the chamber, visibly relieved that the vote had gone in favor of the Treaty, but the tension in their faces and the strain in their smiles indicated an acute awareness of the trouble to come.

We hadn't seen Michael after the session adjourned. He was swallowed up in another round of meetings, this time to cobble together a plan to proceed without half the Dáil. But obviously, Michael had found Thomas. I recognized the burr of his brogue rising up through the vents even though I couldn't hear what he was saying. Thomas, his voice soft and low when he spoke at all, was clearly soothing his friend. I waited to see if I would be summoned to look into my crystal ball but heard the front door close and a hush descend on the house once more. I slid out of bed, pulled my robe around my naked body, and padded down the stairs to the warm kitchen and my brooding husband. He *would* be brooding, I had no doubt.

He sat at the kitchen table, knees splayed, head bowed, coffee cradled in his hands. I poured myself a cup, doused it with milk and sugar until it was the color of caramel, and drank deeply before I parked myself on the table in front of him. He reached out and wrapped one of my long curls around his finger before letting his hand fall back in his lap.

"Was that Michael?" I asked.

"Yes."

"Is he okay?"

Thomas sighed. "He's going to kill himself trying to give the people what they want while trying to appease the few who want the opposite."

It was exactly what he would do. For the final months of his life, Michael Collins would be a man slowly being drawn and quartered. My stomach twisted, and my chest burned. I steeled myself against it. I would not think about that now. Not now.

"Have you slept at all, Thomas? Has he?" I asked.

"You wore me out last night, lass. I slept hard for a few hours," he murmured, touching a finger to my lips, a touch meant to remind me of our kisses, but he pulled away again, as if he felt guilty about the peace and pleasure I had given him. "But I doubt Michael has slept," he finished quietly. "I heard him rooting around in the kitchen at three a.m."

"It's almost dawn. Where is he going?"

"Mass. Confession. Communion. He goes to Mass more than any murderous traitor I know," he whispered. "It comforts him. Clears his head. They mock him for that too. It's an Irish trait. We refuse a man communion while berating him for his sins. Some say he's too pious; others say he's a hypocrite for even setting foot in a church."

"And what do you say?" I asked.

"If men were perfect, we wouldn't need to be saved."

I smiled sadly, but he didn't smile back.

I took the cup from his hands, set it aside, and climbed onto his lap, my hands splayed lightly on his shoulders. He didn't wrap his hands around my hips and pull me into his body. He didn't bury his face in my neck or lift his face for my kiss. His despondence filled the space between us and tightened the muscles of his thighs, which were bracketed between my knees. I began to unbutton his shirt. One button.

Two. Three. I paused to press a kiss to the exposed skin at his throat. He smelled of coffee and the rosemary-scented soap Mrs. O'Toole made.

He smelled of me.

Heat coiled in my belly, crowding out my fear, and I rubbed my cheek against his, back and forth, nuzzling him, my hands continuing their work. He would need to shave again soon. His jaw had grown rough, and his eyes were bruised as he watched me remove his shirt. When I urged his arms over his head to pull his undershirt free, he wrapped one hand around my jaw, drawing my mouth within a breadth of his.

"Are you trying to save *me*, Anne?"

"Always."

He shuddered, letting me kiss the corners of his mouth before I touched my tongue to the crease between his lips. His chest was warm and firm beneath my hands, and I felt the quickening of his heart, the parting of the darkness from the dawn, as he closed his eyes and opened his mouth against mine.

For a moment we communed in caresses, in kisses that deepened and drew us out of ourselves only to softly set us down again. We rose and fell into each other, mouths sated and slow, lips languorous and lush, tongues tangling only to unravel and reunite.

Then his hands were sliding up my calves beneath the blue robe cinched at my waist, gripping the length of my thighs and kneading the flesh of my bottom. His palms skimmed, frantic, over my ribs and across my breasts only to circle back, cupping and cradling, worshipful but insistent. He slid, taking me with him, abandoning the chair for the floor, forsaking misery for commiseration. His mouth made the journey of his hands, parting my robe and pushing it aside until I was naked beneath him, breathing love into his skin and life into his body and being saved in return.

17 January 1922

On 14 January, the Dáil met again, its numbers almost halved by the exit of de Valera and all those who refused to recognize the vote. Arthur Griffith had been voted president of the Dáil upon de Valera's resignation, and Mick was appointed as the chairman of the new provisional government organized under the terms of the Treaty.

Anne and I had not remained in Dublin after the final debate and the vote that shattered the Dáil. We were anxious to escape Dublin, to return to Eoin and the peace of Dromahair, relative as it was. But we returned, Eoin in tow, to watch as Dublin Castle, the symbol of British dominion in Ireland, was handed over to the provisional government.

Mick was late for the official ceremony. He rolled up in an open-top government car, his old Volunteer uniform pressed, his boots gleaming. The people roared their approval, and Eoin waved madly from where he was perched on my shoulders, calling out, "Mick, Mick!" as though he and Michael were old friends. I was so moved that I couldn't speak, and Anne cried openly beside me.

Mick later told me that Lord FitzAlan, the viceroy who had replaced Lord French, sniffed and said, "You are seven minutes late, Mr. Collins," to which Mick responded, "We've been waiting seven hundred years, Governor. You can wait seven minutes."

On Tuesday, we watched as the Civic Guard, Ireland's newly formed police force, marched towards Dublin Castle in their dark uniforms and emblemed caps to assume their new duties. Mick says they are the first recruits, but there will be more. Half the country is out of work, and applications are pouring in.

Whatever the people have said about Mick or about the Treaty, watching the peaceful transfer of power was a moment I will never forget. In every home, on the streets, and in the papers, Dubliners are marveling that this day has come. And the effects of the Treaty are not just evident in the city. Everywhere in Ireland, at all but three of the port garrisons, British troops are preparing to leave. The Auxiliaries and the Black and Tans are already gone.

T. S.

22

CONSOLATION

How could passion run so deep
Had I never thought
That the crime of being born
Blackens all our lot?
But where the crime's committed
The crime can be forgot.

—*W. B. Yeats*

The hope and symbolism of a departing British military at the end of January was overshadowed and forgotten in the months that followed. Just like the Irish and the British had done during the lull of the Anglo-Irish truce, the two opposing Irish factions—pro-Treaty and anti-Treaty—began frantically shoring up their walls and marshalling support while trying to advance their positions to the public at large. The Irish Republican Army was split down the middle, half joining Michael Collins and the Free State supporters, half refusing to compromise and assembling under the banner of republicans, meaning those who wouldn't settle for anything less than a republic.

De Valera had been actively campaigning for anti-Treaty support, pulling in huge crowds filled with citizens sorely disappointed with the Free State solution. So many had suffered terribly at the hands of the British and were unwilling to compromise with an unreliable adversary. The British were notorious in Ireland for breaking the Treaty of Limerick of 1691, and many who supported de Valera believed the British would break the Irish Free State (Agreement) Act as well.

Michael Collins began a campaign of his own, traveling from county to county, drawing thousands anxious to stave off conflict and more war. Thomas started traveling long distances to see him, to succor him, and to gauge the pulse of the public at large. In Leitrim and Sligo, like in every county in Ireland, sides were being taken and lines were being drawn. The tension in the streets once due to the Auxies and the Tans was redirected; hostility between neighbors and distrust between friends was the new strife. Eoin's nightmares increased; Brigid's nerves were stretched thin, divided by her loyalty to Thomas and her love for her sons. When Thomas traveled with Michael, I remained at Garvagh Glebe, afraid to leave them behind.

As February rolled into March and March into April, the crack in Ireland's leadership became a chasm in the country from which chaos climbed. Hell nipped at her heels. Raids on banks and outposts were the order of the day as the guns and money needed to overthrow the new government became paramount. The newspapers were ransacked or overrun, and the propaganda machine began in earnest. Anti-Treaty brigades of the IRA—brigades that behaved more like conquering warlords—began invading entire towns. In Limerick, where command of the city meant control of the River Shannon bridges and dominance over the west and the south, both pro- and anti-Treaty forces were burrowed in. The anti-Treaty IRA commandeered barracks newly evacuated by British troops, set up their headquarters in hotels, and occupied government buildings. It would take force to dislodge them, and no one wanted to use force.

On April 13, Michael spoke to a thousand people in Sligo at a pro-Treaty rally only to be rushed off the stage as fighting broke out in the crowd and shots rang out from a window overlooking the square. He was shoved into the back of an armored car, Thomas on his heels, and whisked away to Garvagh Glebe while order was restored. He spent the night in Dromahair, two dozen Free State soldiers surrounding the house to protect him while he planned his next move. We sat at the dining room table, the remnants of dinner all around us. Brigid was in her room, and Eoin was playing marbles in the adjoining parlor with Fergus, who showed him no mercy but a good deal of patience.

"A British ship off the coast of Cork was seized by anti-Treaty forces. The ship was filled with arms. Thousands of guns are now in the hands of the men who want to destabilize the Free State. What in the hell was a ship full of arms doing off the coast of Cork? The British are behind this," Michael said, rising to his feet to circle the table, his belly full, his nerves taut.

"The British?" Thomas asked, surprised. "Why?"

Thomas stopped in front of the window, peering out into the darkness, only to have Fergus call out, demanding he move.

"If I can't pull this off, Thomas, if Ireland can't pull this off, the British will say they have no choice but to return to restore order. The agreement will be void. And Ireland will slide right back into British hands. So they quietly pull our strings behind the scenes. I sent Churchill a cable, accusing him of collusion. It may not be him. Or Lloyd George. But there is collusion. I have no doubt."

"What did Churchill say?" Thomas gasped.

"He denied it outright. And he asked if there is anyone in Ireland willing to fight for the Free State."

Silence fell over the room. Michael returned to his chair and sat, his elbows on his knees and his head in his hands. Thomas gazed at me, his eyes tragic, his throat working.

"I fought the British, Tommy," Michael said. "I killed and ambushed and outmaneuvered. I was the Minister of Mayhem. But I don't have the bloody stomach for this. I don't want to fight my own countrymen. I keep trying to make deals with the devil—and now the devil has too many faces. I'm capitulating there, making promises over here, trying to keep it all from falling apart, and it's not working."

"Fighting for the Free State means killing for the Free State," Thomas said, his countenance grave. "There are good men on every side of this. And good women. Emotions are high. Tempers are hot. But underneath it all, no one wants to fire on their own. So we scramble and plot and dig in and argue, but we don't want to kill each other."

"It's a helluva lot easier to kill when you hate the people you're shooting at," Michael admitted heavily. "But even Arthur Griffith, the man who is all about peaceful resistance, says force is inevitable."

Arthur Griffith was scheduled to speak on Sunday at the Sligo Town Hall with other pro-Treaty politicians. Considering what had just happened during his own speech, Michael had already arranged for Free State troops to be sent in to keep the peace and allow Sunday's meeting to take place. The provisional government had passed a law with Royal Assent that stated that a general election would be held before June 30. Both pro- and anti-Treaty supporters were scrambling to connect with—or intimidate—voters.

We were interrupted by Robbie, who was hovering at the dining room door, his boots muddy, his hat in his hands, and his coat misted with rain.

"Doc, apparently one of the boys caught some shrapnel during the shooting in Sligo. He bandaged himself up and didn't say anything, but now he's sick. I thought you might take a look."

"Bring him around to the clinic, Robbie," Thomas ordered, throwing his napkin on the table and rising.

"And tell the lad that it's the height of stupidity to ignore a wound when there's a doctor on the premises," Michael groused, shaking his head wearily.

"Already did, Mr. Collins," Robbie answered. He saluted Michael, nodded at me, and followed Thomas from the room.

"I wanna watch, Doc!" Eoin cried, abandoning Fergus and the marbles for a front-row seat in the surgery. Thomas didn't refuse him, and Fergus took the opportunity to make his rounds.

Michael and I were left alone, and I stood and began stacking plates, needing something to occupy my head and my hands. Michael sighed wearily, but he didn't rise.

"I've brought chaos into your home. Again. It follows me wherever I go," he said wearily.

"There will never be a day when you are not welcome at Garvagh Glebe," I answered. "We are honored to have you here."

"Thank you, Annie," he whispered. "I don't deserve your good will. I know that. Because of me, Thomas is rarely home. Because of me, he's dodging bullets and putting out fires he didn't start."

"Thomas loves you," I said. "He believes in you. We both do."

I felt his eyes on my face and met his gaze, unflinching.

"I'm not wrong about much, lass, but I was wrong about you," he murmured. "Tommy has a timeless soul. Timeless souls need soulmates. I'm glad he found his."

My heart quaked, and my eyes filled. I stopped my mindless stacking and pressed a hand to my waist, clinging to my composure. Guilt rose in my chest. Guilt and indecision mixed with dread and despair. Every day, I struggled between my responsibility to warn and my desire to shield, and every day I tried to deny the things I knew.

"I have to tell you something, Michael. I need you to listen to me, and I need you to believe me, if not for your sake, then for Thomas's," I said, the words like ash in my throat, like Eoin's remains on the lake, billowing around me. But Michael was already shaking his head, refusing me, as if he knew where such words would lead.

"Do you know that the day I was born," he said, "my mother worked up to the very moment of delivery? My sister Mary saw that she was in pain, that there was something happening, but my mother never complained or rested. There was work that needed to be done. And she kept moving." His eyes never left my face.

"I was her eighth child, the youngest, and she delivered me during the night, all by herself. My sister told me she was up again almost immediately, not missing a step. My mother worked like that until the day she died. She was an unstoppable force. She loved her country. Loved her family."

Michael took a deep breath. Clearly speaking of her still hurt him. I understood. I couldn't think of my grandfather without pain. "She died when I was sixteen, and I was heartbroken. But now? Now I'm grateful she's gone. I wouldn't want her to worry about me. I wouldn't want her to have to choose sides, and I wouldn't want her to outlive me."

My heart roared in my ears, and I had to look away. I knew that what happened here, in this room, had essentially already happened. My presence was not a variation of history but part of it. The pictures had proven that. My grandfather himself was a witness to the fact. Anything I said or didn't say was already part of the fabric of events; I believed that.

But I knew how Michael Collins died.

I knew where it occurred.

I knew when.

It was something I'd kept from Thomas, and something he'd never asked. Knowing would only make life unbearable for him, and I kept the knowledge close. But guarding the secret made me feel like a coconspirator. It gnawed in my belly and haunted my dreams. I didn't know who was responsible, and I couldn't protect Michael Collins from a faceless foe—his killer had never been named—but I could warn him. I had to.

"Don't tell me, Annie," Michael ordered, divining my internal struggle. "When it comes, it will come. I know it. I feel it. I've heard the banshee crying in my dreams. Death has been dogging my footsteps for a long time. I'd rather not know when the bitch will overtake me."

"Ireland needs you," I implored.

"Ireland needed James Connolly and Tom Clarke. She needed Seán Mac Diarmada and Declan Gallagher. We all have our part to play and our burdens to carry. When I'm gone, there will be others."

I could only shake my head. There would be others. But never again would there be another Michael Collins. Men like Collins, men like Thomas, and men like my grandfather were irreplaceable.

"It weighs on you, doesn't it? Knowing things ye can't prevent?" he murmured.

I nodded, unable to hold back the tears. He must have seen the desperation on my face, the confession on the tip of my tongue. I wanted so badly to tell him, to unburden myself. He stood abruptly and approached me, shaking his head, his finger raised in warning. He pressed it to my lips and leaned into me, holding my gaze.

"Not a word, lass," he shushed. "Not a word. Let the fates unravel as they must. Do this for me, please. I don't want to live counting the days I have left."

I nodded, and he straightened, tentatively removing his finger as though he feared I wouldn't hold my tongue. For a moment we studied each other, arguing silently, wills warring and walls rising, before we both exhaled, having reached an agreement. I brushed at the tears on my cheeks, oddly absolved.

"You have a look about you, Anne. Does Tommy know?" Michael asked softly, the tumult clearing from his expression. I stepped back in surprise.

"W-what?" I stammered. I wasn't even sure myself.

He smiled broadly. "Ah, I thought so. I'll keep your secret if you keep mine. Deal?"

"I don't know what you're talking about!" I huffed, still reeling.

"That's the spirit. Deny. Deflect. Refute," he whispered conspiratorially, and he winked. "It's always worked for me."

He turned to leave the room, but not before he snatched another slice of turkey and a hunk of bread from the basket, his appetite plainly restored by his teasing.

"I'm guessin' Tommy already knows, though. He doesn't miss much. Plus, it's written all over your face. You have roses in your cheeks and a sparkle in your eye. Congratulations, lass. I couldn't be happier if it were mine," he teased, winking again.

Michael Collins will go to Cork on August 22, 1922. Those closest to him will beg him to reconsider, to remain in Dublin, but he won't listen. He will die in an ambush in a little valley they call Béal na mBláth—the mouth of flowers.

I wrote of what was to come, every detail, every theory I could remember about Michael's death: 8.22.22; 8.22.22. The date had become a pulse in my head, the title of a terrible story, and once a story consumed me, I had to write it down. It was my compromise with Michael Collins. I would stay silent as the day approached, just as he'd asked me to do. I would keep the words in my mouth, bitter and brackish. But I would not, could not, be quiet in the end. When the day came, I would tell Thomas. I would tell Joe. I would lock Michael Collins in a room, tie him up, and put a gun to his head to keep him from his fate. These pages would be my insurance, my backup plan. Even if something happened to me, they would speak for me, and Michael's story would have a new ending.

I wrote until my hand cramped, unaccustomed to composing without keys beneath my fingers. It had been a long time since I'd done any serious writing freehand. My penmanship was atrocious, but the action soothed me like nothing else could.

When I'd written all I could remember, I folded the sheets into an envelope, sealed it shut, and slid it into my dresser drawer.

On April 14 in Dublin, the Four Courts building on the quay side of the River Liffey was taken by anti-Treaty forces and declared the new republican headquarters. Several buildings along O'Connell Street as well as Kilmainham Gaol were also occupied. Raids were being made on Free State stores and munitions, the goods stockpiled in the occupied buildings. It was the beginning of the protracted end.

"Ya could'na given me some warning about this, eh Annie?" Michael complained, and Thomas shot him a look of such censure that Michael wilted and ran his hands through his hair.

"I'm sorry, lass. I forget myself sometimes, don't I?"

Michael left Garvagh Glebe in a rush, his convoy, including the shrapnel-wounded soldier, trailing behind. Thomas debated remaining at home but at the last moment packed a bag and prepared to follow, worried that a battle over the Four Courts might ensue, and his skills would be needed.

Eoin sulked, sad to see the excitement end and our visitors leave. He begged Thomas to take him along, to take us both along, but Thomas refused, promising he'd be home in a few days. The occupation of the Four Courts was an escalation between the two sides that promised bloodshed, and I couldn't remember enough of the particulars to reassure him. I simply knew a battle would break out. The Four Courts building would sustain an explosion caused by the stolen munition stores, and men would die. Good men. I just couldn't remember the timeline or the technicalities.

"Michael's right, you know," I said to Thomas as he gathered his things. "I've been preoccupied. Some dates are like constant lights in my head. Some details won't leave me alone. But there are other things, other events, that I should remember and don't. I'll do better," I mumbled.

"Mick lashes out at those he loves. Consider it a sign of trust and affection." Thomas sighed.

"Is that why you looked at him as though you wanted to box his ears?"

"I don't care how much he loves you or trusts you, he will mind his manners."

"So fierce, Dr. Smith."

He smiled and closed his suitcase before approaching me slowly, his hands in his pockets, his head tilted in inquiry.

"Is there anything else you've forgotten to tell me, Countess?" he murmured, drawing so close my breasts touched his chest. They were swollen and tight, and I moaned a little, wanting to embrace him and protect them at the same time. His lips skimmed my hair, and he pulled his hands from his pockets and ran them up my sides until his thumbs brushed the tender tips.

"You're sore. You're beautiful. And you haven't bled since January," he murmured, stroking me so gently the ache became longing.

"I've never been very regular," I hedged, my heart pounding. "And I've never been pregnant, so I don't know for sure."

"I do," he said, tilting my face to his. For a moment he simply kissed me, careful and adoring, as though my mouth held his child and not my womb.

"I'm so happy," he confessed against my lips. "Is it wrong to be this happy when the world is so upside down?"

"My grandfather told me once that happiness is an expression of gratitude. And it's never wrong to be grateful."

"I wonder where he learned that?" he murmured, his eyes shining and so blue I could only stare, lost in him.

"Eoin wished for a whole family," I said, suddenly pensive. "I don't know how any of this is going to work. I get scared when I try to make sense of it, when I think about it for too long, or when I try to unravel it all in my head."

He was quiet for a moment, considering, his eyes never leaving mine. "What did your grandfather tell you about faith?" he asked.

The answer came like a whisper, fluttering past my heart, and I was back in my grandfather's arms on a stormy night in a world so far away and long ago, it hardly seemed real.

"He told me everything would be okay because the wind already knows," I whispered.

"Then that's your answer, love."

16 April 1922

*I've a head full of thoughts and little room to write them.
This journal is full, and I have so much more to say and
too much time till dawn. Anne bought me a new journal
for my birthday, but it waits to be filled on my bedside
table back at home.*

*I awoke in a cold sweat, alone in my bed. I hate
Dublin without Anne. I hate Cork without Anne, Kerry
without Anne, Galway without Anne, Wexford without
Anne. I've discovered I'm not especially happy anywhere
without Anne.*

*It was the rain that woke me. Dublin is caught in
a deluge. It's as though God is trying to douse the flames
of our discontent. If there is to be a battle for the Four
Courts, it won't be right away. Mick says they will do
their best to avoid it. I fear that his reluctance to engage
the anti-Treaty wing will only embolden them. But he
doesn't need to know what I think. I wish I'd stayed at
Garvagh Glebe. I would head back now, but the rain
is insistent, the roads will be mud, and I'm better off to
wait it out.*

*The sound of rushing water infiltrated my sleep,
making me dream of the lough. I was pulling Anne from
the water all over again. Like most dreams, it turned*

strange and disjointed, and Anne was suddenly gone, leaving me wet, my arms empty, her blood staining the bottom of my boat. Then I was crying and screaming, and my screaming became a wail. The wail came from an infant in my arms that was swaddled in Anne's bloody blouse. The infant morphed into Eoin, clinging to me, cold and terrified, and I held him, singing to him the way I sometimes do.

"They can't forget, they never will, the wind and waves remember Him still."

Now I can't get that song out of my head. Bloody rain. Fecking lough. I never thought I'd hate the lough, but I do. Tonight, I do. And I hate Dublin without Anne.

"Don't go near the water, love," I always whisper when we part. And Anne nods, her eyes knowing. This time I forgot to remind her. My head was filled with other things. With her. With thoughts of a child. Our child, growing inside her.

I wish the rain would stop. I need to go home.

T. S.

I pulled you from the water
And kept you in my bed
A lost, forsaken daughter
Of a past that isn't dead.

Somehow love from sweet obsession
Branched and broke a heart of stone
Distrust became confession
Solemn vows of blood and bone.

But in the wind, I hear the strain,
Pilgrim soul that time has found,
It moans to whisk you back again
Bid me follow, sweetly drown.

Don't go near the water, love.
Stay away from strand or sea.
You cannot walk on water, love;
The lough will take you far from me.

23

TILL TIME CATCH

Dear shadows, now you know it all,
All the folly of a fight
With a common wrong or right.
The innocent and the beautiful
Have no enemy but time;
Arise and bid me strike a match
And strike another till time catch.

—*W. B. Yeats*

I spent Sunday morning feeling peaked and tired, as though admitting my pregnancy to Thomas had freed me to act on my condition. Eoin woke with a chest cold, and I remained at home with him while Brigid and the O'Tooles attended Mass. The skies were overcast—a storm was brewing in the east—and Eoin and I climbed into Thomas's big bed and read all the Eoin adventures, one by one, leaving Michael Collins's tale for last. Eoin was very aware that he'd been appointed caretaker of Michael's book, and he hardly breathed as we read, turning the pages gingerly so we wouldn't crease or sully them with our use.

"We should write a story about us," he suggested as I closed the last page.

"You, me, and Thomas?"

"Yes," he murmured, yawning widely. He'd coughed through the night and clearly needed a nap. I pulled the blankets around his shoulders, and he snuggled down and closed his eyes.

"And what should we do? Where should we go?"

"I don't care. Just as long as we're together." His sweetness brought a lump to my throat.

"I love you, Eoin."

"I love you too," he mumbled.

I watched as he drifted off, overcome with the need to gather him up and hold him close, to press kisses all over his little face, to tell him how happy he made me. But he was already snoring softly, his breath slightly labored by his cold. I settled for kissing his freckled forehead and brushing my cheek over his crimson hair.

I slipped from the room, pulling the door closed behind me, and made my way down the stairs. Brigid and the O'Tooles were back from Mass, and a light lunch was being prepared. I needed to get dressed and fix my hair; Robbie wanted to go to Sligo to see Arthur Griffith at Town Hall. Thomas had ordered him to be my shadow while he was gone, sleeping at Garvagh Glebe at night and leaving any duties that took him too far from the house to his brothers. We hadn't seen or heard from Liam or Ben since Thomas had made his wishes known in December. It had been months without the slightest threat or incident, but Thomas had not relaxed his instructions. I knew Robbie wouldn't go to the election meeting if I didn't go with him. I wasn't in the mood for people or politics, but I wouldn't mind hearing Arthur Griffith speak again and hated for Robbie to miss the opportunity to hear a truly great man.

We lumbered down the lane a half hour later, promising Brigid we wouldn't be late. Eoin was still sleeping, the storm had kept its distance, and Brigid seemed content to spend the afternoon in front of the fire, knitting and listening to my gramophone.

Sligo's streets were filled with soldiers, and the tension in the air hummed in my chest as Robbie found a place on Quay Street to park the O'Tooles' farm truck. A lorry full of anti-Treaty forces rumbled past, armed and grim, letting their presence be known. If intimidation was the goal, they accomplished it. Robbie and I climbed out of the truck and made our way toward the cobbled courtyard that rimmed Town Hall. People scurried alongside us, doing their best to stay off the street, even as they collected outside the palazzo-style edifice, their eyes scanning the growing crowd for trouble. At least three dozen Free State troops had created a perimeter around the building in an effort to protect the proceedings. Another lorry filled with IRA men approached, and every head turned and watched them amble by. I caught a quick flash of a familiar face.

"Robbie, is that Liam?" I hissed, grabbing his arm. The man was in the front of the lorry, facing the other side of the road, his body obscured by other men, his hair covered by an ordinary peaked hat. The lorry continued down the street without either of us making a positive identification.

"I don't know, Mrs. Smith." Robbie hesitated. "I didn't see him. But maybe this wasn't a good idea."

"Robbie!" someone shouted, and we turned toward the rounded Romanesque entrance as the bell in the gabled tower began to toll the hour, a dismal clanging in the cloud-covered sky. As if the ringing woke the rain, the heavens rumbled, and fat drops began to soak the cobbles around us.

"There's Eamon Donnelly. He said he'd save us a spot," Robbie said, and we dashed to the limestone steps, our decision made.

The meeting went without incident. We'd missed some of the earlier speeches, but listened, captivated, to Arthur Griffith, who spoke without notes, his hands resting on his cane. He wasn't a flamethrower or a booming orator. He was measured and committed, urging the people to vote in favor of the Treaty and the candidates who supported it, not because it was perfect or solved all of Ireland's problems, but because it promised the best path forward.

He had received a rousing welcome and enjoyed a standing ovation when he was through. As the crowd roared and stomped, Robbie and I vacated our seats, stealing out of the meeting room ahead of the throng, hurrying down the wide staircase with the wrought-iron balustrade. The building was beautiful with its glazed cupolas and carved sandstone, and I wouldn't have minded a closer look, but Robbie was nervous and eager to go, and he wasted no time herding me back to the truck. He didn't relax until we reached Garvagh Glebe an hour later.

He dropped me off at the front of the house so I didn't have to walk from the barn, thanking me for accompanying him on the afternoon's excursion.

"I'll be out back for a bit," he reported. "I told Da I'd feed the animals before Mass. I didn't get it done, and he's not gonna be happy with me when he finds out I went to town instead. Hopefully, he'll never know."

I jumped out and waved him away.

The house was quiet. I walked through the foyer and into my room. I slept in Thomas's bed, but his wardrobe was too small for the two of us. I had kept my things in the room on the ground floor, retreating there when I wanted to write or have a minute to myself. We would have to reconfigure the living situation at some point, especially with a baby on the way. There were half a dozen empty rooms at Garvagh Glebe, plenty of space to arrange a marital suite and a nursery while still keeping Eoin close by.

I took off my hat and coat and hung them in the wardrobe before turning to my dresser for a sweater. The drawers were open. Clothing spilled out as though someone had riffled through each one, looking for something, and not bothered to cover their tracks. The narrow top drawer, where I kept my jewelry and the few odds and ends I'd acquired in my ten months at Garvagh Glebe, had been completely upended. I picked it up, unalarmed but confused, and began restoring order to my drawers.

"Eoin?" I called. Surely, he was awake by now. He and Brigid were somewhere in the house. He hadn't felt well enough to be outside, and he'd obviously been searching for something in my drawers. He was the only one who would leave such a mess behind.

I finished straightening my things and made an inventory of my jewelry and the small stack of gramophone discs, trying to figure out what he'd been looking for. I heard a soft tread outside my door and called out again, not looking up.

"Eoin? Did you go through my drawers?"

"It wasn't Eoin," Brigid said from the doorway, her voice odd. She clutched a sheaf of paper to her chest, her face stricken, her eyes wild.

"Brigid?"

"Who are you?" she moaned. "Why are you doing this to us?"

"What have I done, Brigid?" I asked, my blood beginning to thunder in my ears. I took a step toward her, and she took an immediate step back. Liam, a rifle in his arms, stepped around her. He pointed the gun at my chest, his gaze flat, his mouth grim.

"Brigid," I pled, my eyes riveted on the weapon. "What's going on?"

"Liam told me. From the first day. He told me you weren't our Anne, but I didn't want to believe him."

"I don't understand," I whispered, wrapping my arms around my waist. *Oh my God. What is happening?*

"Eoin was looking for something. I caught him in your room. I scolded him and began putting everything back in your drawers. The envelope was on the floor," Brigid explained, her words rapid, her voice hoarse.

"And you opened it?"

She nodded. "I opened it. And I read it. I know what you're planning. You have Thomas fooled. Michael Collins fooled. But you didn't fool Liam. He warned us! And to think Thomas trusted you. He married you. And you're plotting to kill Michael Collins. It's all written out." She held the pages out in front of her, her hands shaking so hard the paper danced.

"No. You've misunderstood," I said quietly, my voice and eyes level. "I only wanted to warn him."

"How do you know all of this?" she shrieked, shaking the papers again. "You've been working with the Tans. It's the only thing that makes sense."

"Brigid? Where's Eoin?" I whispered, not even bothering to defend myself or remind her that the Auxies and the Black and Tans were gone. She'd drawn the worst possible conclusion, and I didn't know if anything I said would help my case.

"I'm not telling you! You're not his mother, are you?"

I took a step toward her, hand outstretched, a plea for calm.

"I want you to leave," she said, raising her voice. "I need you to go. Walk out of this house and never come back. I'm going to show this to Thomas. He'll know what to do. But you have to leave."

Liam motioned toward the front door. "Go," he clipped. "Move."

I walked on wooden legs, leaving my room and moving into the foyer. Brigid stood with her back against the wall, the papers clutched in her hands. I ignored Liam, directing my pleas to his mother.

"Let's call the Dublin house. On the telephone. We'll call Thomas, and you can tell him everything. All of it, right now," I suggested.

"No! I want you to leave. I don't know what I'm going to tell Eoin. He thought his mother had come home." Brigid began to cry, her face crumpling like the pages she clutched in her fist. She dropped them to mop at her streaming eyes, and Liam stooped and picked them up, stuffing them into the waistband of his trousers.

"Is Eoin all right, Brigid? Is he safe?" I asked, my eyes clinging to the wide staircase that led to the second floor where I'd left Eoin a few hours earlier.

"What do you care?" she cried. "He's not your son. He's nothing to you."

"I just need to know if he's all right. I don't want him to hear you crying. I don't want him to see the gun."

"I would never hurt Eoin! I would never lie to him, never pretend to be something I'm not!" she shrieked. "I'm protecting him from you. Like I should have done the moment you arrived."

"All right. I'll go. I'll walk out of this house. Let me get my coat and my handbag—"

The outrage that bloomed in her eyes and cheeks was more frightening than her trembling and her tears.

"*Your* coat? *Your* handbag? Thomas bought those for you. He sheltered you. Cared for you. And you tricked him! You tricked that good, generous man," she raged.

"Go," Liam demanded, waving his rifle toward the door. I obeyed, abandoning every action except the one that got me out of the house uninjured. Liam followed me, the gun pointed at my back. I opened the door and walked down the front steps, Liam on my heels.

Brigid shut the door behind us. I heard the locks engage, the old-fashioned bolt sliding into place. My legs gave out beneath me, and I collapsed onto the grass in a quivering heap.

I didn't cry. I was too stunned. I simply knelt, head to my chest, hands in the damp grass, trying to formulate a plan.

"You're gonna wanna start walkin'," Liam demanded. I wondered if Brigid was watching from behind the curtains. I prayed Eoin wasn't. I rose slowly to my feet, my eyes on the gun Liam held with such ease. He had not hesitated to shoot me once, with two men looking on.

"Are you going to shoot me again?" I said, my voice loud and ringing. I hoped Robbie would hear and intervene. I felt a flash of shame and prayed Robbie would stay away. I didn't want him to die.

Liam's eyes narrowed, and he cocked his head, considering me, not lowering the rifle from the crook of his arm.

"I suppose I am. You just keep coming back. You have nine lives, Annie girl."

"Annie? You told Brigid I was someone else. Did you tell her you tried to kill me too?" I challenged.

Fear flickered across his face, and his hands tightened on the gun. "I didn't mean to shoot you. Not the first time. It was an accident."

I stared, not understanding, not believing, and even more afraid than I'd been before. What was he talking about? The first time? How many times had he tried to kill Anne Gallagher?

"And on the lough? Was that an accident?" I asked, desperate to understand.

He approached me, nervous, his gaze sharp. "I thought it was the fog playin' tricks on me. But you were real. Brody and Martin saw you too. And we got the hell outta there."

"I would have died," I said. "If Thomas hadn't found me, I would have died."

"You're already dead!" he shouted, his temper flaring suddenly, and I flinched and stumbled back.

"Now I need you to walk down along the trees there," he ordered. His hand shook as he pointed toward the trees, and I realized he was frightened too. "I heard one of my boys is buried in the bog. That's where we're heading, by way of the lough."

I wasn't going anywhere with him. Not to the bog. Not to the lough. I didn't move. In a flash he was on me, one hand fisted in my hair, a barrel in my belly.

"Turn and walk," he hissed, pressing his mouth to my ear. "Or I'll shoot you right here, right now."

"Why are you doing this?"

"Move."

I began to walk, helpless to do anything else. His hand was so tight in my hair that my chin was forced upward. I couldn't see where I was placing my feet and stumbled repeatedly as he pushed me toward the trees.

"I saw you in Sligo today with one-eyed Robbie. I figured Tommy was out of town if Robbie was with you. So I thought I'd pay a quick visit to my mother. Imagine my surprise when I arrived and found her crying, upset, telling me you're working with the Tans. Are you workin' for the Brits, Annie? Are you here to kill Collins?"

"No," I panted, my scalp screaming. I tripped, and he yanked me forward again.

"I don't care if you are. I just want you gone. And you've given me the perfect excuse."

We cleared the trees lining the lough and began sliding down the embankment to the beach. Eamon's boat was pulled up on the shore, and Liam strode toward it, urging me along.

"Push it out," Liam demanded, releasing my hair and shoving me forward as we neared it. He kept the gun pointed at my back, clearly not trusting me not to flee. I hesitated, my eyes on the lapping tide.

"No," I moaned. *Don't go near the water, love.*

"Push it out," Liam yelled.

I obeyed, my limbs heavy, my heart on fire. I pushed the boat into the lough. Water filled my shoes, and I stepped out of them, leaving them behind. Maybe Thomas would find them and know what happened.

"Oh, Thomas," I whispered. "Eoin . . . my Eoin. Forgive me." The water was at my knees. I began to cry.

"Now get in the boat," Liam commanded, wading out behind me. I ignored him and kept walking, knowing what I had to do. The water lapped at my thighs, clinging and ice cold.

"Get in!" he shouted and pressed the barrel of the gun between my shoulder blades. I pretended to stumble, falling forward, arms extended, and let go of the boat. The frigid water rushed up to catch me, covering my head and filling my ears. I felt Liam's hand in my hair, grasping, desperate. His nails scored my cheek.

A shot rang out, oddly amplified by the water, and I screamed, expecting pain—expecting the end. Water flooded my nose and my mouth, and I tried to stand, choking. But Liam was pressing me down, his body heavy above me. I struggled, kicking and scratching, trying to free myself from his arms, to break the surface. To live.

For a moment I was weightless, free, cocooned in a breathless bubble, and I fought to stay conscious. The weight pressing me down became hands pulling me forward, grasping, lifting, dragging me onto the pebbled shore. I flopped onto the sand, gagging, choking, and retching as the lough lapped at my feet, penitent. The taste of the lake, the grit between my toes—all of it was the same. But there was no fog, no gloom, no overcast sky. The sun caressed my shivering shoulders. It was as though the world had flipped, tipping toward the sun, and dumped me out of the lough.

"Where did you come from, miss? Good God almighty. Scared me to death, you did."

I still couldn't speak, and the man above me was silhouetted by the setting sun. I couldn't see his features. He pushed me onto my stomach, and I coughed up another bellyful of water.

"Take your time. You're okay," he soothed, crouching beside me, patting my back. I knew his voice. Eamon. It was Eamon Donnelly. Thank God.

"Liam. Where's Liam?" I rasped. My lungs burned, and my scalp screamed. I laid my head on the shore, grateful to be alive.

"Liam?" he pressed. "Can you tell me more, ma'am?"

"Eamon," I coughed. "Eamon, I need Robbie, and I can't go home."

"Robbie?" Eamon pressed, his voice rising in confusion. "Robbie or Eamon? Or Liam? I'm sorry, ma'am. I don't know what you're asking or who you're asking for."

I rolled back onto my side, too tired to push up to my hands and knees. I peered up at Eamon, a Herculean effort. But it wasn't Eamon.

I stared, trying to orient myself to the face above mine, the face that didn't match the voice.

"Jaysus wept!" he gasped. "It's you, lass. Dear God. What the . . . where the hell have you been? W-what . . . w-when," he stammered, asking questions that I couldn't process.

"Mr. Donnelly?" I cried, the horror rasping in my throat. Oh no. No, no, no.

"That's right. You rented the boat from me, miss. I didn't want you to take that damn boat out. You know I didn't. Thank Mary, you're all right. We thought you'd drowned in the lough," he confessed, horrified.

"What day is it? What year?" I mourned. I couldn't look around to ascertain for myself. I didn't want to see. I pushed up to my hands and knees, struggled to my feet, and stumbled back into the water.

"Where're you goin'?" Jim Donnelly asked. Not Eamon Donnelly. Jim Donnelly, who lived in the cottage by the dock and had rented me a boat. In 2001.

I fell into the lough, desperate to return, even as I refused to admit I'd left.

The man yanked me up. "What are you doing? Are ya out of yer mind?"

"What day is it?" I cried, fighting him.

"It's July the sixth," he bellowed, wrapping his arms around my upper body, dragging me back to the shore. "It's a feckin' Friday!"

"What year?" I panted. "What year?"

"Huh?" he stammered. "It's 2001. We've been lookin' for you for more than a week. Ten days. You never came back to shore. The boat, everything, was just gone. The rental company came and took your car when the Gardai were done with it." He pointed toward the parking lot that didn't exist when Thomas lived at Garvagh Glebe. When Eoin lived at Garvagh Glebe. When I had lived at Garvagh Glebe.

"No," I wept. "Oh no."

"The Gardai have been here. They've been over the lake with equipment. They even sent divers down," he said, shaking his head. "What happened?"

"I'm sorry," I said. "I don't really know what happened. I don't really know."

"Is there someone I can call, ma'am? Where the hell did you come from?" he muttered, trying to coax me back to his cottage, to warmth, to the call he was desperate to make. I wanted him to leave. But he kept his arm firmly around my shoulders, leading me away from the lough. I needed to return to the water, to slip beneath the surface and back to the time before, to the place I'd left, to the life I'd lost.

Lost. Gone. Just like that. A breath, a submersion, and I died and was born again. Liam had tried to kill me. And he'd succeeded. He'd taken my life. Taken my love. Taken my family.

"What happened to ya, lass?"

I could only shake my head, too distraught to speak. I'd been through this all before. And this time, Thomas and Eoin weren't here to help me through it.

26 April 1922

Anne's gone. She's been gone for ten days. I returned to Garvagh Glebe late on Sunday, the sixteenth. My home was in chaos. Maggie held Eoin, who was feverish and ill in her arms. His crying made each breath a struggle. Maggie could hardly look at me, she was so distraught, but she murmured one word—lough—and I was out the door, running through the trees to the beach where Robbie and Patrick were scouring the shore for Anne's body. Robbie, doing his best to explain the unexplainable, wept as he relayed the day's events.

Liam had tried to force Anne into a boat on the lough at gunpoint, and Robbie had shot him. When Robbie ran into the water to pull Liam off her, she was gone.

Robbie said he searched the water for an hour. All he found were her shoes. He thinks she drowned, but I know what happened. She's gone, but she's not dead. I try to console myself with that.

Robbie dragged Liam back to the house where Brigid did her best to tend to him. Liam has a bullet wound in his shoulder, and he lost a lot of blood. But he'll live.

I want to kill him.

I removed the bullet, cleaned the wound, and sutured it. When he cried in pain, I showed him the morphine, but I didn't give him any.

"Thomas, please," he moaned. "I'll tell you everything. All of it. Please."

"And how will you ease my pain, Liam? Anne is gone," I hissed. "I'm letting you live. But I will not ease your pain."

"That wasn't Annie. She wasn't Annie. I swear it, Tommy. I was trying to help you," he moaned.

Brigid claims she found a "plot" in Anne's drawer, a list of dates and details outlining the assassination of Michael Collins. Brigid doesn't know what happened to the pages. She said Liam took them, and he said he must have lost them in the lough. They are both convinced my Anne was an imposter. They are right. And they are horribly wrong. I want to wrap my hands around Liam's neck and howl my outrage into his ears.

"She looked like Annie. But that wasn't Annie," he said, shaking his head, adamant.

I was flooded with a sudden, terrible knowledge.

"How do you know this, Liam?" I whispered, almost afraid to ask, yet filled with a dizzying reassurance that I would finally know the truth. "Why are you so sure?"

"Because Annie's dead. She's been dead for six years," he confessed, his skin damp, his eyes pleading. I could hear Brigid approaching, shuffling towards the room I used as a clinic, and I rose, slammed the door, and locked it. I couldn't deal with Brigid. Not yet.

"How do you know?" I demanded.

"I was there, Thomas. I saw her die. She was dead. Anne was dead."

"Where? When?" I was shouting, my voice so loud it echoed in my grief-soaked brain.

"At the GPO. Easter week. Please give me something, Doc. I can't think straight through the pain. I'll tell you. But you have to help me."

With no fanfare or finesse, I jammed the syringe into his leg and depressed the morphine, pulling it free and tossing it aside as he wilted into the bed beneath him. His relief was so pronounced, he began to laugh softly.

I was not laughing. "Tell me!" I roared, and his laughter turned into chagrin.

"Okay, Tommy. I'll tell you. I'll tell you." He sighed heavily, his pain retreating, his mind travelling some-where else. Somewhere far away. I could see it in his eyes, in the way his voice fell into a storyteller's rhythm as he shared an account he'd probably relived a thousand times in his head.

"That last night . . . at the GPO, we were all trying to be nonchalant. Trying to act like we didn't care that the roof was about to cave in on us. Every entrance was in flames but the one on Henry Street, and getting down Henry Street was like running a feckin' gauntlet. Men were running with their weapons, shooting at sounds, and in the process, shooting each other in the back. I was the last to go. Declan had already gone on ahead with O'Rahilly. They were going to try to clear Moore Street for the rest of us, but right away the word came back that they'd all been shot down. My little brother was always so feckin' willing to be a hero."

I felt the memory rise, thick and hot, like the smoke that had filled my lungs as I'd gone to Moore Street that long-ago Saturday, looking for my friends; 29 April 1916 was the worst day of my life. Before today. Today was worse.

"Connolly told me to make sure everyone was out of the GPO before I evacuated," Liam continued, the morphine slowing his cadence. "That was my job. I had to watch as men ran for their lives, one after another, dodging bullets and tripping over bodies. That's when I heard her. She was suddenly there, in the GPO, walking through the smoke. She scared me, Thomas. I was half blind and so tired, I would have shot my own mother had she come up behind me."

I waited for him to say her name yet recoiled when he did.

"It was Annie. I don't know how she got back inside the post office. The place was an inferno."

"What did you do?" The words were a rasp in my throat.

"I shot her. I didn't mean to. I just reacted. I shot her several times. I knelt beside her, and her eyes were open. She was staring at me, and I said her name. But she was dead. Then I shot her again, Thomas. Just to make sure she was real."

I couldn't look at him. I was afraid I would do to him what he'd done to Declan's Anne. To Eoin's mother. To my friend. I remembered the madness of that night. The exhaustion. The strain. And I understood how it had happened. I would have understood then. I would have forgiven him then. But he'd lied to me for six years, and he'd tried to cover his sins by killing again.

"I took her shawl—she'd been holding it—it was too hot in the GPO to wear it. It didn't have a single drop

of blood on it." He was obviously still awed by the fact. I grimaced, imagining the blood that must have pooled beneath her bullet-ridden body.

"And her ring?" It was all so clear to me now.

"I took it off her finger. I didn't want anyone to know it was her. I knew if I left her in the GPO, her body would burn, and no one would ever have to know what I'd done."

"Except for you. You knew."

Liam nodded, but his face was blank, as though he'd suffered so long with the sharp edge of guilt it had carved him into an empty shell.

"Then I walked out. I walked to Henry Place, Anne's shawl in my hands, her ring in my pocket. I felt the bullets whizzing past me. I wanted to die. But I didn't. Kavanagh pulled me into a tenement on Moore Street, and I spent the rest of the night burrowing through the walls, from one tenement to the next, working my way towards Sackville Lane with some of the others. I left the shawl in a pile of rubble, and I kept the ring. I've carried it in my pocket ever since. I don't know why."

"Ever since?" I asked, disbelieving. How was that possible? Anne had been wearing the ring when I'd seen her last. My Anne. My Anne. My legs buckled, and for a moment I thought I would fall.

"Surely you noticed that Anne was wearing the same ring," I moaned, covering my face with my hands.

"Those English bastards thought of everything, didn't they? Feckin' spies. But they didn't count on me. I knew it wasn't her all along. I told you, Doc. But you wouldn't listen, remember?"

I stood abruptly, knocking over my stool in my haste and moving away from him so I wouldn't strangle the righteous indignation from his face.

Anne told me her grandfather—Eoin—gave her the ring along with my diary and several pictures. They were the pieces of the life he had wanted her to reclaim. Oh, Eoin, my precious boy, my poor little boy. He would have to wait so long to see her again.

"Where's her ring now?" I asked, overcome.

Liam pulled it from his pocket and held it towards me, seemingly relieved to be rid of it. I took it from him, reeling with the knowledge that someday I would give it to Eoin. Eoin would eventually give it to Anne, his granddaughter, and she would wear it back to Ireland.

But that chapter had already been read, and my part in the rippled progression of future and past had already been played. My Anne had crossed the lough and gone home again.

"Last July, when you were moving guns on the lough, why did you shoot Anne when you saw her? I don't understand," I asked, seeking the final piece of the puzzle.

"I didn't think she was real," Liam murmured. "I see her everywhere I go. I keep killing her, and she keeps coming back."

Oh God. If only she would come back. If only she would.

The next morning, I told Liam to go. To never come back. I promised him if he did, I would kill him myself. I gave Brigid the choice to go with him. She stayed behind, but she and I both know I wish she was gone. I can't bring myself to forgive her. Not yet.

I don't know how I will go on. Breathing hurts. Speaking hurts. Waking is agony. I cannot comfort myself. I cannot comfort Eoin, who does not understand any of this. He keeps asking me where his mother is, and I have no idea what to tell him. The O'Tooles are insisting we have a service for her, even without a body. Father Darby said it would help us move on. But I will never move on.

T. S.

24

WHAT WAS LOST

I sing what was lost and dread what was won,
I walk in a battle fought over again,
My king a lost king, and lost soldiers my men;
Feet to the Rising and Setting may run,
They always beat on the same small stone.

—W. B. Yeats

Jim Donnelly was Eamon Donnelly's grandson, and he was kind. He brought me a blanket and some wool socks and threw my wet dress in his dryer. Then he called the police—the Gardai—and waited with me, making me drink a glass of water while he patted my back and guarded the door. He thought I was going to run. And I would have.

I couldn't hold on to a thought, couldn't stop shuddering, and when he asked me questions, I could only shake my head. He began talking to me instead, keeping his voice low as he checked his watch every few minutes.

"You called me Eamon. That was my grandfather's name," he said, trying to distract me. "He lived here on the lough too. We Donnellys have lived here for generations."

I tried to sip my water, and it slipped from my hand and crashed to the floor. He jumped to his feet and brought me a towel.

"Can I bring you some coffee?" he asked as I took the towel from his hand.

My stomach roiled at the mere mention of coffee, and I shook my head and tried to whisper my thanks. I sounded like a shuddering snake.

He cleared his throat and tried again, his voice conversational. "There was a woman who drowned in that lough a long time ago. A woman named Anne Gallagher. My grandfather knew her, and he told me the story when I was a boy. It's a small place, and she was a bit of a mystery. Over the years, the story's taken on a life of its own. The police thought I was pulling a wee joke when I called them and told them your name. It took me a while to convince them that I wasn't kidding." He grimaced and fell silent.

"They never knew what happened to her?" I asked, the tears streaming down my face.

"No . . . not really. They never found her body, which was where the mystery started. She lived at Garvagh Glebe—the manor there, behind the trees," he said, his face reflecting my distress. He rose and came back with a box of tissues.

"And her family?" I whispered. "What happened to them?"

"I don't know, miss. It was a long time ago. It's just an old story. Probably half true. I didn't mean to upset you."

When the police arrived, Jim Donnelly leapt from his chair in relief, ushering them in, and the questions began again. I was taken to a hospital and admitted for observation. My pregnancy was confirmed, my mental health questioned, and numerous calls were made to ascertain whether I was a threat to myself or others. I grasped very quickly that my freedom and independence relied on my ability to reassure everyone I was all right. I wasn't. I was destroyed. Devastated. Reeling. But I wasn't deranged or dangerous. Deny, deflect, refute, Michael Collins had said, and that's what I did. In the end, I was released.

It hadn't taken the police long to ascertain where I was staying and collect my suitcases from the Great Southern Hotel in Sligo. They had jimmied the locked door on my rental car and found my purse beneath the seats. My possessions had been combed through but were readily handed over when the investigation was closed. I paid my hospital bill, made a donation to the county search-and-rescue services, and quietly checked back in to the hotel. The desk clerk didn't flinch when she saw my name; the police had been discreet. I had my purse, my passport, and my clothing, but I needed to rent another car. I bought one instead. I had no intention of leaving Ireland.

I'd left Manhattan one week after Eoin died. I left his clothes in his drawers, his coffee cup in the sink, and his toothbrush in the bathroom. I locked his brownstone in Brooklyn, put off the calls from his lawyer about his estate, and told my assistant and my agent to tell everyone I would deal with what was left of Eoin's life and mine when I returned from Ireland.

His death had sent me running away. His request to have his ashes brought back to his birthplace had been a blessing. It had given me something to focus on besides the fact that he was gone. And I wasn't in any state to go back and deal with it now.

The police had discovered a business card inside my purse with my agent's name, Barbara Cohen, printed directly below my own. They contacted her, the only person on earth who might know where I was or where I'd gone, and they'd been in constant touch throughout the investigation. When I called her the day after being released from the hospital, she cried across the miles, yelling and blowing her nose and telling me to come home immediately.

"I'm going to stay here, Barbara," I said softly. Speaking was painful. It jarred my bruised spirit.

"What?" she gasped in the middle of her rant. "Why?"

"Ireland feels like home."

"It does? But . . . you're an American citizen. You can't just live there. And what about your career?"

"I can write from anywhere," I answered, and I winced. I'd said the same thing to Thomas. "I'll apply for dual citizenship. My grandfather was born here. My mother was born here too. Citizenship shouldn't be especially difficult to acquire." I said the words as if I meant them, but everything felt difficult. Blinking was difficult. Speaking. Staying upright.

"But . . . what about your apartment here? Your things? Your grandfather's home?"

"The best thing about money, Barbara, is that it makes so many things easier. I can hire someone to handle all of that for me," I soothed, already desperate to get off the phone.

"Well . . . at least you have property there. Is it livable? Maybe you won't need to buy a home."

"What property?" I said wearily. I loved Barbara, but I was so tired. So very tired.

"Harvey mentioned your grandfather owned property there. I just assumed you knew. Haven't you talked to Harvey?" Harvey Cohen was married to Barbara, and he just so happened to be Eoin's estate lawyer. It was all a little incestuous, but it was also convenient and streamlined, and Harvey and Barbara were the best at what they did. It made sense to keep it all in-house.

"You know I haven't talked to him, Barbara." I hadn't talked to anyone before I left. I'd shoved everything away, sending emails and leaving messages and avoiding everyone and everything. My heart picked up its pace, thundering clumsily, angry that I was making it move when it was so sore. "Is Harvey there now? If there's a house, I want to know about it."

"I'll get him," she said. She was quiet for a moment, and I could tell she was moving through her home. When she spoke again, her voice was gentle. "What happened to you, kiddo? Where have you been?"

"I guess I got lost in Ireland," I murmured.

"Well," she harrumphed. "Next time you decide to get lost, give the Cohens a heads-up, will you please?" She was back to her salty self when she handed Harvey the phone.

Harvey and Barbara flew to Ireland two days later. Harvey brought all
Eoin's personal papers, our family records, and documents—birth cer-
tificates, naturalization and medical records, deeds, wills, and financial
statements. He even brought the box of unaddressed letters from Eoin's
desk drawer, stating that Eoin had been adamant that I have them. Eoin
had named me executor of the Smith-Gallagher family trust—a trust I
knew nothing about—of which I am the sole beneficiary. Garvagh Glebe
and her surrounding properties were included in the trust. Thomas was a
very wealthy man, he left Eoin a very wealthy man, and Eoin gave it all
to me. I would give it all away to have one more day with either of them.

Garvagh Glebe belonged to me now, and I was desperate to return
to her, even as I shuddered at the thought of living there alone.

"I've made all the calls," Harvey said, checking his watch and eyeing
the list in front of him. "We have a meeting at noon with the caretaker.
You can walk through the property. It's huge, Anne. I never understood
Eoin's attachment to it. It's not a moneymaker, and he never visited.
In fact, he didn't want to talk about it at all. Ever. But he wouldn't sell.
However . . . he made no stipulation on your selling. I have an appraiser
and a realtor scheduled to meet us there, just so you have an idea of
what it's worth. It will give you more options."

"I need to go by myself," I whispered. I didn't bother to tell him I
wouldn't be selling the house under any circumstances.

"Why?" he gasped.

"Because."

Harvey sighed, and Barbara bit her lip. They were worried about me.
But there was no way I could walk through Garvagh Glebe, listening for
Eoin, looking for Thomas, and seeing only the years that stretched between
us. I couldn't return to Garvagh Glebe with an audience. If Barbara and
Harvey were worried about me now, it would be a hundred times worse
when they saw me weeping as I haunted the halls of my home.

"You go ahead. Meet with the realtor and the appraiser. When you
are finished, I will look through the house. By myself," I suggested.

"What is it with this house?" Harvey groaned. "Eoin acted exactly the same way."

I didn't answer. I couldn't. And Harvey sighed and ran his hands through his white mane and looked around the sparsely populated dining room at the Great Southern Hotel.

"I feel like I'm on the bloody *Titanic*," he grumbled.

I smiled wanly, surprising myself and them.

"You and Eoin had an incredible bond," Harvey murmured. "He loved you so much. He was so proud of you. When he told me about his cancer, I knew you would be devastated. But you are scaring me, Anne. You aren't just devastated. You're . . . you're . . ." He searched for the right word.

"You're lost," Barbara supplied.

"No, not lost," Harvey argued. "You're missing."

Our eyes met, and he reached for my hand.

"Where are you, Anne?" he pressed. "Your spirit is gone. You seem so empty."

I wasn't just grieving for my grandfather. I was grieving for the little boy he'd been. For the mother I'd been to him. For my husband. For my life. I wasn't empty, I was drowning. I was still in the lough.

"She just needs time, Harvey. Give her time," Barbara protested.

"Yes," I agreed, nodding. "I just need time." I needed time to take me back, to whisk me away. Time was the one thing I wanted and the one thing no one could give me.

"Are you related to the O'Tooles, by any chance?" I asked the young caretaker when Harvey and his entourage drove away. The caretaker couldn't have been more than twenty-five, and there was something in the tilt of his head and the set of his shoulders that made me think he belonged in the family tree. He'd introduced himself as Kevin Sheridan, but the name didn't fit him.

"Yes, ma'am. My great-grandfather was Robert O'Toole. He was the caretaker here for years. My mother—his granddaughter—and my father took care of the place when he died. Now it's my turn . . . for as long as you need me, that is." A cloud passed over his features, and I knew the sudden interest in the property was concerning to him.

"Robbie?" I asked.

"Yes. Everyone called him Robbie. My mother says I look like him. I'm not sure that's a compliment. He wasn't much to look at—only had one eye—but his family loved him." He was trying to be self-deprecating, to make me laugh at his unimpressive lineage, but I could only gape at him, stricken. He did look like Robbie. But Robbie was gone now. They all were.

Kevin must have seen how close I was to crumbling, and he left me alone to wander around, promising he would be on the grounds if I needed him and mentioning in a cheerful, tour-guide tone that Michael Collins himself had stayed at Garvagh Glebe many times.

I wandered for close to an hour, moving silently through the rooms, looking for my family, for my life, and finding only pieces and parts, whispers and wisps of a time that existed only in my memory. Each room had an emptiness and an expectancy that pulled at me. New king-sized beds heaped with pillows and comforters that coordinated with the updated window coverings were the centerpiece in every room. One or two pieces of the original furniture remained to give each chamber a touch of nostalgia—Thomas's writing table and his chest of drawers, Eoin's rocking horse and a high shelf of his "antique" toys, and Brigid's vanity and her Victorian chair, which was reupholstered in a similar floral fabric. My gramophone and the huge wardrobe still stood in my old room. I opened the doors and stared at the empty interior, remembering the day Thomas had come home from Lyons with all the things he thought I needed. That was the night I knew I was in trouble, in danger of losing my heart.

The oak floors and cabinets in the kitchen were the same but had been resurfaced and were gleaming. The stately staircase and the oak balustrade remained, warm and reliable with years and use. The baseboards and the moldings had all been maintained, the walls painted, and the countertops and appliances upgraded to reflect the times. It smelled like lemons and furniture polish. I breathed deeply, trying to find Thomas, to coax him from the walls and the wood, but I couldn't smell him. Couldn't feel him. I moved on trembling legs toward his library, to the shelves filled with books that he wouldn't read anymore, and halted at the door. A painting, framed in an ornate oval, hung on the wall where a pendulum clock used to toll away the hours.

"Miss Gallagher?" Robbie called from the foyer. Not Robbie. Kevin. It was Kevin. I tried to answer him, to tell him where I was, but my voice shook and broke. I wiped desperately at my eyes, trying to find my composure, but I was unsuccessful. When Kevin found me in the library, I pointed up at the picture, overcome.

"Uh . . . well, that's a picture of the Lady of the Lough," he explained, trying not to look at me and call attention to my tears. "She's famous around here. As famous as an eighty-year-old ghost can be, I suppose. The story goes that she only lived at Garvagh Glebe for a little while. She drowned in Lough Gill. Her husband was devastated and spent years painting pictures of her. This is the one he kept. It's beautiful, isn't it? She was a lovely woman." He hadn't noticed the resemblance, proof that people weren't very observant. Or maybe I wasn't especially lovely now.

"She never returned?" I whimpered, my voice a childlike cry. Jim Donnelly had said the same thing.

"No, ma'am. She, uh, she drowned. So she never returned," he stammered, handing me a handkerchief. I grabbed it, desperate to stem my tears.

"Ma'am, are you all right?"

"It's just sad," I whispered. I turned my back on the picture. *She never returned.* I never returned. God help me.

"Yes. But it was a long time ago, miss."

I couldn't tell him it was only a week and a handful of days.

"Mr. Cohen told me you lost someone recently. I'm sorry, ma'am," he added softly. Kindly.

I nodded, and he hovered nearby until I regained control.

"I know what Mr. Cohen said, Robbie. But I'm not selling Garvagh Glebe. I'm going to be staying here. Living here. I still want you to remain on as caretaker. I will raise your salary for any inconvenience that causes, but we won't be renting out the rooms. Not for a while . . . all right?"

He nodded enthusiastically.

"I'm a writer. The quiet will be good for me, but I can't take care of this place by myself. I am also expecting . . . a child . . . and will need someone to come in and clean and occasionally cook. I tend to get lost in my work."

"I already have someone who cooks and cleans when we have guests. I'm sure she would be glad to have regular employment."

I nodded and turned away.

"Miss? You called me Robbie. It's . . . Kevin, ma'am," he said gently.

"Kevin," I whispered. "I'm sorry, Kevin. I won't forget again. And please, call me Anne. Anne Smith is my married name."

I forgot again. I kept calling Kevin Robbie. He always quietly corrected me, but it never seemed to bother him too much. I was a guest that slowly became a ghost, flitting through the halls, not disturbing anyone or anything. Kevin was patient with me and stayed out of my way for the most part. The barn behind the house had been converted into living quarters, and when he wasn't working, he was there, letting me haunt the big house alone. He checked on me every day and made sure the girl from town—Jemma—kept the house clean and the fridge stocked. When my things arrived from the States, he unloaded boxes and assisted me in setting up a new office in my old room. He marveled at the books I'd written, the languages they'd been translated into, the framed bestseller lists, and the random awards, and I was thankful for him, even though I know he thought I was a little crazy.

I waded out into the lough at least once a day, reciting Yeats and pleading with the fates to send me back. I sent Kevin to buy a boat from Jim Donnelly—I didn't dare approach him—and rowed it out into the middle of the lake. I stayed all day, trying to recreate the moment I'd fallen through time. I willed the mist to roll in, but the August sun did not cooperate. The beautiful days played dumb, and the wind and the water were silent, pretending innocence, and no matter how much I recited and raged, the lough denied me. I started plotting ways to get my hands on human ashes, but even clouded by desperate grief, I recognized that if the ashes had played a role, it was most likely because they were Eoin's.

About six weeks after I'd moved into Garvagh Glebe, a car rolled through the gates that were erected sometime in the last eighty years and proceeded up the lane, shuddering to a stop in front of the house. I sat in my office, pretending to work but staring out the window, and I watched as two women climbed from the car, one young and one old, and approached the front door.

"Robbie!" I yelled, and then caught myself. His name was Kevin. And he was mowing the acres of grass behind the house. Jemma had already come and gone. The door chimed. I considered ignoring the visitors. I didn't need to answer the door.

But I knew them.

It was Maeve O'Toole, old again, and Deirdre Fallon from the library in Dromahair. For whatever reason, they'd come to call, and they'd made time for me once, when I'd needed help. I should return the favor. I smoothed my hair and thanked heaven that I had found the will to shower and dress that morning, something I didn't always do.

Then I answered the door.

16 July 1922

Anne was right. The Free State Army fired on the Four Courts building in the early morning hours of 28 June, placing field guns at strategic locations and shooting high-explosive shells into the buildings where the anti-Treaty republicans were hunkered down. An ultimatum had been sent to the Four Courts and was ignored, and Mick had no choice but to attack. The British government was threatening to send troops to handle it if he didn't, and no one wanted Free State troops and British troops fighting alongside each other against the republicans. The buildings occupied by republicans on O'Connell Street and elsewhere in the city were also blockaded to prevent anti-Treaty forces from running to assist the besieged Four Courts. The hope was that when the republicans saw that actual artillery was being used, they would give in and give up.

The siege lasted three days and ended with an explosion in the Four Courts that destroyed precious documents and brought the whole debacle to an end. Good men died, just like Anne predicted. Cathal Brugha wouldn't surrender. Mick wept when he told me. He and Brugha didn't see eye to eye much of the time, but Cathal was a patriot, and there is little Mick respects more than that.

I stood in front of the burned-out shell of the Four Courts today. The stolen munitions kept exploding, making it impossible for the firemen to put out the blaze. They had to let it burn itself out. I wonder if all of Ireland will have to burn itself out as well. The copper dome is gone, the building destroyed, and what the hell for?

An agreement was forged in May between the republicans and the Free State leaders to defer the final decision on the Treaty until after the election and after the Free State Constitution had been published. But the compromise devolved before it could gain any traction; Mick says Whitehall got wind of it and didn't like the sound of a delayed decision on the Treaty. Too much was at stake, too much money had been spent, too much ground covered. The six counties in Northern Ireland not included in the Treaty have descended into bloodshed and chaos. The sectarian violence is unfathomable. Catholics are being slaughtered and run from their homes, and new orphans are being made every day.

My heart is numb to it all. I have an orphan of my own to worry about. Eoin sleeps in my bed and shadows me wherever I go. Brigid has tried to console him, but he refuses to be alone with her. Brigid's health is failing. Stress and loss have made us all phantoms of ourselves. Mrs. O'Toole has stepped in to watch him when I cannot take him with me.

Mick called two Sundays after Anne disappeared, asking about her health, seeking her counsel, and I had to tell him she was gone. He shouted into the phone like I had lost my mind and showed up four hours later in an armoured car, Fergus and Joe with him, ready to do war. I am no longer equipped to do war, and when he demanded answers, I found myself weeping in his arms, telling him what Liam had done.

"Oh, Tommy, no," he wailed. "Oh no."

"She's gone, Mick. She was worried about you, and she'd written out a warning and tucked it away. I think she intended to give it to me or Joe, hoping we'd be able to keep you safe. But Brigid found it. She thought she was plotting against you. Brigid told Liam, and he dragged Anne out to the lough. Robbie thinks he intended to kill her and hide her body in the marsh. Robbie tried to stop him. He shot him, but it was too late." I didn't bother with the whole truth, with all of Liam's sins. I couldn't condemn myself or Anne to Mick's disbelief or burden him with distrust.

He stayed with me until the following day, and we drank ourselves into a stupor. Neither of us was comforted, but for a while I forgot, and when they left, Fergus at the wheel, Joe beside him, and Mick hungover in the backseat, I slept for fifteen hours. He gave me that, and I was grateful for the brief reprieve.

I don't know if Mick put out a hit on him, or if Fergus carried it out on his own because he was worried about Liam's volatility, but Liam Gallagher's body washed up on the strand in Sligo three days after Mick came to Garvagh Glebe. Mick was always pragmatic and principled in the terror he unleashed. I saw him scream in the faces of his squad and threaten them with discharge if they even hinted at a revenge hit. His tactics had always been about bringing Great Britain to her knees, not reprisals. The only time I'd suspected Mick of retaliation was when the Irishman who pointed out Seán Mac Diarmada to British soldiers after the Rising was found dead. Mick had seen the man do it, and he'd never forgotten the betrayal.

We haven't spoken of Liam Gallagher's death. We haven't spoken of many things. Brigid said Anne wrote about an assassination attempt—she remembers something about August and flowers and a trip to Cork—but the pages disintegrated in the lough. It's not much to go on, and Mick doesn't want to hear it. He feels responsible for Anne's death, just another weight he carries, and I cannot relieve him of it, try as I might. Robbie feels responsible too. We are all convinced we could have saved her, and I am devastated that I have lost her. We are united in our self-loathing.

Last week, while setting traps, Eamon found a small red boat in the bog. It had been washed up onto a muddy shelf, and he dragged it home. He found an odd satchel pushed up under the seat, a corked urn and a leather journal inside. Both had been protected from the worst of the elements. He read the first page of the journal and realised right away that the book was mine. The urn and the satchel were Anne's; I have no doubt. I put the boat in the barn, tying it to the rafters to keep Eoin out of it, and gave Eamon a finder's fee for bringing his treasures to me.

I puzzled over the journal, trying to ascertain how it could have been inside a bag in the marsh when it already sat high on the shelf in my library. I was convinced my copy would not be there. But it was. The pages of my book weren't yellowed, and the leather was suppler, but it was there. I held the aged journal in my left hand and the newer one in my right, confounded, my mind tripping and tumbling, trying to formulate a plausible explanation. There wasn't one. I set them side by side on the shelf, almost expecting one to dissolve into the other, restoring balance and oneness to the universe. But they lay against each other, past and present, today and tomorrow, unaffected and unaltered by my limited understanding. Perhaps at some point, the two books will become one again, each existing in their own moment, just like Anne's ring.

I walk along the beach every day, watching for her. I can't help myself. Eoin walks with me, his gaze continually returning to the glassy surface. He asked me if his mother is in the lough. I told him no. He asked me if she had crossed the lough into another place, like he did in his adventures. I said that I believed she had, and it seemed to reassure him. It occurs to me that Anne might have created the stories to comfort Eoin in the event that she couldn't.

"You won't go too, will you, Doc?" Eoin whispered, taking my hand. "You won't disappear into the water and leave me behind?"

I promised him I wouldn't.

"Maybe we can both go," he mused, looking up into my face, trying to ease my pain. "Maybe we can get in that boat in the barn and go find her."

I laughed then, grateful I'd had the foresight to put the boat where he couldn't reach it. But my laughter didn't ease the ache in my chest.

"No, Eoin. We can't," I said gently, and he didn't argue.

Even if I knew how, even if we could both follow her across the lough into another time, we could not go. Eoin must grow up in this day, in this age, and have a son who grows up in the next for Anne to exist at all. Some sequences must unfold in their natural order. Of that much, I am sure. Anne will need her grandfather even more than Eoin needs a mother. He has me. Anne has no one. So Eoin will have to wait, and I have promised to wait with him, even if it means I will never see her again.

    T. S.

25

LOVE'S LONELINESS

The mountain throws a shadow,
Thin is the moon's horn;
What did we remember
Under the ragged thorn?
Dread has followed longing,
And our hearts are torn.

—*W. B. Yeats*

Deirdre had a large canvas bag over her shoulder, and she clung to the strap nervously, clearly standing on my doorstep against her will. Maeve looked perfectly comfortable as she gazed at me through her thick glasses, unblinking.

"Kevin says you always call him Robbie," she said without preamble.

Deirdre cleared her throat and stuck out her hand. "Hello, Anne. I'm Deirdre Fallon from the library, remember? And you've met Maeve. We thought we'd welcome you to Dromahair officially since you've decided to stay. I didn't realize you were Anne Gallagher, the author! I've made sure we have all your books in stock. There's a waiting list for your titles. Everyone in town is so excited you're living here in our little village." Each sentence was punctuated with enthusiasm, but I sensed she was more nervous than anything.

I clasped her hand briefly and ushered them both inside. "Come in, please."

"I've always loved the manor," Deirdre gushed, her eyes on the wide staircase and the huge chandelier that hovered over our heads. "Every Christmas Eve, the caretakers open the house to the town. There's dancing and stories, and Father Christmas always comes for the children. I got my first kiss here, under the mistletoe."

"I'd like tea in the library," Maeve demanded, not waiting for an invitation and veering through the foyer toward the large French doors that separated the library from the entrance hall.

"M-Maeve," Deirdre stuttered, shocked at the old woman's impudence.

"I don't have time for niceties, Deirdre," Maeve snapped back. "I could die at any moment. And I don't want to die before I get to the good stuff."

"It's all right, Deirdre," I murmured. "Maeve knows her way around Garvagh Glebe. If she wants tea in the library, then she shall have tea in the library. Please make yourself comfortable, and I'll get the tea."

I already had a kettle on; I drank peppermint tea all day long to soothe the nausea that was now my constant companion. The doctor in Sligo said it should ease in the second trimester, but I was almost twenty weeks, and it hadn't ebbed at all. I'd wondered if it wasn't nerves more than anything.

Jemma had shown me where the tea service was—a service I'd been convinced I would never use—and I arranged a tray with more enthusiasm than I'd felt in two months. When I joined Deirdre and Maeve in the library, I expected them to be seated in the small grouping of chairs surrounding a low coffee table. They were standing beneath the portrait instead, their heads tipped back, quietly arguing.

I set the tray down on the table and cleared my throat.

"Tea?" I said.

They both turned to look at me, Deirdre sheepish, Maeve triumphant.

"What did I tell you, Deirdre?" Maeve said, satisfaction ringing in her voice.

Deirdre looked at me and looked back at the portrait. Then she looked at me again. Her eyes widened. "It's uncanny . . . I'll give you that, Maeve O'Toole."

"Tea?" I repeated. I sat down and spread a napkin over my lap, waiting for the women to join me. Deirdre abandoned the portrait immediately, but Maeve was slower to follow. Her eyes ran up and down the shelves, as if she were looking for something in particular.

"Anne?" she mused.

"Yes?"

"There was a whole row of the doctor's journals in this library at one time. Where are they now? Do you know? I don't see as well as I once did."

I stood, my heart pounding, and walked to her side.

"They were on the top shelf. I dusted those books at least once a week for six years." She extended the cane above her head and rapped it against shelves, as high as she could stretch. "Up there. Do you see them?"

"I would have to climb the ladder, Maeve." There was a ladder on runners that could move from one end of the shelves to the other, but I hadn't felt any compunction to climb since moving to Garvagh Glebe.

"Well?" Maeve sniffed. "What are ya waitin' for?"

"For God's sake, Maeve," Deirdre huffed. "You are being incredibly rude. Come sit down and drink your tea before this poor woman has you bodily removed from her home."

Maeve grumbled, but she turned away from the shelves and did as she was told. I followed her back to the coffee table, my thoughts on the books on the highest shelf. Deirdre poured, making polite conversation as she did, asking me if I was enjoying the manor, the lough, the weather, my solitude. I answered briefly, vaguely, saying all the expected things without really saying anything at all.

Maeve harrumphed into her teacup, and Deirdre threw her a warning glare.

I set my cup down. "Maeve, if you have something to say, please do. You've obviously come for a reason."

"She's convinced that you are the woman in the painting," Deirdre rushed to explain. "She's been asking me to bring her here ever since word spread that you were living at Garvagh Glebe. You must understand . . . the whole village was abuzz when it was believed that another woman drowned in the lough. A woman with the same name! You can't imagine what a stir it caused."

"Kevin told me your name is Anne Smith," Maeve interjected.

"You are Kevin's great-great—" I paused to calculate how many greats. "He's your nephew?" I asked.

"Yes. And he's worried about you. He also says you are expecting a child. Where is the child's father? He seems to think there isn't one."

"Maeve!" Deirdre gasped. "That is none of your business."

"I don't care if she's married, Deirdre," Maeve snapped. "I just want to hear the story. I'm tired of gossip. I want to know the truth."

"What happened to Thomas Smith, Maeve?" I asked, deciding I would ask a few questions of my own. "You and I never talked about him."

"Who was Thomas Smith?" Deirdre said between sips.

"The man who painted that picture," Maeve said. "The doctor who owned Garvagh Glebe when I was a girl. I left when I was seventeen, after passing all my accounting examinations. I went to London to work at the Kensington Savings and Loan. It was a grand time. The doctor paid for my schooling and my first year's room and board. He paid for all our schooling. Every O'Toole held him in the highest regard."

"What happened to him, Maeve? Is he in Ballinagar too?" I asked, bracing myself. My cup rattled against the saucer, and I set both down abruptly.

"No. When Eoin left Garvagh Glebe in 1933, the doctor left too. Neither of them ever came back, as far as I know."

"Now, who was Eoin again?" Poor Deirdre was trying to keep up.

"My grandfather, Eoin Gallagher," I supplied. "He was raised here, at Garvagh Glebe."

"So you're related to the woman in the picture!" Deirdre crowed, mystery solved.

"Yes," I said, nodding. Closely related.

Maeve was having none of it. "But you told Kevin that Anne Smith is your name," she insisted again.

"She's a famous author, Maeve! Of course she has aliases." Deirdre laughed. "I must say, though, Anne Smith isn't terribly original." She laughed again. When Maeve and I didn't laugh with her, she finished her tea in a gulp, her cheeks scarlet. "I brought something for you, Anne," she rushed. "Remember the books I mentioned to you? About the author with the same name? I thought you might like your own copies, with a little one on the way." She flushed again. "They're delightful, really." She opened the big bag beside her chair.

She drew out a stack of brand-new children's books, shiny black rectangles, each one with a little red sailboat drifting across a moonlit lake on the cover. *The Adventures of Eoin Gallagher* was written across the top in Thomas's bold hand. Along the bottom, each title was printed in white.

"My favorite is the adventure with Michael Collins," Deirdre said, browsing through the stack to find it. I must have moaned in distress because her eyes shot to my face, and Maeve cursed on a sigh.

"You are a ninny, Deirdre," Maeve groused. "Those books were written by Anne Gallagher Smith." Maeve pointed up at my portrait.

"The woman in the picture, the woman who drowned in the lough, Thomas Smith's wife, and the woman who wrote those children's books are all the same person."

"B-but . . . these were published last spring and donated to commemorate the eighty-fifth anniversary of the Easter Rising. Every library in Ireland received a box of them. I had no idea."

"May I see them?" I whispered. Deirdre set them reverently on my lap and watched as I looked through them with shaking hands. There were eight of them, just like I remembered.

"Written by Anne Gallagher Smith. Illustrated by Dr. Thomas Smith," I read, running my thumb across our names. That part was new. I opened the cover on the first book and read the dedication: *In loving memory of a magical time.* Beneath the dedication it said, "Donated by Eoin Gallagher."

They'd been professionally reproduced on thick glossy paper and machine bound. But each picture and each page, from the cover to the last line, was identical to the original.

"My grandfather did this. These were his books. He didn't tell me . . . didn't show me. I knew nothing about this," I marveled, my voice hushed in tearful wonder.

"Those copies are yours, Anne," Deirdre pressed. "A gift. I hope I haven't upset you."

"No," I choked. "No. I'm just . . . surprised. They are wonderful. Forgive me."

Maeve looked as if the wind had been knocked out of her. Her vinegar was gone; her questions quieted. I had a feeling she knew exactly who I was but had decided it served no purpose to make me admit it.

"We loved Anne," she muttered. Her lips began to tremble. "Some people talked. Some people said terrible things after she . . . died. But the O'Tooles loved her. Robbie loved her. I loved her. We all missed her dreadfully when she was gone."

I used my napkin to blot my eyes, unable to speak, and noted that Deirdre was wiping her eyes as well.

Maeve stood, leaning heavily on her cane, and headed for the door. The visit was apparently over. Deirdre rushed to rise as well, sniffling and apologizing for leaving mascara on my cloth napkin. I placed the books carefully on a shelf and followed them out, feeling overwrought and weak-kneed.

Maeve hesitated at the door and let Deirdre exit first.

"If his journals are still on that top shelf, they will tell you all you need to know, Anne," Maeve said. "Thomas Smith was a remarkable man. You should write a book about him. And don't be afraid to go back to Ballinagar. The dead have a great deal to teach us. I've got my own plot picked out."

I nodded, emotional once more. I longed for the day when my pain and my tears weren't so close to the surface.

"Come visit me, will you?" Maeve grumbled. "All my other friends are dead. I can't drive anymore, and I can't speak freely with Deirdre listening. She'd have me committed, and I don't want to spend my last years in the loony bin."

"I'll visit you, Maeve," I said, giggling through my tears, and I meant it.

I couldn't face the top shelf. Not right away. I waited several days, hovering in the library only to retreat again, arms wrapped around myself and barely holding on. I'd been standing on a ledge since leaving 1922. I couldn't move forward or back. Couldn't move to the left or the right. I couldn't sleep or breathe too deeply for fear of falling. So I held perfectly still on my ledge, making no sudden moves, and in that stillness I existed. I coped.

Kevin found me in the library, clinging to the ladder, not climbing, not moving, my eyes glued to the top shelf.

"Can I help you, Anne?" he asked. He still wasn't comfortable calling me Anne, and his hesitation to say my name made me feel as old as Maeve and separated from him by six decades instead of six years.

I moved away from the ladder gingerly, still firmly on my ledge. "Will you see if there are some journals on the top shelf?" I pointed. "Maybe you could hand them down to me." In my mind, I could hear a rush of smattering pebbles; I was standing too close to the edge. I closed my eyes and sipped the air, willing myself to be calm.

I heard Kevin climbing the ladder, the rungs protesting each step. "There are journals, all right. Looks like six or seven of them."

"Will you just open one and read the date at the top of the page . . . please?" I panted.

"All right," he said, and I heard the reservation in his voice. Pages ruffled. "This one says 4 February 1928 . . . um, it looks like it starts in '28 and ends"—the pages ruffled again—"in June of 1933."

"Will you read me something? It doesn't matter which page. Just read whatever it says."

"This page says 27 September 1930," Kevin reported.

> *Eoin's grown so tall, and his feet and hands are as big as mine. I caught him trying to shave last week and ended up giving him a lesson, the two of us standing in front of the mirror, bare-chested, our faces lathered, razors in hand. It'll be a while yet—a long while—before he needs to remove his beard with any regularity, but now he knows the basics. I told him how his mother used to steal my razor to shave her legs. It embarrassed him and embarrassed me. It was too intimate a detail for a boy of fifteen. I forgot myself for a moment, remembering her.*

It's been more than eight years, but I can still feel Anne's smooth skin, still see it when I close my eyes.

Kevin stopped reading.

"Read something else," I whispered.

He turned the pages and began again.

Our child would have been ten years old now had Anne stayed. Eoin and I don't talk about Anne as much as we used to. But I'm convinced we think about her even more. Eoin is planning to go to medical school in the States; he's got Brooklyn in his head. Brooklyn and baseball and Coney Island. When he goes, I'll go too. I've fallen out of love with the view from my window. If I'm to be alone for the rest of my life, I'd just as soon see the world as sit here watching the lough, waiting for Anne to come home.

"Can you hand it down?" I interrupted, needing to hold the book in my arms, to hold what was left of my Thomas.

Kevin bent down, the book dangling from his fingers, and I took it from him, drawing it to my nose and inhaling desperately, trying to find the smell of Thomas lingering in the pages. I sneezed violently, and Kevin laughed, surprising me.

"I need to tell Jemma she isn't doing a very bang-up job of dusting," he said. His laughter eased the tight knot in my chest, and I made myself set the book aside for later.

"Will you open another one, please?" I asked.

"All right. Let's see . . . this journal is from, eh, 1922 to 1928. It looks like they're in order up here."

My lungs bellowed, and my hands grew numb.

"Want to hear something from this one?"

I didn't. I couldn't. But I nodded, playing Russian roulette with my heart.

Kevin opened the book and flipped through the first section. His fingers whispered past the pages of Thomas's life.

"Here's a shorter one, 16 August 1922." Kevin began to read, his Irish brogue the perfect narration for the heartbreaking entry.

> *Conditions in the country have disintegrated to the point where Mick and other members of the provisional government are at constant threat of being picked off by a sniper or shot in the street. Nobody goes on the roof to take a smoke anymore. When they're in Dublin, nobody goes home. They are all living—all eight members of the provisional government—in government buildings surrounded by the Free State Army. They are young men constantly on the knife's edge. The only senior member among them, Arthur Griffith, suffered a brain haemorrhage on 12 August. He's gone. We've lost him. He'd been confined to his bed but kept trying to carry out his duties. He's found the only rest available to him.*
>
> *Mick was in Kerry when the news reached him about Arthur's death, and he cut his southern inspections short to attend the service. I met him in Dublin today and watched as he walked at the front of the funeral procession, the Free State Army marching behind him, every face bleak with sorrow. I stood with him for some time at the graveside, staring down into the hole which held the body of his friend, each of us lost in our own thoughts.*
>
> *"Do you think I will live through this, Tommy?" he asked me.*

*"I'll never forgive you if you don't," I answered. I
am terrified. It is August. Brigid remembers August from
Anne's pages. August and Cork and flowers.*

"Ye will. Just like ye forgave Annie."

*I've asked him not to say her name. I can't bear it.
It makes her absence too real. And it makes a mockery
of my secret hope that someday I will see her again. But
Mick forgets. He has too many things to remember. Stress
is eating a hole in his gut, and he lies to me when I press
him about it. He's moving slower, and his eyes are dim-
mer, but maybe it is my own pain and fear I'm seeing.*

*He is insisting on resuming his southern tour and
continuing on to Cork. He has meetings scheduled with
the key players causing havoc in the region. He says he's
going to end the bloody conflict once and for all. "For
Arthur and Annie and every feckin' lad that's hung on
the end of a rope or faced a firing squad trying to do my
bidding." But Cork has become a hotbed for the republican resistance. Railroads have been destroyed, trees are
downed all over the roads to prevent safe passage, and
mines have been set throughout the countryside.*

I begged him not to go.

*"These are my people, Tommy," he snarled at me.
"I've been all over Ireland, and no one's tried to stop
me. I want to go home, for God's sake. I want to go to
Clonakilty and sit on a stool at the Four Alls and have a
drink with my friends."*

I've told him if he goes, I'm going with him.

For a moment the library rang with those words, and Kevin and I
were silent, wrapped in the memory of men who were larger than life
until life rose up and snuffed them out.

"These are incredible," Kevin marveled. "I know a little about Arthur Griffith and Michael Collins. But not as much as I should. Do ya want me to read more, Anne?"

"No," I whispered, heartsick. "I know what happens next."

He handed the book down, and I set it aside.

"This journal is a lot older. It's in bad shape," Kevin mused over another volume. "No . . . it's the next one," he reported, turning the pages. "It starts in 1916, May, and ends—" He flipped the page. "It ends with a poem, it looks like. But the last entry is 16 April 1922."

"Read the poem," I demanded, breathless.

"Um. All right." He cleared his throat awkwardly.

*I pulled you from the water, and kept you in my bed, a
lost, forsaken daughter of a past that isn't dead.*

When I stared at him in stunned silence, he continued, his face as red as Eoin's hair. With each word, I felt the wind roaring in my head and the lough gathering beneath my skin.

*Don't go near the water, love. Stay away from strand or
sea. You cannot walk on water, love; the lough will take
you far from me.*

There was no ledge beneath my feet, and I sat down on Thomas's desk, dizzy with disbelief.

"Anne?" Kevin asked. "Do you want this one too?"

I nodded woodenly, and he climbed down, the book still clutched in his right hand.

"Can I see it, please?" I whispered.

Kevin placed it in my hands, hovering and clearly rattled by my shock.

"I thought this journal was lost . . . in the lough," I breathed, running my hands over it. "I . . . I don't understand."

"Maybe it's a different one," Kevin supplied hopefully.

"It's not. I know this book . . . the dates . . . I know that poem." I gave it back to him. "I can't look at it. I know you don't understand, but can you read the first entry to me, please?"

He took it back, and as he thumbed through the pages, several pictures fluttered to the ground. He stooped, scooping them up and glancing at them curiously.

"That's Garvagh Glebe," he said. "This picture looks like it's a hundred years old, but she hasn't changed much." He handed the picture to me. It was the picture I'd shown Deirdre that day in the library. The picture I'd tucked into the pages of the journal before rowing out into the middle of the lake to say goodbye to Eoin. It was the same picture, but it had aged another eighty years.

"This one is something else," Kevin breathed, his gaze captured by the next picture in his hand. His eyes widened and narrowed before lifting to meet mine. "That woman looks just like you, Anne."

It was the picture of Thomas and me at the Gresham, not touching but so aware of each other. His face was turned toward me—the line of his jaw, the slice of his cheekbone, the softness of his lips beneath the blade of his nose.

My pictures had survived the lough. The journal too. But I had not. We had not.

28 August 1922

We left for Cork early on the twenty-first. Mick tripped going down the stairs and dropped his gun. It went off, waking the entire house and increasing my sense of foreboding. I saw Joe O'Reilly framed by the window, watching us depart. He, like all the rest of us, had begged Mick to stay out of Cork. I know he felt better because I was with Mick, though my value in a fight has always been when it's over. My war stories are all the surgical kind.

It started well enough. We stopped at Curragh barracks, and Mick carried out an inspection. We stopped in Limerick and in Mallow, and Mick wanted to swing by an army dance, where a priest called him a traitor to his face, and I had a pint poured down my back. Mick didn't even flinch at the insult, and I finished my whiskey with a wet arse. Mick showed a little more outrage when the lookouts at the hotel in Cork were fast asleep in the lobby when we arrived. He grabbed each boy by his hair and knocked their heads together. If it had been Vaughan's Hotel in Dublin a year ago, he would have left immediately, certain that his safety had been compromised. He didn't seem especially concerned and fell asleep as soon as his head hit the pillow. I dozed sitting in a chair in front of the door, Mick's revolver in my lap.

Maybe it was my weariness, or the fog of grief I've been walking in since Anne disappeared, but the next day unfolded like a motion picture, jerky and dreamlike, with no colour or context to my own life. Mick had meetings with family and friends in the early part of the day, and it wasn't until late afternoon that we left for Macroom Castle. I didn't accompany him inside but waited in the courtyard with the small convoy—Sean O'Connell and Joe Dolan from Mick's squad and a dozen soldiers and extra hands to clear any barricades—assigned to escort Mick safely through Cork.

We ran into problems near Bandon when the touring car overheated twice and the armoured car stalled on a hill. One debacle fed into another. Trees were cleared, only to discover trenches had been dug behind them. We took a detour, got lost, got separated from the rest of the convoy, asked for directions, and eventually reunited for the last appointment of the day, heading towards Crookstown through a little valley called Béal na mBláth. The mouth of flowers.

The road, narrow and rutted, was more suited to a horse and a buggy than a convoy. There was a hilly rise on one side and an overgrown hedge on the other. Daylight was slinking away, and a brewery cart missing a wheel lay tipped on its side in the middle of the road. Beyond that, a donkey, freed from the cart, grazed benignly. The convoy slowed, and the touring car veered into the ditch to avoid the obstacles blocking the road.

A shot rang out, and Sean O'Connell yelled, "Drive like hell! We're in trouble."

But Mick told the driver to stop.

He picked up his rifle and tumbled out the door, eager for the fight. I followed him. Someone followed me. Shots rained in from the left, high above us, and Mick whooped, ducking behind the armoured car where we crouched for several minutes, punctuating the steady stream from the Vickers machine gun with shots of our own.

The back-and-forth continued, riddling the air with volleys that thunked and whistled over and around us. We had the firepower on our side, but they had the better position. Mick wouldn't keep his head down. I kept pulling him back to the ground. He kept popping back up. For a moment there was a lull, filled only with the ringing in our ears and the echo in our heads, and I dared hope.

"There they are! They're running up the road," Mick yelled, standing to get a better shot at the party of ambushers scurrying up the hill. He ran out from behind the car, and I immediately followed, shouting his name. A single shot rang out, clean and sharp, and Mick fell.

He lay crumpled, facedown in the middle of the road, a yawning hole at the base of his skull. I ran to him, Sean O'Connell at my heels, and we dragged him by his ankles back behind the car. I fell to my knees and began tearing at the buttons of my shirt, needing something to make a compress. Someone said an Act of Contrition, someone else began to rage, and others ran down the road, firing at the fleeing shooters. I pressed my shirt to the back of his head and rolled Mick towards me. His eyes were closed, his face young and loose in repose. Night had fallen, and the Big Fella was gone.

I cradled him in my arms, his head against my chest, his body across the seat as we headed back to Cork. I was not the only one weeping. We stopped for water to wash the blood from his face, and shell-shocked and unaccustomed to our surroundings, we got lost again. We were caught in a hellish maze of felled trees, blown up bridges, and railroad crossings, and we drove aimlessly in the dark. At one point, we pulled over to ask for help and direction at a church. The priest came within several feet of the car, saw Mick propped against my blood-soaked chest, and turned and ran back inside. Someone screamed for him to come back and threatened to shoot. The weapon discharged, but thankfully the priest didn't fall. Maybe we misjudged him, but we didn't wait for him to return.

I don't remember finally coming into Cork, only that we eventually did. Two members of the Cork Civic Patrol led us to Shanakiel Hospital, where Mick's body was taken away, leaving us covered in his blood and stranded in the corner of the world that should have loved him most. He had been so sure they were his people.

A cable was sent, warning London, alerting Dublin, and informing the world that Michael Collins had been brought down just a week after Arthur Griffith was laid to rest. They sent his body by boat from Penrose Quay to Dún Laoghaire. They wouldn't let me go with him. I took the train, crowded among people who talked of his loss, of Ireland's loss, and then talked of hats and the weather and the neighbour's bad habits. I became so angry, so irrationally livid, that I had to get off at the next stop.

I am not fit to be around people, yet I don't want to be alone. It took me two days to get back to Dublin.

They buried him today in Glasnevin, and I was there among the mourners, huddled with Gearóid O'Sullivan, Tom Cullen, and Joe O'Reilly. Their love for him is a balm to me; I won't have to carry his memory by myself.

I am selling my house in Dublin. After today, I have no desire to return. I am going home to Eoin, to my little boy. Ireland has taken everyone else, and I have nothing left to give her.

T. S.

26

A MAN OLD AND YOUNG

She smiled and that transfigured me
And left me but a lout,
Maundering here, and maundering there,
Emptier of thought
Than the heavenly circuit of its stars
When the moon sails out.

—*W. B. Yeats*

The last day in August, I returned to Ballinagar and climbed the hill behind the church, my breath hard to catch, my lungs crowded by my ever-expanding abdomen. My doctor, an ancient ob-gyn practicing in Sligo, said I was due the first week in January. At my first appointment, the nurse had tried to calculate my pregnancy based on my last menstrual cycle. I couldn't tell her it had been in mid-January of 1922. I'd had to plead ignorance, even though I suspected I was about twelve weeks along when I returned to the present. My first ultrasound confirmed my estimate, though the dates did not align. Time travel or not, I would still be carrying this child for nine months, and I had four months more to go.

I crouched in front of Declan's stone and ran my palm over the surface, saying hello. Anne Finnegan's name was still engraved beside his; that had not changed. I pulled the weeds around Brigid's grave. I could not find it in my heart to be angry with her. She'd been tangled in a web of deceit and impossibility, and none of it was her fault. She thought she was protecting Eoin, protecting Thomas. My eyes kept flickering to the stone with Smith written on the base; it was set back from the Gallagher graves, a slim shadow covered in lichen. With a deep breath, trusting that Maeve had not been mistaken when she told me Thomas was not buried here, I approached it and knelt beside it, raising my gaze to the words on the rock.

Anne Smith—April 16, 1922—Beloved wife of Thomas.

The grave was mine.

I didn't gasp or cry out. I simply sat, barely breathing, looking at the monument he'd erected for me. It was not macabre or frightening. It was a memorial to our life together, to the love we shared. It testified that I was, that I had been, and that I always would be . . . his.

"Oh, Thomas," I whispered, resting my head against the cold stone. I cried, but the tears were a release, a relief, and I made no attempt to staunch their flow. He was not there in Ballinagar. He was not in the wind or in the grass. But I felt closer to him in that moment than I'd felt in months. The baby fluttered inside me, and my stomach tightened in response, drawing around the new life that bore witness to the old.

I lay down at the base of the stone, talking to Thomas the way I'd felt him talking to me through his journals, telling him about old Maeve and young Kevin and Eoin publishing our stories. I told him how the baby was growing and how I thought it was a little girl. I discussed names and what color to paint the nursery, and when the sun began to set, I said a tearful goodbye, wiped my eyes, and made my way down the hill again.

I began reading the journals in small pieces, opening the books to random pages the way Kevin had done. I read Thomas's final entry first, dated 3

July 1933, and could not read another for days. I kept going back to it like a moth to a flame; the pain I felt when I read it was almost joy.

Eoin turns eighteen next week. We booked his passage last spring and made all the arrangements for his room and board. He was accepted at the Long Island College of Medicine, though he's quite a bit younger than most of the other students. I bought myself a ticket as well, intending to go with him. I want to get him settled, to see the streets he will walk and the places he will be, so that when I think about him, I can picture him in his new surroundings. But he is adamant that he go alone. He reminds me of Mick sometimes. An iron will and a soft heart. He promised me he would write, but we both laughed at that. I won't be getting any letters.

In many ways, I have been given more than a parent could ask for; I have the reassurances Anne gave me. I know the pattern of his days and the path his life will take. I know the kind of man he is and what he will become. The adventures of Eoin Gallagher are just beginning, even as our time together has come to an end.

There were some entries and dates I avoided completely. I couldn't face 1922. I didn't want to read about Michael's death—I'd been unable to save him—or about the continual collapse of the Irish leadership on all sides. I knew from my earlier research that after the death of Arthur Griffith and the assassination of Michael Collins, the scales tipped violently, the way they always do, and the provisional government granted special powers to the Free State Army. Under these special powers, well-known republicans were arrested and executed, without appeal, by firing squad. Erskine Childers was the first to be executed, but he was not the last. In a period of seven months, seventy-seven republicans were arrested and executed by the Free State Army. In return, the IRA began to kill prominent Free State figures. Back and forth the pendulum swung, leaving the earth scorched with every swath.

I spent most of my time in the years from 1923 to 1933, soaking up every mention of Eoin. Thomas loved him well, and his entries revolved around him. He reveled in Eoin's victories, took his cares personally, and fretted like a father. In one entry, he talked about catching sixteen-year-old Eoin kissing Miriam McHugh in the clinic and worried that Eoin would lose focus on his studies.

> *There is little that is more intoxicating than being in love and in lust, but Miriam isn't the girl for Eoin. And this is not the time for romantic attachments. Eoin sulked a little when I counseled him to talk to Miriam instead of kissing her. Kisses can fool a man but deep conversation seldom does. He scoffed and questioned my experience. "How would you know, Doc? You never talk to women. And you sure as hell aren't kissing them," he said. I reminded him that I'd loved a woman who had excelled at conversation and kissing—a woman who'd ruined me for all others, and I damn well did know what I was talking about. Mentioning Anne always makes Eoin contemplative. He didn't say much after that, but tonight he knocked on my bedroom door. When I opened it, he put his arms around me and embraced me. I could tell he was close to tears, so I just held him until he was ready to let go.*

I had to put the journals away for a few days after that, but I found more comfort in them than pain. When it hurt too much to think of Thomas and the little boy I'd left behind, I sifted through the pages and turned back the years, reading their triumphs and troubles, their joys and their struggles, and I watched them go on together.

I found an entry written on the day that Brigid died. Thomas wrote about her with compassion and forgiveness. I was grateful she was not alone in the end. I read about illnesses and deaths in Dromahair and about new treatments and advances in medicine. Sometimes Thomas's journals felt like a patient log, detailing a myriad of ailments and remedies, but he never wrote about politics. It was as though he had divorced himself entirely from the fray. The patriot heart he spoke of in his early years had been replaced by a nonpartisan soul. Something died in him when Michael was killed. He lost his faith in Ireland. Or maybe he just lost his faith in men.

There was one entry in July of 1927 where Thomas mentioned the assassination of Kevin O'Higgins, the minister for home affairs. O'Higgins had been responsible for the implementation of the special powers in 1922 that had created so much bitterness. The assassination came on the heels of the establishment of a new political party, Fianna Fáil, which was organized by Eamon de Valera and other prominent republicans. Public sentiment was with de Valera. Someone had asked Thomas which party he would support in the upcoming election. His failure to publicly support any of them had upset more than a few candidates who sought his approval and his financial backing. His response had me gasping and rereading his words.

There are some paths that inevitably lead to heartache, some acts that steal men's souls, leaving them wandering forever after without them, trying to find what they lost. There are too many lost souls in Ireland because of politics. I'm going to hold on to what's left of mine.

The first few lines were the words Eoin had quoted the night he died. Any questions I'd had about Eoin's knowledge of the journals, of his intimate understanding of the man who had raised him, were gone. He'd only taken one journal with him when he left home, but he'd read them all.

I bought Maeve a stack of romance novels in Sligo after my doctor's appointment, along with an assortment of little cakes in pale pastels. I showed up unannounced; I didn't have her phone number. She came to the door wearing a royal-blue blouse, yellow slacks, and cheetah-print house slippers. Her fuchsia lipstick was fresh, and her pleasure at seeing me was genuine, though she feigned irritation.

"It took you long enough, young lady!" she scolded. "I tried walking to Garvagh Glebe last week, and Father Dornan dragged me home. He thinks I have dementia. He doesn't understand that I'm just old and rude."

I followed her into the house, pushing the door shut with my foot as she prattled on. "I'd begun to think you were rude too, Anne Smith. Not coming to see me when I asked so nicely. Are those cakes?" She sniffed the air.

"Yes. And I've brought you books too. I distinctly remember you telling me you liked big books best. The ones with lots of chapters."

Her eyes grew wide and her chin wobbled. "Yes . . . I remember that too. So we're not going to pretend?"

"If we pretend, then we can't talk about the old days. I need to talk to someone, Maeve."

"So do I, lass," she murmured. "So do I. Come sit down. I'll make some tea."

I took off my coat and set out the cakes—one of each kind—and left the rest in the box for Maeve to nibble on later. I stacked the new books near her rocking chair and took a seat at her small table as she returned with the kettle and two cups.

"Eoin insisted you weren't dead. He said you were just lost in the water. Everyone was worried about him. So Dr. Smith had a stone engraved, and we had a small service for you to give us all some peace and comfort. Father Darby wanted to have your name taken off Declan Gallagher's headstone, but Thomas insisted it be left alone, and he refused to put a birthdate on the new one. The doctor was stubborn, and he was rich—he gave lots of money to the church—so Father Darby let him have his way.

"Eoin threw a fit when he saw the grave. It didn't comfort him one whit to have his mother's name on a marker. Thomas didn't even stay for the service. He and Eoin went for a long walk, and when they came back, Eoin was still crying, but he wasn't screaming, poor mite. I don't know what Doc said to him, but Eoin stopped saying daft things after that."

I sipped my tea, and Maeve smirked at me over the edge of her cup. "He wasn't daft though, was he?"

"No." Thomas wouldn't have told Eoin everything. But he would have told him enough. He would have told him who I was and that he would see me again.

"I'd forgotten all about Anne Smith. I'd even forgotten about Doc and Eoin. It's been seventy years since I last saw them. Then you showed up at my door. And I started to remember."

"What did you remember?"

"Don't be coy, lass. I'm not twelve years old anymore, and you are not the lady of *this* house." She thumped her slippered foot on her carpeted floor. "I remembered you!"

I smiled at her vehemence. It felt good to be remembered.

"Now, I want to know everything. I want to know what happened to you. Then and now. And don't leave out the kissing scenes," she barked.

I refilled my cup, took a huge bite of a frosted pink pastry, and I told her everything.

In September, I awoke to news that the Twin Towers had fallen, that my city had been attacked, and I watched the television coverage, clutching my growing belly, sheltering my unborn child, wondering if I'd returned from one vortex only to be plunged into another. My old life, my streets, my skyline, was forever changed, and I was grateful Eoin was no longer alive in Brooklyn to witness it. I was grateful I was no longer there to witness it. My heart was incapable of holding more pain.

Barbara heard the planes—they shook the agency as they passed overhead—before they hit, and called me in a state days later, repeating over and over again how glad she was that I was safe in Ireland. "The world has gone mad, Anne. Mad. It's upside down, and we are all holding on for dear life." I knew exactly what she meant, but my world had been spinning for months, and 9/11 just added another layer of impossibility. It distracted Barbara from her worry over me, from my midlife crisis, and I could only retreat further into the corners of Garvagh Glebe, unable to absorb the magnitude of such an event, unable to process any of it. The world was upside down—just like Barbara said—but I'd been falling when it tipped, and I already had my sea legs. I turned off the television, begged my city for forgiveness, and pled with God to keep us all—even me—from losing ourselves. And I continued on.

In October, I ordered a crib, a changing table, and a rocking chair to match the old oak floors. Two weeks later, I decided that the floor in the nursery needed to be carpeted. The house could be drafty, and I had visions of my baby tumbling out of her bed and onto the unforgiving slats. The carpet was installed, the furniture assembled, and the curtains hung, and I told myself I was ready.

In November, I concluded that the soft-green paint on the nursery walls would look better with white stripes. Green-and-white stripes would work for a girl or a boy, and it would give the room some cheer. I bought the paint and supplies, but Kevin insisted that pregnant ladies should not paint and hijacked my project. I made a halfhearted protest, but my enormous belly made a mockery of my ambitions. I was thirty-two weeks along and could not imagine getting any bigger or being any more uncomfortable. But I needed something to do.

Barbara had called earlier in the week to see how my next book was coming along. I had to confess it wasn't coming at all. I had a story to tell, a love story like no other, but I couldn't face the ending. My words were a tangled mess of agony and denial, and whenever I sat down to plot or plan, I ended up staring out the window, traipsing through the yellowed pages of my old life, searching for Thomas. There were no words for the things I felt; there was only the rise and fall of my breath, the steady slog of my heart, and the unrelenting ache of separation.

Unable to paint and unwilling to write, I decided to walk. I pulled a pink cashmere shawl over my shoulders and stuffed my feet into a pair of black Wellies so they wouldn't get wet when I walked to the lough. My hair danced in the gloom, waving at the naked branches of the shivering trees. No need to tame it now. No one cared if it hung halfway down my back and curled around my face. No one would look twice at my black leggings or disapprove of the way my cotton tunic hugged the swell of my breasts or clung to my pregnant belly. The beach was empty. No one would see me at all.

Western Ireland was caught in the damp doldrums of a dying fall, and the moldering mist licked at my cheeks and hovered over the lake, obscuring the sky from the sea, the surf from the sand, and the silhouette of the opposite shore. I stood facing the lough, letting the wind lift my hair and let it go again, watching the fog gather into ghosts and shift in the tepid light.

I'd stopped going into the water. I'd stopped rowing out, away from the shore. The water was cold, and I had a child to consider, a life beyond my own. But I still came at least once a day to plead my case to the wind. The blanket of fog cushioned the air, and the world was hushed and hiding. The lapping of the water and the squelch of my boots were my only company.

And then I heard whistling.

It stopped for a moment and it came again, faint and far away. Donnelly's dock was empty, his business closed for the season. Light shone from his windows, and a tendril of smoke rose from his chimney, merging with the hazy sky, but nothing moved along the shore. The whistling was not on the land but in the water, like a foolish fisherman was hiding in the fog.

The sound grew stronger, drifting in with the tide, and I stepped toward it, listening for the whistler to finish his tune. It warbled and broke, and I waited for an encore. When none came, I pursed my lips and finished the song for him, the sound breathy and soft and a little off-key. But I recognized the melody.

They can't forget, they never will, the wind and waves remember Him still.

"Thomas?"

I'd called to him before. I'd screamed his name across the water until I was hoarse and hopeless. But I called to him again.

"Thomas?"

His name hung precariously in the air, weighty and wishful, before it teetered and fell, sinking like a stone beneath the surface. The lough whispered back with liquid lips, slow and sighing. *Tho-mas, Tho-mas, Tho-mas.*

The bow appeared first, shifting in and out of sight. The lough was playing hide-and-seek. There it was again. Closer. Someone was rowing with steady strokes. The pull and release of the paddle through the water mocked a hushed endearment, the sound of his name becoming the sound of his voice. *Coun-tess, Coun-tess, Coun-tess.*

Then I saw him. A peaked cap, broad shoulders, a tweed coat, and pale eyes. Pale-blue eyes clinging to mine. He said my name, low and disbelieving, as the small red boat split the fog and slid toward the shore, so close I heard the oar scrape the sand.

"Thomas?"

Then he was standing, using the oar like a Venetian gondolier, and I was sinking to my knees on the rocky shore, crying his name. The little boat bellied up to the beach, and he stepped out onto solid ground, tossing the oar aside and pulling his hat from his head. He clutched it against his chest, like a nervous suitor come to call. His dark hair was shot with silver, and a few more lines creased the corners of his eyes. But it was Thomas.

He hesitated, teeth clenched, gaze pleading, as though he didn't know how to greet me. I tried to rise, to go to him, and he was suddenly there, swooping me up and holding me against him, the swell of our child cradled between us, his face buried in my hair. For a moment, neither of us spoke, our burning lungs and pounding hearts stealing our speech and robbing our senses.

"How is it that I've lost eleven years, and you haven't aged at all?" he cried into my curls, his joy tinged in sorrow. "Is this my child, or have I lost you too?"

"This is your child, and you will never lose me," I vowed, stroking his hair, touching his face, my hands as delirious as my heart. Thomas was wrapped around me, so close I felt every breath, but it wasn't enough. I drew his face to mine, frantic, afraid I would wake without kissing him goodbye.

He was so real and so wonderfully familiar. The scrape of his cheeks, the press of his lips, the taste of his mouth, the salt of his tears. He kissed me like he'd kissed me the first time and every time after that, pouring himself out, holding nothing back. But this kiss was flavored with long absence and new hope, and with every sigh and second that passed, I began to believe in an afterlife.

"You stayed in Ireland," he choked, his lips skimming across my cheeks, down my nose, and over the point of my chin, his fingers cradling my face.

"Someone told me once that when people leave Ireland, they never go back. I couldn't bear the thought of never going back. So I stayed. And you stayed with Eoin," I said, overwhelmed.

He nodded, his eyes so full and fierce that tears trickled down my face and pooled in the palms of his hands.

"I stayed until he told me it was time to go."

On July 12, 1933, the day after Eoin's eighteenth birthday, Thomas lowered the little red rowboat from the rafters in his barn and packed a small suitcase with a box of gold coins, a change of clothes, and a few photographs. He thought he might need something that had belonged to me in 2001, something that would guide his travel, and slipped the diamond earrings I'd sold Mr. Kelly into his pocket; he'd bought them back the day after I pawned them. He had the empty urn that once held Eoin's ashes, and he knew the verse I'd recited that day on the lough, the poem by Yeats that spoke of fairies and riding on the wind.

But Thomas was convinced the diamonds, the dust, and the fairy words made no difference whatsoever. When it was all said and done, he simply hitched a ride to 2001. The moment the boat was returned to the lough, it began to sail toward home, slipping through the ages, parting the waters, and calling the mist. Eoin had watched it disappear.

We left the boat on the shore, the paddle in the sand and the lough behind us. Thomas was wide-eyed but unafraid, his suitcase in his hand, his cap back on his head. I doubted much about Thomas would change, regardless of the decade he called home. For eleven years, two months, and twenty-six days, he had patiently waited. He'd worried that I would be gone, that he would have to find me in an unknown world and across an ocean. He expected to find a son or daughter half grown, if he found us at all. And what if time took him somewhere he didn't want to go, and he lost everything? It was the legend of Niamh and Oisín all over again.

And still he came.

13 November 2001

Friday, 9 November 2001, was the day I arrived. Eleven years, two months, and twenty-six days were condensed to one hundred thirty-four days. Anne's ten months in 1921–22 were reduced to ten days when she returned. I've tried to puzzle it out, but it's like trying to wrap my mind around the creation of the universe. I spent ten minutes studying a child's toy in Lyons department store yesterday—the store still exists! The expansion and contraction of the toy—Anne called it a Slinky—made me consider time in a whole new way. Maybe time is coiled into ever-widening (or tightening) circles, layered and wrapped around the next. I spread my arms as wide as I could, lengthening the coils of the Slinky, and then I pressed my hands together, flattening it between my palms, intrigued. Anne insisted on buying it for me.

I told her my new theory on time and toys last night as we laid in her glorious bed. It is enormous, yet we sleep spooned together, her back to my chest, her head beneath my chin. I can't quit touching her, but she suffers from the same insecurity. It will be a while before either of us can bear any type of separation. I was in the shower—so much hot water coming at such a wonderful velocity—and she joined me after a few minutes, her eyes shy and her cheeks pink.

"I was afraid . . . and I didn't want to be alone," she said. She didn't need to explain or apologize. Her presence there led to another discovery. The shower is delightful for a variety of reasons. But apparently there is a limit to the hot-water supply.

The trip to Sligo made me appreciate Anne a little more, if that is possible. I can't imagine the fear and intimidation she must have felt that first time, trying to navigate a new world (and new clothes) while pretending to be someone who was well accustomed to it. We ended up purchasing a wardrobe that looks much like my old one. Peaked hats, white button-downs, and trousers haven't gone out of fashion. Suspenders have. Vests have. But Anne says the style suits me, and I can wear whatever I like. I've noticed I dress like the old men. But I am an old man—even older than Maeve, who has taken all of this in remarkable stride. We went and paid her a visit today. We talked for hours of the years I missed and the loved ones who are now gone. When we left, I embraced her and thanked her for being a friend to Anne, both now and then.

Anne's going to write our story. I've asked if I can pick my character's name, and she agreed. She also wants me to pick our child's name. If it's a boy, he will be Michael Eoin. I've had more trouble thinking of a name for a lass. I don't want her to be named for the past. She will be a girl of the future, like her mother. Anne says maybe we should call her Niamh. It made me laugh. Niamh is one of the oldest names in Ireland. Niamh, the Princess of Tír na nÓg, the Land of the Young. But perhaps it is fitting.

Anne is even more beautiful than I remember. I haven't told her—I don't think women like comparisons, even with their old selves. Her hair is glorious. She makes no effort to control it here, and it curls with complete and joyous abandon; it curls the way Anne makes love. She laughs at her burgeoning belly and her swollen breasts and the way she waddles and can't see her toes, but all I want to do is look at her.

We're going to Dublin in the morning. Anne says eventually we will see all of Ireland together. I recognize old Ireland beneath her new clothes. She hasn't changed much, Éireann, and when I look out at the lough and up into the hills, she hasn't changed at all.

Dublin might be hard for me. I went back very little in the ten years after Mick died. He lurked around every corner, and I had no wish to be there without him. I wish he could see Dublin with me now, and I wonder what the world would have looked like had he lived.

We'll go to his grave at Glasnevin when we're through, and I'll describe all the ways the world has changed for the better, even in Ireland. I'll tell him I found my Annie. I wish I could see his face; he took her loss so hard. I'll tell him I found my girl, and I'll ask him to keep an eye on my boy.

*Eoin is very present. He's in the wind. I can't explain it, but I have no doubt he's here. Anne showed me the books—*The Adventures of Eoin Gallagher—*and I felt him beside me, turning the pages. Then she handed me a box teeming with letters Eoin had insisted she keep. Hundreds of them. Anne says she never understood why he hadn't sent them. They are dated and bundled in decades. There are more from the early years, but at least two for every year of his long life, and all of them are addressed to me. He promised he would write. And he did.*

T. S.

AUTHOR'S NOTE

In the summer of 2016, after doing a little research on my family tree, I traveled to Dromahair, Ireland, to see the place where my great-grandfather, Martin Smith, was born and raised. He emigrated to the States as a young man; my nana said he got involved with the local IRB, and his parents sent him to America because they didn't want him getting into trouble. I don't know if that's true, as Nana has been gone since 2001, but he was born the same year as Michael Collins, in a period of reformation and revolution.

Nana had written a few things on the back of a St. Patrick's Day card one year about her father, my great-grandfather. I knew when he was born, I knew his mother's name was Anne Gallagher, and his father was Michael Smith. But that's all I knew. Just like Anne, I went to Dromahair with the hopes of finding them. And I did.

My parents and my older sister took the trip with me, and the first time we saw Lough Gill, my chest burned, and my eyes teared. Every step of the way, it felt like we were being guided and led. Deirdre Fallon, a real-life librarian—libraries never let you down—in Dromahair, directed us to the genealogical center in Ballinamore. We were then directed to Ballinagar, a cemetery behind a church in the middle of fields. When I asked how we would find it, I really was told to pray or pull over and ask someone, just like Anne was told to do in this book. I won't ever forget how it felt to walk up that rise among the stones and find my family.

The townland where my grandfather was born was called Garvagh Glebe, just like in the story. But Garvagh Glebe is not a manor, and it is not next to Lough Gill. It is a rather barren and rocky stretch of land, a true "rough place" up in the hills above Dromahair where there is a wind farm now. When I saw those big windmills, the title was born. *What the Wind Knows* was inspired by these events and by ancestors I've never met but feel like I know.

I couldn't give my main character my great-great-grandfather's name (Michael Smith) because Michael Collins was such a central figure in the book, and I didn't want two Michaels. So Thomas Smith was named for two of my Irish grandfathers, Thomas Keefe of Youghal, County Cork, and Michael Smith of Dromahair, County Leitrim. We also have a Bannon branch that I can't get a lock on. Maybe there will be another book about John Bannon.

Even though this book has a strong dose of the fantastical, I wanted it to be a historical novel as well. The more research I did into Ireland, the more lost I felt. I didn't know how to tell the story or even what story to tell. I felt like Anne when she told Eoin, "There is no consensus. I have to have context." It was Eoin's response to Anne, "Don't let the history distract you from the people who lived it," that gave me hope and direction.

Ireland's history is a long and tumultuous one, and I did not wish to relitigate it or point fingers of blame in this story. I simply wanted to learn, understand, and fall in love with her and invite my reader to love her too. In the process, I immersed myself in the poetry of Yeats, who walked the streets my great-grandfather walked and who wrote about Dromahair. I also fell in love with Michael Collins. If you want to know more about him, I highly suggest Tim Pat Coogan's book *Michael Collins*, to gain a deeper appreciation of his life and his place in Irish history. There is so much written about him, and so many opinions, but after all my research, I am still in awe of the young man who committed himself, heart and soul, to his cause. That much is not in dispute.

Of course, Thomas Smith is a fictional character, but I think he embodies the kind of friendship and loyalty Michael Collins inspired among those who knew him best. I did my best to blend fact and fiction, and many of the events and accounts I inserted Thomas and Anne into actually happened. There was no assassination attempt or arson at the Gresham Hotel in August of 1921, and that event is fictional, but it mirrors many of the attempts that were made on Michael Collins's life during the time. The night Michael and Thomas spent inside the records room was based on actual events, as were Michael's friends—Tom Cullen, Joe O'Reilly, Gearóid O'Sullivan, Moya Llewelyn-Davies, Kitty Kiernan—and historical figures like Constance Markievicz, Arthur Griffith, Cathal Brugha, Eamon de Valera, Lloyd George, and so many more. Terence MacSwiney, his sister Mary, and others mentioned in a historical context were also real people, and I tried to stay true to the record where they are referenced. A bodyguard for Michael Collins was alluded to in several accounts—one with details very similar to the events at Garvagh Glebe and the shooting in the marsh—but his name was not Fergus as far as I know. Brigid McMorrow Gallagher was named for my great-great-great-grandmother, Brigid McNamara, and her relationship to Seán Mac Diarmada's mother was completely fictional.

Any mistakes or embellishments to the actual record to fill in the historical gaps or to further the story are well intentioned and are completely my own. I hope when you are finished with *What the Wind Knows,* you simply have a greater respect for the men and women who came before and a desire to make the world a better place.

I must give huge thanks to my friend Emma Corcoran of Lusk, Ireland, for her input and Irish eyes on this novel. She kept the narrative authentic and my facts straight, as well as helped me with the Gaelic at every turn. Grateful thanks to Geraldine Cummins also, for reading and enthusiastically reporting back.

Big thanks to my friend Nicole Karlson, for reading each section as I wrote it and for leaving me long messages filled with encouragement and praise. This was a hard novel to write, and her enthusiasm kept me optimistically plodding away more times than I can count.

To my assistant, Tamara Debbaut, who is always a steady source of support and so much more. She does all the things I can't ever seem to do for myself. There would be no Amy Harmon, author, without Tamara Debbaut. I am quite useless without her.

Karey White, my personal editor, must also be mentioned for her time and care on perfecting my manuscripts long before my agent and publisher ever see them. To my agent, Jane Dystel, for believing in my books and making big dreams happen. For my Lake Union team, particularly Jodi Warshaw and Jenna Free, for enthusiastically embracing my efforts and walking with me through the publishing process once more.

Finally, my never-ending gratitude to my dad for giving me Ireland, to my husband for giving me unfailing belief, and to my children for not caring one whit about my books and reminding me what is truly important in my life. I love you all very much.

Amy Harmon